Running Hot

Jayne Ann Krentz, who also writes under the names Amanda Quick and Jayne Castle, has more than forty *New York Times* bestsellers under various pen names and more than twenty-five million copies of her books are in print. She lives in the Pacific Northwest.

Visit her website at www.jayneannkrentz.com

Also by Jayne Ann Krentz

Light in Shadow
Truth or Dare
Falling Awake
All Night Long
White Lies
Sizzle and Burn

Jayne Ann Krentz writing as Amanda Quick

Wait Until Midnight
The Paid Companion
Lie By Moonlight
Second Sight
The River Knows
The Third Circle
Affair
Mischief
With this Ring
I Thee Wed
Slightly Shady
Wicked Widow

Running Hot

Jayne Ann Krentz

PIATKUS

PIATKUS

First published in Great Britain in 2009 by Piatkus Books
First published in the United States in 2008 by G. P. Putnam's Sons,
A member of Penguin Group (USA) Inc., New York

A CIP catalogue record for this book
is available from the British Library

ISBN 978-0-7499-0898-0 [HB]
ISBN 978-0-7499-0901-7 [TPB]

Printed and bound by CPI Mackays, Chatham, ME5 8TD

Papers used by Piatkus Books are natural, renewable and recyclable
products made from wood grown in sustainable forests and certified
in accordance with the rules of the Forest Stewardship Council.

Mixed Sources
Product group from well-managed
forests and other controlled sources
www.fsc.org Cert no. SGS-COC-004081
© 1996 Forest Stewardship Council

Piatkus Books
An imprint of
Little, Brown Book Group
100 Victoria Embankment
London EC4Y 0DY

An Hachette Livre UK Company
www.hachettelivre.co.uk

www.piatkus.co.uk

For Steve Castle, with love.
I am so lucky to have you for a brother.

Running Hot

Prologue

Martin was going to kill her.

She stepped off the gangway and onto the sleek, twin-engine cabin cruiser, wondering why the cold despair was hitting her so hard. If there was one thing you learned fast when you were raised by the state, it was that ultimately you could depend only on yourself. The foster home system and the streets were the ultimate universities, awarding harsh degrees in the most basic kind of entrepreneurship. When you were on your own in the world, the laws of survival were simple. She had learned them well.

She thought her past had prepared her for any eventuality, including the possibility that the only man she had ever trusted might someday turn on her. She had been mistaken. Nothing could blunt the pain of this betrayal.

Martin emerged from the cabin. The dazzling Caribbean sunlight glinted off his mirrored glasses. He saw her and gave her his familiar charismatic smile.

"There you are," he said, coming forward to take the computer case from her. "You're late." He glanced at the man in the white shirt and dark blue trousers coming up the gangway with her suitcase. "Weather problems?"

"No, sir." Eric Schafer set down the small suitcase. "We landed on time. But there's some kind of local holiday going on. The streets were jammed. You know how it is here on the island. Only one road from the airport and it goes straight through town. No way to avoid the traffic."

Eric straightened and wiped the sweat off his forehead with the back of his hand. His shirt, embroidered with the discreet logo of Crocker World, had been military-crisp that morning when he climbed into the cockpit of the small corporate jet in Miami. It was now badly wilted from the island heat.

"The Night and Day Festival," Martin said. "I forgot about it. Big event down here. A combination of Mardi Gras and Halloween."

He was lying, she thought. She watched the strange dark energy flash in his aura. It was all part of the plan to kill her. The festival would provide excellent cover for a murder. With so many strangers on the island, the local authorities would be too busy to notice if Mr. Crocker returned from his private island alone.

"Will there be anything else, sir?" Eric asked.

"Where's Banner?"

"Left him back at the airport. He's keeping an eye on the plane."

"You two can take the jet back to Miami. No point both of you cooling your heels on this rock for an entire week. You've got wives and kids who will probably be very happy to see you. I've been keeping you guys busy these past few months."

"Yes, sir. Thanks."

Eric's gratitude was real. Martin knew how to bind his people to him with a combination of generous salaries and benefits and his own natural charisma. She had often thought that he could have been a very successful cult leader. Instead, he had chosen a different career path.

He went up the short flight of teak steps to take the helm.

"Get the lines for me," he called down to Eric.

"Sure thing, Mr. Crocker." Eric crouched to uncoil the ropes that secured the powerful boat to the dock.

She wondered what he and the others on the staff would think when she disappeared. Martin had probably already prepared a convincing story for them. Something to do with falling overboard, perhaps. The currents around the island were notoriously tricky.

She felt the vibration beneath her feet as the boat's engines started to churn. Eric gave her a friendly wave and dashed more sweat off his forehead.

There was no veiled look of masculine speculation in his expression, no sly wink or grin. When he got back to the airport he and his copilot, John Banner, would not make any comments about the boss going off with one of his girlfriends. No one on Martin's staff had ever mistaken her for one of Martin's many lovers. His women tended to be tall, willowy and blond. She was none of those things. She was just the hired help.

Officially she was Martin's butler, the one person who traveled with him everywhere. She kept his life organized and oversaw the operation of his many residences. Most important, she supervised the entertaining of his friends, business associates and the occasional visiting politician, lobbyist or head of state.

She raised her hand in farewell to Eric and squeezed back tears. Regardless of what happened today, she knew that she would never see him again.

The boat slipped gracefully away from the dock, headed toward the entrance to the small harbor.

Like many who moved in the stratospheric circles inhabited by those of great wealth, Martin owned several houses and kept a number of apartments in various locales around the world. The Miami mansion was his main residence but the place he considered home was the small island he had purchased a few years ago. The only way to get to it was by boat. There was no landing strip, just a single dock.

Unlike his other residences, which were always maintained in a state of readiness, Martin kept no staff on the island. The house was much smaller and far more modest than his other dwellings. He considered the place his private retreat.

Once past the stone pillars that marked the harbor entrance, Martin revved the engines. The boat picked up speed, slicing eagerly through the turquoise blue water. He was busy at the wheel, not paying any attention to her as he concentrated on piloting the craft. She heightened her other senses and took another look at his aura. The dark energy was stronger now. He was getting jacked up.

The boat felt very small around her. There was nowhere to hide; nowhere to run.

She had known for days—weeks, if she was brutally honest with herself—that Martin was planning to get rid of her. She was even sure she knew why. Nevertheless, some small part of her had clung to the slender thread of denial, even as it unraveled. Maybe there was some logical explanation for the disturbing changes in his aura. Maybe the new darkness was the result of mental illness. As dreadful as that possibility would be, at least it would allow her the comfort of knowing that he was no longer in his right mind; that the real Martin would never plot her death.

But her own finely honed survival instincts had refused to let her deceive herself any longer. Martin might have had some affection for her at one time, but deep down she had always known that their relationship was rooted in her usefulness to him. Now he had concluded that she had become a liability so he was going to get rid of her. In his mind the situation was not complicated.

She stood at the stern and watched the harbor and the small town grow smaller and smaller. When they became tiny, indistinct blobs, she turned around. Martin's private island was very close now. She could make out the house perched on the hillside.

Martin slowed the boat and brought it neatly alongside the wooden dock.

"Get the lines," Martin said sharply, his attention on maneuvering the boat.

That did it. For some inexplicable reason the simple, routine order flipped the last switch somewhere in her head. The unholy brew of pain, sadness, disbelief and mind-numbing fear that had been swirling through her in alternating currents for days was suddenly swept away by icy-cold rage. Her other senses leaped violently in reaction to the adrenaline rush.

The son of a bitch was planning to murder her. Now. Today.

"Sure thing, Martin," she said, amazed by how cool and controlled she sounded. But then, she'd had a lot of practice concealing her emotions and reactions behind a gracious, exquisitely polite façade. She could have given a geisha lessons. But she was no geisha.

She grabbed the stern line, stepped lightly out of the boat and onto the narrow dock. It didn't take long to tie up. She had done it countless times in the past.

Martin left the wheel and came back down the steps.

"Here, take this," he said, handing her the computer. "I'll get your suitcase and the supplies."

She took the computer from him and waited while he swung the suitcase and the two bags of groceries up onto the dock. He glanced around, making sure he had everything he wanted out of the boat. Then he stepped onto the dock.

"Ready?" he said.

Not waiting for a reply, he scooped up the bags of groceries with an easy motion and tucked one into the crook of each arm. His aura flashed with impatience and a really scary excitement. The pulses of dark energy were becoming increasingly agitated. This wasn't just business, she realized. He was actually looking forward to murdering her. Her own fury flared higher.

"Of course." She gave him her best professional smile, the one she used to greet his guests and business associates. She thought of it as her stage smile. "But just out of curiosity, when do you plan to do it?"

"Do what?" he said. He was already turning away from her, heading toward the small SUV parked at the end of the dock.

"Kill me."

He froze in mid-stride. She watched the torrent of shock crash through his aura. The indescribable colors flashed across the spectrum. She really had taken him by surprise, she realized. Had he actually believed that he could plot her death without her sensing it? Evidently the answer to that question was a resounding yes. Then again, she had never told him all of her secrets.

When he turned to face her his expression was a mix of anger and impatience.

"What the hell are you talking about?" he said. "Is this your idea of a bad joke?"

She folded her arms, hugging herself a little.

"We both know it isn't a joke," she said quietly. "You brought me here with the intention of murdering me."

"I haven't got time for this. I've got work to do."

"I assume I'm going to be the victim of a tragic drowning accident?" She smiled bleakly. "So sad. The butler went swimming and went under. Happens all the time."

He searched her face as though wondering if she had a high fever and then shook his head. "I don't believe this."

"I didn't, either. But in hindsight I saw it coming weeks ago."

"All right, let's play this out," he said with the air of a man who has begun to suspect that he is dealing with a crazy person. "You and I have been a team for a long time. Twelve years. Why would I want to kill you now?"

"I think there are a couple of reasons. The first one, of course, is that I recently discovered that for the past few months you've been allowing some very nasty people to use the resources of Crocker World as a cover for illegal arms dealing. All that agricultural equipment you so generously donated to various developing countries? Turns out those tractors and plows fire real bullets. Imagine my surprise."

For an instant she thought he was going to continue the charade a little longer. But this was Martin. He could get to the bottom line faster than anyone else she had ever met. That was part of his talent.

He smiled with just the right touch of genuine regret and put down the grocery bags. "I knew you would have problems with my little sideline. That's why I didn't bring you on board at the start of the project."

"It isn't just what you're dealing, although that's bad enough. It's the people you're working for."

Fury sparked in his eyes and in his aura.

"I don't work for anyone else," he said through his teeth. "Crocker World is mine. I built the company, damn it. I am Crocker World."

"You *were* Crocker World. But you've handed the company you built, that I *helped* you build, to some sort of criminal organization."

"You had nothing to do with my success. You should be down on your knees thanking me for what I did for you. If I hadn't come along, you'd still be working in that low-rent flower shop, living all by yourself with a couple of cats because you scare off every man you meet. Hell, sometimes you even scare me."

That shook her. "What?"

"The way you take one look at a person and figure out what makes him tick. What he'd kill for. What scares the shit out of him. His strengths and weaknesses. It's damned spooky. Why do you think I'm getting rid of you?"

"You're forgetting something, Martin. If you hadn't offered me a job twelve years ago, you'd still be operating a cheap way-off-the-strip casino in Binge, Nevada. I'm the one who identified the cheats who were robbing you blind. I'm the one who helped you pay off that mob boss. If it hadn't been for me, you'd have been buried in some shallow grave out in the desert by now."

"That's a lie."

"And I'm the one who identified those first investors for you, the venture capitalists who backed you when you decided to sell the casino and start building condo towers."

Martin's aura was an inferno now.

"I would have found the investors on my own," he shouted.

"That's not true. You're a mid-range strategy talent, Martin. You can sense opportunities and put together a plan with a skill few can match because you're psychic in that way. But you're no good when it comes to reading people."

"Shut your stupid mouth."

"Without that talent, all the business insight in the world is useless. Building a financial empire isn't just about numbers and the bottom line. It's about identifying and exploiting your opponent's strengths and weaknesses."

He gave her a sharklike smile. "You think I need a lecture on the art of the deal from you?"

"For twelve years I've been your personal profiler. I'm the one who tells you when a business associate is in trouble, either financially or in his personal life. I warn you when someone is trying to con you. I identify the strengths and weaknesses of your opponents and your partners. I tell you exactly what you need to offer to someone in order to close the deal, and I'm the one who tells you when your best option is to walk away from the table."

"You had your uses, I'll grant you that. But I don't need you anymore.

Before we finish this, though, I'd really like to know how you tumbled on to my little arms-dealing sideline."

"As far as your guests and business associates are concerned, I'm just a trusted member of the staff. No one looks twice at me. No one notices me. But I take a good look at them. That's what you pay me to do, after all. Sometimes I see things and sometimes I hear things. And I am very, very good when it comes to research, remember?"

"How much do you know?"

"About the people you're involved with?" She raised one shoulder slightly. "Not a lot. Just that it's some sort of cartel run by very powerful sensitives and that they've seduced you into doing their dirty work."

Martin's aura flared higher. "No one has seduced me."

"Until recently I would never have believed that anyone could buy you," she said. "I mean, what could a bunch of gangsters offer one of the most successful men on the planet that would make it worth his while to risk his freedom, his reputation and his life?"

Martin's rage showed in his eyes now. "You don't know what the hell you're talking about. The organization isn't some mob."

"Yes, it is, Martin. The first time you brought those two men to the Miami residence, I told you they were very, very dangerous."

"So am I," Martin hissed. He reached up and slowly removed his mirrored glasses. "More dangerous than you can imagine, thanks to my new business associates. And thanks to them, I no longer need you."

"What are you talking about?"

"The organization those two men represent is about much more than money. It's all about power, real power; the kind that world leaders and warlords and billionaires can only dream about."

Suddenly she understood. She had not thought that she could be any more appalled than she already was but she had been wrong.

"I guess this explains the changes in your aura in the past couple of months," she said.

Martin looked startled.

"What changes?" he demanded.

"I thought perhaps you had become the victim of some kind of mental illness that affected your parasenses."

"I am not sick, damn you."

"Yes, you are, but not because of some natural disease process. You did this to yourself. With a little help from your new friends, of course."

Martin took a step closer. He didn't look horrified. He looked eager. Excited. "You can see the effects of the drug in my aura?"

"A drug," she repeated. "Yes, that's the only logical explanation. Those two men supplied you with some sort of drug that affects your parasenses."

"There's an excellent likelihood that it will also increase my natural life span, maybe by as much as a couple of decades. What's more, they'll be good decades. I won't be weak and frail. I'll maintain my powers."

"I can't believe I'm hearing this. Martin, you're a brilliant businessman. Don't you know when you've been sold a bill of goods? The promise of longevity is the oldest scam in the world."

"The reason the researchers aren't certain about the extended life span is because the new drug hasn't been around long enough to test the theory. Those at the top have been using the stuff for only a few years. But the lab data look very promising."

"You're a fool, Martin."

"It's true," he insisted. "Even if they're wrong about the drug's ability to lengthen my life, that doesn't alter the fact that the formula *works*. It can kick a level-seven strategy talent like me all the way up to a nine or a ten."

"You're not a nine or a ten. I'd know. Something has changed in your aura, though. Whatever it is, it isn't—" She broke off, groping for the right word. "It isn't wholesome."

"Wholesome?" He laughed. "Now there's a silly, old-fashioned word.

Do you think I care how *wholesome* I am? For your information, you're right, though. The drug they gave me didn't elevate the level of my talent. It wasn't intended to have that effect."

"I don't understand."

"The drug can be genetically altered in a variety of ways to suit an individual's psychic profile. The version I'm taking has provided me with an entirely new talent."

"If you believe that, you really have gone off the deep end."

"I am not insane," Martin shouted.

The words seemed to echo around them. A few seconds of terrifying stillness followed. Then Martin's aura flared with a sickening heat.

She knew, then, that the moment had come. He was going to try to kill her now. The only question was whether he intended to use a gun or his bare hands. One thing was certain, standing there at the end of the dock left her nowhere to run.

The mind-searing blast of energy came out of nowhere. It roared over her, bringing disorienting pain and the promise of an endless plunge into the abyss.

Not a gun. She fell to her knees under the force of the lightning that slashed at her senses. *Not his bare hands, either.* A slight miscalculation on her part.

Martin stared down at her, enthralled with his own power.

"They were right," he breathed. "They told me the truth about the drug. Congratulations. You are about to become the first person to witness what I can do with my new talent."

"Don't touch me."

"I'm not going to touch you. It isn't necessary. I'm going to incinerate your psychic senses. You will go into a coma and then you will die."

"Martin, no, don't do this." Her voice was steadier now. So were her senses. She had recovered somewhat from the initial traumatizing shock. She was getting a handle on the pain, which meant that she was pushing back the invading waves of energy. "Maybe it's not too late. Maybe some of the experts in the Society can help you."

"You're pleading with me. I like that."

"I'm not going to beg for my life. But there is one thing you should know before you do this."

"What?"

"If you hadn't come along, I would have owned that florist shop by now, a whole chain of flower shops."

"That was always your greatest flaw," Martin said. "Your dreams and ambitions were so much smaller than mine."

He heightened the psychic heat of the dark energy he was generating, his face tightening with effort. She pushed back harder, pulling energy from her own aura. The pain lessened some more.

"Die, damn you," he hissed. He took another step closer. "Why don't you *die*?"

Her strength was coming back. She was able to focus clearly on maintaining the energy shield that her aura had become.

Martin staggered but he did not seem to notice that she was fighting him. Instead, he appeared disoriented.

Angrily, he pulled himself together and took another step toward her, almost touching her. He forced more energy through the murky bands of dark lightning he was generating.

"You're supposed to die," he shouted.

He reached down to seize her by the throat. She raised her arms in a reflexive, defensive gesture. He grabbed her hands. She gripped his wrists.

Her palms burned. The world exploded, sending jolt after jolt of shock waves through her senses.

Martin Crocker convulsed once. He looked at her with the eyes of a man who is peering into hell.

"No," he screamed.

He reeled, lost his balance and went over the side of the dock into the water. His aura winked out with terrifying suddenness.

She rose, heart pounding. For the second time in her life, she had killed a man. Not just any man this time—a very powerful, influential multibillionaire who just happened to be involved in a dangerous criminal enterprise.

And her hands still burned.

One

WAIKIKI . . .

The big man in the short-sleeved, orange and purple flowered shirt was going to be a problem in about five minutes. It didn't take a psychic to sense the angry, volatile energy stirring the atmosphere around table five. Any experienced bartender would have picked up on it. For a bartender who just happened to be psychic and who was also an ex-cop, the invisible warning signs had started blazing neon-bright when Mr. Orange and Purple Flowers walked into the Dark Rainbow half an hour earlier.

Luther Malone gave the mai tai a quick stir with a swizzle stick and set it on Julie's tray next to the beer and the Blue Hawaii. Julie leaned over the bar to pluck a cherry and a slice of pineapple out of the chilled containers.

"Got trouble on five," she said quietly. "The idiot is picking on Crazy Ray. Fortunately for the big fool, Ray hasn't noticed yet."

"I'll take care of it," Luther said.

Although the hole-in-the-wall establishment was located in Waikiki, they didn't get much tourist trade. Tucked away in a small courtyard half a block off busy Kuhio Avenue, the Rainbow catered to an eccentric group of regulars. Some of the customers, Crazy Ray among them, were more eccentric than others. Ray had long ago dedicated himself to the gods of surfing. When Ray was not surfing, he went into a Zen-like state. Everyone who knew him acknowledged that he was best left in that otherworldly zone.

"Be careful," Julie said. She garnished the mai tai with the pineapple and the cherry. "A lot of that bulk is muscle, not fat."

"Yeah, I can see that. I appreciate the tip."

Julie flashed him a quick smile. "I'd really hate to have anything happen to you, boss. The hours on this job mesh perfectly with my work at the hotel."

Like so many others employed in the tourist trade throughout Hawaii, Julie held down two jobs. Life in the islands had its benefits but it was expensive. Friday and Saturday nights she showed up at the Dark Rainbow to help with the dinner rush. Her regular day job was working the front desk at one of the countless small, faded, budget hotels that somehow managed to survive in the shadows of the big beachfront resorts and high-rise condos.

In addition to Julie two nights a week, the Rainbow usually employed a dishwasher. That position, however, was currently open. Again. Dishwashers came and went with such relentless frequency that the proprietors, Petra and Wayne Groves, no longer bothered to remember names. They called each one Bud and let it go at that. The most recent Bud had quit the previous night. Evidently the job had interfered with his regular appointments with his meth dealer.

The door to the kitchen swung open. Wayne Groves, half owner of the Rainbow, emerged with a tray of platters, each laden with mounds of deep-fried food. Pretty much everything that came out of the Dark Rainbow's kitchen was fried.

Wayne came to an abrupt halt, his attention riveted on the man in the orange and purple shirt.

Wayne had a lean, rangy build and hard, sharp features that would have suited an old school gunslinger. His eyes went with the image. They were ice cold. He was sixty-five but could still read the last line on the chart at the eye doctor's. The truth was he could have read a few more lines below that but they didn't design eye tests for people with preternatural vision.

Wayne was covered from head to foot in tattoos, the most distinctive one being the red-eyed snake coiled around his gleaming bald scalp. The head of the snake was positioned high on his forehead, a dark jewel in an ominous crown.

Wayne was a very focused person. Most of the time the full force of his concentration was directed at taking orders for fish and chips and hamburgers or polishing glassware. But at the moment he was locked on another target. Flower Shirt didn't know it but he was now squarely in the sights of a man who had once made his living working as a sniper for a clandestine government agency.

Luther grabbed the cane that was hooked over the counter. Time to get moving. The last thing they needed at the Rainbow was an incident that would result in a visit from the Honolulu PD. The neighboring business establishments would not appreciate it. Around here, everyone liked to keep a low profile. That went double for the Rainbow's regulars, most of whom were badly damaged sensitives like Crazy Ray.

He maneuvered his way out from behind the bar. He paused briefly near the still and silent Wayne.

"It's okay," he said. "I'll handle it."

Wayne blinked and snapped out of his lethal stillness.

"Whatever," he growled. He turned and glided toward a nearby table.

The kitchen door opened again on a wave of grease-scented heat. Petra Groves, the chef and co-owner of the restaurant, appeared. She raked the room with an assessing expression while she wiped her hands on her badly stained apron.

"Had a feelin'," she said. She hadn't lived in Texas since childhood but the laid-back accent still clung to every word she spoke.

Petra's intuition, like Wayne's ability to take down a target with an impossibly long-range rifle shot, was well above normal. Actually, it could only be described as paranormal.

Both Wayne and Petra were mid-range sensitives; both had retired from the same no-name agency. Petra had been Wayne's spotter in the days when Wayne had worked as a sniper. Together they had formed a lethal team. They had also become another kind of team—partners for life.

Petra was a sturdily built woman in her early sixties. She wore her long gray hair in a braid down her back. A badly yellowed chef's toque sat squarely atop her head. A gold ring glinted in one ear. While Wayne carried a concealed gun in an ankle holster, Petra favored a knife; a big one. She kept it in a sheath beneath her long apron.

"I've got it handled," Luther said.

"Right." Petra nodded once and stalked back into the hot kitchen.

Luther tapped his way across the tiled floor. The overall level of tension in the room was rising fast. The crowd was getting restless. The study of parapsychology had been thoroughly discredited by the modern scientific establishment. Because of that, a lot of folks went through their entire lives ignoring, suppressing or remaining willfully oblivious to the psychic side of their natures. But in situations like this, even those with normal sensitivity found themselves looking around for the nearest exit well before they had registered exactly what was wrong. The crowd at the Rainbow was anything but normal.

Flower Shirt didn't seem to be aware of Luther or the restless energy of the regulars. He was too busy poking at Crazy Ray with a sharp, verbal stick.

"Hey, Surfer Bum," he said loudly. "You make a good living screwing female tourists? How much do you charge the ladies for a peek at your little surfboard?"

Ray ignored him. He continued to sit hunched over his beer, munching steadily on his deep-fried fish and fries. He had the broad-shouldered build and the burned-in tan of a man who spends his days riding the waves. His lanky brown hair had been bleached by the sun. Couldn't blame Flower Shirt for picking the wrong target, Luther thought. Ray didn't look crazy, not unless you could see his aura.

"What's the matter?" Flower Shirt said. "Got a problem answering a simple question? Where's that aloha spirit I'm always hearing so much about?"

Ray put down his beer and started to turn. Luther jacked up his senses until he could see the auras of those around him. Light and dark reversed but not in the way they did in a photographic negative. When he was running hot like this the colors he viewed were anything but black and white. The hues came from various points along the paranormal spectrum. There were no words to describe them. Energy pulsed and flared and spiked around every person in the vicinity.

The growing tension had been palpable to his normal senses, but perceived through his parasenses, it had already escalated into a flood tide of dangerously swirling currents.

The brief moment of vertigo that always accompanied the shift in perception evaporated between one step and the next. He was accustomed to the short flash of acute disorientation. He had been living with his talent since he had come into it in his early teens.

He concentrated on Ray first. Flower Shirt was the most obnoxious person within range but Ray was the most unpredictable. The seething, barely controlled craziness showed clearly in the murky hues and erratic pulses of his aura. The most alarming stuff took the shape of sickly, greenish-yellow filaments that flashed and disappeared in no discernible pattern. The tendrils gathered strength rapidly as Ray's frail grasp on reality started to weaken. He slid rapidly into his uniquely paranoid universe.

"Keep away from me," Ray said softly.

A smart man, hearing that voice, would have backed off immediately, but Flower Shirt grinned, unaware that he was about to let a very un-stable, unpredictable genie out of its bottle.

"Don't worry, Surfer Bum," he said. "The last thing I want to do is get too close to you. Might catch whatever diseases you picked up from those tourists you service."

Ray started to rise, muscled shoulders bunching beneath his ripped T-shirt. Luther was less than two feet away now. He concentrated on the unwholesome greenish-yellow spikes of energy that snapped and cracked in Ray's aura. With exquisite precision—mistakes often had extremely unpleasant consequences—he generated a wave of suppressing energy from his own aura. The pulses resonated with Ray's in a counterpoint pattern. The green-yellow tendrils of energy weakened visibly.

Ray blinked a few times and frowned in confusion. Luther tweaked his aura a little more. With a sigh, Ray lost interest in Aloha Shirt. Suddenly exhausted, he sank back down into his chair.

"Why don't you finish your beer?" Luther said to him. "I'll take care of this."

"Yeah, sure." Ray looked at the bottle on the table. "My beer."

Grateful for direction in the midst of the overwhelming ennui, he picked up the bottle and took a long swallow.

Deprived of his prey, Flower Shirt reacted with spiraling rage. His face scrunched up into a snarl. He leaned to one side and peered around Luther.

"Hey, I'm talking to you, Surfer Asshole," he yelled at Ray.

"No," Luther said, using the same low voice he had employed with Ray. "You're talking to me. We're discussing the fact that you would like to leave now."

Flower Shirt's aura was a lot more stable than Ray's. That was the good news. The bad news was that the colors were those of frustration and fury.

The politically correct view of bullies was that they suffered from low self-esteem and tried to compensate by making other people their victims. As far as Luther was concerned, that was pure bull. Guys like Flower Shirt felt superior to others and lacked all traces of empathy. Bullies bullied not out of some unconscious desire to try to compensate for their low self-esteem. They did it because they could and because they enjoyed it.

The only way to stop a bully was to scare him. The species had a strong sense of self-preservation.

There was nothing tricky or mysterious about the wavelengths of energy in Flower Shirt's pattern. The hot rush of the man's unchecked lust for verbal abuse spiked and pulsed very clearly. Luther generated the suppressing patterns. The compelling urge to hurt and dominate Ray died instantly beneath the heavy, crushing weight of exhaustion but Flower Shirt was already on his feet, turning his attention to Luther.

"Get out of my way, bartender, unless you want a fist in your face."

He grabbed Luther's arm, intending to shove him aside. That was a mistake. Physical contact intensified the force of the energy that Luther was using.

Flower Shirt swayed a little and nearly lost his balance. He grabbed the edge of the table to keep himself upright.

"What?" he got out. "I think I'm sick or something."

"Don't worry about the bill," Luther said. He took hold of Flower

Shirt's arm and steered him toward the door. "The drinks are on the house."

"Huh?" Flower Shirt shook his head, unable to focus. "Wh-what's goin' on?"

"You're leaving now."

"Oh." Flower Shirt's brow creased. "Okay. I guess. Kinda tired all of a sudden."

He made no attempt to resist. A hush fell over the crowd. The other diners watched in silence as Luther guided Flower Shirt outside into the night.

When the door closed behind them the noise level inside the Dark Rainbow went back to normal.

"What's going on?" Flower Shirt rubbed his eyes. "Where are we going?"

"You're going back to your hotel."

"Yeah?" There was no defiance in the word, just dazed confusion.

Luther guided Flower Shirt through the small courtyard, steering him around the sickly-looking potted palms that Wayne had set out in a misbegotten effort to add a little authentic island atmosphere.

It was going on ten o'clock. The proprietor of the gun club on the second floor had taken in the sign that promised tourists a *Safe Shooting Environment, Real Guns, Factory Ammo* and *Excellent Customer Service*. For reasons Luther had never fully comprehended, businesses that allowed visitors to the island the opportunity to shoot in indoor ranges thrived in Waikiki.

The Red Skull Tattoo and Body Piercing Parlor and Zen Comics were also closed for the night but the rusty window air conditioners of the adult video arcade were grinding away as usual. It was the only way to know if the place was open. No light ever showed through the grimy, blacked-out windows of the arcade. The customers slipped in and out like so many wraiths, preferring the cover of darkness.

Luther prodded his zombie-like companion beneath the antique wooden surfboard that marked the entrance to the courtyard and walked him along the narrow lane to Kuhio Avenue. At this hour there was plenty of traffic and the open-air restaurants and taverns were crowded.

He debated taking Flower Shirt another block to Kalakaua, where the brilliantly lit windows of the high-end designer boutiques and the more upscale restaurants lured herds of visitors out into the balmy night. No need to go to the trouble, he decided. He could do what needed to be done right here.

Unfortunately, it would do little good to merely dump Flower Shirt on the street. The effects of the suppression energy were short-lived. Luther knew that once he released Flower Shirt from the extreme ennui, the guy would bounce right back to whatever state was normal for him.

When he came out of the fugue he would remember that his attempt to bait Ray had somehow stalled and that the bartender had gotten in his way. He would also recall that he had been escorted off the premises in an ignominious fashion by a gimp on a cane. Those memories would be more than enough incentive to bring him back to the Rainbow in search of revenge.

Fear was one of the most primitive emotions, a core survival instinct that, like all such instincts, was hardwired into the brain. That meant it was experienced across the spectrum of the senses from the normal straight into the paranormal. It was also one of the easiest emotions to trigger, if you had the knack. And once triggered, it tended to hang around for a while.

Bullies comprehended fear well because they spent so much time instilling it in others.

Luther took a breath and let it out slowly. He wasn't looking forward to this part but a bartender does what a bartender's got to do.

He went hotter, revving up his senses. Then he turned his unresisting zombie so that Flower Shirt faced the entrance to the lane that led to the Rainbow.

"You don't ever want to go down there," he said. "Folks in that little restaurant are all crazy. No telling what they'll do. Like walking into a room full of nitroglycerin. You're way too smart to go back."

He accompanied the words with little pulses of energy aimed at the latent fear points on Flower Shirt's paranormal spectrum, deliberately stirring and arousing as many as he could identify. There was a reason for the term "panic button." He tweaked and fiddled until Flower Shirt was sweating and shaking and staring into the dark lane as though it were the gate to hell.

With luck, when he recovered from the experience, the memory of the lane and the Dark Rainbow would be inextricably linked to a sub-liminal sense of deep unease. Flower Shirt would never be able to ex-plain it; probably wouldn't even try. But if he happened to pass this way again, he would instinctively avoid the lane. That was how fear worked on the psychic level. Usually.

The problem with trying to establish a fear response was that there was always the possibility that it would backfire on you. Some people felt compelled to confront their fears. But in Luther's experience that wasn't true of the bully mentality.

He eased off the psychic pressure. Flower Shirt calmed.

"You want to go back to your hotel room," Luther said. "Had a little too much to drink tonight. Go sleep it off."

"Yeah, right," Flower Shirt whispered, anxious now. "Too much booze."

He hurried toward the intersection and crossed the street. He disap-peared around the corner, heading toward Kalakaua and the safety of the bright lights of the beachfront hotels.

Luther leaned heavily on his cane, feeling the dark weight of what he had done. He hated this part. There was always a price to pay when he used his talent on someone like Flower Shirt.

The bastard may have deserved what he got but the reality was that the battle had been unequal from the get-go. He never stood a chance; never even knew what hit him.

Yeah, that part sucked.

Two

After they closed the restaurant for the night they followed their usual custom and walked down Kuhio to the Udon Palace. Milly Okada, the proprietor, brought them huge bowls filled with steaming, aromatic broth and plump noodles. She gave Luther a knowing look when she set the soup down in front of him.

"You okay?" she asked.

"I'm fine, Milly." Luther picked up the chopsticks. "I just need some of your udon, that's all. Been a long night."

"You're depressed again," she announced. "You should be feeling better now that your leg is almost healed."

"For sure," Petra agreed. "But he's not feelin' better. He's feelin' worse."

The wound had healed but his leg was never going to be the same. The damned cane would be a part of his life from now on. He was still coming to terms with that fact but that was not why he was feeling low tonight. He did not know how to explain the real problem to anyone.

"I am feeling better," he insisted. "Just a little tired, that's all. Like I said, it's been a long night."

"I'll get you another beer," Milly said.

She disappeared through the fluttery panels of red-and-white cloth that screened the kitchen from the dining area.

"Milly and Petra are right, you're depressed again." Wayne used his chopsticks to slurp up a mouthful of noodles. "Take the J&J job. That will make you feel better."

"Yeah," Petra said. "That will get you out of this little funk you've been in for the past couple of months."

Luther glared at them across the small table. "The job Jones offered is make-work. A two-day babysitting gig on Maui."

"So what?" Wayne tapped the chopsticks on the rim of his bowl. "It's work. Means you're back in the game."

"No," Luther said. "It doesn't mean that. It means that Fallon Jones is feeling sorry for me, maybe even a little guilty because of what happened on the last job. He's decided to throw me a bone."

Petra snorted. "Get real. Fallon Jones doesn't do sympathy and he wouldn't recognize a guilt trip if one bit him on the ass."

"Okay, I'll concede that Fallon is not given to indulging the finer feelings," Luther said. "That leaves only one other reason why he left that message in my voice mail."

"What?" Petra demanded.

"The job is so low-rent he doesn't want to waste money paying for an agent to fly from the mainland."

"Huh." Petra shrugged. "Maybe. My advice is to take the bone."

"Why?" Luther asked.

"Because you need to gnaw on something besides your own thoughts. Working for J&J again, even if it is just a two-day bodyguard job, will be good for you."

"Think so?"

"Yeah," Petra said. "And there's another reason you should take the job."

"What?"

"I've got a feelin' about it."

"You had a feeling about the last job," Luther reminded her.

They all looked at the cane hooked over the back of a chair.

"This feelin' is a little different," Petra said.

Three

It was after two in the morning by the time he limped up the steps to the second floor of the old, two-story Sunset Surf Apartments. Bruno the Wonder Dog yipped wildly when he went past the owner's unit. Bruno was small and fluffy and probably weighed less than five pounds but he had the guard instincts of a Doberman. No one gained access to the grounds of the Sunset Surf without Bruno announcing the fact.

Inside 2-B, he flipped a switch, illuminating the threadbare carpet, the aging paint and the yard-sale furniture he'd bought two years ago when he moved to the islands. He'd been paying off his second divorce at the time. Money had been tight. Money was still tight.

He'd been using the J&J work to help build up his bank account. Things had just started to turn around and he'd even been contemplating a move into a more upscale apartment when he took the job Fallon had offered two months ago. Getting shot had not only hurt like hell, it had proven to be a major financial setback.

Wayne and Petra were right. He should accept the babysitting job Fallon had offered. His pride would take a hit but he could use the money. J&J paid well.

He went into the small kitchen and took down the bottle of excellent whiskey that Wayne and Petra had given him for his birthday. He poured a healthy dose, opened the sliding glass doors and went out onto the microchip-sized lanai.

He leaned on the railing and took a swallow of whiskey. The silken night closed around him like an unseen lover, soothing all his senses. The Sunset Surf was one of innumerable small apartment houses tucked away in the maze of Waikiki's backstreets and alleys. It did not have a view of either the sunset or the surf. It also lacked air-conditioning and a pool. What it did have was a massive, heavy-limbed banyan tree in back that helped keep things cool during the hot summer months.

His neighbors consisted of the owner, a senior citizen he knew only as Bea, a couple of retirees from Alaska, an aging surfer with no discernible means of support and some guy who claimed he was writing a novel. It was not what you could call a sociable crowd.

The whiskey was doing its job. He was starting to feel if not exactly mellow, at least a tad more philosophical.

As if on cue his cell phone vibrated and buzzed. He unclipped it from his belt and opened it without bothering to look at the ID of the incoming call. There were only three people who had his number and he was pretty sure Petra and Wayne were asleep by now.

"Do you know what time it is here, Fallon?" he asked.

"Hawaii is two hours earlier than California this time of year." Fallon sounded irritated, a normal state of affairs for him. "What does that have to do with anything?"

Fallon Jones was the head of Jones & Jones, a very low-profile psychic investigation agency. He had a few redeeming qualities, including a powerful talent for spotting patterns and links where others saw only random chance or murky coincidence. Other assorted virtues such as good manners, thoughtfulness and patience, however, eluded him.

"I was going to call you in the morning," Luther said.

"It's four A.M. here. That's morning. I can't wait any longer for you to think about whether or not you're going to take the job. I need an answer now. I don't have time to cater to your delicate sensibilities."

"Translated, you don't have anyone else available who just happens to be in the neighborhood."

"Yeah, that, too. You're good and you're convenient. A real win-win combination in my book. What's the problem? This isn't like you."

Why was he hesitating? Luther wondered. Fallon was right. It wasn't like him. He'd been taking contract jobs with J&J ever since he resigned from the Seattle PD two years ago. He liked the work. Okay, except when he got shot. Fact was, when he was in this kind of mood he craved J&J assignments.

The agency was unique. It was established during the Victorian era, and it was always understood that its chief client was the Governing Council of the Arcane Society. Its highest priority was to protect the Society's deepest secrets.

But somewhere along the way, the Council had acknowledged that most police departments simply weren't equipped to deal with certain types of psychic sociopaths. Few members of modern law enforcement were even willing to acknowledge that some killers were endowed with talent. By and large, the Council considered that a good thing. The paranormal got enough bizarre press as it was, most of it in the harmless form of outrageous tabloid headlines and silly television talk shows. No one wanted the police to start making serious announcements to the media about psychic killers.

As far back as the Victorian era, the Council had reluctantly accepted responsibility for hunting down certain dangerous, renegade talents on the theory that it was better to handle such problems internally rather than risk allowing the freaks to continue to operate.

The Maui job might be a routine bodyguard assignment but it was something and he could use the money. And Petra had a feeling about it.

"I'll do it," he said.

"About time you came to your senses," Fallon grumbled. "By the way, you'll be working with a partner this time."

"Whoa. Hold it right there. In your voice mail you said it was a bodyguard gig."

"More like a chaperoning gig."

"What the hell does that mean?"

"The person you're going to be looking after is not one of my regular agents. She's what you might call a specialist. A consultant. It's her first time in the field. Your job is to make sure she doesn't get into trouble. Let her do her job and then get her out of there. Simple."

"I'm not mentor material, Fallon."

"Don't go into your lockdown stubborn mode on me, Malone. You'll definitely be in charge of the operation."

"That's supposed to reassure me? In my experience specialists and consultants don't take orders well."

"Damn it, we've got a real shot at nailing Eubanks here. I'm not about to see it blown just because you don't fancy working with a specialist."

Eubanks was a suspect in the recent murder of a young woman whose family were all registered members of the Society. After the police officially ruled the death a tragic accident, the victim's parents asked J&J to investigate the death. A psychic profiler who visited the scene of the crime prepared a profile that Fallon then handed over to one of the librarians in the Society's Bureau of Genealogy. The librarian ran the data through the department's latest whizbang computer program and produced three possible suspects. Eubanks's name was at the top.

"I think you'd better find someone else," Luther said.

"There is no one else. I need you and Grace Renquist on the scene by tomorrow. Eubanks is due in the following day. If he's worried about being followed, he's more likely to be watching to see who arrives after him, not who is at the hotel before he gets there."

"I know how surveillance works," Luther said patiently. "Who's Grace Renquist?"

"Among other things, she's an aura talent like you but with a twist."

"Every talent has a twist. What's hers?"

"She can read auras like no one I've ever known." Fervent admiration hummed in Fallon's voice. "When she gets a look at Eubanks, she'll be able to tell me whether he matches the psychic profile that was prepared by the agent who investigated the crime scene. What's more, she'll probably be able to tell if Eubanks committed an act of extreme violence anytime within the past few months. Our client's daughter was murdered six weeks ago."

"Give me a break. No one can see that kind of detail in an aura."

"Grace Renquist can. You know that old saying about murder leaving a stain? She says it's true in the sense that it taints an aura in some unusual ways."

"Uh-huh. And just how would she know that?"

"With Grace I don't ask too many personal questions," Fallon said.

"Look, even if she can make a positive ID for you, that's not going to be of much help. You need solid evidence to give to the police in cases like this. Oddly enough, they hesitate to arrest people on the basis of an aura reading."

"Which is a major pain in the ass," Fallon grumbled. "But I'll worry about digging up hard evidence after I know whether or not we've got the right guy. I'm still looking at two other possible suspects."

"You said Grace Renquist is not one of your regular agents. What does she do?"

"She's a reference librarian in the Society's Bureau of Genealogy."

"A *librarian?*"

"Specializes in the familial patterns of genetically inherited psychic traits."

The Arcane Society had kept extensive genealogical records of its members since its inception in the late 1600s. It had not escaped the notice of the founder of the Society, Sylvester Jones, a brilliant if decidedly twisted alchemist, that psychic talent could be passed down through families. In the past few years, the Bureau of Genealogy had put the contents of its extensive collection of dusty tomes containing the family trees of generations of members into a computer database.

"I don't believe this," Luther said. "You want to pair me with some gray-haired little old lady from Genealogy? Is this your idea of a joke?"

"Now do you see my problem? I can't send a sweet, innocent elderly librarian into a situation like this alone. She wouldn't have a clue. With my luck she'd give herself away to Eubanks, who would bop her on the back of her bun and dump her body. Next thing you know, I'd have Old Beak yelling at me for getting one of his people killed on the job."

Harley Beakman was the notoriously obsessive and powerful head of the Bureau of Genealogy. The name Old Beak had been bestowed on him decades earlier because of a certain unmistakable aspect of his profile. The moniker had stuck because he possessed the personality of a bad-tempered rooster.

"You can skip the high drama," Luther said wearily. "I get the point."

"I depend on Genealogy for a lot of my research. I need the cooperation of Old Beak and his staff. If I let anything happen to one of his people, I'll be screwed."

"I admire the way you're always thinking of others, Fallon."

"Listen, this is just a fast in-and-out job. Two days max. You and Miss Renquist go to the resort on Maui. You hang out awhile until she makes the ID, and then you put her on a plane home before she can muck up my investigation. How complicated is that?"

"Let me guess, I'm going to pose as a dutiful son escorting his elderly mom on a Hawaiian vacation, right? Please tell me I'm not going to be one of those guys going on forty who's still living with his mother."

"I'm having the documents related to your covers couriered to Renquist tonight," Fallon said a little too smoothly. "She'll have them with her when she meets you in Honolulu tomorrow."

"You're sure you don't mean this morning?"

"I don't make mistakes like that. She's booked on a flight from Portland, Oregon, tomorrow morning that leaves at eight. Got a pen?"

Luther went back inside the apartment. He found a pen and a pad on the kitchen counter.

"Go," he said.

Fallon rattled off the flight number and repeated the date. "She lands in Honolulu at eleven thirty-five. The two of you will travel on to Maui under your new IDs and check into the hotel."

"She lives in Portland?" Luther asked.

Not that it mattered where Renquist lived.

"No, a little town on the Oregon coast," Fallon said. "Place called Eclipse Bay."

"Never heard of it."

"Yeah, well, I get the impression that's why Miss Renquist likes it there."

"A lot of senior citizens get off the planes here," Luther said. "How will I recognize her?"

"She'll probably be wearing gloves."

"Gloves? In Hawaii? It'll be eighty-one degrees here tomorrow."

"Miss Renquist likes to wear gloves," Fallon said. "She's a little eccentric that way."

"She'll stand out in the crowd, all right. Tell her I'll be in khakis and a dark brown shirt."

"Is the shirt with or without flowers?"

"Without."

"I'm sure the two of you will find each other without too much trouble."

Fallon ended the sentence with a couple of odd snorts and cut the connection.

Luther left the piece of paper with Grace Renquist's flight information on the counter and went back out onto the balcony. He would get a few hours' sleep and then he would call Petra and Wayne and tell them he had taken the Maui job. At least they'd be pleased.

He finished the whiskey and thought about the strange vocalizations Fallon had made just before ending the call.

If it had been anyone other than Fallon Jones, he would have sworn that the odd snorts were laughter.

Four

ECLIPSE BAY, OREGON . . .

She would get a dog when she returned from the Maui assignment.

The decision made, Grace Renquist turned away from the dresser and placed the neatly folded nightgown into the suitcase. There was nothing sexy about the plain white cotton garment. The sleeves were long and the hemline fell to her ankles. It had not been purchased for purposes of seduction and enticement. She had selected the cozy gown for its practical virtues. Winter nights were chilly on the Oregon coast.

The nightgown was all wrong for Hawaii and so was everything else she was putting into the suitcase, especially the spare pair of thin black leather gloves. A year ago she had fled her old life with only the clothes on her back. She did not even own a bathing suit; hadn't needed one in Eclipse Bay. But she was not about to buy a whole new wardrobe for what she had been informed would be a very short trip to Maui. The Arcane Society paid well but not nearly as well as her previous job. In her new life as a psychic genealogist, she had to exercise some financial restraint.

The work was fascinating and rewarding but it wasn't enough to banish the increasing gloom of loneliness. *Should have gotten a dog months ago.* But she knew why she had resisted the temptation. There had been so many uncertainties during this first year as Grace Renquist. What if the Florida authorities tracked her down? What if the two men whose auras pulsed with dark energy found her? What if her new identity didn't survive scrutiny by J&J? She had wanted to be prepared to disappear again in the blink of an eye. A dog would have complicated any escape plan. She knew that she would not have been able to abandon it.

But it had been a little over twelve months since Martin Crocker had died. Surely if anyone had been looking for her she would have sensed it by now. Her survival instincts were inextricably linked to her peculiar version of aura talent. Both had been honed razor sharp at the age of fourteen. Even more reassuring, she had made it through the J&J background checks. She was safe now; tucked away in that great dusty vault of the Arcane Society officially known as the Bureau of Genealogy. True, the contents of the vault these days were housed online and she accessed them with a computer; nevertheless, the metaphor still applied.

She was safe. It would be okay to get a dog.

Her cell phone rang. She glanced at the coded number and answered immediately.

"Good morning, Mr. Jones," she said. The formality was automatic, one of the many tools she employed to keep some distance between herself and others.

"Are you packed yet?"

She had never met the man in person. Fallon Jones ran J&J from a one-man office tucked away in a little town on the northern California coast. Some said he was an obsessively paranoid recluse. Others claimed that the reason he lived and worked alone was because no one could stand being around him for more than five minutes. It was true that he had the personality of an annoyed rhinoceros. He was also a brilliant talent.

She had done some off-the-books genealogical research shortly after her boss, Harley Beakman, had begun referring Jones's queries to her. Evidently she was the only one in the department who had the patience to put up with the ceaseless demands of the notoriously difficult head of J&J.

It hadn't taken much sleuthing to discover that Fallon was a direct descendant of Caleb Jones, the founder of Jones & Jones. That much was not a secret. There was also no question but that Fallon ranked very high on the Jones Scale, probably off the charts. She knew from her work that the members of the Jones family—many of them legends in the Society—were not above fudging their talent rankings with a view to making themselves appear less psychically powerful than they actually were. She did not hold that against them. She had discreetly cranked her own ranking back to a more respectable and far less intimidating level seven.

The exact nature of Fallon's talent, however, had proved elusive, probably because no one had yet come up with a polite, scientifically neutral term for what most people referred to as a full-blown conspiracy theorist.

The thing that set Fallon apart from the general run of committed conspiracy nuts was the fact that the mysterious patterns he identified and which he wove into his elaborate theories were not a product of his feverish fantasies. They were real. Most of the time.

"Almost finished," she assured him. "I'll be on my way to Portland in an hour or so. Before I leave I have to drop by the post office to ask Mrs. Waggoner to hold my mail, and then I have to notify my landlady that I'll be out of town for two or three days. That's it."

"You have to make an announcement about this trip to the whole damn town?" Fallon growled.

"Trust me, if I don't inform my landlady about the trip and leave word at the post office, there will be rumors within twenty-four hours. The next thing I know, the police chief will be knocking on my door wanting to see if I'm alive. This is a very small town."

"Yeah, yeah, I know how it is with small towns. Same story here in Scargill Cove. Do what you have to do and then get moving."

"Yes, sir."

"You're booked into an airport hotel in Portland tonight. The ID you and Malone will be using will be delivered to you there by a Society courier. Your flight to Honolulu leaves tomorrow morning. Malone will meet you at the gate in the Interisland Terminal at Honolulu International. That's where the two of you will catch the connecting flight to Maui."

"How will I recognize Mr. Malone?"

"Well, let's see. He's a level-eight aura talent. With your sensitivity you'll be able to pick him out in a crowd. Can't be that many level eights running around Honolulu International."

Luther Malone was the one factor in the venture that bothered her. She had not had an opportunity to research his family tree but she was not worried about his level-eight ranking. It certainly indicated above-average strength but nothing out of the ordinary, at least not within the Society. What concerned her was the fact that Malone had once been a cop, specifically a homicide detective. What's more, his record for closing cases was extraordinarily good. Cops could be tricky. But she had dealt with a number of them over the years. She could handle one more.

"All right, I'll watch for an eight aura," she said. "Anything else?"

"His picture is on the driver's license the courier will give you this evening," Fallon said. "But let's see, I think he said he'd be wearing khakis and a dark brown shirt. No flowers. I told him you'll have on a pair of gloves. Don't sweat it. I doubt that the two of you will miss each other at the airport."

She looked down at the gloves in the suitcase and sighed. Like everyone else she met these days, Luther Malone would think she was weird. She was getting very tired of being weird.

"Right," she said.

"I should probably warn you that Malone isn't thrilled about working with a partner. He'll want to know as much about you as possible. Probably try to interrogate you a little. He's an ex-cop. He won't be able to help himself."

It would be okay, she thought. If she could deceive Martin Crocker and conceal her secret from Fallon Jones, she wouldn't have any trouble dealing with an above-average aura talent. Malone wasn't interested in Crocker's death, anyway. He had no reason to be suspicious of her, merely cop-curious about his new partner.

"I'm sure we'll get along just fine," she said, going for smooth competence. She could do smooth competence very well. She'd had a lot of practice during her twelve years with Martin.

"This is your first time in the field as a J&J agent," Fallon continued. "You're going to have to do a little acting on this job but I don't want you to take any risks. That's what Malone will be there for."

"To take the risks?"

"No, to make sure *you* don't. This is a routine surveillance and identification operation, not a takedown. Once you've confirmed Eubanks's psychic profile, your job is done. Malone will get you off Maui and you'll be on the plane back to Oregon ASAP. Understood?"

"Yes, Mr. Jones."

"Look, between you and me, Malone can be a pain in the ass but he's good at what he does. If he starts giving orders, which he probably will, just shut up and do what he says. Any questions?"

"No, sir."

"I love it when my agents call me sir. Almost forgot, there is one more thing that might help you identify Malone on sight."

"Yes?"

"He'll be on a cane."

That stopped her cold. "You've assigned me a bodyguard who has to use a cane to get around?"

"He had a little accident a while back. Unfortunately, the doctors told him that the leg would never really be right. He'll be on that cane for the rest of his life."

"I see. Does Mr. Malone perhaps carry a gun?"

"Not since he left his job in the police department. He told me once that he's not comfortable with guns. Between you and me, he was a lousy shot, anyway."

Great. She was getting a bodyguard who couldn't shoot straight and who relied on a cane.

"I have the impression that this mission isn't exactly a high priority with J&J," she said.

"No, it's not." Fallon exhaled heavily. "Don't get me wrong. If Eubanks killed that young woman, I want him off the street. But essentially, this is a routine case. J&J handles dozens like it every year. Clients come to me and I hand them off to one or more of the agents on my list. It's their job to bring in evidence that will stand up in court."

"But you've got higher priorities?"

"Yes, Grace, I do." Fallon sounded grim and oddly weary.

She wanted to ask what those other priorities were but she knew Fallon well enough to realize she probably wouldn't get an answer if she asked the question. He could be maddeningly secretive.

"I understand, sir," she said instead. "Are you sure that Mr. Malone is the right man for this mission, though? It sounds like he should be thinking about retirement."

"Thing is, he's right there on Oahu. Convenient. And he needs the money."

"On top of everything else he's broke?"

"Two divorces in four years will do that to a man. He's been getting by tending bar in a little place called the Dark Rainbow."

"I see. Well, I suppose there's something to be said for the convenience factor."

"Damn straight," Fallon agreed. "Look, I gotta go. Got the new Master of the Society on the other line. Have fun on Maui."

There was an odd chortling sound in Grace's ear. It was immediately followed by a click as Fallon ended the call.

She closed the phone and contemplated it thoughtfully for a couple of seconds. Had she just heard the sound of Fallon Jones's laughter?

Impossible. Everyone knew that Fallon Jones had no sense of humor.

She put the phone into her purse and went back to packing. The last thing she tucked into her carry-on was her computer. You never knew when you might have to do a little research while on a mission. She closed the lid and zipped the small suitcase closed.

After a year of hiding out and licking her wounds, she was ready to live again. The opportunity for an exciting adventure had been handed to her on a silver platter and, somewhat to her own amazement, she had seized it. Time to start living in the now.

TWENTY MINUTES LATER she emerged from the post office and walked quickly toward her car. An SUV painted camouflage green and brown wheeled into the parking lot. The door popped open. A spry-looking senior citizen climbed out. Her bubble of steel-gray hair was partially covered by a billed cap. She wore military-style fatigues and heavy black boots. Her eyes were shielded by a pair of mirrored sunglasses. The utility belt around her waist was studded with various and assorted implements including binoculars, a flashlight and a high-tech camera.

The look was Arizona Snow's day uniform. At night when she went out on her endless reconnaissance patrols of Eclipse Bay, she switched to black trousers and pants and added a set of night-vision goggles to her ensemble.

"'Mornin', Grace," Arizona called. "Heard you're fixin' to go on a little vacation."

Grace smiled. Arizona Snow was Eclipse Bay's resident eccentric. She must have been in her early eighties but aside from some trouble with arthritis she showed no signs of slowing down. Her commitment to protecting the town from some mysterious, unnamed conspiracy that, as far as anyone knew existed only in her mind, never wavered.

"News travels fast," Grace said, coming to a halt a short distance from Arizona.

"Not everything you hear around here is accurate," Arizona muttered ominously. She took a notebook and pen out of one of the half-dozen pockets that festooned her fatigues. Flipping the notebook open, she clicked her pen. "Goin' to Hawaii, eh?"

"That's right."

Arizona made a note. "Return date?"

"Well, I'm not sure yet. I probably won't be gone long, though. A couple of days, maybe three at the most. Why?"

Arizona looked up, shaking her head at the naive question. "I need to know when you'll be back so I can alert the chief in case you don't return on time."

Grace was touched. Arizona had taken a keen interest in her right from the start and had been happy to rent the cottage to her. As a rule, Arizona viewed every outsider in town with acute suspicion. But with Grace she had assumed an air of comradely understanding. It was as if she had concluded that the two of them had unspoken secrets in common.

That assumption was probably not too far from the truth, Grace thought. One thing she had discovered in the past few months was that, although Arizona had lived in Eclipse Bay for several years, no one seemed to recall exactly when she had moved into town and no one seemed to know where she had come from.

There were rumors about her, the most dramatic being that she had once worked for a mysterious government intelligence agency. The theory was that she had either resigned or been forced to retire when she became permanently lost in her own strange world.

"I'm afraid we'll have to leave my return date open," Grace said gently.

"Understood." Arizona snapped the notebook closed and looked around, making certain there was no one in the vicinity who might be eavesdropping.

Satisfied that they had privacy, she edged a little closer, respectful, as always, of the distance that Grace preferred to keep between herself and others. Arizona was one of the few people Grace had met who seemed to sense intuitively that she did not like to be touched. The leather gloves offered a degree of protection but they were by no means foolproof. Touching the wrong individual, however fleetingly, could be an ordeal.

"So, the agency is finally sending you out on a field assignment," Arizona said in low tones. "You be careful now, honey. From what I can tell, you're an analyst, not a trained operative. I'll bet your experience has all been at a desk with a computer. I hope they're supplying some muscle to keep an eye on you."

The irony of the situation made Grace smile. Arizona filtered everything through her skewed view of the world. Because of that, she was the only person in Eclipse Bay who had come close to guessing the truth. If Arizona ever found out that the Arcane Society existed and that it was a secretive, centuries-old organization devoted to research and study of the paranormal, she would have no problem weaving it into her own worldview.

"Don't worry about me," Grace said. "I'll have a partner."

"Someone with field experience." Arizona nodded, satisfied. "Excellent. You tell him I said to take good care of you."

"Okay." Like heck she would tell Luther Malone that he was supposed to take care of her. She didn't need any help in that department. She had been taking care of herself since the day her mother died.

"I'll keep an eye on your cottage while you're gone," Arizona added. "Make sure the sons a bitches don't try to get into your files."

"Thanks. I appreciate that."

"Stay alert, stay alive," Arizona said. She snapped off a quick salute and stalked off across the parking lot, heading for the glass doors of the post office.

Grace got into her car. She thought about her landlady as she drove out of the parking lot and turned toward the highway that would eventually take her to Portland.

Arizona was a powerful sensitive, although she was probably unaware of it. Her talent was similar to Fallon's. She could see patterns in chaos. But somewhere along the line she had lost control of the paranormal side of her nature. Perhaps if she had been raised as a member of the Arcane Society community, things would have been different for her. Perhaps she could have been taught how to control her talent. Or maybe not.

There was no question but that it was far too late to intervene now. Arizona had gone too deep into her strange, private world. Now her talent controlled her.

Grace wondered if Fallon Jones ever worried that he, too, might someday get trapped forever in his own world of plots and counterplots, unable to find his way back to reality. He was trying to do too much, she thought. On several occasions during the past few months she had heard the exhaustion in his voice. Running the West Coast office of J&J was obviously too big a job for one person. He needed an assistant.

It started to rain. Fat drops spattered on the windshield. She turned on the wipers and wondered if it was raining in Hawaii. When she got bored thinking about the weather in the islands she wondered if she was pushing her luck by taking this assignment from J&J. The *what-ifs* loomed in her imagination. What if she couldn't handle the mission? What if Luther Malone uncovered her secrets?

Don't think like that, she mentally scolded herself. How much trouble could a guy on a cane possibly be? *You've been hiding in Eclipse Bay long enough.*

THE COURIER from the Arcane Society—a young man who seemed thrilled to be performing a role, however small, for the legendary firm of J&J—delivered the packet to Grace at the airport hotel. He handed it to her in the lobby, so close she could feel the pulse and power of his talent. A para-hunter, she thought. She didn't have to jack up her own senses to know that he was strong.

"What's your name?" she asked, automatically stepping back to put some distance between them.

"Sean Jones, ma'am," he said.

Of course, she thought. The Jones family tree was filled with hunter talents of various kinds.

She thanked him and hurried back to the elevator, ripping open the sealed packet as soon as she reached the privacy of her room. The contents tumbled onto the table—Luther Malone's phony driver's license on top. She picked it up and studied the picture, consumed by a curiosity she could not explain.

Like most license photos, the shot was not intended to be flattering. It was possible that it was the lighting that made Malone look so hard but her intuition told her that the brutal planes and angles of his face would look just as austere in person. His dark hair was cut short. The note said his eyes were brown but in the picture they looked unreadable, the eyes of a lone wolf.

The picture should have been off-putting. Malone appeared to be stone cold. But for some reason she could not stop staring at the image.

Reluctantly she put the license down and reached for her plane ticket and the resort reservation.

Approximately sixty seconds later—the length of time it took her to get her shaking fingers under control—she dialed the now-familiar number in Scargill Cove.

"You didn't tell me that Malone and I would be registering as Mr. and Mrs. Carstairs," she said, her voice rising in spite of her determination to remain cool and professional. "There's only one room."

"Take it easy," Fallon said, uncharacteristically soothing. "I made sure you got a suite. Take the bedroom. It has its own bath. Tell Malone he can have the pull-out bed in the living room."

"I don't know if I can do this, sir. You should have warned me."

"I knew you'd panic if I told you that you and Malone would be checking in as husband and wife." Fallon sounded aggrieved, the voice of a put-upon employer forced to work with a difficult, temperamental employee.

"You were right."

"There's absolutely nothing to worry about. Malone is a pro. He's there as your bodyguard and this is the only arrangement that will allow him to do his job."

She swallowed hard. Fallon was right. Malone was a professional. She was the amateur. If she wanted to become a real agent for J&J, she had to start acting like one.

"Mr. Malone agreed to this plan?" she asked warily.

"He'll be fine with it."

"Wait a second, are you saying he doesn't yet know that he and I are supposed to pose as a married couple on this assignment?"

"Thought I'd let you break it to him," Fallon said.

"Oh, gee, thanks."

For the first time in her association with Fallon Jones, she ended the call before he could cut the connection.

For a long time she stood there, looking at Malone's phony driver's license and the hotel registration.

Got to learn to live in the now.

Five

The concourse was crowded with tourists and business travelers from around the world. The planes landing and taking off on the runway bore the logos of nations from every part of the globe, including a few from countries that would have been unfamiliar to most people living outside the South Pacific. The warm, silken breeze carried the twin scents of jet fuel and the light mist that was sweeping down from the mountains.

Luther lounged against the wall, his hand wrapped around the handle of the cane, and watched the dark-haired woman walking toward him. She had come into view at the far end of the walkway a couple of minutes ago. For some reason, he found his attention shifting back to her again and again.

What the hell, he had a few minutes to kill. According to the monitors, Grace Renquist's plane had landed on time a short while ago at the main terminal but it would take her a while to find her way to the inter-island terminal. She was an elderly lady so she would probably wait for the Wiki-Wiki bus that connected the terminals rather than make the long hike along the concourse.

The dark-haired woman disappeared behind a large tour group of senior citizens heavily draped in leis. Anticipation zinged through him while he waited for her to reappear. When she popped back into view she was closer, still coming his way. He could see her more distinctly now. She was pulling a carry-on suitcase with one hand. Her stride was lithe and purposeful and somehow sexy. A frisson of excitement hummed through his senses, *all* his senses. That hadn't happened in longer than he cared to think about.

Her hair was cut at a dramatic angle that started high at the nape of her neck and ended in two sweeping wings just below her cheekbones. She had him riveted now but damned if he could figure out why. She was attractive in some indefinable, out-of-the-ordinary way but she was no glossy cover model; far from it. There was something proud and determined about the strong lines of her nose and jaw; a cool, touch-me-not attitude that radiated sexual challenge, at least to him. Dark glasses veiled her eyes. That was hardly unusual in Hawaii where everyone wore shades, but for some reason the glasses seemed to add to the air of exotic, sensual mystery that stirred the atmosphere around her.

She must have just arrived from the mainland, he concluded; someplace where it had been raining probably because she wore a lightweight trench coat. Was he an ace detective or what? The coat was unbuttoned over a pair of dark pants and a classically cut shirt in a deep coppery color. The collar of the shirt was pulled up high and flared out a little, framing her throat and somehow subtly protecting it. A black leather handbag trimmed with bronze buckles was hooked over one straight shoulder. The hand that wasn't wrapped around the handle of the suitcase was tucked into the pocket of the trench.

He could not take his eyes off her. Maybe it was just him. No one else seemed to be paying any attention to the woman. This was a fine time for his long-dormant sexual appetite to wake up and go on the prowl.

Life had been so peaceful since he'd sunk into his own private well of gloom. Maybe Wayne and Petra and Milly were right. Maybe he had been flirting with depression. But at least life had been calm.

It had also been damned uninteresting.

She was close enough now. He jacked up his senses. Light and dark inverted. Most of the people in the crowded concourse were instantly transformed into human glowworms, their auras flaring and pulsing in the usual hues and patterns that he had learned to associate with those who did not possess strong psychic talents.

Power flared around the dark-haired woman, however. She stood out in the crowd like some incandescent butterfly surrounded by a swarm of pale, nondescript moths.

She was a strong talent of some kind. That was probably what his senses were responding to. Even on the normal plane he had picked up the exciting strength of her psychic energy. Here in the paranormal realm, it was just as compelling. He wanted to get closer, a lot closer.

He tightened his hand on the handle of the cane and straightened away from the wall. He had a few more minutes until the elderly genealogist arrived.

He took one step forward and halted abruptly. What was he thinking? He was here to do a job. *Let her go, you idiot.* Just two psychics passing in the night. It happens.

Yes, but it had never happened like this, not to him. He'd met other strong sensitives before, lots of them. Two months ago one had tried to kill him. He'd never responded to any of them with this kind of gut-deep awareness.

She was less than six feet away now. Before he could move to intercept her, she halted directly in front of him, dazzling him with a fire that threatened to ignite his senses. He knew in that moment that she had made him as another sensitive, just as he had recognized her.

Damn. What were the odds?

"Mr. Malone?" she said quietly.

He snapped back into normal focus. The iridescent fire around the woman disappeared but his hungry fascination did not. The memory of Fallon Jones laughing on the other end of the phone flashed through him. *An elderly, gray-haired librarian, my sweet ass.*

"I'm Malone," he said. "Grace Renquist?"

"Yes."

"Well, what do you know. Fallon Jones has a sense of humor, after all."

She smiled slightly. "Badly warped, I'm afraid."

"Only to be expected. He's still Fallon Jones." He held out his hand. "A pleasure, Miss Renquist. Uh, it is Miss, isn't it? Or did I get that wrong, too?"

"It's Miss." She inclined her head politely. "Who or what were you expecting?"

He glanced down and saw that she was still gripping the suitcase handle with one gloved hand. Her other hand was firmly planted out of sight in the pocket of the trench coat. He lowered his own hand.

"Let's just say I had the impression you would look a lot more mature," he said.

She removed the dark glasses. Dry amusement gleamed in a pair of smoky, sage-green eyes.

"Gray-haired, perhaps?" she said. "Maybe equipped with a hearing aid?"

"Fallon encouraged me to leap to a few conclusions."

"If you think I'm something of a surprise, wait until you see your new ID packet."

She took her hand out of her pocket for the first time, revealing another thin, expensive-looking leather driving glove.

"Little warm for a coat and gloves," he said neutrally.

She ignored the comment just as she had his attempt to shake hands earlier. Instead, she took the leather bag off her shoulder, opened it and reached inside for an envelope. When she handed it to him she was careful not to let her gloved fingers brush against his bare skin.

Just his luck. The most exciting woman ever to walk into his life had some kind of serious phobia about touching other people. *Well, hey, it's not like I'm real normal, either.*

He opened the envelope and removed a driver's license, a couple of credit cards and the folded hotel registration. A quick glance at the license and the plastic told him that his new name was Andrew Carstairs and that he lived in L.A. The registration informed him that he was married. He looked up.

"Nice to meet you, Mrs. Carstairs," he said, refolding the form.

To his surprise, she blushed and quickly shoved her gloved hands back into the pockets of her coat. "Mr. Jones didn't tell me about our cover until it was too late for me to back out of the assignment."

"Jones has a way of getting what he wants from his agents." He glanced at his watch. "We've got some time before we leave for Maui. Want something to eat?"

"I'm not hungry but I could use a cup of coffee."

"Sounds good."

They walked a short distance to a coffee bar. Grace ordered her coffee black, he noticed. It was how he drank his. *Hey, something in common. Focus on the positive.*

They sat together at one of the tiny tables.

He studied Grace's hand, which was currently wrapped around her cup.

"You're going to have to lose the gloves before we get on the plane to Maui," he said quietly.

She paused, the cup halfway to her mouth. "Why?"

"Because if you insist on wearing them, you're going to stand out like, well, like a sore thumb."

She winced and looked at her gloved fingers. "I was afraid you would say that."

"How big a problem is it?" he asked.

"I have some issues," she said coolly.

He angled his chin toward the cane hooked over the edge of the table. "So do I. Mine are physical. Yours?"

"Psychical. But the problem is linked to my sense of touch, which makes things complicated at times."

"Seen one of the Society's shrinks?"

Her eyes narrowed. He could practically feel her withdrawing from him.

"No," she said coolly.

"Look, I realize that under normal circumstances this wouldn't be any of my business, but given that we've got a job to do on Maui, I need to know what I'm getting into here."

She went very still. "There's no cause for concern. I assure you that my phobia doesn't interfere with my aura-reading talent."

"Fine. You're still going to have to lose the gloves. Can you deal with that?"

For a few seconds he thought she was going to tell him to go to hell. Then, very deliberately, she stripped off first one glove and then the other. She stuffed the pair into her handbag and picked up her coffee.

"Satisfied?" she asked.

Her hands were surprisingly delicate-looking, the nails neatly tapered and unpolished. There was no ring.

"Yes," he said. He let out some air. "Sorry about that."

"Uh-huh." She did not look impressed with the apology.

"Are you going to be okay?" he asked quietly.

"Don't worry about me," she said coldly. "I can take care of myself."

"Been doing that awhile, have you?"

"Yes," she said. "I have."

Six

The rental car that had been booked for Andrew Carstairs was waiting at the end of the short flight to Maui. J&J was nothing if not efficient, Grace thought.

"Want the AC on?" Luther asked, getting in behind the wheel.

"No thanks. I don't like air-conditioning unless it's absolutely necessary. I'd rather roll down the windows."

"Same here." He put the car in gear and drove out of the parking lot.

She contemplated her initial impressions of Luther Malone. They could be summed up in three potent words: *Powerful, controlled, fascinating.* Okay, there was a fourth word that came to mind: *exciting.* There was something indefinably electric in the atmosphere, at least on her side of the car. At various times in her life she had found other men attractive but she had never experienced anything quite like this fluttery little rush of sensual anticipation. It stirred all her senses in unusual and interesting ways.

Power was always interesting; power that was ruled by the kind of exquisite control that Luther wielded was especially intriguing, at least to her. One glance at his aura had told her that he was no level eight—

more like a level ten or higher. Obviously he'd managed to keep that little fact out of the files. She couldn't hold it against him. She'd faked her own ranking, too. Powerful talents were slapped with the label "exotic" within the Society. The term did not convey admiration or respect. At best, other sensitives tended to view strong sensitives of any kind with a degree of caution. At worst, they avoided them. Power might be interesting but it could also be dangerous.

The photo on Luther's new driver's license had not lied. He was as hard-looking in person as he was in the picture. His eyes were brown, too, as advertised. But it was an almost feral shade of amber. It made her think of dark jungles and forbidden passions. Not that she'd had much experience with either.

"I love the air here," she announced, inhaling deeply. "It's intoxicating. Makes me want to put my head out the window like a dog."

"Hawaii has that effect on a lot of people." He glanced at her, his eyes unreadable behind his dark glasses. "How are you doing without the gloves?"

The question annoyed her. She looked briefly at her hands, neatly folded in her lap, and then raised her chin.

"I told you, I can deal with it."

"You're sure? I noticed that you kept your hands under your raincoat on your lap for most of the flight."

"I would not have taken this assignment if I thought I couldn't handle it."

"Sorry."

"No, you're not." She wrinkled her nose. "You're fretting. I'm making you nervous."

"Maybe I'm just curious?"

"You're fretting," she repeated evenly. "I suppose I can't blame you for your lack of confidence but try looking at this situation from my perspective."

"Which is?"

She raised her brows. "I've got a bodyguard who isn't comfortable carrying a gun and needs a cane to get around."

"Fallon told you about the gun thing?"

"Yes."

He meditated on that for a long moment and then nodded once. "You know, you're right. From your perspective, those facts would not at first glance appear to be reassuring."

"Luckily for me," she said coolly, "I took a second glance."

"At my aura," he said. It wasn't a question.

"I'm an aura talent. That's what I do."

To her surprise, he smiled faintly. "What did you see that was reassuring?"

She sat back in the seat and concentrated on savoring the wonderful air.

"I saw a lot of sheer bullheaded determination," she said.

"Bullheaded determination is a good quality?"

"It means you'll do whatever you need to do to complete this mission. What's more, you know your own power and how to control it. You feel confident about your talent so I do, too."

She saw a lot more than that but she was not prepared to go into details. Some things you just did not talk about on a first date. The thought made her smile.

Luther was silent for a moment, processing what she had said. Then his hands tightened on the steering wheel. "You can see things like determination in an aura?" he asked, half curious, half disbelieving.

She turned her head to look at him. "Didn't Mr. Jones tell you about the little twist in my talent?"

"He said you could read a person's psychic profile. Guess I didn't understand exactly what that meant. I'm surprised they haven't got you working as a parapsychologist."

"I don't have the academic background to work as a counselor."

"How did you end up in Genealogy?"

"I applied for a position in the Bureau. I like psychic genealogy. It suits my talents. How did you end up as a bartender in Waikiki?"

"It suits my talents."

She knew a conversational dead end when she ran into one.

"Right. Speaking of your talents, what's the plan for finding our bad guy?" she asked. "Do I just stroll around the resort like a drug-sniffing dog looking at auras?"

His mouth twitched a little. "We'll try to be a little more cool than that."

"Even if we're very cool, it probably won't take long to spot Eubanks. Powerful talents of any kind are rare. What are the odds that there will be more than one level-nine strat staying at the resort?"

"That's what Fallon Jones said."

"If anyone knows probabilities, it's Mr. Jones."

"I'll tell you a little secret about Fallon Jones," Luther said.

"What's that?"

"Most of the time he's right but occasionally he screws up and when he does, it's never in a small way."

She thought about that. "Maybe that's because he's so sure of himself and his talent that he doesn't always allow for other possibilities. Or maybe because he's overworked. I have the impression that he's under a tremendous amount of pressure these days."

"You do realize that he's a first-class conspiracy theorist who just happens to have a good track record?"

"Yes." She cleared her throat. "But I admit that it is a bit unsettling to think of Mr. Jones in those terms."

"Pay is good, though," Luther said.

She smiled. "Yes, it is."

Seven

It was after four o'clock by the time they checked into the beachfront hotel in the Wailea resort community. The suite was on the fourth floor with a view of the pool, the gardens and the ocean beyond. There were deeply shaded lanais off both the master bedroom and the living room. The perfect spot for a honeymoon, Luther thought, morosely. Not that he would know. He'd gone to Vegas for both of his.

He carried his small leather travel kit into the second bath and set it on the counter next to the sink, aware of Grace unpacking in the master bedroom. For a moment he indulged in a pleasant little erotic fantasy, thinking that it would have been very nice to be the real Mr. Carstairs on a real honeymoon with his real wife.

Don't go there. She's not your wife, she's the partner you never wanted; one with zero field experience. That is not a good thing.

She was also the only woman who had revved up his senses and made him seriously hard in months. No way that could be a *bad* thing. It was distracting, however. He was going to have to work in order to stay focused.

His leg ached. The combination of the flight from Honolulu and the drive from the airport had taken its toll. Annoyed, he removed the bottle of anti-inflammatory tablets from his kit and shook out four. He managed to resist the almost overwhelming urge to hurl the bottle across the room. The damn leg was never going to be the same. Get over it.

He dropped the bottle back into the kit, tightened his hand on the cane and made his way out of the bathroom. Grace was waiting for him. She had changed into a pair of lightweight trousers and another long-sleeved shirt. At least she wasn't wearing the trench coat.

It occurred to him that she did not seem overly impressed with the suite. He was. He'd spent time in the army, put in several years as a cop and now he was a bartender and part-time contractor with J&J. None of those career paths had paid the kind of money that allowed him to check into classy suites like this one. Grace, however, seemed unfazed by the luxury accommodations. Maybe he should consider a position in the Bureau of Genealogy.

"Going somewhere?" he asked.

"Thought I'd take a walk on the beach," she said. "I've been in a plane or on the road for most of the day. I'd like to unwind before dinner."

It was time to explain the facts of life, he decided.

"Got one rule on this job," he said. "We'll call it Rule Number One."

She raised her brows. "And that would be?"

"I give the orders, and the first order is that you don't leave this room alone. No wandering off on your own unless I give permission."

She inclined her head very politely. "I take it that means you're coming down to the beach with me."

"What the hell. I need to get a feel for the terrain, anyway." He opened the door for her. "But the order still stands. You don't go out of here on your own. Got it?"

She went past him, neatly avoiding any accidental contact. "Fallon Jones said that you were in charge on this mission."

"I'll take that as a yes."

He followed her out into the hall and closed the door, waiting a beat until he heard it lock securely. Satisfied, he walked with Grace toward the elevator lobby, fighting the temptation to move into the invisible Don't Touch Zone that enveloped her like another kind of aura. He noticed that her arms were folded beneath her breasts in a seemingly casual manner. If you looked closely, however, you could see that her fingers were tucked safely out of sight.

He brooded on what might have happened to a woman to make her dread touching another human being. The realization that a little skin-to-skin contact with him might actually cause her psychic pain was troubling. It just didn't seem right that she might not be able to abide his touch; not when he was so certain that touching her would bring him nothing but pleasure.

"I'm starting to feel guilty about the glove thing," he said.

"As well you should."

"Damn it—"

"Don't worry, I understand," she said. She smiled wryly. "Wearing them on this mission would not be at all professional."

He searched for another path through the Don't Touch Zone.

"How long have you been in Genealogy?" he asked.

"A year."

"That's all? Fallon implied that he considered you very valuable."

She glowed. "I'm delighted to hear that. Mr. Jones is not what you would call forthcoming with positive feedback."

"He's never going to be up for Boss of the Year, that's for sure. But take it from me, he wouldn't have used your professional services more than once if he hadn't been impressed."

"That's good to know."

"What did you do before you went to work for the Society?"

"Didn't Mr. Jones tell you?" she asked.

"Fallon can be vague about details that he doesn't consider important."

"I used to work for a company called Crocker World."

He stopped in front of the elevators and pressed the call button. "Martin Crocker's company?"

"Yes." She looked politely surprised. "You were aware of the company?"

"Crocker's death made headlines. It was also big news within the Society. He was a member. Funded a lot of research projects."

"Yes, I know."

"What did you do at Crocker World?"

"I was on the corporate research library staff. After Mr. Crocker died, it became obvious that the firm was in trouble. Everyone knew that the company would fall apart without him at the helm. I could see the writing on the wall, so I started job hunting immediately."

It was all said very smoothly, very casually, but there was something ever so slightly off. Luther jacked up his senses until he had a clear view of her aura. He might not be able to see details the way she apparently did, but he could make out certain strong emotions. There was tension in the energy field that blazed around her, the kind that, as a cop, he'd learned to associate with a well-crafted lie.

"How long have you been a member of the Society?" he asked.

"My mother registered me when I was born." She paused a beat. "You?"

"My folks were both members. They registered me at birth."

The elevator doors slid open, revealing a cab packed with people. He assessed the situation in a single glance. Joining the crowd would mean forcing Grace to run the risk of someone brushing against her. He could feel her sudden tension.

Luther smiled benignly at the cluster of faces.

"We'll wait for the next one," he said.

The elevator doors closed.

"Thank you," Grace said quietly.

"No problem," he said. "I'd suggest we take the stairs but—" He broke off, giving the cane a disgusted look. He refused to tell her that his leg was acting up and that descending four flights of stairs would make things worse. "I can make it down but it's not the most graceful sight in the world," he said instead.

"No problem," Grace said gently. "It's not as if we're in a hurry."

They stood together in silence and watched the illuminated numerals over the three elevators. Grace's expression was calm and composed. It was impossible to tell what she was thinking.

Luther used the time to wonder why she had lied about the job at Crocker World.

Eight

They had a drink in the open-air bar and ate red snapper garnished with a light ginger and miso sauce in the restaurant. There were candles on the tables, moonlight on the sea and a slack-key guitar playing softly. If she closed her eyes and surrendered to the wonders of magical thinking, she could almost pretend she was on a real date, Grace thought. Of course, you had to overlook the fact that she did not dare to even hold her escort's hand. Not that Luther had made any attempt to initiate such intimate contact, she reminded herself. Just the opposite. He seemed to be going out of his way to keep plenty of distance between them, no doubt afraid that if he even brushed against her by accident, she'd freak and destroy their cover.

She was more than a little surprised when he suggested a walk on the oceanfront path after dinner. Her first instinct was to refuse. She always felt more vulnerable after dark. The old fear that someone was creeping up on her was strongest at night, probably because that was when the Monster had visited her bedroom. But this evening she would not be facing the night alone. In spite of her own secrets, she felt curiously safe with Luther.

He was careful to keep at least a foot away from her as they made their way along the dimly lit path that linked the beachfront hotels. His cane tapped softly on the pavement. She sensed his barely suppressed irritation.

"Does your leg hurt?" she asked.

"Just a little stiff," he muttered.

He was lying, she thought. But then, she had lied to him earlier when he tried to interrogate her. She knew that he had not been completely satisfied with her answers. The conversation in the hotel hallway after they had checked into their room had been the one that she worried about the most. She had gone over it again and again in her mind, however, and she knew she had aced it. Luther's cop intuition might have been aroused, but if Fallon Jones hadn't penetrated the veil of her carefully manufactured past, it was unlikely that Luther would discover the truth.

"How long have you lived in Hawaii?" she asked, watching the moon-lit surf crash on the rocks below the path.

"Couple of years. Moved here after my second divorce. Quit my job with the department at the same time. Figured I needed a change of scene."

"Sorry about the divorce," she said quietly.

"Yeah, well, it wasn't the biggest surprise in the world."

"Were you deeply in love?"

"Whatever I felt for Tracey died the day I found her in bed with my partner."

"Funny how finding out that someone you trusted has betrayed you can kill a relationship."

"Been there?" he asked.

"Yes."

"Ex-husband?"

"No. We were never married."

Good grief, what was she doing? Even with the names changed to protect the guilty, any attempt to explain her complicated association with Martin Crocker would not only be difficult, it would be extremely dangerous. She had kept secrets most of her life. She was a pro. But something about being out here in the night with Luther was threatening to make her careless.

"Does aura talent run in your family?" she asked.

"Sporadically. My grandfather was a strong aura. He told me that my father was a high strat talent though, and my mother had a mid-range talent for color and design, of all things."

"Raw psychic power tends to be a strong genetic trait but the form the talent takes is often hard to predict. Your grandfather told you about your parents?"

"My folks were killed in a car crash by a drunk driver when I was a baby. I never knew them. My grandfather raised me."

"Is your grandfather still alive?" she asked.

"No. He died the year I graduated from high school and went into the army."

She told herself she should stop right there. But she couldn't seem to help herself. "Is there anyone else in your family?"

"Maybe some distant cousins somewhere." He sounded disinterested. "If they're out there, they never bothered to show up after my parents were killed."

"In other words, there's no one?"

"Got a couple of good friends over on Oahu. They own the restaurant where I work as a bartender. What about you?"

"My mother died when I was thirteen. Some kind of rare infection."

"Tough," he said.

"Yes, it was."

"Your dad?"

"I never knew him." She kept her voice perfectly neutral. "When my mother decided to have a child, she went to a sperm bank clinic."

"Oh, shit," he said softly.

She almost smiled. In that single, pithy statement he had told her in the most eloquent terms that he understood.

"Yes," she said. "Oh, shit, indeed."

"Talk about having a psychic hole in your life." He turned his head to look at her. "You're a genealogist. Ever try to find your father?"

"Of course. A lot of sperm bank kids go looking for their fathers. I eventually found the name of the facility that my mother used, the Burnside Clinic. It was established by a member of the Society. Dr. Burnside catered to clients who were members of the Arcane community. He guaranteed that all of his donors were high-level sensitives of one kind or another. He also promised absolute confidentiality to both donors and clients."

"Were you able to find your father's file?" he asked.

"No. The clinic burned to the ground a few years ago. All the records were destroyed. Arson was strongly suspected but no one was ever arrested."

"Probably one of the donors who didn't want to be found."

"Do you think so? I did wonder about that possibility."

"There are others," he said, sounding thoughtful now. "Maybe one of the mothers who didn't want a donor to find his offspring. Or maybe one of the kids who couldn't find his father and got really pissed off. It also could have been someone who didn't approve of the services the clinic offered."

"In other words, the list of suspects would be a very long one."

"Sounds like it."

She was quiet for a moment. "I was never able to identify my father, but after I went to work in the Bureau of Genealogy` I found some information about him that my mother had entered into the genealogical records when she registered me with the Society. Mostly a health and talent history."

"And?"

She shrugged. "What can I tell you? My father was descended of sound genetic stock and he was a strong talent. But then, Dr. Burnside would have insisted on those qualities in all of his donors."

"Sure."

"I got my eyes from him," she whispered after a while. "But that's about it. He wasn't even an aura talent. My mother listed him as a strat."

"Knowing that you're a green-eyed aura talent descended from a green-eyed strat wouldn't have given you much to go on."

"No," she said. "It didn't. Strat talents are very common within the Society. There are literally thousands registered. Narrowing the field by age and gender and eye color didn't help. I eventually gave up."

A couple strolled toward them, hand in hand, lost in each other, taking up a good portion of the path. Luther thumped the cane loudly a few times. In response, the pair moved hurriedly to the far side of the pavement.

With the force of long habit, Grace shook off the old melancholy that always came over her when she thought about her own unknown history.

"You're good with that thing," she said.

"It has its advantages. People tend to get out of my way. No one wants to be responsible for making a guy on a cane go down. Lawsuit city."

"How did you end up on it in the first place? Fallon said something about an accident."

"I got careless."

And that, she knew, was the end of that conversational topic. At least for now. She was trying to think of a clever way to dig deeper when ghostly fingers touched the nape of her neck. She tensed instinctively and folded her arms beneath her breasts, shielding her hands.

There were a number of people on the path but the man coming toward them out of the shadows was moving a little differently from the rest. He was still several yards away. It was too dark to make out his features but there was something about his stride that disturbed her senses. He didn't stroll or jog or walk in a normal fashion. He exhibited the easy, predatory glide of a big cat on the hunt.

Part of her was aware that a subtle shift of awareness had come over Luther. She knew that he, too, had noticed the figure coming toward them.

She jacked her parasenses to the max. One look at the powerful aura that enveloped the approaching man and she knew him instantly for what he was. Para-hunter.

Every instinct screamed at her to turn and run even though the logical side of her brain knew it would be useless. If the pacing man was hunting her, he could easily run her down. Those endowed with his brand of talent were not supermen by any means, but their natural human hunting abilities were psychically enhanced. They could see very well in the dark. Their reflexes were on a par with those of any other wild predator. They could detect the psychic spoor of their quarry, and their favorite prey was human.

A lot of hunters wound up in the military or in security work. But she knew all too well that, given their natural aptitude, it was inevitable that some became dangerous predators.

Luther's aura was running hot, too, but he gave no outward indication of his tension. His halting stride did not alter but somehow he was a little closer to her now, making certain that the hunter would pass on the opposite side, as far from her as possible.

Take it easy, she thought. *Whoever that guy is, he isn't after you. If they had found you, they would have sent someone to Eclipse Bay to get you. They wouldn't have waited until you took a Hawaiian vacation.*

Then again . . .

The hunter was less than two yards away, closing the distance fast. Somehow she managed to keep moving alongside Luther, matching his slow, careful stride. There was no change in the *tap-tap-tap* of the cane.

She was calmer now. Logic and common sense were kicking in, overriding the more primitive side of her brain.

No, not logic and common sense, something else was neutralizing her fear. By rights she should still be scared out of her wits. What's wrong with this picture? That thought was almost as frightening as the approaching hunter.

Instinctively she tried to beat back the calming influence. She should be scared. It was the appropriate response under the circumstances. Damn it, she *would* be scared.

The unnatural calm wavered and dissolved. The terror of the hunted rushed back but so did a sense of rightness. This was the way she ought to feel.

Before she could adjust to the transition back to a state of fear, she became aware of Luther's aura. It was pulsing at unusual points along the spectrum. Power resonated in the night.

The two men were close now, within touching distance. Suddenly, as if a psychic switch had been turned off, the pacing man's aura dimmed, becoming markedly less intense. It was still the aura of a para-hunter but not one who is on the prowl. Instead, his energy field took on the colors and wavelengths of a person who is calm to the point of being sleepy. Whoever he was, the hunter was not interested in her or in Luther.

He went past, showing no signs of curiosity about the couple to his left. She had to fight the urge to look over her shoulder.

"It's okay," Luther said quietly. "He's gone."

"Hunter," she whispered.

"Yes."

She glanced at him, half afraid of what she might see. But his aura was normal again. Maybe she'd been mistaken a moment ago. Perhaps the proximity of the hunter's fierce aura had confused her senses.

"You could tell he was a hunter?" she asked.

"I don't have your brand of aura-reading talent but it isn't hard to identify that kind of energy, especially when the guy's running hot. Didn't you notice how everyone else on the path unconsciously got out of his way? Even nonsensitives can detect a high-level predator in the vicinity. What did you pick up?"

"I have to admit I wasn't taking notes. He was powerful, though, and, as you said, he was running wide open."

"Hunting?"

She thought about it. "No. I didn't get that from his aura. He wasn't focused. I don't think he was after anyone in particular. Maybe he was just out for an evening stroll and felt like running jacked. You know how it is. Sometimes you use your parasenses just because you can."

"He could have been checking out the terrain," Luther said. "Doing a little recon work."

"That's certainly a possibility. But for what purpose?"

"Good question. Anything else I should know?"

"One thing," she said. "Whoever he was, he's comfortable with violence."

"A killer?"

She hesitated. "I think he has killed, yes, but he's not a rogue or a freak. He wasn't crazy or out of control. He wasn't a sociopath, either. Those are easy to spot. What I saw indicated a cold, almost businesslike approach to violence."

"Think he might have been military or maybe a cop?"

"Possible. Or maybe he's a professional gangster. Whoever he is, he knows how to compartmentalize."

"What the hell does that mean?"

She wrinkled her nose. "It means that regardless of what he does in his day job, he's quite capable of having a loving wife and family."

"About that conversation we had earlier," Luther said evenly. "The one in which we discussed Fallon Jones's probability theory as it relates to this job."

She swallowed hard. "That would be the theory which, roughly paraphrased, was 'What are the odds that there will be more than one high-grade talent at that resort?'"

"Yeah, that theory," Luther said. "I think it may be flawed."

"I agree. But I suppose it's theoretically possible that guy we just passed was an innocent tourist who happens to be staying at one of the nearby resorts. There are a lot of hotels on this beach."

"Still."

"Right. Still. Hunters that powerful aren't exactly common on the ground."

"No, they aren't. Neither are high-level aura talents like us." Luther came to a halt. "So the question becomes, what are the odds that three very strong sensitives would show up on this stretch of beach on the same night?"

"You're wondering if this little coincidence is connected to our mission, aren't you?"

"Looks like I'm going to have to call Fallon. Talk about a fast way to ruin the evening."

She knew the exact instant when he reached for his cell phone because he had to release his tight grip on her arm to do it.

Nine

He couldn't see her expression clearly in the moonlight but he didn't need to in order to know that she was stunned. So was he, but not because he had just touched her.

They both looked down at where, until a moment ago, his fingers had been firmly wrapped around her upper arm.

"Damn," he said. "I'm sorry. I wasn't thinking. Just wanted to steer you as far out of his path as possible. Are you okay?"

"I'm okay," she said. Wonderingly, she touched his bare arm with her fingertips. "There's no pain. None. I'm all right. It's been so long, more than a year. You can't imagine what a relief it is to know that I'm more or less normal again."

"You're sure you're all right?"

"Yes." She sounded elated, almost euphoric. "Yes, I'm fine." She paused, staring down at her hands. "At least with you."

He liked that, he realized; liked the idea that he was someone special, at least as far as she was concerned. She could not even begin to guess how she had just rocked his already slightly weird world. No one had ever detected his subtle aura manipulation, let alone actively resisted it.

The hunter had passed blithely by, never even noticing that his jacked-up senses had been temporarily suppressed. Yet Grace had pushed back at the quick, light attempt to calm her panic as easily as she would have closed a door that had been blown open by a breeze. Now, why was that so damn intriguing?

"Blame it on the magic of Hawaii," he said. "Come on, let's get somewhere private where I can call Fallon."

They left the path, heading away from the beach, and moved deep into the heavily landscaped gardens of the nearest hotel. He stopped beneath the low-hanging branches of a large tree. Grace halted nearby. He fired up his senses again, this time to make sure there were no auras in the vicinity. No human lightbulbs appeared in the shrubbery. Satisfied that they were alone, he punched Fallon's code into the phone.

He watched the dark silhouette that was Grace while he waited for Fallon to answer. She stood quietly beside him, arms folded beneath her breasts again. He wondered what she was thinking.

It was probably a very good thing that she did not seem to know what he had tried to do to her back there on the path. He got the feeling that she hadn't been consciously aware of what she had done, either. Her attention had been riveted on the hunter.

Fallon answered on the second ring. That was unusual for him.

"What's up, Malone?" he growled.

"I was starting to think you weren't home. You usually jump on the phone halfway through the first ring."

"I was making another pot of coffee. Been a long night. Why are you calling?"

Luther provided a brief run-through of the encounter and waited patiently while Fallon brooded on the new factor in the equation.

"I agree that it's unlikely that you and Ms. Renquist would run across a high-grade hunter within a short distance of your hotel," Fallon said finally. "It's a red flag but not a huge one. Sensitives go on vacation in Hawaii like anyone else. Hell, it could have been a Jones."

"I know there are a lot of hunters hanging around your family tree, Fallon, but what are the odds that one of them is here at the same time that Grace and I are supposed to be conducting surveillance on a high-grade killer?"

"Probably somewhere in the neighborhood of twelve percent. Lot of Joneses live on the West Coast and a lot of 'em like to vacation in Hawaii. Been there myself."

"You took a vacation?"

"It was a long time ago. Before I got this job. You're sure the guy was a hunter? Any chance he might have been some other kind of talent? Maybe Eubanks got in early?"

"You said Eubanks is a level-nine strategist. This guy was definitely a hunter. Grace and I both made him."

"Okay, I'm a little tired at the moment," Fallon said. "Not at my best. Let me think about this some more. Meanwhile, stick to the original plan. If Eubanks shows up on schedule tomorrow, we can probably assume that the hunter's presence in the area is just a coincidence."

The weariness in Fallon's voice was extremely unusual. In the two years Luther had been working for him, he had never heard the head of J&J sound so exhausted.

"Thought you didn't believe in coincidences, Fallon."

"No," Fallon said. "I don't. Keep an eye out for the hunter. If he shows up again, I want an ID on him, too."

"Figured you'd say that. I'll look for him after I put Grace on a plane back to Oregon."

In the shadows, Grace stiffened. Her chin came up at a stubborn angle.

"You're going to need her to spot him again," Fallon said.

"No, I won't. I just told you, I had no trouble identifying him as a hunter tonight."

"Only because he was jacked up. If he had been cranked back, just sitting around a pool, would you have been able to spot him?"

They both knew the answer to that question.

"Probably not," he admitted. "But I don't want Grace getting near him."

"She's a J&J agent, just like you. She has the right to make her own decisions in situations like this."

"She's a specialist, not a trained field agent."

"Damn it, Malone—"

"I'll get back to you."

The phone went dead in his ear. He closed it and clipped it to his belt.

"Well?" Grace said. "What now?"

"We stay with the plan. Wait for our target to arrive and ID him."

"And then we try to find out the identity of the hunter," she said briskly.

"Fallon would like to know who he is, if possible, but I can find him on my own."

"It would be easier if I stick around to help you."

"Grace—"

"I can handle it. I'll be prepared next time. I won't freak out on you, I promise."

"Forget it."

"I overheard that conversation with Fallon," she said, going mutinous. "He told you it's my choice to make, didn't he?"

"There are times when I don't pay any attention to Fallon Jones. This is one of those golden moments."

"You need me," she insisted. "Admit it."

"I need you to be reasonable. Chasing down hunters is not your area of expertise."

"This is all because I got a little anxious tonight when we passed that hunter, isn't it? That's hardly fair."

He felt his temper start to slide. "Fair has nothing to do with this. You're not a trained agent. You're a genealogist who got drafted for an emergency field trip. When it's over, you're going home as fast as I can get you on a plane."

She drew herself up in the shadows. "Mr. Jones obviously has other ideas. I work for him, not you."

"Got news for you. When you're with me, you take orders from me."

"Oh, for Pete's sake," she snapped. "Give the bullheaded, I'm-in-charge-here thing a rest."

"That's not what us bullheaded, I'm-in-charge-here types do. I think we'd better talk about this in the morning when you're in a more reasonable mood."

"Now you're patronizing me."

"Is that what it's called? I think of it as just doing my job. Let's go back to the hotel. You've had a long day."

Automatically, he started to reach for her arm, intending to steer her out of the gardens. She took a quick step back out of reach. So much for thinking he was special because she could touch him. He let his hand fall to his side and tried to suppress the wave of gloom that resonated through him.

"One thing before we leave here," she said softly.

"What now?"

"Would you mind very much if I tried touching you again?"

The gloom dissolved in a heartbeat, replaced by a thrill that zapped across all his senses. In the next instant comprehension struck. His initial excitement faded.

"You want to run an experiment?" he asked. "See if things are different this time now that you're not distracted by the hunter?"

"Well, yes," she said. "Look, if you'd rather I didn't touch you, I certainly understand. Better than most people, in fact. I mean, I *really* understand why someone wouldn't want to be touched."

"No," he said. "No, It's okay. I don't have a problem with the experiment."

He held out his hand, palm up. Great. He'd been reduced to the level of a lab rat.

She took a cautious step forward, as wary as any wild bird being offered food by a human. Slowly she put out her hand.

Her fingertips hovered just above his for a few seconds, and then she brushed them across his palm, alighting briefly before immediately taking flight. He resisted the urge to capture her wrist and draw her closer.

Slowly she lowered her hand again until they were skin to skin. This time she did not flutter away. He could feel fine tremors going through her.

"Are you all right?" he asked.

"Yes. I'm fine." She sounded entranced. "This is amazing. Last week I accidentally touched a clerk's hand in the grocery store and got another bad jolt. I was starting to think that maybe I wasn't going to recover this time."

He wanted to ask her how often she'd experienced the problem in the past but he sensed that this was not the moment for that kind of question.

"Feel anything?" he said instead.

"Yes, but nothing bad."

"You know, a compliment like that could really go to a man's head."

"Sorry. It's just that for the past year I haven't been able to touch anyone without getting a strong psychic shock. Just going to the dentist was an ordeal. I had to take a dose of anti-anxiety meds to get through a simple cleaning. You can't imagine how it feels to know that my senses are returning to normal."

Slowly he closed his fingers around hers. The fine bones of her hand felt delicate and incredibly sensual. Her skin was warm and soft. She did not try to pull away.

"I wonder if it's just you," she said, very thoughtful now. "I suppose it could have something to do with the fact that we're both aura talents. Maybe I'm not cured, after all."

He tightened his grip a little. She did not flinch.

"If you're thinking of grabbing every man we pass just to see if you can replicate this little experiment, I have a few objections I'd like to raise," he said.

She laughed, a soft, low, utterly feminine sound that galvanized his senses. He leaned closer, savoring the sweet, hot energy that shimmered around her.

"Maybe not *every* man," she said. "But a representative sample might ensure a more reliable scientific test."

"If you're in the mood for further experimentation, I hereby offer my services."

"How altruistic of you."

"Yeah, that's my middle name," he said. "Altruistic."

She brushed the fingers of her other hand against the side of his face.

"You're running hot," she said. "I can feel the heat."

"Something tells me it's going to be even more fun this way."

"What will be more fun?"

"Kissing you at full throttle."

She knew what he meant.

"Ever tried it with anyone else?" she asked.

Well, at least she hadn't said no.

"Occasionally," he admitted.

"And?"

"And it didn't work very well. Mostly I scared the hell out of the other person. Invading someone else's energy field with a strong aura makes even nonsensitives nervous."

"So this kiss we're discussing is something of an experiment for you, too?"

"Definitely."

He braced himself against the trunk of the tree, legs slightly spread, and propped the cane nearby. Reaching out with both hands, he drew her into the intimate cage formed by his thighs. She did not resist.

"You don't scare me," she whispered.

It wasn't a challenge, he thought. She was simply telling him the truth.

"I know," he said. "You don't scare me, either."

"You're sure?" There was a sultry smile in the words.

He traced the outline of her lips with one finger. "Do I look scared?"

"No."

He took her mouth, slowly, deliberately, knowing that, whatever happened, he was going to remember this moment for the rest of his life. Her arms went around his neck; tightened. And then she was kissing him back, leaning into him, pressing him against the trunk of the tree.

The light around her flared into a glowing aurora. Waves of unnamed colors ebbed and flowed, clashing and resonating with his own energy. The incredibly intimate sensation had a lot in common with putting a match to a dry forest in August. The night was suddenly on fire.

He'd thought he was already jacked. Now he was at flashpoint. The rush dazzled his senses. It was also disorienting. The only thing that kept him on his feet was the tree at his back. Come to think of it, he did not want to be on his feet, anyway. He'd much rather be down on the ground, on top of Grace.

He had intended this first kiss to be gentle, nonthreatening. After all, the woman hadn't touched anyone in a year, at least not without shocking her senses. A gentleman would go slowly in a situation like this. Instead, he was in hand-to-hand combat with the forces of his own self-control. A devouring urgency cascaded through him.

Grace seemed to be as caught up in the whirlwind as he was. Her arms were wound fiercely around him. Her mouth was soft and open beneath his. Maybe her desire for him was just the result of being freed from a year of misery. He'd worry about that later. Right now the only thing that mattered was that she wanted him as much as he wanted her.

The scorching kiss blazed across his senses, hotter than any sex he'd ever had.

"I could come right now," he muttered against her mouth. "Just kissing you is enough."

"This is amazing." She shuddered in his arms and pulled back a little to look at him. "I haven't ever felt like this, not even before my senses got fried. It must have something to do with the fact that we're both aura talents. Nothing else explains it."

"Do me a favor. Stop trying to analyze it."

"Sorry," she said. "It's just that it's all so weird—"

He crushed her mouth with his own to silence her. She responded by wrapping her right leg around his calf as if she intended to climb up onto his erection.

He reached down, found the zipper of her pants and lowered it. She made a small, desperate little sound when he got his hand inside her panties and between her legs. She was hot and wet and full. He found the tight little bundle of nerve endings with his thumb. She gasped.

He slid a finger inside her tight core. She clenched around him immediately, as if she had been waiting for him forever.

"Yes." Her hands tightened around his shoulders. *"Yes."*

He stroked her, learning her. It was almost impossible to concentrate but he forced himself to pay attention to her aura, watching for the extra spikes of heat that told him he was touching the right places, using the right amount of pressure.

"Luther."

She sounded shocked. There was no other word to describe her startled, breathless gasp. For one awful instant he thought that her senses had rebelled after all. The possibility that he was giving her pain, not pleasure, was too terrible to contemplate.

But she did not try to escape. Instead, she buried her face against his neck and clung to him. He felt the small contractions of her climax ripple through her body; sensed them flashing through her aura.

When it was over he was almost as relieved as she was.

"Hell," he said into her hair. "Don't ever scare me like that again. For a second there I thought I was hurting you."

She made a weak, muffled sound into his shirt. It took him a while to realize that she was laughing. She was limp against him. Her breathing was that of a swimmer who had just made it back to the surface after nearly drowning.

He held her tightly, trying to get his own breathing as well as his raging need under control.

After a while he realized that she was no longer laughing. The front of his shirt was soaked with tears.

"Grace?"

"Don't worry." She did not raise her face from his shirtfront. "I'm all right. It's just that I haven't felt anything quite like that before."

He smiled into her hair. "Neither have I."

She stilled and then raised her head. "But you didn't—"

"It's okay." He stroked the wings of her hair back behind her ears. "I think you need some time to process this."

"I think you're right. I feel like I've been on a roller coaster all day."

"You're not the only one."

"I'm sorry," she said, chagrined. "I never meant that to happen. I realize it's highly unprofessional."

He covered her mouth with his fingertips, silencing her.

"Whatever you do," he growled, "don't tell me you're sorry about what just happened. That's the one thing I do not want to hear. Are we clear on that?"

She hesitated and then nodded once.

He took his hand off her mouth, eased her away from him and grabbed the cane. They walked back to the hotel in moonlight and silence, not touching.

Ten

Harry Sweetwater felt the faint vibration of his cell phone just as he left the beach path and started up the steps to his hotel. He checked the incoming number and then stopped in the shadows of a large palm to take the call.

"Hello, Gorgeous," he said.

"Hello, Handsome," Alison said.

The ritual greeting between them was as old as their relationship. It had started on their first date thirty-four years earlier.

"Are you in position?" Alison asked.

He pictured his wife at her pristine desk, heavily encrypted computer and phones neatly at hand. The desk was in a small, anonymous office housed in a large commercial tower located on a convenient, offshore island. Most of the other firms in the building offered financial assistance to those who found it necessary to give their money a thorough cleansing before investing it in legitimate enterprises. Among such a group of discreetly run businesses, a small, family-owned enterprise that offered special services to an exclusive clientele went unnoticed.

"All set," he said. "Got a room in the hotel next to the one the target is going to check into tomorrow."

"I'm starting to think that we may have a problem with the client, Harry."

He didn't question the conclusion. Alison was a high-level intuitive.

"We've done a lot of work for Number Two," he said.

They only had two clients. It kept things simple in the customer relations department.

"Everything looks right," Alison said. "Two is using the right security codes. I'm not sure what's bothering me about this job. Maybe something to do with the way the client is trying to micromanage it."

"You got another e-mail?"

"Yes. It came in a few minutes ago requesting another update. That's not routine. In the past, once Two has commissioned a job, there has been no further contact unless something changes. When the contract is completed, the money shows up in our account and that's the end of the matter."

That was true. In his experience, neither of the two clients ever wanted to know anything more than what was absolutely necessary about the details of the work that had been commissioned. Ignorance was bliss or maybe it just let the clients sleep better at night.

"Did you initiate a reverse security check?" he asked.

"Yes. I got the right response but something just doesn't feel right."

"Think we've been hacked?"

"I've got Jon checking that angle now. He doesn't think our computers have been invaded but there's always the possibility that someone has gotten inside Two's system."

He felt a flash of fatherly pride. His youngest son was brilliant when it came to computers; preternaturally so. Jon was a crypto, a strat talent with a twist that made it possible for him to plot patterns and follow complex paths in the new dimension that was cyberspace. He wasn't a true hunter like most of the other males in the Sweetwater family, but he possessed all the right instincts. If anyone could track a hacker back to his lair, he could.

"Tell Jon to keep looking," he said to Alison. "We've got time. Mistakes are embarrassing."

"I'll get back to you as soon as I know anything more."

"I'll be waiting."

"How's Maui?"

"Warm. Balmy breezes. Palm trees. Beach. Hell, it's an island."

Alison laughed. "I can always tell when you're working. You never take time to stop and smell the plumeria flowers."

"Not when I'm on a job."

But even as he said the words, an uneasy sensation twisted through him. A few minutes before, he had been running wide open, doing some basic recon on the beachfront path. But somewhere along the line he had unintentionally relaxed and slipped back into his normal senses. That wasn't like him. He always stayed at least partially alert while on a job. He had been taught from the cradle that it was critical to maintain constant awareness of the immediate environment. The smallest details could lead to disaster. Screwups were not good for business.

So what the hell had happened to him out there on the path? The thought that he might be losing his edge at the grand old age of fifty-nine was depressing. His father and grandfather had worked into their seventies. Sure, they had slowed down a little with the passage of the years, but experience had more than compensated for what they lost in raw speed and psychic sensitivity. In the end it wasn't a decline in talent that had forced them into retirement. They had both been dragged into it, kicking and screaming, by their wives.

"How's Theresa doing?" he asked.

"She's fine, just a little impatient. She's more concerned about Nick. He's turning into a basket case. It's been a long nine months for him."

He smiled. His eldest son was a stone-cold hunter when he was working but when it came to his beloved wife and his soon-to-be firstborn kid, there was nothing icy about him. Nick had scheduled his jobs so that he could attend prenatal classes with Theresa. He had devoured every book on the subject of birth and parenting that he could find on the Internet. He had even insisted on hiring a decorator to design the baby's room in order to create what one of the texts had called a "nurturing environment." Now he was determined to assist at the birth.

"He'll survive," Harry said. "I did."

"Hah. Every time you came into the delivery room with me, I was afraid you would faint."

"Okay, maybe I got a little pale around the edges but I didn't keel over."

They chatted for a few more minutes and then signed off with their customary ritual.

"Good night, Gorgeous."

"Good night, Handsome."

The phone went silent in his hand. He dropped it into his pocket and stood looking out at the black mirror of the ocean. Something had definitely happened back there on the path. He tried to remember exactly when his other senses had shut down. He had passed an elderly couple who had been holding hands. Next he'd noticed a man using a cane and a woman. They had been walking side by side, not touching. Something about the man had drawn his attention. His jacked-up hunter instincts had recognized another potential predator. But an instant later he had lost interest.

The next thing he knew he was several yards down the path, cranked back to normal. Relaxed on a job when he had no business being relaxed.

Eleven

The dream was familiar, one of a handful of repeat nightmares connected to the day she killed Martin Crocker. But there was something different about it this time. For one thing, she was aware that she was dreaming. The most striking aspect, however, was that she was not afraid.

> *. . . Martin was coming toward her, only a couple of yards away. The bags of groceries had fallen from his arms. A loaf of bread, a package of coffee beans and a plastic bag filled with lettuce lay scattered on the dock. She wanted to run but she could not. Soon the pain would slash across her senses. Martin would reach down to take hold of her.*
>
> *But something was wrong. She was not stricken with fear. Instead she felt calm. That wasn't right. She should be mortally afraid, not only of Martin but of what she was about to do. . . .*
>
> *"No."*
>
> *She pushed through the veil of unnatural serenity, searching for the right emotion.*

She came awake suddenly but her heart was not pounding the way it usually did after the dock scene dream. She wasn't even breathless, and her nightgown was not stuck to her skin with icy sweat.

She opened her eyes and looked out through the sliding glass doors. The outline of the lanai railing and part of a lounge chair were etched against the pale gray light of dawn. *You're not in Eclipse Bay anymore.*

Right. She was in Maui; here on a mission for J&J and, oh, by the way, trying to learn to live in the moment.

"Are you okay?" Luther said from the doorway.

Startled, she sat up and turned to look at him. He had put on his pants but that left a lot of him uncovered. She was intensely aware of his bare feet and the broad expanse of his strong shoulders and well-muscled chest. Clearly, the fact that he used a cane did not keep him from working out.

Vivid memories of how those shoulders and that chest had felt beneath her fingers the night before cascaded through her.

Sex. She'd had *sex* with this man. The most intimate kind of human contact. Okay, technically there had been no penetration, at least not by the portion of the male anatomy that was, by tradition and in legal terms, generally considered the penetrating object. "Heavy petting" was probably the correct term. Still, there had been a lot of skin-to-skin contact. Also an overwhelmingly powerful climax, at least for her. She felt a little guilty about that part.

The truth was, she had been too shattered by the experience to reciprocate. Just staying on her feet had required most of her strength and willpower. The whole experience had left her oddly disoriented, balanced precariously on a knife edge of exquisite relief and anxious amazement. Was she cured of her phobia or had last night been some bizarre interlude created by the close brush with the hunter?

Luther seemed to have understood. Either that, or he had lost interest when she had collapsed, crying on his chest. Men were not keen on dealing with tearful women. That probably went double when it came to women who cried after an orgasm. She couldn't blame him.

Whatever the answer, he had seen to it that they returned immediately to the hotel. The elevator had been empty, thank goodness. She didn't think she could have managed the stairs. When they reached the suite, he'd ushered her into the bedroom and then closed the door very deliberately.

Obviously at some point during the night he'd opened the door. Well, he was a bodyguard, after all.

"I'm fine," she said. She drew her knees up under the bedding and wrapped her arms around them. "Just a bad dream." Alarm sparked through her. If she had awakened him, she must have cried out. "Did I say anything?"

"No."

"Good." She relaxed a little.

"You said no," he explained. "You were thrashing around a lot and you said no a couple of times. Must have been bad."

"Well, it wasn't terribly pleasant." She sank back against the pillows. At least she hadn't mumbled Martin's name in her sleep. But there was no getting around the fact that it had been a very close call.

"Probably brought on by that brush with the hunter last night," Luther suggested. "That kind of thing can affect the dream state in people like us."

"People like us?"

"Sensitives."

"Right."

But it wasn't the hunter who had invaded her dreams. The memory of the way her nerves had quieted when he went past returned in a rush. She had been too occupied with other things, including her first orgasm in longer than she cared to recall, to think about what had happened out there on the path. But now it occurred to her that last night she had experienced the same eerie, unnatural sense of calm that had made the dream feel so very different. In both instances the ratcheting down of the panic had been unnatural. She had fought it instinctively.

"If you're sure you're okay, I'm going to finish getting dressed," Luther said. He started to retreat into the other room.

"Hold it right there."

Obediently he paused. "Something wrong?"

"Yes, I think there is something wrong." She pushed aside the covers, got to her feet and faced him across the tumbled bed. "I want an explanation."

"Of what?"

"You used your aura energy to squelch some of mine out there on the path last night, didn't you? Admit it. I'll bet you did it again a few minutes ago while I was dreaming. How *dare* you?"

He stood very still in the doorway. "Take it easy, you've had a long day and you've just come out of a nightmare. Your nerves are probably still a little unsettled."

"My nerves are fine, thank you very much. What did you do to me?"

"You felt it?" he asked, frowning a little as if he was not certain that he had heard her correctly.

"Well, of course I did. I didn't have time to think about it last night because I was focused on the hunter and the fact that he wasn't paying any attention to us and—" She broke off, astonishment shooting through her. "Good grief, you did it to him, too, didn't you? You defused him or—or something. He was running hot and you cooled him down. You used your own aura to suppress his."

"You seem to have figured it out pretty damn fast." He watched her with a shuttered, wary expression. "No one else ever has, with the possible exception of Fallon Jones."

"He's aware of what you can do?"

"There's no telling what Fallon knows."

"Well, it certainly explains your success as a bodyguard." She thought about it. "And as a cop and a bartender, too, I suppose. No wonder you don't like guns. You don't need them. All you have to do is focus on a bad guy and just switch him off."

His hand clenched around the handle of the cane. "Unfortunately, it's not that simple. The effect diminishes rapidly with distance. If the bad guy is too far away from me, I can't do much except try to talk him into range. I couldn't suppress the aura of a sniper on a rooftop."

She smiled a little. "How many of your clients need protection from professional snipers?"

"Doesn't come up a lot in my line," he admitted. "The threat is usually much closer to home."

"Your ability must have been useful when you were a cop."

"My talent was why I quit the force," he said without inflection.

"I don't understand. Why wouldn't it have been helpful?"

"It's a long story."

"And you're not in the mood to tell it?"

"No," he said.

He had a right to his secrets, she thought. She was certainly keeping some of her own. She slipped into her other senses and studied his aura. There was a lot of tension in it, much of it sexual. She felt herself redden.

He smiled faintly. "See anything interesting?"

Shocked, she opened her mouth, closed it, then finally opened it again. "You can tell when I'm looking at your aura?"

"Sure. Don't you know when I'm viewing yours?"

Appalled, she could only stare at him. "Uh, I don't know."

"You don't know?" he repeated, disbelief underscoring every word.

She swallowed hard. "I mean, sometimes when I'm near you I sense an unfamiliar kind of energy, but I thought it had something to do with, uh—" She broke off, mortified.

"Something to do with the fact that we're attracted to each other?" He shrugged. "Maybe it does. You must have felt me watching you yesterday at the airport. I didn't know who you were but I couldn't take my eyes off of you. I remember thinking that you looked like some kind of incredibly brilliant psychic butterfly."

"Oh, jeez, I didn't realize what the sensation meant."

She thought about the excitement and anticipation she had experienced the day before when she first noticed him on the concourse. Her cheeks got warmer. How much had he seen? Not that it mattered, given what had happened last night. He'd obviously known from the start that she was attracted to him.

No one had ever been able to read her. She had always been the one who did the reading; the one who knew what others were going to do, sometimes before they did. That was how she had kept her secrets secure.

"Well, this is awkward," she said, cheeks burning.

He looked amused. "Takes some getting used to but I'm okay with it if you are."

This was very dangerous ground. She had to be careful. She could not afford to jeopardize the new life she had so carefully crafted.

"I need to think about it a little more," she said weakly.

"You do that. Meanwhile, why don't you tell me your real Jones Scale number?"

Thoroughly rattled now, she tried to compose herself.

"Didn't Mr. Jones tell you?" she said.

"He gave me some line about you being a level seven with an unusual ability to profile the auras you read. That's a flat-out lie, though, isn't it? I'm betting you're a level ten, at least. Wouldn't be surprised if you've got an asterisk after your number, too. You're an exotic."

She could not afford to panic, she reminded herself. Anger was a much safer response.

"I don't know where you got that idea," she said coldly. "My level seven is as official as your level eight."

He nodded, satisfied. "Like I said, a flat-out lie."

"You admit it?" she demanded, incredulous.

"Where's the harm? You probably already know it, being such a hot-shot talent and all. I doubt that you're going to run around telling everyone you meet."

"Well, no. It's just that Mr. Jones assured me that you were an eight."

"The sooner you learn that Fallon Jones lies through his teeth whenever it suits him the better off you'll be."

She sank down on the edge of the bed, her hands clasped in her lap, her back to him. She looked out at the lanai. "I don't think he lied for the sake of it. I think he was trying to protect your secret."

"You want to be careful about attributing good intentions to Fallon Jones. His only priority is protecting the Society's secrets. He'll do whatever it takes to accomplish that objective."

"I suppose you're right," she said. She wondered uneasily how much Fallon knew or suspected about her own Jones Scale number.

"Fallon tweaked my file to make sure my rank stayed under the radar," Luther said. "He wanted to keep my abilities under wraps. But how the hell did you manage to alter your own number?"

"What makes you think that I did?"

"Because I can see your power wavelengths," he said quietly. "I can feel them. Whatever you are, you're no seven."

Maybe she could finesse this.

"I told you, my mother died when I was thirteen, shortly before I was due to be tested at Arcane House. I went straight into the foster care system where no one knew or cared about the Society. The result was that I wasn't tested until I applied to join the Bureau. By then I knew how to control my talent. It was no big deal to make sure I scored a seven. You know how people react to nines and tens within the Society."

"Sure. They think we're freaks of nature. Freaks, especially powerful freaks, make people nervous. So, what are you? A ten?"

She cleared her throat. "A nine."

"Bullshit. You should see your aura. It's pulsing like crazy. You're a ten plus, aren't you?"

That much was true.

"Yes," she said.

"Like me."

She sighed. "The Jones Scale stops at ten."

"Only because they haven't found a way to measure psychic energy beyond that point. That's why they came up with the damned asterisk. Think Fallon Jones knows your real number?"

"Until this morning, I would have said no." She unclasped her hands. "Now, I'm not so sure. Given the nature of his own talent, I suppose it's possible he's guessed that I'm a little higher than my file indicates."

"You're an exotic," he said, very sure. "Like me."

One secret in exchange for another. As he had pointed out, where was the harm in acknowledging a piece of the truth to another aura talent? It was a relief to admit it to someone who truly understood.

"Yes," she said. She made a face. "But I hate that word."

"Exotic?"

"It's just a semi-polite term for psychic freak."

"You're no freak." He started toward her, cane thudding softly on the carpet. "But you are a very rare creature in my book."

She stood, turning to face him.

"I am?" she said.

Another wave of hot, sensual energy whispered through her. He was revved up again, watching her aura. She could feel the light pulses of heat from his energy field. Now she knew just what that meant. The sensation was exquisitely intimate. *He sees the real me,* she thought. *He's the only man who ever has.*

He came to a halt directly in front of her, smiling a little. "This is where I get to say here's looking at you, kid."

She laughed, feeling suddenly light and very highly charged; sexy. Adventurous. Living in the moment.

"Like the view?" she asked. Good grief, she was actually flirting with him.

"Oh, yeah," he said. He touched her cheek. "No one has ever noticed me screwing around with their auras, let alone pushed back."

She held her breath but there was no psychic jolt. Experimentally she put her fingertips on his bare chest. She felt nothing except warm skin and sleek, strong muscle. Last night hadn't been a fluke. She really could touch him without pain. She flattened her hand against him.

She could feel the intense, very focused energy of his desire sweeping around her, enveloping her in powerful and possibly quite dangerous currents. But she no longer cared about the warning signs.

"Are you telling me that you're attracted to me just because I can keep you from manipulating my aura?" she asked.

His smile was wickedly sexy. "And because you're hot, of course."

She blinked. "You really think I'm hot?"

He moved the cane behind her back and grasped the other end in his right hand, trapping her. He pulled her closer and lowered his mouth to hers.

"Very, very hot," he said against her lips.

The words thrilled all her senses. He wanted her. So what if part of the attraction was based on the fact that he saw her as an interesting challenge? At least she didn't scare him, the way she did other men. That was a really big plus. And she could touch him.

Live in the moment.

"Yes," she said. "But it's cool to hear the words."

"How about actions? Don't they count?"

"Oh, yes." She was breathless now. "Actions are very important."

"That's good because I'm in the mood for a little action."

His mouth closed over hers. She wrapped her arms around his neck and kissed him back, throwing herself into the embrace with all her might. Caught off balance by the sudden impact of her weight, Luther dropped the cane and staggered back a step. They collapsed together onto the rumpled bed.

She landed on top. Dazzled and energized, she started kissing his throat. He moved his hands down the sides of her body to her hips and tugged the hem of her nightgown upward. A moment later she felt his fingers close around her bare bottom.

He squeezed gently. She shuddered in response and dug her nails into him.

"Oh, yeah, definitely hot," he said, his voice tight and ragged.

He raised one knee, cradling her between his thighs and pressed the hard, demanding shape of his erection against her leg.

Enthralled, she slipped one hand down his chest and over his flat belly until she found his zipper. She started to tug. The zipper did not slide readily due to the presence of the large object in the way.

Luther drew in a harsh breath and eased back a little.

"I'll get it," he said.

"Okay. Hurry."

He sat up on the side of the bed. "Trust me, I'm moving as fast as I can."

She rolled onto her side to admire the powerful shape of his shoulder and hip while he got rid of the trousers. When he pushed the pants down she saw the ragged, newly healed scar that marked his thigh half-way between his hip and his knee. Shock lanced through her.

"Oh, Luther," she whispered.

He looked down, his mouth twisting. "Not very attractive, is it? One of the doctors talked about plastic surgery to make it look better, but at the time the last thing I wanted to do was go back into a hospital."

"Who cares how it looks?" She sat up beside him and gently put her fingertips on the savage brand. "You must have lost a lot of blood. You could have been killed."

"I told you, it was my own fault." He paused, watching her very steadily. "Does it bother you?"

"Of course it does. It was obviously a very serious injury."

"That's not what I meant. Does it turn you off?"

"Don't be ridiculous. I was just concerned, that's all. Was it a car accident?"

"No." He opened his wallet and took out a condom packet.

"Does it still hurt?"

"Aches a little sometimes." He sheathed himself in the condom. "If you don't mind, I'd rather not discuss it. Sort of takes the glow out of the moment, if you know what I mean."

She blushed. "Wouldn't want to do that."

He gave her another sexy smile and settled her back down onto the bed and loomed over her.

"On that we are in perfect agreement," he said softly.

He put one hand on her breast. She was intensely aware of the heat of his palm through the fabric of the nightgown. She closed her hands around his shoulders. A shudder swept through him. His aura flared higher. It seemed to her that in some way it was starting to resonate with hers. A glorious sense of her own feminine power soared within her.

He moved his hand deliberately up the inside of her thigh to the hot, full place between her legs. He started to stroke her the way he had the night before, as though he knew exactly what she wanted and needed. She sensed the now-familiar pulse of his energy.

Damn. He *did* know exactly what she wanted and needed. He was reading her aura to see what worked and what didn't.

"Wait a second," she gasped. "I think that's cheating."

"All's fair in love and war."

He did something with his fingers that shocked her senses in the most delicious way. Of their own accord, her legs stirred amid the rumpled sheets, opening for him.

Impulsively she reached down and wrapped her fingers around him. He sucked in a deep lungful of air and exhaled on a groan. She did not need to see his aura to know that she was pressing all the correct buttons.

"You're right," she said, savoring his reaction. "All's fair."

He was hard and solid and very erect. She watched him with her other vision as she explored him, discovering exactly where and how to touch him. The sexual excitement in his hot energy field began to resonate harder and faster, emboldening her. She had never tried anything like this with anyone else. The game was compelling, addictive; and her learning curve was very fast, thanks to the feedback she got from his aura.

She heard a low, husky laugh and knew that Luther knew that she was watching him in the same incredibly intimate way that he was watching her.

"You are definitely getting the hang of this," he growled. He captured her wrists and pinned them over her head. "But I'm not going to let you end things too soon."

She smiled sweetly and raised one hip a little, nudging him. Distracted, he reached down with his free hand, bringing his shoulder within range of her mouth. She nipped him lightly, letting him feel her teeth.

"I should have seen that coming," he muttered. "Okay, you've made your point."

He freed her wrists and she went back to her explorations. So did he. The sensual battle grew increasingly fierce and exciting, each of them trying to push the other to a higher level of excitement.

And then Luther was on top of her, driving himself deeply into her. She gripped his shoulders, raised her knees and tightened around him. Invisible light and fire flashed in the atmosphere of the bedroom. She held him even closer, possessive and demanding in a way she had never been with any other man. She felt his muscles harden under her clutching hands. Her insides clenched tighter and tighter.

Luther's entire body went rigid. Beneath her palms, the muscles of his back could have been sculpted from steel. With an effort, she managed to open her eyes. The morning light revealed the savage set of his hard face. It was the expression of a man on the verge of either sexual release or lethal violence.

He opened his eyes and saw her watching him. He did not speak. She knew that, like her, he could not. They were both too far gone into the whirling fire. But in that heartbeat of time she sensed a flash of intense awareness—a kind of mutual recognition—resonating between them.

Before she had time to analyze the strange new energy, her climax rolled through her, stealing her breath. A heartbeat later Luther followed her over the edge.

For a timeless moment she could have sworn that their auras fused into a single energy field that enveloped them both.

Which was, of course, quite impossible according to the laws of paraphysics.

Twelve

There was only one other person in the elevator, a woman swathed in one of the hotel's plush white spa robes. Luther stifled a grin when he sensed Grace's disappointment. He knew that she had been hoping to test her sense of touch on someone else to determine the extent of the "cure."

When they reached the terrace where the open-air restaurant was located, Grace got out first. He followed, thinking that he couldn't remember the last time he had felt so good, so *refreshed.*

"Can you use that aura manipulation trick to make a woman get instantly hot for you?" Grace asked with what sounded like academic curiosity.

The urge to smile vanished instantly. He knew a trap when he saw one.

"Damn it, Grace, keep your voice down."

He looked around quickly, hoping for a distraction. But none of the half-dozen people in the airy colonnade that led to the restaurant were close enough to eavesdrop. So much for that excuse. He lowered his own voice and injected as much steel into it as possible.

"Doesn't work like that," he said.

"You can't blame me for being curious. I haven't come across your particular talent in any of my genealogy research."

He put on his sunglasses and looked at her. She had taken a shower after the hot, sweaty sex. Her still-wet hair was combed back behind her ears. She had on a pair of trousers and another one of her long-sleeved shirts. The sleeves of the shirt were rolled up almost to her elbows, though. A very daring move.

"I'm not some small electric you can plug in whenever it's convenient," he muttered.

"No," she agreed. "You are definitely not a *small* appliance. So? What's the answer?"

"We're about to eat breakfast. Usually I read newspapers when I'm eating breakfast. Could we have this conversation some other time?"

"A simple yes or no will do."

"There is no such thing as a simple yes or no when it comes to sex," he said.

That was good, he thought, pleased. Smart answer, Malone. Brilliant, in fact.

She tilted her head to look at him, eyes veiled by the dark glasses.

"That's not an answer," she said.

He exhaled slowly and went for *deeply offended.* "You're asking me if I can use my talent to seduce any woman I want."

"No." She stopped and turned toward him, clearly shocked. "I know you wouldn't do anything that unethical."

He stopped, too. "Yeah? How do you know that?"

"I'm an aura profiler, remember?"

He frowned. "You profiled me?"

"Of course," she said coolly. "Do you think I'd go to bed with a man I haven't analyzed? Especially given my issues?"

"I guess I haven't thought about it quite that way." He paused. "I, uh, passed the profile test?"

"Oh, yes." She gave him a smile that was brighter than the light of the tropical morning. "You definitely passed."

"And here I've been wondering if the reason you were attracted to me was because you could touch me without getting fried."

"What?" It was her turn to be outraged. "How dare you think I would fall into bed with a man simply because I could touch him."

"You did say you haven't been able to get close to a man for over a year."

"My phobia issues had nothing to do with what happened last night or this morning," she snapped. "At least, not in the way you mean. I am insulted."

"Take it easy."

"I will not take it easy. I am more than insulted. You just made me mad. Really, really mad."

"I know. I can see it," he said, admiring the heat leaping around her.

"Let's get something clear," she said evenly. "I would never go to bed with a man just because I could *touch* him."

The fires of her feminine outrage were resonating nicely with the hot, exciting wavelengths of desire. She was furious but she wanted him. He suddenly felt much more cheerful again.

"You can't blame a man for leaping to the obvious conclusion," he said.

"Yes, I can."

"Ever heard the phrase 'You're cute when you get mad'?"

For a few seconds he thought she was going to explode. But she made a face instead.

"Fine," she said. "Be that way. I'm hungry. Let's eat."

She turned on her heel and took off very quickly, heading toward the entrance to the restaurant. He retaliated by playing the injured card, making a show of limping after her. By the time he reached the podium, the hostess was waiting with menus in her hand and pity in her eyes.

Grace glared. He smiled, satisfied with his petty revenge.

"That sort of behavior is called passive-aggressive," she said when they were seated.

"I know." He picked up the menu. "But it feels good. Look, I'll try to answer your question but don't blame me if things aren't clear. It's a very murky subject."

She raised her brows. "I'm listening."

"Manipulating sex energy is very complicated," he began, assuming what he hoped was an air of scholarly authority.

"More complicated than tweaking other elements of an aura?"

"Yes."

"Why?" she asked.

"How the hell should I know? Blame it on biology." So much for sounding scholarly.

"You're not getting off that easily."

"For starters, I can't work with what doesn't exist," he said.

"I beg your pardon?"

"If a woman isn't already attracted to me, there's no energy. I can't create it out of thin air."

"But what about her natural desire for sex? Couldn't you just—" She made a little motion with one hand. "Enhance it a little? Put her in the mood?"

If only it were that simple.

"Maybe," he said. "If she wasn't concentrating on something else, like, say, painting or cooking or teaching a class in physics or listening to music."

"Why would that be a problem?"

"Because sexual energy is a raw fuel that can be channeled into a lot of different engines or, in this case, passions. I might be able to heighten a woman's sense of physical excitement under the right circumstances, but sadly, there's no guarantee she would focus that excitement in my direction. She might decide that the guy she saw going down to the beach with a surfboard earlier in the afternoon looked a lot more interesting."

Grace pursed her lips, thoughtful now. "But if she was interested in you in a casual way, could you intensify that interest?"

"Theoretically, maybe. But even if it were possible to get her into bed by fiddling around with her aura, what would be the point? The next morning she'd wonder what the hell she saw in me. That would not be good for the ego."

"There are men who wouldn't care at all about what the woman thought the next morning."

"Yeah, well, I'm not one of them."

"No," she said, very serious, "you're not."

He frowned, unsure how to take that. "Even if there was no ego issue, there's one other big reason why manipulating a woman's aura in bed wouldn't work well, at least not for long."

"What's that?"

"Viewing someone's aura requires only a small amount of energy and effort. But take it from me, manipulating a person's energy field requires enormous concentration and the maximum amount of power. The evening would be ruined for me because I'd have to work constantly every minute just to keep her interested on the psychic level. There wouldn't be much left over to concentrate on the, uh, physical aspects of the situation."

She tapped the menu lightly against the edge of the table. "I hadn't thought about the heavy energy drain."

"There's no ducking the laws of physics." He picked up his own menu. "Energy is energy. For every action there is an equal and opposite reaction. If you use a lot of power, it takes time to recover."

The waiter showed up with coffee, took their orders and left. Luther saw Grace glance at a nearby table. An oddly wistful look crossed her face before she turned back and picked up her coffee cup.

He looked at the table that had drawn her attention and saw a family of four. The attractive, stylishly dressed blond mother was several years younger than her silver-haired husband. There was a lively little boy of about five and a small blond princess who was probably seven.

He picked up his own cup. "Don't know about you," he said in low tones, "but when I was a kid, Granddad and I didn't do vacations at ritzy hotels in Maui. Camping in a state park was about as fancy as it got."

Her fingers tightened around the handle of the cup but the expression on her face remained perfectly neutral. "That situation isn't as perfect as it looks. Second marriage for him. He's got kids by his ex-wife who are now adults and are not thrilled about having a couple of half siblings."

"Especially when it comes to sharing the trust funds and the inheritance?"

"The battle over the inheritance will be all the more bitter because the first family didn't get what the second family is getting."

He cocked a brow. "Lots of attention from a doting father who is enjoying a do-over?"

"Yes," she said.

"What about her?"

Grace moved her hand in a dismissing gesture. "The usual story when a young woman marries a much older man. She's in it for the money and the status. For now she's satisfied with the bargain but one of these days, she'll take a lover."

"Are you guessing or can you really see those things in their auras?"

"I can't see the precise details. There's no such thing as true mind reading, you know that. But I can detect patterns and themes and chords in auras. My talent allows me to interpret those elements and make certain kinds of inferences. It's an intuitive process."

"No wonder Fallon finds you useful." He contemplated the couple with the two kids. "But I don't think you have to be psychic to figure out the dynamics in that family. Older man, beautiful young wife and very young children. It's a common enough scenario."

"True," she agreed. "But I happen to be very good at this game. Want to try another table? One where the dynamics aren't so obvious?"

"Game?"

She shrugged. "I invented it when I was a kid. I call it the There's No Such Thing as a Perfect Family game. I've played it a lot over the years. Show me a family, any family, and I'll tell you where the fault lines are."

He whistled softly. "Wow. That's cold."

She flushed, embarrassed. "Yes, I suppose it does sound that way. It's a self-defense mechanism, of course. When I was younger I didn't have to feel so bad about not having a family of my own if I could look around and see all the tensions and problems in other people's families. Somewhere along the line the game became a habit."

"Damn. I think you're even more cynical than I am."

"Wouldn't be hard." Her eyes gleamed with sudden amusement. "You're a genuine romantic."

"How the hell can you say that?" It was his turn to be offended. "I haven't got a romantic bone in my body. Just ask either of my exes."

She gave him first a surprised and then a considering look. "Your exes didn't know you very well, did they?"

They sure as hell didn't know me the way you do after only one night, lady, he thought. But he decided this was probably not a good time to say that out loud.

"According to them, I didn't understand them," he said instead. "They were right. The divorces were my fault."

"Why do you say that?"

He shrugged. "Because it's true. In hindsight, I think I scared both of them. Just took them a while to realize that they were scared. About a year in each case."

"Were either of your wives sensitives?"

"No."

She nodded sagely. "And you kept your little secret from them until after you were married, right?"

He felt himself redden. "Figured it would be easier to explain once they got to know me better. But it was the same pattern both times. Things started off with a bang and then went south. They would hear rumors about me from the spouses of some of the other people in the department. They asked questions. Each time I tried to ease into an explanation of how psychic talent works but that just made things worse. Eventually they decided that I wasn't just weird, I was delusional. Possibly dangerous. They filed for divorce."

"I think it was probably a little more complicated than that."

"What do you mean?"

"Power of any kind is attractive at first. I'm sure each of your wives sensed your strength and found it exciting, even though they didn't understand what it was that got their attention. But after a while they became uncomfortable because they intuitively knew that you were too strong for them. They probably began to feel intimidated, maybe a little overwhelmed, even though they could not explain why. The bottom line is that the balance of power was never even remotely equal. Unequal relationships are always treacherous."

"Yeah? So what makes you so sure I'm a romantic?"

"It's in your aura," she said simply. "And in your career path, of course."

"Of course?"

"You didn't become a cop by accident, and it's no coincidence that you work for J&J these days. You were born to protect and defend."

"I'm also a bartender," he said, wanting to challenge her. He wasn't sure he liked being analyzed. In fact, he was very sure that he didn't like it. "How does that fit into your little theory?"

"I don't know yet but I'm sure it does, somehow. Tell me, did you ever think of trying arcanematch-dot-com?"

"No," he said. "I've always heard that the Society's matchmakers aren't very good when it comes to matching exotics, especially when it comes to clients who lie about their Jones numbers. Too many unknowns and unpredictables. You?"

"No," she said. She did not offer an explanation.

"Ever been married?" he pressed.

She shook her head again. "No."

"Why not?"

She smiled sweetly. "Unlike you, I'm not a romantic."

"Liar," he said. "I think the reason you never married is because you've been waiting for Mr. Right."

"Call me picky."

Thirteen

The new arrivals began checking in early that afternoon. Luther sat beside Grace on the hotel's wide, shaded veranda. To the left he could see the pool terrace and the beach beyond. To the right was an unobstructed view of the open-air lobby and the front desk. There were two glasses of iced tea on the small round table between the two rattan chairs. He had a copy of *The Wall Street Journal.* Grace appeared immersed in a paperback novel that she had brought with her. They both wore sunglasses.

He fine-tuned the pleasant little fantasy he had been concocting while he watched the bell staff unload an expensive set of golf clubs from the back of a limo van. The latest version of the fantasy involved Grace and himself on a Maui honeymoon that he, not J&J, had paid for. Also The Fantasy 2.0 did not include keeping an eye out for a psychic killer.

A man and a woman got out of the limo. They were greeted with orchid leis and escorted to the front desk by a member of the hotel staff. Automatically Luther looked at them with his other vision. The man was sending out the quick, green vibes indicative of a simmering irritation that could spill over into anger, given the right provocation.

"She's a low-range intuitive talent," Grace said without looking up from her book. "A three maybe. Strong enough to give her an edge when it comes to picking a husband who is as ambitious as she is. As far as she's concerned, she's made him what he is today."

"Think she knows about the psychic side of her nature?"

"I doubt it. Not at that level. Like most women, she probably takes her intuition for granted."

"What about the husband?"

Grace turned a page. "He's annoyed."

"Yeah, I got that. Probably a long flight with a few of the usual travel glitches. Anything else?"

"His wife holds the reins of power in the relationship. He knows she's smarter than he is and that he needs her to climb the corporate ladder. But that just makes him all the more resentful. Based on that analysis, I'd guess he has a mistress who knows how to make him feel like the strong one."

"You're good, aren't you?"

"Yes." She turned a page. "That's why Mr. Jones sent me on this mission."

"I hate to shatter your image of yourself as a female James Bond but I'm not sure this trip to Maui rises to the level of a mission."

"What would you call it?"

"A job."

"I think I'll stick with mission. Sounds more exciting."

He nodded. "Things have certainly been exciting in the past twenty-four hours, I'll give you that."

Another limo arrived at the front of the hotel. More bags of golf clubs and what looked like diving gear were unloaded. Luther watched the bell staff spring into action. A sophisticated-looking man in his early forties got out. His companion was an attractive redhead of about the same age who looked like she spent a lot of time in spas and high-end hairstyling salons.

"I give the marriage six more months," Grace said coolly. "He's headed into a full-blown midlife crisis and wants a trophy wife to impress his friends."

"Kids?"

Grace studied the couple for a moment. "Yes. I'm sure he'll tell the children that it's for the best."

"You're right," he said. "You're good at this game. Must get a little depressing at times, though."

"I like to think of it as being realistic."

He glanced at the cover of her book. The illustration showed the shadowed profile of a woman. She had a gun in her hand. The title was equally ominous.

"Looks like a murder mystery," he said.

"Romantic-suspense," she corrected.

"Meaning?"

"Meaning it's got both romance and a couple of murders in it."

"You like books like that?"

"Yes."

He smiled. "Thought you said you weren't a romantic."

"I'm not." She turned another page. "Doesn't mean that I don't like to read about romance."

"What about the murders?"

"They get solved by clever sleuthing on the part of the hero and heroine. It's very satisfying."

"You know, in real life the motivation for murder is usually a lot more straightforward than it is in fiction," he said. "Somebody gets pissed off, picks up the nearest gun and shoots the guy who pissed him off."

"Really?" She did not seem particularly interested.

"What's more, the majority of cases get solved because someone talks, not because of forensics or clever sleuthing."

"If I want real police work, I'll read the newspapers, not a book," she said.

"Probably a good idea. Let me know how that one ends."

She turned another page. "I already know how it ends."

"You read the ending first?"

"I always read the ending before I commit to the whole book."

He looked at her, baffled. "If you know how it ends, why read the book?"

"I don't read for the ending. I read for the story." She looked toward the entrance, watching a cab that had pulled up in front. "Life is too short to waste time on books that end badly."

"By badly you mean unhappily, right?"

"As far as I'm concerned, the two are synonymous."

"Okay, so how does that book end? Wait." He held up a hand. "Let me guess. The butler did it."

She flinched visibly, her lips parting as though in shock. He could have sworn that the book shook a little in her hand. He raised the volume of his senses.

The normal hues and colors of the world faded. The myriad shades of the paranormal spectrum shimmered into view. He was startled to see unmistakable spikes of fear in Grace's aura. Before he could ask her what was wrong, he realized she was watching the lobby entrance.

He followed her gaze and saw a man climb out from behind the wheel of one of the newly arrived vehicles. He had the heavy, overmuscled build of a weight lifter on steroids. His head was shaved and he wore a pair of mirrored sunglasses.

But it was his aura that grabbed Luther's attention. It was not only strong, there was something *wrong* with it. Sparks of dark energy flickered and flashed in the field. Wherever they rippled through the pattern, they created disturbing pulses.

"What the hell?" he said softly.

"Hunter," Grace said quietly. "Sort of."

"Damn. So much for Fallon's probability theory."

"It's not just the odds that are bad here." There was a shiver in her voice. She appeared transfixed. "The profile isn't that of a normal hunter."

"How is it different?"

"For one thing, it's unevenly developed. It doesn't reflect the full range of abilities that generally go with that type of talent. There are whole sections missing or blunted along the spectrum."

"Such as?"

"Well, for starters, I'd say he doesn't possess the ability to detect the psychic spoor of violence, which is a common aspect of an above-average hunter talent. He's got the night vision and the strength and speed, though."

"Anything else missing?" he asked. He did not take his attention off the man.

"Yes. There's usually a strong correlation between intelligence and a high level of any kind of psychic ability. A level-eight or -nine hunter like him should possess above-average intelligence."

"He doesn't?"

"No. He's not stupid but he's not an independent thinker, that's for sure. You're looking at a guy who can be easily manipulated by someone who knows how to handle him; a man who would never question orders."

"Not the brightest bulb on the tree, huh?"

"No."

"Any chance that's Eubanks?"

She shook her head. "Not unless the profile I was given was very badly flawed, which I doubt."

Luther watched the driver open the rear door of the car. Another man climbed out. He looked to be in his late thirties, tall and square-jawed with a too-perfect tan that could only have come out of a spray can.

Grace drew a sharp breath and tensed again.

"That's Eubanks," she whispered. "High-level strat talent. Everything else fits, too."

"You're sure?"

"Positive."

"What's with the rogue waves?" he asked.

She turned her head very quickly, stunned. "You can see them?"

"No offense, but I think they'd be hard to miss. I've seen some crazy people in my time. A lot of them have an erratic pulse in their auras. But not like those."

Eubanks left the luggage to the driver and the bell staff, ignored the lei offered by the greeter and walked quickly toward the front desk.

"Junkies develop bizarre patterns, too," Grace said hesitantly.

He studied Eubanks, thinking about that possibility. "A heavy user will throw off a lot of weird vibes. But in my experience, junkies' auras resemble those of the crazies. You get a lot of what look like misfires or short-circuiting going on. The pattern is inherently unpredictable and makes it hard for the normal wavelengths to resonate, at least not for very long."

"But this is a regular, repeating pattern," she said, still speaking in that odd, soft tone. "A consistent rogue wave."

"Which sounds like an oxymoron."

"Why do you think Eubanks brought a hunter along?" she asked.

"Probably for the same reason that I'm here with you. The hunter is a bodyguard."

He watched the way the hunter quartered the lobby, checking out each sector. The bodyguard's gaze passed lightly over them and then moved on. There was no flicker of alarm in the pattern.

Grace seemed to relax a little. "He didn't pay any attention to us."

"Like you said, he's not that sharp. Whatever the case, you've done your job. Time to get you off this island." He hated the thought of sending her back to that little town on the Oregon coast, but he sure as hell did not want her anywhere near Eubanks.

"We're not done yet," she said. "You need me to help profile that hunter we ran into last night, remember?"

"The situation has become complicated."

"I can do complicated."

"You're not going to do it here," he said.

"You need a partner," she insisted. "And I'm the only one handy. Eubanks is a very, very dangerous man and so is that hunter."

"I know the cane doesn't make a reassuring impression, but I do know how to do this kind of stuff."

"I am well aware of what you can do," she said. "I saw you in action last night. But you're not crazy."

That was interesting. "You think Eubanks is?"

"I think," she said carefully, "that there's something more than a little off about him, just like there is something off about his bodyguard."

"The rogue waves?"

"Yes. I think you should stay away from both of those men."

His first reaction was to start brooding over her obvious lack of confidence. Okay, so he wasn't in the best of shape at the moment. Then it occurred to him that she was genuinely worried about his safety. He wasn't sure how to take that. Go with the positive, he thought. She cares enough to be concerned.

"I'll be fine," he said. "You know, instead of flying home to Eclipse Bay, you could go back to Honolulu and wait for me there. I won't be here long. As soon as I phone Fallon, he'll make arrangements for Eubanks to be put under long-term surveillance. I'll hang around, see if I can find that hunter and then—"

He broke off because he realized she was not listening. Her attention was no longer on Eubanks, who had received his card key and was already striding impatiently toward the elevator lobby, the hunter by his side. Instead, she was watching another new arrival, a woman who had just gotten out of a white limo.

An executive, he decided, watching the woman direct the bell staff with an authoritative air. She was accompanied by a muscular man dressed in an ill-fitting jacket.

The woman ignored the proffered lei, just as Eubanks had done, and walked briskly through the lobby toward the front desk.

"Look at them," Grace said urgently.

"I am looking at them. What is it?"

"*Look* at them."

"Right." Obediently he jacked up his senses again.

The woman's aura flared, a cold array of icy blues and glassy greens.

"Wouldn't be a good idea to get between her and whatever she happened to want," he said mildly. "Had a captain like that once. All he cared about was getting into the commissioner's office. He left footprints on the back of everyone who stood in the way."

"I doubt if your captain's aura looked like hers."

And then he saw the pulses—short little stabs of darkness that crackled through the blues and greens, briefly altering the resonating patterns. The rogues were not identical to those in Eubanks's and the hunter's aura but there was a distinct similarity.

He switched his attention to the woman's companion and saw the same bad energy.

"Hunter," Grace said. "Incomplete, like the other one."

"Another bodyguard. That explains the bad jacket. He's carrying."

"Carrying what?"

"A gun."

"Oh, right." She assumed a knowing air. "Definitely carrying."

Another vehicle halted at the entrance. This time two men got out. One of them supervised the unloading of a set of golf clubs. The other headed for the lobby.

"High-level probability talent and his bodyguard," Grace said. "Same dark energy spikes in their fields."

"What the hell is going on here? I've never seen anything like those weird rogue waves."

"I have," Grace said softly.

"I did get that impression." He reached for his cane. "You and I need to talk."

Fourteen

"What the hell is going on and what do you know about it?" Luther asked. He used his flat, unemotional cop voice.

She'd had enough for one day. Her temper spiked. "Don't talk to me like that."

"Like what?"

"Like I'm a suspect that you've got cornered in an interrogation room."

He looked at her, eyes veiled by his dark glasses, and said nothing. He waited the way cops and psychiatrists did sometimes, hoping you'd get nervous and start talking.

They were standing in the shade of the very same tree that had concealed them the previous evening when he touched her for the first time. But it wasn't the precious memory of what had happened the night before that slammed through her now. It was the fragment of the Martin Crocker dream that had awakened her that she found herself remembering.

She concentrated on the ocean while she composed her thoughts. Luther had a right to know whatever she could tell him about the auras

of the strange group that had just arrived. But she was under no obligation to confess all her secrets. It wouldn't be the first time she had lied to
a cop. She could do this.

"I once knew someone else whose aura developed a similar distur-
bance," she said quietly.

"Go on."

"You know this would be a whole lot easier if you played Good Cop
instead of Bad Cop."

"Talk to me, Grace."

"This man I knew, the rogue waves, as you call them, started to appear after he began taking a drug."

"What drug?" Luther did not stir beside her but she knew that he had
heightened his senses. He was watching her with his other vision, searching for signs of anxiety, fear, anger or any other strong emotion that
might signal to him that she was lying or evading. *Let him look. So what
if I'm scared? He should be scared, too.*

"I don't know the name of whatever he was using," she said, "but I'm
very sure it was illegal. It had a weird effect on him. It gave him a new
kind of talent, one he definitely did not have before he started taking the
drug. It's hard to explain, but—"

"Shit," Luther said, interrupting her very softly. "Nightshade."

Startled, she turned to face him, her own senses flaring. His aura
flashed with a cold, controlled excitement that did not show on his face.
She knew he was running hot, not just psychically but physically. Adrenaline.

"What is Nightshade?" she asked warily. "Some new street drug?"

"No. It's the code name that Fallon gave to a new organization of
rogue sensitives that has managed to re-create the founder's formula."

"The formula?" She was beyond startled, she was stunned. "But that's
just an old Society myth," she managed weakly.

"Not any longer. Hunting down Nightshade operatives and identifying the group's leaders is J&J's number one priority these days. Everyone in the agency knows that."

"No one told me anything about Nightshade."

"Probably because Fallon considers you temporary help. But I've got a hunch your status in the firm just got changed but good. What do you know about Nightshade?"

Careful. You don't have to tell him everything.

Who was she kidding? Her private Pandora's box of horrors had just been opened. There was no stuffing the bad news back inside. Her survival instincts kicked in. She hastily assessed her options and decided there were two. She could disappear again, a risky proposition because she had a hunch that J&J would pull out all the stops to hunt her down. The second option was to cooperate in the hunt for Nightshade. It was a dicey maneuver but if she was very careful, she might be able to pull it off without revealing her own secrets.

She straightened her shoulders, the decision made. She would give Luther the information that might be helpful to J&J. But she didn't have to throw herself under the bus.

She had one very big factor going for her in the equation, she decided. J&J clearly needed the data that she could supply. That gave her some negotiating power. If worst came to worst, she could work with that.

"I told you that until I joined the Bureau of Genealogy, I worked as a librarian in a large corporation," she said.

"Crocker World."

"Right. A lot of my time was spent doing Internet searches that were commissioned by various executives, including Mr. Crocker. On a few occasions I was called into the executive suite to deliver the results of my research."

"Martin Crocker summoned a librarian into his office?"

There was irritation and impatience in Luther's voice. He didn't believe her.

"Mr. Crocker was a strat talent. People like that love background and research. The more facts and details they can gather before they make a decision, the better. I did a lot of work for him."

She was pleased with the way that came out. Let him look. Every word was true.

"Go on," Luther said.

"During the years that I worked at headquarters in Miami, I saw Mr. Crocker many times." More truth.

"On your trips upstairs to the executive suite," Luther said without inflection.

Damn. Was he buying this or not?

"What I'm trying to tell you is that I had several opportunities to examine his aura," she said. True.

"What made you do that?"

The question threw her for a couple of seconds. Why would the company librarian care about the boss's aura?

"I suppose," she said simply, "because he was Martin Crocker. In the world in which he moved, he was a rock star. And he was my boss."

"I assume you profiled him?"

She nodded and concentrated on the horizon. "He was a complicated man. Driven."

"Were you attracted to him?"

"Not in the way you mean." More truth. "But I suppose you could say I admired him. Everyone in the company respected his business abilities. He was Martin Crocker, after all. He built an empire."

"Go on."

"During the last few months of his life, Crocker was working on a major project. He requested a number of detailed searches."

"All of which were hand delivered by you?"

"Yes. I made a number of trips to the executive suite and on several of those trips I saw Crocker. Something changed in his aura during that time. I noticed the dark energy waves. They were small, almost undetectable at first. But they grew stronger as the weeks went by."

"What did you think was happening?"

She folded her arms very tightly. "It occurred to me that he might be developing some sort of mental illness that was psychic in origin. Something about his dark energy scared the living daylights out of me."

He considered that a moment. "Okay, it's spooky stuff, I'll give you that."

"One day when I was summoned to the executive suite, I noticed two men going into Crocker's office. Both gave off bad vibes. You couldn't miss them, not if you were an aura talent."

"You checked out their patterns."

"Sure."

"And?" he prompted.

"And I saw the same dark energy patterns in their fields."

"What did you do?"

"Started working on my résumé. What else? I've been around enough freaks in my life to know when it's time to bail. But before I could land another job, the news broke that Crocker had disappeared while on a trip to his private island. There was a lot of speculation. If you followed the story, you know that everyone had a theory. There were rumors. Some of them hit the papers."

"What rumors?" he asked.

"That Crocker was involved with some drug lords and there was a falling-out. That was when I assumed that Crocker himself was doing drugs." Okay, that was a minor tweaking of the truth.

"The theory was that the drug lords got rid of him?"

"It wasn't exactly an off-the-wall conclusion," she said. "Crocker World was headquartered in Miami, after all."

Luther was silent for a long time, his expression cop-hard. Quickly she reviewed her story. It sounded tight. She was satisfied with it, especially given the fact that she'd had only a few minutes to put it together. It helped, of course, that most of the facts were true, including the rumors about Martin's involvement in drug trafficking.

She risked a peek at Luther's aura. Her heart sank. He believed parts of her story but not all of it. Maybe it was time to pull out one of the handful of identities she had constructed from the Society's genealogy files and disappear. Good thing she hadn't gotten a dog. She was surprised by how much the thought depressed her, though. One night with Luther and she had begun building a fantasy of happily ever after. She, of all people, should have known better.

"I'm going to call Fallon," Luther said.

He took out his phone.

Fifteen

"You've got *three* Nightshade operatives under surveillance?" Fallon demanded. The fierce excitement in his voice vibrated through the phone. "Eubanks is one of them?"

"Three *possible* Nightshade operatives," Luther said, clamping a lid down on his own adrenaline rush. "Plus their bodyguards. There is also that unidentified hunter in the vicinity, the one we ran into last night. Don't forget him. Looks like we have a regular little convention of psychics here."

"You say that you and Grace can both identify the Nightshade people by the patterns in their auras?"

"Slow down, Fallon. I'm telling you that we can see some very unusual energy in their fields, and Grace says that the psychic aspects of all of the profiles are abnormal. We think the effect is caused by some kind of drug. That's all we know for certain at this point."

"Any drug that has such a consistent effect on psychic talent in several different people has got to be based on the founder's formula."

"Okay, I agree that sounds like a reasonable assumption. But what if there's another drug out there that produces similar effects?"

"That would be one hell of a coincidence," Fallon said. "No, this is Nightshade. Don't forget, Eubanks is a respected member of the Society. All the evidence indicates that the Nightshade organization has some high-ranking, well-connected talents planted within the Arcane community. That's probably how they got their hands on the formula in the first place, and that's how they've managed to stay one step ahead of us."

"Wait a second. Are you telling me that you think Nightshade still has people planted within the Society?"

"Yes. What's more, Zack Jones agrees with me. We've been talking about the problem damn near every day since he took over the Master's Chair a few weeks ago."

Fallon had been known to leap off the deep end occasionally when it came to his beloved theories. But Zack Jones, the new Master of the Society, was, by all accounts, cool-headed, smart and highly intuitive. If he was on the same page with Fallon when it came to Nightshade, there was a good chance Fallon's conclusion was right.

"Okay," he conceded. "Here's something else to chew on. Grace has seen similar waves before."

"Shit. *Where?*"

"In the aura of her old boss, Martin Crocker, and in the auras of two men with whom he had dealings."

"Son of a bitch," Fallon said softly. "So Crocker was Nightshade."

"You're leaping to conclusions again."

"It's what I do. Damn. You know, I was getting suspicious of Crocker. He was high profile and he was Arcane so he popped up on my radar occasionally. I had started to wonder if he was into some dirty side business. Figured it was either arms dealing or drugs, though. Never made the Nightshade connection."

"What happened?"

"He died before I decided whether or not to fire up an investigation. Do you realize what this means? If we've got a way of identifying Nightshade's people on sight, we'll have a huge advantage. There are a lot of aura talents registered with the Society. I need to start recruiting some and get them trained."

"It's not going to be that easy," Luther warned. "Grace thinks that only high-level auras will be strong enough to see the dark energy. Most people with the talent can perceive only vague stuff like whether or not the person is ill or mentally disturbed."

"Which means I need you and Grace to keep up surveillance there on Maui until I can get people in place."

"You've got me," Luther said. "But I want Grace off the island as fast as possible."

"Put her on the phone."

"No," Luther said.

"Figured you'd get stubborn."

Luther heard Grace's phone burble. Startled, she opened her purse.

"You're a real SOB, Fallon," Luther said.

Grace had her phone open. "Hello?"

"Hang on," Fallon said in Luther's ear. "I'll be right back."

Luther cut the connection.

"Oh, hello, Mr. Jones," Grace said. "I thought you were talking to Luther. Yes. Quite near the hotel. We just stepped out to discuss the situation. What? No, the hunter we ran into last night did not have those rogues in his pattern. Yes, I'm sure Mr. Crocker did. When did I last see him? Uh, well, let me think. It would have been shortly before he disappeared. His office requested some research. I delivered a report to him before he left for his private island."

Luther braced his back against the tree and watched Grace's aura as she talked to Fallon.

"The subject of the research?" She frowned in thought. "It's been over a year, but as I recall it had something to do with some agricultural equipment requests from a charitable foundation that was doing work in developing countries. The two other men I saw who had similar wave patterns were supposedly representatives of the foundation."

There was a pause while she listened intently.

"Yes, sir, of course," she said. "Glad to help. Please feel free to call back if you have any more questions. Yes, sir, I'll tell Luther."

She ended the connection, slipped the phone back into her purse and looked at Luther.

"You're not going back to Eclipse Bay today, are you?" he said.

"Mr. Jones instructed me to stay here with you. We're to return to the hotel immediately and see if we can spot any other Nightshade operatives."

"And you agreed."

She raised her chin. "Yes, I did."

"I don't like it."

"I am aware of that but it's my decision."

"What makes him think there will be more than just the three of them and their bodyguards?"

"Mr. Jones said that where there are a few snakes, there may be a whole nest."

"What are the odds that there's a whole bunch of Nightshade folks hanging out together at a resort on Maui?" he asked.

"Very good, actually. Mr. Jones pointed out that Nightshade is an organization. That means it has a formal structure and a strict hierarchy. No organized group of any kind can survive without at least occasional face-to-face meetings. What's so strange about holding a conference of senior management on Maui? Pharmaceutical companies and insurance firms do it all the time."

Excitement had replaced the tension in her voice. He knew when he was beaten.

"You're really enjoying the role of secret agent, aren't you?" he said.

"I didn't get out much this past year in Eclipse Bay."

He used the cane to push himself away from the tree. "All right. We'll watch the hotel guests for a day or two. See what turns up. But remember Rule Number One on this job."

"I'm afraid that in all the excitement, I forgot it."

"Rule Number One is that I give the orders in the field."

"I'm your partner and I'm also J&J's special consultant on the scene, the only one the agency has available at the moment."

"You do what I say or you'll find yourself on a plane before you can get packed, partner."

"But Mr. Jones said—"

"Fallon Jones isn't here. I am."

Sixteen

Damaris Kemble's hands curled into fists on the keyboard as she read the e-mail message from the mysterious contractor. She swallowed hard, fighting the rage and frustration that threatened to swamp her.

Job declined. There will be no refund, as it has come to our attention that you misrepresented your references.

"Damn, damn, *damn.*"

Somehow the contractor had discovered that she was not the real Winthrup. She had failed Daddy.

The plan had been brilliant in concept, beautifully simple and daring. But it had not worked. Unfortunately, time was running out fast. Eubanks and the others would be together on Maui for only a few days. She shoved herself away from the computer and picked up the phone.

Her call was answered on the first ring.

"The contractor refuses to go through with the job," she said.

"What went wrong?"

The voice on the other end was reassuringly calm, cool and controlled. Her father's voice. She relaxed a little at the sound of it.

"The contractor somehow discovered that my credentials were false."

"You used the correct security codes?"

"Yes, of course. I just rechecked them. They were the codes you provided. But somehow the contractor discovered that I wasn't the real Winthrup."

"Interesting. The codes must have been changed quite recently." There was a pause. "The important thing is that there is no way this can be traced back to either of us. The contractor will assume that someone hacked into the government agency's computers and stole the codes. He'll probably notify the agency that they've got a security leak. But there's no reason the contractor or the agency would look twice at J&J or suspect that someone within the Society was involved."

"You're sure we're safe, Daddy?"

"Honey, I've been playing this game a long time. I know what I'm doing. What's done is done. Now we have to concentrate on our next move. All we've got is a three-day window. There's no time to line up another professional contractor. We have no choice but to go with our fallback scenario."

She slumped in her chair. "I had a feeling you were going to say that. I told you it would be risky."

"You're in no danger. I'll take care of you."

"You're the one I'm worried about. If this goes wrong—"

"It won't."

His certainty had the effect of steadying her nerves somewhat. She had been so jumpy lately, easily startled and hyperalert. She hadn't slept well since she had started taking the drug. When she did manage to get to sleep, she was frequently awakened by bizarre nightmares. Daddy had explained that the problems were merely short-term side effects of the drug. He said that once the formula had finished ramping up her crystal working talent, her nerves would calm down.

"Call her," Daddy said.

"All right." She paused and lowered her voice. "When can I see you again?"

"We agreed it would be best if we did not have any further contact until after this is over."

"I know, but it's been weeks. After all these years of not even knowing you existed, I want as much time together as possible."

"Soon, honey. For now, my main goal is to protect you. You're my true heir but we need to allow time for the drug to take effect and bring you into your full powers. I also want to make sure that you're fully trained before I let you take too many risks. You're the future of the organization. I can't put you in harm's way."

There was a more formal title for the organization, but it had adopted the name that the Arcane Society had given it. *Nightshade*. And she was its future.

"I understand, Daddy." That's what fathers did, she thought. They took care of their daughters.

"Don't worry. Once Eubanks is dead, things will fall into place very quickly. Within a few months we'll be ready for phase two of the operation. Go make the call."

"All right. Daddy?"

"Yes, honey?"

"I love you."

"I love you, too."

She ended the connection, feeling markedly better. She always did after she talked to her father. But she was not looking forward to Plan B. It meant dealing with a killer who was not only a consummate professional but also mentally unbalanced. Her sister.

Seventeen

She did not need to hear the key played in order to find the right note. She was La Sirène. Endowed with perfect pitch, she plucked the A out of thin air and launched straight into the Queen of the Night's second aria.

The elegant, acoustically precise practice room had been designed and built for her by her current lover. Newlin Guthrie, a billionaire who had made his fortune by inventing any number of boring computer gadgets and high-tech security software programs, had spared no expense in the construction. The room was on the second floor of the Mediterranean-style villa he had purchased for her shortly after she drew him to her with her Siren's talent. The lovely mini palazzo was perched above the bay in Sausalito and offered stimulating views of San Francisco.

She had chosen the florid "Der Hölle Rache" for the very private performance on Maui for two reasons: The first was that it was good practice for her role in the upcoming production of *The Magic Flute*. The second reason was that it was ideally suited to her unique talent. The challenging high F, the note that hardly any sopranos could sing full voice, was one of the few that allowed her to project and focus the specific wavelengths of psychic energy required to interfere with certain critical neurological functions of the human brain. Glass had been known to shatter when she sang that note; people had died.

Besides, when you set out to kill a man, you could hardly go wrong with a song that had a title that translated as "The Revenge of Hell Cooks in My Heart." She had learned long ago that the music chosen for a performance—especially one of her unique *private* engagements—had to be right. Art was all about the communication between artist and audience.

She had not planned on going to Maui. In a week she was scheduled to sing the Queen of the Night at the opening of the new opera house in Acacia Bay. The engagement, arranged by dear Newlin, was critical to the rejuvenation of her career. Things had not been going well since that dreadful night at La Scala two years ago when the claque had dared to boo her.

But when her sister had called and begged her for a favor, she had been unable to refuse. Damaris was family, after all, the only family she had. *Daddy* didn't count.

Nevertheless, she was annoyed to find herself preparing to board a plane for Maui on such short notice. It was not as if she did not have a great deal to do between now and opening night. Furthermore, she knew that the only reason Damaris wanted her to give this particular performance was because of *Daddy*.

Personally, she despised the father who had shown up out of nowhere to claim his daughters. How on earth Damaris could care for a man whose only contribution to their lives had been to ejaculate into a glass vial and deposit the result in a sperm bank was beyond her. *Daddy* could keel over tomorrow as far as she was concerned. In fact, she often fantasized about giving one of her private performances just for him. The problem with that little scheme, unfortunately, was that Damaris would very likely guess the cause of death and have a fit. There was another issue, as well. *Daddy* had his own psychic talent, and it was lethal.

Although the Maui trip was an imposition, she was starting to look forward to it in spite of herself. Successful performances of any kind always gave her a euphoric sensation that was impossible to achieve in any other way. For hours afterward she felt gloriously powerful. But there was nothing like the absolutely dazzling rush that followed one of her special *private* performances. Following those engagements, she knew what it was like to be a true goddess. The sensation of immortality sometimes lasted for days.

She had been twenty-three years old, at the very start of her career, when she first discovered the ultimate power of her talent. Her singing had always been special, of course. Mother had planned her future before she was born, having chosen the sperm donor with great care, not for his particular psychic ability but for the strength of his raw energy.

Descended from a long line of sensitives herself, Mother had studied the complex laws of psychic inheritance with attention to detail. Everyone was endowed with some degree of talent, but at the lower end of the scale—the so-called normal end—it usually appeared in the form of a murky sense of intuition that an amazing number of people either took for granted or willfully ignored.

But there were others, those who were gifted with a considerable degree of psychic power: too much to be overlooked or suppressed. When that talent was strong enough to register at level five or higher on the Jones Scale, it tended to differentiate into specific, more narrowly focused types of abilities. It was a given that when it came to the most powerful talents, no one got more than one. Mother had explained that it was some sort of evolutionary law, nature's way of preventing the creation of super predators.

Mother had also understood that certain talents, including the near-mythic Siren talent, were dominant and sometimes gender-related traits.

Historically all Sirens had been female, probably because only females—musically trained females at that—could hit the so-called money notes, the glorious, almost surreal high D's, E's, F's and even G's that were the only ones capable of focusing a Siren's particular type of psychic energy. Not all coloratura sopranos were Sirens, by any means, but all true Sirens were capable of singing the coloratura repertoire, provided they had been trained.

Mother had also comprehended another one of the complicated laws of psychic genetics: When a strong dominant trait such as the Siren talent was enhanced by the power of almost any other type of talent, the result was an even more powerful Siren. Hence Mother's choice of sperm donor.

Singing and music lessons had begun before La Sirène could walk.

"You will be more famous than Sutherland or Sills or Callas," Mother had assured her. "You have the power to become the most brilliant soprano of your generation, perhaps of any generation. The talent is in your bloodline."

She had, indeed, skyrocketed to fame and stardom but not without having to overcome a few obstacles. The first serious glitch had been an ambitious young rival who had shown up at that important audition in her twenty-third year. The creature had walked off with the title role in the production of *Lucia di Lammermoor* even though it was obvious that she could barely pop off the E-flat in the Mad Scene, let alone embellish it with the high F the way La Sirène could. The rumor that the untalented bitch was sleeping with the wealthiest and most influential backer had spread quickly. It certainly explained a few things.

La Sirène had known for some time that it was theoretically possible to kill with her voice. Her mother had told her that some of her female ancestors had done just that. Nevertheless, she never quite believed it, not until the night when she cornered the bitch in a practice room backstage and sang the Mad Scene the way only she could sing it.

The autopsy had revealed the cause of death as an aneurism. Very tragic, promising young singer cut down on the brink of what could have been a spectacular career, blah, blah, blah. But the show must go on. And it did, with the hot new coloratura soprano who would soon be known as La Sirène in the role of Lucia.

Come to think of it, maybe the Maui engagement wasn't such an imposition, after all. She always sang her best in the days and weeks following one of her private performances. The Voice needed to be exercised to the fullest extent occasionally in order to remain flawless.

The performance in Acacia Bay had to be perfect.

Eighteen

By ten-fifteen that evening they had identified a total of ten rogue auras, five of whom looked like executives. The other five appeared to be bodyguards with incomplete hunter profiles.

Grace sat with Luther in the shadows at the edge of the hotel's open-air bar, sipping sparkling water, listening to the slack-key guitar player and watching their quarry.

The five execs sat together, drinking and chatting in a way that Grace had witnessed a thousand times over the years. Their bodyguards hovered at a nearby table, looking tense and uncomfortable against the laid-back island atmosphere.

"You know, if you ignore the evidence of the drug in their auras and the fact that they're all strong talents and that they're all traveling with bodyguards, their profiles are pretty much what you'd expect from people in senior management," she said. "I think Mr. Jones is right. We've stumbled into some sort of high-level Nightshade business meeting."

"We still don't have any proof that they're Nightshade," Luther said. "But I agree that, whoever they are, they look like corporate suits. Wonder where Eubanks ranks in the hierarchy?"

She contemplated the auras again. "I'd say that they see themselves as roughly equal, which means they're probably at the same level in the organization. Judging by those luggage tags you saw earlier, they're all from the West Coast plus the one from Arizona."

"According to Fallon, the Nightshade organization appears to be concentrated on the West Coast and in Arizona," Luther said. "Maybe these guys are regional managers."

"Everyone's certainly being very chummy and convivial," she said, "but there's a lot of aggression just below the surface."

"Now, that I *can* see," Luther said. "I'd bet any one of those five would be willing to slit the throat of any of the others if he or she thought it would be useful. Nightshade is a very Darwinian organization. Only the strong and the ruthless make it to the top."

She shuddered. "The level of potential violence surrounding them is very strong but the really worrisome thing is that a couple of them seem to be developing additional talents."

"Thought that was genetically impossible."

"Not quite. I can tell you from my genealogy work that it's true that multiple talents are extremely rare. But there have been a handful of exceptions over the centuries. The thing is, the exceptions all went insane and died young. Something to do with overstimulation of the brain."

"So these multitalents are artificially induced by the drug."

"Yes," she said. "I saw the same thing in Mr. Crocker's aura after the dark energy appeared, although I didn't know what it meant at the time."

"We need more information on Eubanks. I want to see just how he's connected to Nightshade."

"What do you suggest?"

He put his sparkling water down on the table. "I'm going to pay a visit to his room while he's occupied down here."

A shiver went through her. "I don't like that idea."

"What's the problem? We know where he is. You can keep an eye on him while I take a look around his suite."

"How am I supposed to warn you if he leaves the bar?"

"You call my cell. From here it's a five-, maybe eight-minute walk back through the lobby, up the elevators and down the hall to number six-oh-four. Plenty of time for me to get out before he sees me."

"Luther, I know this is going to sound wimpy, but I've got a bad feeling about this."

"You're right, that sounds wimpy." He got leisurely to his feet. "Call me if he makes a move to head back to the room."

She swallowed her next argument, which wasn't any more convincing than the first. She watched carefully but none of the executives or their bodyguards appeared to notice Luther leaving the bar.

She settled down to wait, the cell phone cradled in one hand.

Nineteen

He got the door open with the useful little J&J gadget that Fallon issued to all his agents. Automatically he heightened his senses and moved inside.

The only warning he got that he was not the only one in the room was the hot flash of a seriously jacked-up aura. *Hunter.*

He spun around to face the threat. The cane went out from under him. He went down hard on the carpet. The fall saved him.

The hunter's thwarted rush carried him straight into the bed. He recovered with the lightning-swift reflexes that were the hallmark of his talent, seeming to bounce off the comforter and back onto his feet.

Luther didn't even try to rise. No one without a similar talent could hope to defeat a hunter in hand-to-hand combat. Instead he focused quickly and slammed everything he had at the attacker's pattern, dousing the fiery energy with a tsunami wave of crushing ennui.

The hunter staggered and reeled back, disoriented. He sank onto the bed.

"Shit," he muttered. "How the hell do you do that?"

"Who are you?" Luther kept the suppressing energy flowing at full power while he got to his feet. "What are you doing here?"

The room was in near total darkness but that wouldn't bother the hunter. With his talent powered, he had excellent night vision. Luther couldn't see a thing except the other man's aura. That was enough.

"I think it's a good bet that we're both here for the same reason," the hunter said. "To get some information on Eubanks."

"You sure you aren't here to take him out?"

"Plans have changed."

The hunter started to come up off the bed. He made no sound but his aura shifted a split second before he did.

"Don't move," Luther said. He accompanied the warning with an extra shot of energy.

The hunter sank back down onto the bed, literally too weary to get to his feet.

"That really is a nifty trick," he said. "How long can you keep it up? Must be a hell of an energy drain."

It was true that he was using an enormous amount of energy to immobilize the hunter. He saw no reason to admit that, however. But the casual manner in which the other man had used the term "energy drain" was interesting. Few people outside the Society, even those comfortable with their psychic natures, would have phrased it quite that way.

"Are you Arcane?" the hunter asked.

"You could say it's in the blood. You?"

"J&J."

"Of course you are. No wonder she had a bad feeling about this job."

"Who?"

"My scheduler. Last night she informed me that she was having doubts about the client and the whole damn situation. This morning she canceled the contract and told me to go home. But I just had to have a look at Eubanks's room. After all these years, you'd think I'd know enough to pay attention to her intuition."

"Who is the client?"

"Called herself Winthrup. That's the code name for our Number Two client. Her story checked out."

"She identified herself as female?"

"No. The real Winthrup is male. Like I said, my scheduler is a strong intuitive. She had a hunch that whoever contacted us was not the real deal."

"Any idea why this Winthrup wanted Eubanks removed?"

"We were informed that he had murdered two wives and a young woman but that isn't why we were given a contract. His major offense, according to Winthrup, is that he is engaged in laundering money for a group that finances terrorists."

"You work for the government?"

"Private contractor. We've got a very short list of clients. A certain government agency is one of them. That's where the real Winthrup works."

The cell phone in Luther's pocket vibrated urgently. He yanked it out and glanced at the code. Grace.

"Eubanks is on his way back here," he said. "He's got a hunter body-guard with him."

"The hunter will sense that there was some action in this suite."

"I don't think so. My associate assures me that the bodyguard is not a full hunter. Seems to lack a few of the usual skills, including the ability to pick up the spoor of violence."

"Not much of a hunter, then. Well, this is over for me. Good thing, too. My first grandchild is due to arrive at any minute. The family is gathering to celebrate the big event. Mind letting me up?"

"One more thing," Luther said. "Got any proof of your version of events?"

"How about if I say the magic words?"

"Which are?"

"Tell Fallon Jones that Sweetwater sends his regards."

"You know Fallon?"

"We've only got two clients. Number One is J&J."

Twenty

"You ran into Harry Sweetwater in Eubanks's hotel room?" Fallon sounded genuinely startled, a rare state of affairs. "Son of a gun. What are the odds?"

"You keep saying that." Luther reached the sliding glass doors, turned and started back across the suite. The cane thudded heavily on the carpet. "Here's the thing, Fallon. You're supposed to know the damn odds. That's your job, remember? Figuring the odds? Connecting dots? Running probabilities? This is a major screwup. What the hell is going on? Did you forget to mention that you'd sent a pro after Eubanks?"

He was very aware of Grace sitting on the sofa looking concerned. The aftereffects of using such a heavy volume of energy to keep Sweetwater planted on the bed were hitting him hard and she obviously knew it. The adrenaline and other biochemicals that had flooded his bloodstream had worn off, leaving him jittery and cold. He hated this part, hated looking exhausted in front of her. The damn cane was bad enough.

"I didn't send Sweetwater after Eubanks," Fallon said.

"Who else besides J&J would want Eubanks dead?"

Grace raised her hand. "Someone who wants his job?"

"I heard that," Fallon said. "I like it. Makes sense, given what we know about Nightshade. It's a tough outfit."

Luther stopped and looked across the room at Grace. "Sweetwater said his scheduler thinks that the person calling herself Winthrup was a woman. Evidently the real Winthrup is a man."

"Sweetwater's scheduler is his wife," Fallon said. "She's probably right. High-level intuitive."

"I don't believe this. His *wife* schedules the hits?"

"Sweetwater is a family business," Fallon explained. "It was founded shortly after J&J was established. There's been a connection between the two firms ever since. Should be another generation of Sweetwaters coming along soon. Harry's oldest son got married a while back."

"He did say something about having to get home for the birth of a grandchild."

"It's a very close family."

"The family that whacks together, stays together?"

Over on the sofa Grace raised her brows.

"Guess it makes for strong family bonds," Fallon said.

"Just out of curiosity, how often does J&J employ the Sweetwater clan?"

"As infrequently as possible and only when there's no other option. We always make an effort to put together a case that will hold up with regular law enforcement and the courts, you know that. You've helped build some of those cases. But occasionally we find ourselves dealing with a high-level sensitive gone bad who is just too damn clever or simply too powerful. Cecil Ferguson, for example."

"Who was Ferguson?"

"A level-ten hypnotist who was also a serial killer. Murdered twelve people before he came to our attention. Took us that long to realize he was one of us, a sensitive. High-grade hypnos are so rare that I've often wondered if he was formula-enhanced."

"Nightshade?"

"Maybe. But we were never able to prove it. This was back in the early days of dealing with Nightshade. We were just beginning to realize that we were facing a full-blown criminal organization, not just another renegade scientist who had decided to play alchemist. At any rate, I knew we couldn't give Ferguson to the cops, not even with plenty of evidence. Anyone who got within a few feet of him was at risk of being put into a trance. He would simply have walked away from the arresting officers."

"So you sent Sweetwater."

"Who took him out from a safe distance. For the record, I use Sweetwater only as a last resort and then only with the full approval of the Council and the Master. And we sure as hell didn't send him to Maui."

"Whoever did send him knew how to make herself look like she was Client Number Two. Sweetwater said she used all the right codes."

"Interesting," Fallon said, grim and thoughtful.

"All right, getting back to our little problem here, how are you doing getting your long-term surveillance people in place? These guys might leave at any time."

Over on the sofa Grace raised her hand again. "I could follow one of the Nightshade operatives."

He gave her his most intimidating stare. She did not appear to notice.

"Heard that, too," Fallon said. "Unfortunately, Grace isn't trained for that kind of work."

Luther smiled at Grace. "He says you're not trained for that kind of work."

She grimaced and flopped back against the sofa cushions.

"I'm working on the surveillance issue," Fallon said. "I'll have five agents there within the next twenty-four hours. You and Grace will have to keep an eye on things until then."

"We don't need Grace on the scene any longer. I want her out of here."

"More Nightshade people might arrive," Fallon said.

"I can ID them for you."

"Yes, but you can't profile them. Which reminds me, tell Grace I got the profiles she worked up this afternoon. They look very thorough."

The phone went abruptly silent.

Luther looked at Grace. "He liked your profiles."

She brightened. "I'm so glad. I take it we're still partners?"

"Yeah."

"Your overwhelming enthusiasm is so heartwarming." She got to her feet, took his arm and steered him toward the bedroom. "Come with me. You need to get some rest. You're running on fumes."

"Used up a lot of energy on Sweetwater. I'm going to have to crash for a while. Pay attention. Keep all the doors locked. Do not leave this room and do not let anyone in, not even the guy who restocks the minibar. Got that?"

"Understood."

He sank down onto the bed and contemplated his running shoes. A man on a cane probably didn't need running shoes, he thought. Before he could decide whether or not he had enough strength left to remove them, Grace knelt in front of him, her head bent. The soft light gleamed on her dark hair. He watched her untie the laces.

"Do you think it should worry us that the best example of a perfect family that we've run into on this trip is a clan of contract killers?" he asked.

"Family is family."

Twenty-one

He awoke with an awareness that she was in the room. He did not have to open his eyes to see her. He knew in some way that he could not explain that he would always be aware of her when she was close. The sense of recognition that had hit him full force when he saw her walking toward him along the airport concourse had become a hundred times more intense when she shivered through her first release in his arms; a thousand times stronger that morning when it seemed to him that their auras had somehow fused for a timeless moment in a bond that would never be severed.

Hell, maybe she was right. Maybe he was a romantic.

"You're awake," Grace said. "How do you feel?"

He did open his eyes then and levered himself up on his elbows. She stood near the sliding glass doors. The curtains were drawn open a couple of feet, giving him a view of the bright morning.

He noticed that she was still dressed in the same clothes she had been wearing the night before. There was an air of unnatural alertness about her. He recognized it immediately. He'd experienced the same sensation on more than one occasion after a sleepless night.

"I'm fine." He surveyed her. "But you look like you never went to bed."

"You were sleeping very deeply. I thought that, under the circumstances, it might be a good idea if one of us stayed awake."

He turned away and swung his legs over the side of the bed. "In other words, you were afraid that I wouldn't be able to do my job, that I wouldn't be able to protect either of us if someone broke in while I was out of it."

"We're a team, remember?"

He rubbed the back of his neck. He might be linked to her in some special way, but that didn't mean he couldn't get pissed off at her.

"For the record," he said evenly, "I can handle the occasional aftereffects of my job."

"I'm sure you can. I just thought it would be best to take precautions."

"I would have awakened if someone had tried to get into the room. Trust me."

"Do you always wake up this grouchy?" she asked, sounding curious, rather than accusatory.

"No, only on those mornings when I discover that the client I'm supposed to be protecting thinks she has to protect me."

"I'm not your client. I'm your partner."

"I'm here to do my job."

"Last night you did it. For heaven's sake, this is a stupid argument. Why don't you go take a shower?"

He thought about that. It was probably a good idea.

"What about you?" he said. "You need some sleep."

"I rested in the chair. Dozed a bit off and on."

"You didn't have to spend the entire night watching over me."

"It isn't the first time I've gone without a good night's sleep. I'll be fine. Now, go take a shower."

He grabbed the cane and got to his feet. When he looked down he realized that he was still wearing his shirt and trousers. When he looked up he caught sight of himself in the mirror. His clothes were rumpled, his eyes were wells of shadows and he needed a shave. Badly. Not a pretty picture.

On top of all that, he was hungry and not just for food. He looked at Grace, trying to gauge the extent of her fatigue.

"You know," he said, testing the roughness of his morning beard with one hand. "A sensitive guy probably wouldn't ask a woman who'd had a sleepless night if she might be interested in showering with him."

Her brows crinkled together in a repressive glare. "You're right, a sensitive man would certainly not suggest sharing a shower at a moment like this."

He nodded, resigned. "Yeah, I know. I look a little ragged around the edges right now."

"For Pete's sake, it's got nothing to do with how you look," she snapped.

"What, then?" he asked, going blank.

"We just had a fight." She waved her hands. "You were growling at me a moment ago. Now you're talking about having sex as if nothing happened."

"You call what we just had a fight?"

"How would you describe it?"

He thought about it. "It was a discussion. Now it's over and I'm going to take a shower. Just wondered if you'd like to join me, that's all."

"It was a fight," she said.

"You're blowing it out of proportion. Probably because you're tense from lack of sleep."

"It was a fight and I am not tense from lack of sleep."

"You know, showering together would be a good way to relieve that tension."

Her mouth opened and closed a couple of times. Before he had time to say another word, Grace picked up one of the small decorative pillows and hurled it at his head.

He batted the pillow aside and started toward her, circling the bed.

"Now, a pillow fight is something I do understand," he said.

He quickly closed the distance between them. The room was suddenly ablaze with energy.

She took a step back toward the wall. "If you think for one moment that I'm in any kind of mood for sex after our little *discussion,* think again."

"See, that's the thing about men and sex." He tossed the cane onto the bed and braced his hands on the wall behind her, caging her between his arms. "Thinking doesn't usually enter into it."

"That explains so much."

"Always glad to be of service."

He kissed her, a slow, morning kiss; the kind a man gives a woman he knows he has satisfied; the kind that makes it clear he intends to satisfy her again. And be satisfied in return. A claiming kiss.

But she did not respond like a claimed woman. Instead, she kissed him back with the kind of fierce intensity that made it clear she had a claim on him.

"Good," he said against her mouth. "That's how it should be."

She pulled back an inch or so. "How what should be?"

"Forget it. I'll explain some other time."

Her mouth softened, her aura shimmered and began to resonate with his. He savored the knowledge that she was linked to him, whether she knew it or not.

Forty-eight hours, that was all the time they'd had together. How could he be so sure that he would think about her, yearn for her, want her for the rest of his life, even if he never saw her again? How the hell did that work?

But there was no time to think about it because Grace was undoing the fastening of his pants. When he felt her fingers on his erection, cupping him, the lazy heat of his arousal flashed into a wildfire. Her hand tightened around him in response.

He opened her shirt and discovered that sometime during the night she must have removed her bra. He was sure she had been wearing one earlier. He covered her breasts with his palms. The feel of her firm small nipples against his bare skin was exciting beyond belief.

He left her shirt hanging loose and reached down to undo her trousers. By the time he got them pushed to her ankles, she was shivering and whispering his name. Most of all she was touching him everywhere. Her hands glided over his thighs and chest and shoulders as though he was some rare and extremely valuable work of art.

"So good," she said, kissing his shoulder. "It's so good to be able to touch you like this."

"I like it that you like touching me." He captured her face in his hands and raised his head to meet her eyes. "But the thought of you touching anyone else like this would make me crazy."

"The only man I want to touch right now is you."

"That's not quite what I want to hear but we can talk about it some other time."

"I don't understand—"

"Doesn't matter. Not now."

He grabbed the cane, caught hold of her wrist and led her into the gleaming marble-tiled bathroom. There he got both of them out of the rest of their clothes and into the rain forest of a shower.

He lowered himself onto the built-in seat and eased her down so that she could ride him astride. He made love to her beneath the artificial waterfall until they were both locked together in hot climax.

Whatever else happened between them, he thought, she would not forget him.

. . .

SOMETIME LATER she stood in front of the steamy mirror, a huge white towel wrapped around her breasts, another around her wet hair. She felt energized. Invigorated. Who needed a full night's sleep?

Luther was shaving beside her, a towel draped around his waist. She met his eyes in the foggy glass.

"It was a fight," she said.

He grinned. "We should do that more often."

Twenty-two

The housekeeper was humming. She pushed her cart past Grace and continued down the hallway. The melody sounded vaguely familiar. Grace found herself trying to identify it. The harder she concentrated, the more intricate and compelling the tune seemed to become.

The song was definitely not from the contemporary pop repertoire. Not classic rock, either. It was far more elaborate and sophisticated; an aria from an opera, perhaps.

She wondered how many housekeepers hummed opera. Someone had certainly missed her calling. Then again, perhaps the woman sang professionally. Maybe housekeeping was just her day job.

The humming echoed softly in the corridor, growing ever more illusive and more intriguing as it faded.

Music was a form of energy. It acted directly on all the senses and across the spectrum. The proof was evident everywhere. It could stir the passions, excite the nerves or send adrenaline rushing through the veins. Some religions feared its power to such an extent that they tried to ban it. Others harnessed its unique energy to exult and glorify their deities. Music could throw an intoxicating spell over crowds, drawing people to their feet and compelling them to discharge the energy in the form of motion; dancing.

Music could make you want to focus on something very important. *Name that tune.*

An odd chill fluttered through Grace. It suddenly seemed very important that she identify the housekeeper's song. She had attended the opera on several occasions over the years. The over-the-top emotions of the stories appealed to her primarily because she had always been so careful to control her own passions. The singers' astonishing ability to project their impossibly gorgeous voices to the farthest corners of a three-thousand-seat theater without the aid of microphones never failed to amaze her. But she was not a dedicated fan. She lacked an intimate acquaintance with the music. She had heard the housekeeper's piece somewhere on an opera stage, though, she was sure of it.

The inexplicably intense need to recall the name of the song dissipated almost as swiftly as it had come.

Ice touched the nape of her neck. Her pulse beat harder, faster. From out of nowhere an anxious, almost panicky sensation gripped her senses. She recognized the syndrome. Her survival instincts were kicking in hard and fast. *Get out of here.*

Music was a form of energy.

It occurred to her that although she had come within a yard of the housekeeper, she could not recall anything about her, not even her hair color, let alone whether she had been plump or thin or middle-aged or young. Nothing at all except an overpowering urge to focus on the tune that the woman had been humming.

Grace stopped and turned. The housekeeper and her cart had disappeared around the corner at the far end of the long corridor.

She hesitated, uncertain of her next move. She was on her own for the morning. The five Nightshade executives and their bodyguards had left for the golf course an hour ago. Luther had followed them after giving her strict orders to remain either in the suite or in the hotel's public spaces.

She had been on her way back to the room to pick up the hat she had forgotten to take down to the pool when she passed the humming housekeeper. For a moment there, she had been so distracted by the compulsion to identify the song that she had even forgotten the purpose of her return to the suite.

Something was very wrong.

She had to get a look at the housekeeper.

She walked quickly back the way she had come, following the path the housekeeper had taken. When she reached the corner, she heard the humming again, very faintly this time. Once again the urge to focus on the pattern of the music came upon her. But she was ready for it this time. She pushed back, gently but firmly. The urge evaporated.

She went around the corner and saw the housekeeper. The woman was waiting for the freight elevator. Her hair was an explosion of dark curls that partially obscured her profile. A pair of heavily framed dark glasses veiled her eyes. She moved with vigor and grace. There was an air of glowing enthusiasm about her; clearly a woman who loved her work. She didn't appear to be struggling with the heavily laden cart. She manipulated it effortlessly.

Grace slid into her other senses. The housekeeper's aura flared brilliantly. Waves of an unfamiliar but extraordinarily powerful psychic energy pulsed through it. The rest of the profile was complicated. There was also something wrong with it. There was none of the darkness that was the signature of the Nightshade auras; nevertheless, the pulsing bands of energy looked warped in places and very erratic in others.

The housekeeper might enjoy her work but she had some serious mental health issues.

It's not like I'm one to talk, Grace thought. She had just gone an entire year barely able to touch another human being.

The door to the room across the hall from the freight elevator opened. A couple emerged.

The housekeeper stopped humming and started singing. Her voice was soft but it floated down the hallway on wings of energy. Every note was crystalline. Grace had the impression that she was not the intended audience; even so, she had to resist the urge to try to capture the bell-like notes as they drifted through the air.

The couple went past the housekeeper, paying no attention. A lot of people might be inclined to ignore a hotel maid, Grace thought, but surely not one who could sing like this. The expressions on the faces of the man and the woman were utterly blank.

The elevator doors opened. There was a ping and an arrow glowed indicating that the cab was going up. The housekeeper pushed her cart inside. The doors closed, cutting off the song. Grace watched the couple become visibly more animated and engaged. The woman blinked a few times and then looked at her companion.

"My spa appointment is at eleven," she said. "When will you be back from the golf course?"

"Not until five," the man said.

"In that case, I think I'll do some shopping this afternoon."

They nodded politely at Grace and continued along the hall to the guest elevators.

She waited until they were out of sight before she opened the stairwell door and stepped inside. There were two floors above the one on which she stood, five and six.

She rushed up the concrete stairs and listened intently before opening the door. No aria sounded on the other side. Cautiously she opened the door and checked the corridor. Empty.

She hurried up the next flight and again paused at the hall door. She sensed the music pulsing gently, insistently, even though it was almost inaudible.

She opened the door and moved out into the corridor just in time to see the singing housekeeper vanish into a room at the far end of the hall. The woman, her aura flaring hotly, left her cart outside. She did not follow the hotel's usual routine of leaving the door open, however. Instead she closed it firmly behind her.

Grace glanced at the number on the door across from where she stood and did the math. More adrenaline splashed through her. If she had counted correctly, the housekeeper had just vanished into 604, Eubanks's suite.

Mr. Jones, what are the odds?

Whatever was going on here, it was important. She was very sure of that. The question was what to do next. Luther would know but he was not around. A good field agent had to be able to make independent decisions.

It would be no big deal to walk past the room the singing housekeeper had just entered and check the number to make absolutely sure that it was 604. It would not be good for her future as a J&J specialist if she screwed up on something that important.

She started down the hall in what she hoped looked like a leisurely manner, card key in hand, as though she were on her way to her own room. There were no other guests about.

Another housekeeper, pushing a heavily loaded cart, appeared at the far end of the corridor. She paused in front of a room and rapped lightly.

"Housekeeping," she called.

That was something else the operatic maid had failed to do, Grace recalled. The woman had entered the room without knocking and without announcing her presence, as if she knew full well that the occupants were not inside.

Grace reached the singing maid's cart. She looked at the closed door: 604.

She kept going, unsure what her next move should be. It seemed logical, however, that a sharp, independent-thinking J&J agent would keep an eye on the singing housekeeper and follow her after she left Eubanks's suite. This was a surveillance mission, after all.

It was also imperative to notify Luther that a woman with a high-level psychic talent who may or may not have been a member of the hotel staff had just entered the room of one of the Nightshade members.

She took out her phone and entered a quick text message. *Talent entered E's rm. Will watch.*

She dropped the phone back into her purse and looked around for someplace to conceal herself while she waited for the singer to reappear. All she could see were two long rows of doors stretching out ahead of her. The hall ended where it intersected with another corridor. She had two choices, either go back the way she had come and hide in the stairwell or go around the corner at the far end and wait for the door to 604 to open.

She opted for the stairwell. It was closer. She hurried back past Eubanks's suite and was almost at the door when she sensed movement behind her. She turned to look over her shoulder and saw the second housekeeper striding purposefully toward 604.

She switched to her other senses and studied the woman's aura. It was average for a nonsensitive but it was clear the housekeeper was annoyed. The sight of the other cart in the hall bothered her for some reason, perhaps because this was her territory.

Grace was suddenly very certain that it would not be a good idea for the housekeeper to confront the woman who had just disappeared into 604.

Impulsively she started back toward the suite but the housekeeper was already knocking briskly. Without waiting for a response, the maid jammed her master key into the lock and pushed open the door. She stared into the room, her body tense, her aura registering a growing unease.

"Who are you?" she demanded. "This is my floor and I didn't ask for any extra help today. You must be new."

The singing started up inside the room, intense and so darkly compelling that Grace felt as if she were in danger of being extinguished by the crushing weight of impending doom. Power and violence conveyed in a coloratura soprano's pure, utterly mesmerizing voice poured out into the hall.

The second housekeeper's aura pulsed with terror. The woman retreated a step, turning slightly, as though preparing to run. But she went statue-still instead. Then, as though drawn by invisible chains, she started toward the shadowed doorway of 604.

The energy of the song shivered across the paranormal spectrum. Grace could feel its inexorable pull even though she recognized intuitively that it was aimed at the housekeeper, not at her.

The maid was transfixed by the music. She took another step toward the fatal doorway. Soon she would vanish into 604.

"Wait," Grace called loudly, hoping to shatter the spell of the music with the force of a command. "Stop. Don't go in there."

The housekeeper ignored her cry of warning. Her aura was no longer pulsing in a normal manner. As Grace watched, horrified, it became unstable and erratic. Through it all, panic still pulsed. The woman knew that she was being drawn to her doom but she could not stop.

Grace rushed forward, jacking up her own aura to the max. The music was not loud out in the hallway but the controlled power of it seemed to fill all the available space.

She had not had to do what she was about to do for a long time. But she had not forgotten the inevitable reaction of her senses. It was going to hurt.

Bracing herself for the shock of physical contact, she seized the housekeeper's shoulder, simultaneously pushing back hard at the wavelengths of the fearful music, trying to shield the mesmerized woman with her own aura.

Pain splashed through her. The thin fabric of the housekeeper's uniform offered almost no protection. She clamped her teeth tightly together and managed to keep her grip on the woman's shoulder.

Momentum carried the two of them several feet beyond the doorway before they stumbled and fell together onto the carpet. Grace rolled frantically to the side, struggling to free herself from the other woman's unmoving body.

She scrambled to her knees and looked toward the doorway to 604.

The curtains inside had been drawn tightly shut, sealing the room in dense shadows. The singer stood near the bed, her mouth still open on the last notes of her terrible song. The combination of the oversized dark glasses, the heavy wig and the dim light made it impossible to see her face clearly. But Grace was still on high alert. She had no trouble viewing the spiraling rage in the woman's aura.

The housekeeper launched into another fiery cascade of song. Each note struck Grace with the force of a shock wave from some invisible explosion. Her senses reeled beneath the onslaught. She could not breathe. Her heart pounded. The hallway whirled around her.

Instinctively she forced all her energy into a counterpoint pattern. The hallway steadied. Her head cleared.

The rage in the singer's aura grew stronger but the power of her music lessened. The crystal pure note she was singing suddenly fractured.

"Who are you?" the singer shrieked. "How dare you interrupt my performance?"

Grace managed to get to her feet. She stood over the fallen housekeeper. "You were going to kill her."

"The stupid woman deserved to die. She interfered."

"I'm in your way, too," Grace said. "Do you intend to kill me?"

"*Yes.*"

The single word should have come out as a scream. Instead it floated through the shadows on a cloud of dark, exquisitely controlled energy intended to pull Grace into the room. The note was so intense that it *hurt*. Once again Grace felt her heart start to pound.

She resisted the compulsion with everything she had, fighting back with all her power. She could tell that she was having some effect. The singer went higher, apparently in an effort to compensate for the resistance. Sooner or later she was bound to attract attention. There had to be someone in one of the neighboring rooms. Surely not every single guest was at the beach or the spa or the golf course.

But none of the doors in the long hall opened; no one appeared to inquire about the music. A terrible possibility occurred to Grace. Maybe those who heard the music assumed that it was being piped into the hallways by the hotel.

The perfection of the music literally stole Grace's breath. She realized with horror that she was no longer inhaling. Her chest and head were in agony. It was as if she were drowning in an invisible sea.

Breathe, she told herself. *You're going to die if you don't breathe.*

From out of nowhere she managed to summon an extra flicker of power. The killing song weakened again.

She was still dizzy but she managed to use the reprieve to suck in one gasping breath and then another. She lacked the strength to scream for help. It was all she could do to fill her lungs. But the oxygen suddenly flooding her system fueled her will to live. She had not survived the death of her mother, the foster care system, the streets and Martin Crocker only to die at the hands of a killer diva.

She forced herself to concentrate. There were signs of definite instability in the pulses of power that flashed and sparked in the singer's aura. The woman was not only a little crazy, she was on the verge of flying into an inchoate rage. Grace's resistance was infuriating her.

Push her a little harder, Grace thought. *You're going to die here in this hallway if you don't.*

Her intensified resistance had an immediate effect. The singer's aura darkened and flashed with unstable rage. She was losing her emotional control. Surely that would impact her vocal control, Grace thought. She had read somewhere that professional opera singers claim it is fatal to feel too much emotion when they sing. The logic was obvious. It was difficult if not impossible to maintain perfect control over your voice when your chest and throat were tightened by rage or tears, or *fear.*

It dawned on Grace that she had the same problem. If she did not pull herself back from the brink of panic, she would lose her own control. She needed to think of something other than impending death.

Luther.

There was power in a name if the person attached to the name had a strong connection to you. The strength she drew from Luther's name told her just how important he was to her.

The singer screamed. There was no other word for it but the sound was no normal shriek of fear. It was an intense pulse of raw rage. The incredibly high-pitched note was all wrong.

Grace discovered that she could move again. Instinctively she jammed her fingers into her ears. The music and the pain receded slightly.

And then another sound echoed down the hallway: the distinct chime of the elevator bell.

The singer must have heard it, too, and understood that other people were about to appear. Chaos sparked across her aura. Teetering on the edge of insane fury, she launched herself at Grace, fingers hooked like claws.

Grace scrambled out of her path, putting the cart between them. She groped for something to use as a weapon. Her fingers closed around a feather duster.

The singer tried to adjust her trajectory but she stumbled over the unconscious housekeeper and went down, sprawling on the carpet. Grace shoved the cart toward her but it did not roll far enough.

The singer staggered to her feet. Her mouth opened. Her throat worked. But the only sound that emerged was a choked gasp.

She glanced back once toward the elevator lobby. The doors started to open. Logic or maybe her own survival instincts overrode her rage. She fled, running straight past Grace, and vanished around the corner.

Grace waited, clutching the duster, but there was no more singing.

She took a deep breath and started toward the fallen housekeeper, who was just beginning to stir. Something crunched under her foot. She looked down and saw sparkling shards of glass scattered across the carpet. One of the clean drinking glasses that had been sitting on top of the cart had shattered.

It dawned on her that the door to suite 604 was still open. She closed it. Something told her that Fallon would want to keep this incident quiet if at all possible.

She crouched beside the dazed woman.

"Are you all right?" she asked gently.

"Yes, I think so." The housekeeper gave her a blank look. "Did I just faint?"

"Yes. Don't try to get up. There's a house phone down by the elevators. I'll call your supervisor."

"I'm okay, really. Just a little tired, that's all. It's been a long day."

"It certainly has."

The housekeeper would be all right. Her aura had returned to normal. Automatically Grace reached out to pat her in a reassuring fashion. At the last instant she remembered how her palm had burned when she had pulled the woman away from the doorway. The pain was gone but she dared not touch the housekeeper. It would take days or even weeks to recover.

Back to square one.

"Damn," she whispered. "Damn, damn, damn."

She pushed herself to her feet and went down the hall to the phone.

Twenty-three

She was huddled on the sofa, the computer open on the coffee table in front of her, when Luther arrived. He stalked into the suite looking like the Lord of the Underworld—a very pissed-off Lord. He started toward her, using his cane to emphasize each word.

"What" *thud* "the" *thud* "hell" *thud* "did" *thud* "you" *thud* "think" *thud* "you" *thud* "were" *thud* "doing?" *Thud.*

"Don't touch me," she yelped. She leaped off the sofa and backed hurriedly toward the open door to the lanai, shielding her hands under her crossed arms. "I mean it. Please don't touch me."

He halted, thunderstruck. "You think I'd hit you?" he asked, disbelief and pain etched on his face.

"No," she said, chagrined. "Of course not. I just meant don't touch me. Not yet, at any rate. I've been sensitized again."

"Damn." He didn't look any less angry but his pained expression evaporated. "All right, tell me what happened."

She gave him what she hoped was a thoroughly professional report. When it was over she expected him to take out his phone and call Fallon

Jones. Instead he just stood there, regarding her with an unnerving consideration, as if he had never seen anything quite like her before.

"That trick you used on the housekeeper," he said eventually. "You said you've done it before?"

"A few times." She unfolded her arms and looked at her palms. "After my mother died, I went into the foster care system. I left it after about six months. I was on the streets for a while. There are some badly warped people out there."

"No shit," he growled.

She chose to ignore that. "Some of them are sensitives who have learned to use their talents to manipulate others. There was one pimp, some kind of weird charisma talent, I think. He was able to seduce young girls, make them fall in love with him. They'd do anything for him."

"So he sent them out onto the streets to turn tricks for him," Luther said, a savage edge on the words.

"I see you've encountered that particular species of sewer rat," she said quietly.

"Yes." He did not elaborate.

"I used to hang out with some of his girls at night. I'd use my talent to tell them which johns were safe and which ones to avoid. One day the pimp discovered that the girls were turning down some of the dangerous tricks. He was furious. He decided to beat one or two as examples to the others. I figured out what he was planning. I even knew which girl he intended to beat first, the newest and youngest one. I was there when he came to get her that night. She was terrified. There was so much violence surrounding him you could have cut it with a knife. When he reached for her, I took hold of her arm and jacked up to full strength, overwhelming her aura with my own and forming a kind of barrier to his. The instant he touched her he got fried."

"Define 'fried,' " Luther said. "Are we talking dead?"

"No," she said quickly, appalled. "No, I didn't kill him, I swear it."

"I wouldn't give a damn if you did terminate him."

"Oh." She cleared her throat. "Well, I didn't. But something happened when he came in contact with my aura. It was as if his own energy field short-circuited for a few seconds. I can't explain it. All I know is that he went unconscious for a while. So did the girl. But when she woke up she was okay, just a little shaken."

"What about the pimp?"

"He was not okay. It was as if he'd had some kind of mental breakdown. He just sort of fell apart. I think something permanent happened to his talent. Whatever it was affected not just his psychic senses but everything else, as well. He became a basket case and just drifted away from the neighborhood. After a while we heard that he'd been killed in a drug deal gone bad."

"You said there were other incidents like that one?"

"A few," she admitted. "The technique works against nonsensitives, too. After all, everyone has an aura. But every time I do it, I get sensitized again."

"Huh."

She waited but he didn't offer anything further, just stood there, looking lost in thought.

"What?" she prompted.

"Just wondering. Do you think you shorted out the singer's aura today?"

"No. She was much too powerful. Fortunately when she lost her cool a lot of her control went with it. And then the elevator started to open and she panicked and ran."

He watched her very steadily. "What would have happened if the singer hadn't fled the scene?"

"I don't know," she admitted. "I suppose the outcome would have depended on which one of us was the stronger. We didn't get a chance to finish the contest. Guess you could say it was a draw."

"The last thing I want is to see a rematch. Got that?"

She shuddered. "Trust me, I'm not eager for one, either. Okay, you can start yelling again now."

There was another long silence.

"You're not yelling," she pointed out.

"Don't get me wrong, I feel like yelling."

"But?"

"But you saved the housekeeper's life. That's pretty much what a J&J agent is supposed to do in a situation like that."

She suddenly felt much better. "Thanks."

"Are you sure I can't touch you?" Luther asked.

She tensed. "It was a bad burn. It will probably take days, maybe weeks to heal." Her brief moment of professional pride went out like a light. It was all she could do not to burst into tears. "It's so maddening because I just got over the last burn."

"Can I talk you into running an experiment? You said yourself the fact that we're both auras might have some protective effect."

She hesitated. "Okay."

"You do the touching. That way you're in complete control."

For a few seconds she did not move. *You're a J&J agent. Take a risk.*

She walked slowly toward him and stopped when she was a couple of feet away. He held out one hand, palm up. Gingerly she touched it with her fingertips. There was no shock, no jolt of pain. Relief crashed through her. Deliberately she flattened her hand on his, palm to palm.

"This is amazing," she said, awed. "I've never been able to touch anyone so soon after an incident like the one today. Guess I was dating the wrong kind of men all these years."

He groaned, grabbed her hand, pulled her close and kissed her hard. When he released her she was a little breathless.

"Don't tease me like that," he warned darkly. "I'm still getting over the shock I got when I read that text message you sent. Thought my heart would stop."

"They're called Sirens, Mr. Jones," Grace said into the phone. "The talent is extremely rare. That's why you haven't ever heard of them. They crop up so infrequently in the Society's records that many of us in Genealogy have assumed that they're more myth than reality."

She was perched on the sofa again, so exhausted she was amazed that she could make any sense at all out of the data on the computer screen in front of her, let alone deliver a coherent report to her boss. The after-shocks of adrenaline were still shivering through her. It would be a while before her nerves calmed down to the point where she might be able to sleep.

But *she could still touch Luther*. The wonder of that buoyed her spirits as nothing else could have done.

He was at the window, watching the hot afternoon sun spark and flash on the ocean while listening to her conversation with Fallon. He was back in what she was starting to think of as his professional mode—cold, hard and very focused.

"What's a Siren?" Fallon demanded. "Some kind of hypno talent?"

"It's related to hypnosis in that the psychic energy is transmitted via the voice but it requires extremely high, pure notes, the kind that very few people can sing. Also, although there have probably been a fair number of Siren talents in the population, very few of them would have had the power to actually project a killing wave of energy."

"So what happens with the others? Why haven't we heard of non-lethal Sirens?"

She smiled faintly. "You have, sir, you just didn't know it. They're called opera singers."

"Opera singers?" Fallon sounded thoroughly nonplussed.

"Not all of them are Sirens, of course. I suspect just some of the major coloratura sopranos. And those who are Sirens probably aren't even aware of their psychic natures. Wait, I take that back. Opera singers are known for their egos. Some of them probably do consider their talents to be paranormal."

"What the hell do you mean?"

"How many times have you heard an opera singer described as 'mesmerizing'? Historically various singers have been said to be able to transfix or enrapture their audiences."

"Huh."

She concentrated on the computer screen, reading quickly. "The high level of talent required to disrupt the human neurological system appears almost exclusively in females because it requires a true coloratura soprano to reach the high, killing notes. In addition to being linked to their voices, the talent is also connected to their sexuality, hence the Siren label."

"Opera singers are sexy?" Fallon asked, dumbfounded.

"Sir, I hate to break this to you but opera singers as a group, male and female, are legendary for their sexual prowess. Wealthy, powerful men seem to find sopranos, in particular, absolutely riveting. Think Maria Callas and Aristotle Onassis."

Luther turned around at that, brows lifting slightly. She pretended not to notice.

"You said the singer was crazy?" Fallon asked.

"Well, that depends on your definition of 'crazy,' I guess. She emanated some very unstable aspects, but she was obviously capable of making and carrying out an elaborate plan. I'm almost positive that she went into suite 604 intending to do violence to someone, presumably Eubanks."

"You think she planned to wait for him there in his room?"

"I'm sure of it."

"What about the bodyguard?"

"Maybe she wasn't aware that Eubanks has one. Or maybe she assumed she could deal with both of them. Whatever the case, the hotel housekeeper interfered with the scheme. The Siren was furious with her for that." She shivered, remembering the scene. "I swear, the singer acted like a genuine diva who has been interrupted in the middle of a performance."

"Trying to kill the housekeeper seems a little extreme under the circumstances," Fallon said. "You'd think the Siren could have talked her way out of the situation by telling the real maid that she was a new hire or something."

"She's an opera singer and she's mentally unstable. Going over the top is probably second nature for her."

"You really think she's a trained singer?"

"No doubt about it. I'm betting she once sang professionally. Maybe she still does."

"You say she accused you and the housekeeper of interrupting her *performance?*"

"I know, it's an odd choice of words. The Siren may be unhinged but she sees herself as a star. Trust me, it was all there in her profile."

"What about the housekeeper?" Fallon demanded. "Does she remember anything about what happened?"

Luther was still watching her. Grace focused on the computer screen. Lying was always such a tricky business and in her present exhausted state she had to be extra careful. As usual, she left in as much of the truth as possible.

"Not much," she said. *Truth.* "As I told you, she fainted when the Siren started singing to her." *Not quite true. I'm the one who made her faint, not the singer.* "When she woke up she was fine. I checked her aura. It looked healthy." *Truth.* "She remembered going down the hall to see why another housekeeper was cleaning 604 but she didn't recall anything after that."

"What did you tell her?" Fallon asked.

"Just that I had seen her faint and that I went to investigate."

"All true. Good. I like that in a lie. You've got a talent for the business, Grace."

In spite of her weariness, a flash of pride straightened her shoulders and boosted her spirits.

"Thank you, sir."

"So the bottom line here is that no one called hotel security?" Fallon asked.

"Right. The housekeeper and her manager assumed there was some sort of mix-up in the housekeeping schedule, that's all."

"Then Eubanks isn't going to hear about any of this," Fallon said with growing satisfaction.

"No, sir," Grace agreed. "Luther checked on him a short while ago. Eubanks returned from the golf course with the rest of his group and went directly to his room. He doesn't appear to have any concerns because he's now in the spa getting a massage."

"Which means his bodyguard didn't pick up on the spoor of violence that must have been all over the place."

"As I told you, the hunter profiles of all the bodyguards are incomplete."

"Because of the drug, no doubt," Fallon concluded. "Damn, I can't wait to see where the hell this thing is going."

Something in his voice reminded Grace that Fallon Jones came from a long line of hunters himself. It was true that his talent had taken a few unusual twists but the adrenaline rush of the chase came easily to the surface.

"Yes, sir," she said.

"Can you give me a description of the singer?"

"No, sir, I'm very sorry about that. When she came running out of 604 I realized that in addition to wearing a wig and the big glasses, she also had on a lot of heavy makeup. I think she's probably in her mid-thirties, and I can tell you that she was tall and slender and she seemed to have a lot of upper-body strength but that's about it."

"Slender? I thought opera singers were supposed to be built like SUVs."

"That's a generalization, sir. It's true that there are some very large singers. Many of the women who sing Wagner probably shop in the plus-size department. But there are actually lots of body shapes on the stage. Some of the most famous sopranos are downright tiny."

"You're sure this one was a soprano?"

She thought about the shattered glassware. "Definitely. The kind referred to as a coloratura soprano. Those are the ones who can sing the highest ranges. I'm no expert but even I could tell that she had exquisite control on some incredibly high notes. At least she did until her rage got the better of her."

"You saw her aura. I want a full profile."

"Yes, sir. I'll get one to you as soon as possible. But if you don't mind, I'd like some time to think about it. I also want to do some more research in the genealogy files. We're talking about a very rare talent."

"We don't have any time to waste here." Impatience crackled in Fallon's voice.

"I understand, sir. But I want to be accurate. I'm not at my best at the moment."

"All right. Get some sleep and then get back to me."

"Yes, sir."

"Tell Malone that the last of our surveillance people just arrived on the island. They'll take over the job of watching the five Nightshade operatives. The two of you might as well pack."

Grace felt a rush of disappointment. Her grand adventure as a J&J agent was ending.

"What happens now, sir?" she asked.

"In addition to shadowing the Nightshade people, I'm going to contact Harry Sweetwater."

"Why?"

"The Siren you encountered must be a pro."

"A professional opera singer? Yes, I think so."

"No, a professional hit woman," Fallon corrected impatiently. "Someone hired her to take out a Nightshade operative. That means she must be a private contractor available for hire. Sweetwater knows his competition. With luck he'll be able to give me a line on her. Can't be that many Siren talent contractors running around. Hell, you'd think I would have heard of her myself, by now."

"I'm not so sure, sir. I think of professional hit people as being, well, cold-blooded, at least when they're working." She could hardly say that in her former job she had actually met a few killers thanks to Martin's venture into the arms trade. "The Siren was a true diva. I told you, she went ballistic when her performance was interrupted. I wouldn't have thought that a volatile temperament and a lack of emotional control would be an asset in a contract killer."

"Guess you get all kinds in any profession," Fallon said. "Let me talk to Malone."

Obediently she held the phone out to Luther. He snapped it out of her fingers, looking like a man preparing to go into battle.

"What?" he said brusquely. He listened for a minute. "No, she is not going back to Eclipse Bay. Not yet, at any rate. I'm taking her home with me."

Grace felt her spirits start to rise.

"Why?" Luther said. "Because that damn Siren is a nutcase. She became enraged with Grace today. Who's to say she might not develop some sort of obsession? No, I'm not saying I think she'll come after Grace, but I'm not going to take any chances, either. Grace stays with me until you find the singer and neutralize her."

Grace's soaring spirits immediately stalled out. Luther was going to keep her with him but only because he was worried about her safety. Still, she was not about to get picky here. She would take any excuse to prolong their association.

"Call me as soon as you know anything," Luther said. He ended the connection and looked at Grace.

"I know you need sleep," he said. "But you'll have to hang on for a while. I want to get you off this island."

"Okay, I'll go pack." She pushed herself up off the sofa. "I could use some coffee, though."

"I'll order some to go from room service. You can drink it in the car on the way to the airport."

"All right."

"And while you're drinking your coffee, you can tell me what happened a year ago," he added, his voice dangerously soft.

She froze in the doorway to the bedroom. "I beg your pardon?"

"You were sensitized for an entire year. I'm betting that the incident that triggered it was a little more dramatic than what happened today. You seemed to think that it would only take a few weeks to recover from that event. So, doing some quick math, I have to assume that whatever happened last year was worse than what happened today."

She took a shaky breath. "You're acting like a cop."

"Yeah, I do that sometimes. Look, I've got no problem with you lying to Fallon. But I need the truth. Your life may be in danger. You're going to have to trust me."

Twenty-four

By the time they were in the car and headed toward the airport, she had
recovered enough from the initial shock to succumb to a sense of resig-
nation. Maybe she was just too exhausted to resist. No, she decided, the
truth was that she simply didn't want to lie to Luther any longer. She
wasn't sure what was going on between them. She was afraid to use the
word "love" to describe the bond. It was too soon and she'd had too
little experience with that particular feeling to be able to recognize it on
sight. But whatever it was, she wanted desperately to trust him.

She peeled the lid off the coffee cup. "Do you think Mr. Jones knows
that I didn't tell him the full truth about what I did with my aura today?"

"Who knows?" Luther did not take his attention off the road. "He's
damn good at connecting dots, though, so you'd better assume he suspects more than he let on."

"Why didn't he say anything?"

"Probably because it didn't suit him to say anything. Fallon is not
what you would call the communicative type."

She slumped lower into the seat. "Damn."

"The real question is why didn't you tell him what you can do with your talent? After all, you want to be a real J&J agent. Why not try to impress the boss?"

She gazed glumly out at the sugarcane fields. "Keeping my secret is an old habit. You know how it is. You don't go around advertising what you can do, either."

"What happened a year ago? Whatever it was must have been pretty dramatic. Were you assaulted?"

"He tried to kill me with some sort of flash of energy," she said quietly.

Luther's profile hardened. "The guy who attacked you was a sensitive, too?"

"Yes. I fought back with my talent. When he realized he couldn't murder me with his psychic-blast trick, he became enraged and tried to throttle me. I was running hot at the time, jacked to the max trying to defend myself. Something happened when he touched me. It was as if the energy that he was projecting at me rebounded back on him. The next thing I knew he was dead."

Luther was silent for a moment. She waited for what she knew would come next.

"You said he hit you with some kind of psychic energy?"

"Yes. He could focus it somehow. It was incredibly painful. I could feel it killing me."

"Fallon told me that one of his agents encountered a Nightshade operative who could make a person unconscious with a blast of energy. It happened a while back on a case in Stone Canyon, Arizona. The talent was drug-induced. The operative was injecting the formula at the time."

"The man who tried to murder me was also on the drug," she said, letting the rest of the truth spill out. "He told me it gave him the power to kill without a trace."

Luther whistled softly. "Well, I'll be damned. You killed Martin Crocker, didn't you?"

"Yes."

"Let me take a wild guess here. You were not the company librarian."

"I was his butler."

"You're kidding."

"That was my official title," she explained. "No one pays any attention to the hired help, you see. Afterward, the newspapers barely even mentioned the fact that I had died in the same boating accident. It was as if I had never existed, which was fine by me."

"I seem to recall that the search-and-rescue team found Crocker's boat drifting aimlessly in the water. How did you escape?"

She shuddered, remembering the horror and the grim determination to survive that had ridden her hard that night.

"What the searchers didn't know, what no one except Martin and I knew, was that Martin kept a small inflatable boat on the island to use in case of an emergency. I waited until after dark. Then I got Martin's body into the cruiser and took it partway back to the main island. I released the body into the water and left the cruiser to drift. Then I got into the inflatable."

Luther said nothing but he reached over and gripped her hand very tightly for a few seconds, letting her know that he understood both the horror and the will to live.

She took strength from his touch. "The inflatable was unmarked. There was nothing to link it to Martin or to me. I dumped it offshore. The next day I took a commercial flight back to Miami using a fake ID."

"You already had the new ID in place?"

"Along with a small suitcase full of bare necessities. I'd carried both with me everywhere for days." She swallowed hard. "I knew Martin better than he knew himself. It was a matter of when, not if, I'd need the ID and a change of clothes."

"You weren't just Crocker's butler, were you? What else did you do for him?"

"I was his personal profiler," she said. "I read the people with whom he did business, his mistresses and everyone else who came in contact with him."

"The ultimate bodyguard."

"I identified his opponents' strengths and weaknesses. I told him who he could trust and warned him when someone was plotting against him."

"How long were the two of you a team?"

"Twelve years."

"Were you lovers?" Luther asked tonelessly.

"No. Neither of us was attracted to the other in that way. I wasn't his type. In the end he told me he had always found my talent a little scary. For my part, I knew from the start that Martin wasn't capable of anything remotely close to real love or commitment. But we were partners and friends of a sort. I trusted him because I knew he needed me and I knew he understood that."

"What happened?"

"Everything changed after he started taking the drug."

"Why did he try to kill you?"

"He decided that he didn't need me any longer. But I knew all his secrets. As he explained, that made me a serious liability." She shook her head, still amazed. "He actually believed all the lies that the Nightshade people told him, including the myth that the drug would lengthen his life span."

"Why did you create the corporate librarian history for yourself when you went into hiding? Why not fire up a whole new identity, one with no connection to Crocker World?"

"I went with the old theory that the best lies contain a measure of truth. Also, I knew everything about Crocker World, including how to access the computerized personnel files and create an employment record that would stand up to close scrutiny. It worked, too. I made it through a J&J background check."

Luther smiled slightly. "If Fallon ever discovers that, he'll have an attack of the vapors."

She turned her head quickly. "Are you going to tell him?"

"No."

"I didn't think so. Thank you." She drank some more coffee.

"What really happened that day that Martin Crocker and his butler disappeared?" Luther asked.

She told him everything. When she was finished he was silent for a long time.

"Do you believe me?" she asked when she could stand the suspense no longer.

"Yes."

She peeked at his aura and knew that he was telling the truth.

"One more question," he said. "If you were worried that someone might someday find out that you killed Crocker, why in hell did you apply for a job within the Society? You had to know that you'd be surrounded by people endowed with various kinds of psychic talents. Your secret would be at risk every day."

"I wasn't sure if the people who recruited Martin would get suspicious about his death and come looking for me. I also knew from what Martin told me that the organization you call Nightshade is a group of renegade psychics. I figured the one bunch they might want to steer clear of is the Arcane community."

"So you decided to hide in the heart of the Society." Luther's mouth curved faintly. "I like it. Talk about a gutsy move."

"There was another reason why I applied for the post in the Bureau of Genealogy," she said quietly. "I've always heard that when you're in real trouble, you run home."

"So?"

"The Society is the closest thing I have to a family."

Twenty-five

It was intolerable.

La Sirène paced the hotel suite, seething. The Queen of the Night's desire for revenge against Sarastro was nothing, a mere whimper of protest, compared to this clawing need for vengeance against the bitch who had somehow managed to resist her singing. The stupid creature should have died the way all the others had died. Why hadn't she?

Time, she decided. There just hadn't been enough time to finish the job. Another minute and it would have been over. If only the damned elevator hadn't arrived when it did.

She squeezed her hands into fists, still unable to believe that things had gone wrong. The silly housekeeper had been completely under control. The superbly powerful, violent notes of Chiang Ch'ing's "I am the wife of Mao Tse-tung," a coloratura credo from John Adams's *Nixon in China,* had been working perfectly, drawing the woman to her doom. The Voice had been flawless. She had woven the energy into it until it became a lethal force. The maid had been unable to resist. *No one* should have been able to resist.

A tendril of panic slithered through her. There was nothing wrong with the Voice. *Nothing.* The dreadful incident at La Scala two years ago had been no more than a fluke. Yes, she had been booed but sooner or later everyone who was anyone in the world of opera got booed by the damned claques at La Scala. It was practically a rite of passage for a singer. But what if they really had heard the lack of power on the high F?

There was no getting around the fact that things had not gone well the following season. There had been that horrible night in Seattle when she'd had to fake some of the money notes in her Lucia. That critic at *The Seattle Times* had caught it. But she had been coming down with a cold at the time. So what? Every singer had the occasional off night.

Yes, and more than one famous soprano had awakened one morning to discover that her voice had simply vanished. Another chill lanced through her.

The doctors had assured her that there was nothing wrong with her vocal cords but they weren't aware of her psychic side, let alone how it was inextricably entwined with her singing voice. What if the problem lay with her senses? What if her worst nightmare was coming true? What if she was losing her Siren talent?

Impossible. She was too young, only thirty-five. She was in her prime. But there was no denying that her career was in trouble. It was her former agent's fault, of course. The idiot had cost her important engagements. He had actually believed the rumors about her. She'd had no choice but to fire him permanently in a very private performance. The last note he would have heard was the stunningly perfect high G in Mozart's "Popoli di Tessaglia." She hoped he'd had a chance to admire her brilliant passagework.

No, there was nothing wrong with her except a little bad luck and worse management. But that would all change after she sang the Queen for the opening of *The Magic Flute* in Acacia Bay. It was certainly not the Met but Guthrie Hall was an exquisite little jewel of a theater and it was situated close to L.A. As dear Newlin had pointed out, there was an excellent chance that some of the important critics could be enticed to the performance. There they would see for themselves that La Sirène was back, and more brilliant than ever.

Once again the most exclusive designers would be standing in line to beg her to wear their clothes and their jewelry. She would soon be signing autographs just as she had in the old days. She would be booked three years in advance for performances at the most important opera houses in the world. . . .

Her phone warbled, interrupting the glowing vision of her spectacular future. She glanced at the code and winced. The last person she wanted to talk to right now was her sister. With a sigh she opened the phone.

"Hello, Damaris."

"What's going on? I've been waiting for your call. Is everything all right?"

"Calm down, everything's fine. There was a small glitch this afternoon when I went to Eubanks's hotel room, but it was nothing—"

"What happened?" Damaris sounded panicky.

"Take it easy. I used the gadget that *Daddy* provided to get into the suite, as we planned. I was going to wait for Eubanks and his bodyguard. I was preparing for my performance, doing a little warm-up, when one of the hotel housekeepers interrupted me. You know how I hate having my practice sessions interrupted."

"What did you do?" Damaris yelped. "Please don't tell me you killed her."

"Well, no. Unfortunately that performance was also interrupted by an utterly impossible woman. Tell Daddy that I want him to find her for me. He owes me that much."

"You want him to find the maid?"

"No, the horrid bitch who ruined everything. The one who was actually able to resist me for a short time. Can you believe it? She managed to save the housekeeper."

"What are you saying?" Damaris cried. "You were seen by someone besides the maid?"

"Yes. I was forced to leave the stage before I could correct the situation. Some people were getting off the elevator, you see. You know how my talent works. I can handle at most two people in a private performance but no more."

"We're doomed," Damaris whispered. "It's all gone wrong."

"That's ridiculous. Pull yourself together. I've rescheduled my private performance with Eubanks for tonight. I've got a much more appropriate venue in mind. By this time tomorrow, I'll be on a plane back to San Francisco."

"But what about the other woman?" Damaris wailed. "If she was able to resist you, she must be a sensitive. Any possibility she was Nightshade?"

"How should I know? Daddy's the great secret agent in the family. It's his job to find out things like that."

"Is there any possibility that she could identify you?"

"Only if she is a true fan, which I doubt. She gave no indication that she recognized my voice. I was in full costume, as we arranged, so she could not possibly describe me."

"But if she was Nightshade, she'll warn Eubanks," Damaris said.

"Eubanks is still at the hotel if that makes you feel any better. I watched him go into the spa a short time ago."

"She wasn't Nightshade then."

"Probably not."

"Who was she?"

"I have no idea. Ask *Daddy*. When he finds out who she is, I intend to give her one of my private performances. I will not tolerate the sort of interruption I was forced to endure today."

"Vivien, you sound like you're starting to obsess here," Damaris said anxiously. "Are you absolutely certain the woman was able to resist your singing?"

"Only for a short period of time. I'm sure I could have destroyed her, given another minute or two. I'm going to hang up now. It has been a very unsettling day. I need to prepare myself for my next performance. Good-bye, Damaris."

"Wait—"

"Tell Daddy to find the bitch."

La Sirène closed the phone and tossed it aside. Really, it was such a responsibility being an older sister. Poor Damaris was so easily upset these days. It was Daddy's fault, of course.

"She was J&J," Daddy said.

"*What?*"

"Relax. I just pulled up the file. Turns out Fallon Jones has Eubanks under surveillance. But not because he thinks Eubanks is Nightshade."

"Are you sure?" Damaris propped her elbows on the desk, rested her aching head in her hand and clutched the phone to her ear. The hot and cold chills were getting worse. She wondered if she was allergic to the drug. "Maybe J&J turned up a link."

"No." Daddy sounded very certain. "Trust me, if the agency had any suspicions in that regard, the Council would have been notified. Nightshade is its highest priority these days. This is a routine J&J operation."

"How can you call it routine?"

"Eubanks is a registered sensitive who has killed three people," Daddy said patiently. "The parents of the third victim were members of the Society. They asked J&J to investigate. That's the only reason Jones is looking at him. These things happen."

"This is getting complicated."

"Calm down. I'll know if J&J identifies the people on Maui as Night-shade. If that occurs, there are procedures in place designed to handle the problem. Meanwhile, let's hope your sister can finish the job."

"Vivien wants you to identify the woman who rescued the house-keeper."

"Don't worry, I intend to do just that."

"Then what?"

"Then I will take care of the problem," Daddy said.

Twenty-six

Eubanks heard the singing when he emerged from the men's room. It emanated from somewhere in the hotel's extensive gardens and floated upward to the long veranda. The notes were so pure and high and sweet that at first he thought someone was playing a flute.

Some aria from an opera, he thought. He had never been a fan, but then, he'd never heard anything this thrilling. The music aroused all his senses.

The sound was so alluring, so enthralling, that he momentarily forgot that Clayton should have been waiting for him at the entrance to the men's room. Belatedly it dawned on him that his bodyguard was nowhere around. A short time ago Clayton had made certain that the restroom was empty and then, per standard procedure, he had gone back outside to make sure no one entered.

Clayton was nowhere around and that was wrong. But the music could not be ignored. It called to him, seductive and inviting.

He forgot about Clayton again and crossed to the railing to look down. The massed foliage of the gardens was so thick it was like looking at the top of a jungle canopy. The moon gleamed on the long fronds of some of the taller palms. Here and there he could see a few of the low lights that picked out the narrow, meandering path that led to the picturesque wedding chapel.

The song tugged at him. He had never experienced anything like this. The flute-like notes were physically arousing. There was no other way to describe the effect. He was getting hard.

The singer was female and he was consumed with desire for her. She was down there in the gardens calling to him. He had no choice but to go to her.

A moment ago he had been focused entirely on his plans to move up into the highest circle of the Nightshade organization. He was being considered for the recently vacated opening on the board of directors. No one deserved it more. Soon he would be leaving the ranks of upper management and going straight to the top of the organization.

He knew that his superiors were extremely impressed with the recent refinement of the formula that had come out of the lab he supervised. There had been some unfortunate incidents in the early human trials but the organization was not the stodgy, timid FDA. The only thing that mattered to the people at the top was success. And he had delivered, big-time.

He had been told that the reason he was on the short list for promotion to the ultimate level of power was because his lab people had come up with a small but highly significant alteration that made it possible to store and transport the drug without the necessity of refrigeration. What's more, it could now be put into capsule form and taken orally rather than injected. Until now, anyone using the genetically tailored formula had been forced to make certain that the vials were kept on ice or in a refrigeration unit of some kind.

There was no doubt but that he had earned the right to occupy a place on the board. Thanks to the drug, he was becoming a powerful strat talent. It was no secret that most of the people at the highest levels were strats. The ability to outthink, outplan and outmaneuver others was, after all, the master talent. It was what took you to the top.

The other talents had their uses to be sure. But what good did it do to possess a psychic power for charisma or for illusion or for viewing auras if you didn't know how to use it to achieve your objectives? High-level strat talents used other talents as pawns.

Oh, yeah, he was destined for the board.

But first he needed to find the singer. Nothing was more important tonight. He listened closely with all his senses trying to pinpoint her location. Somewhere in the very heart of the darkened gardens, he decided.

He went down the flight of stone steps. At the foot of the staircase, he started along a narrow path following the lure of the music. When he rounded a corner he stumbled against an object. He tripped and almost fell but managed to catch his balance. When he looked down he saw a man's leg sticking out from under the fronds of a mass of ferns. The sight briefly shattered the trance induced by the music.

Shocked, he took a quick step back. Then he realized there was some-thing familiar about the dark trousers and the running shoe. Fear sparked through him.

"Clayton?" he said.

The figure did not move.

He crouched to make sure. There was just enough light from the footpath lamp to reveal Clayton's face. The bodyguard's eyes were closed. He was not moving but he was breathing. Blood that looked black in the poor light partially bathed his face.

Part of Eubanks continued to focus on the lilting music while an-other part tried to concentrate on the fact that someone had lured his bodyguard into the gardens and knocked him unconscious with a seriously blunt object. There wasn't much that could catch a high-level hunter off guard, even one who was only partially enhanced.

Run. Get the hell out of here.

He leaped to his feet, turning quickly to scan his surroundings. It was impossible to make out anything in the shadows. He started back the way he had come.

But the music came to him out of the night, stronger and more powerful now. The singer was close. He could not resist, even though his mind was screaming at him to get to safety.

Against his will, he reversed course and went deeper into the gardens. Slowly, fighting each step, he crossed a small footbridge over an ink-colored koi pond. Something splashed in the dark waters. Now he could see the graceful silhouette of the moonlit wedding chapel. The singing came from within.

He went up the steps and through the open door. The structure was not illuminated but there was enough silvery light filtering through the floor-to-ceiling windows to allow him to see the figure standing at the front of the room. The singer was dressed in a long white spa robe, her features shadowed by the hood drawn up over her head. She looked like some ethereal being from another dimension.

Fascinated, he moved down the aisle, unable to resist the compulsion of the music. The singer opened her arms to him. Her voice rose higher, becoming a splashing crystal fountain of perfect and somehow terrifying notes.

The pain began then, alternately searing and then freezing his senses. It spread swiftly. The sudden headache was excruciating.

He finally understood that the singer was killing him. Someone had arranged his murder.

This could not be happening, not to him. He was destined for power and greatness. He had killed three women to get this far.

He fell, drowning in darkness. A horrifying thought came to him. Was the woman who was killing him with her music the ghost of one of the three he had murdered?

The crystalline notes followed him into the depths.

And then there was nothing.

Twenty-seven

Luther opened his eyes to sunlight streaming through palm fronds, the incredibly satisfying sensation of Grace curled around him, and the annoying trill of his phone. The sunshine and the phone were standard issue when it came to mornings. The feeling of Grace cuddled next to him was anything but. Only one night of having her here in his bed and he was already addicted.

Reluctantly he eased away from Grace's soft warmth, sat up on the edge of the bed and picked up the phone. He got a little jolt of adrenaline when he saw the familiar code.

"What have you got, Fallon?"

"Eubanks is dead," Fallon said. The anticipation of the hunter rumbled through his bearlike voice. "His body was discovered in the wedding chapel by a member of the hotel janitorial staff a few hours ago. Looks like he died around midnight last night. The authorities are calling it a stroke. No signs of violence."

"The Siren made her kill."

"That she did. Now we get to sit back and watch. Can't wait to see who takes Eubanks's place. When we find out, we may know who commissioned the murder."

"What about the Siren?"

"She fulfilled her contract. If she's a real pro, as I suspect, she'll probably just disappear."

"But you're looking for her, right?"

"Sure." Fallon paused. "Well, Sweetwater's looking for her, which is even better."

"This isn't Sweetwater's responsibility. She's a sensitive. That makes her a J&J job, *your* job."

"Malone, I gotta tell you that at the moment she is not high on my to-do list." Fallon's voice was shaded with an uncharacteristic anger. He frequently got impatient and was often annoyed but he rarely succumbed to strong emotion like this. "I've got too many other things going on. As long as she sticks to killing Nightshade people, I've got no beef with her."

"She tried to murder Grace and an innocent bystander."

"From the way Grace described things, the incident sounds like it may have been an accident."

"How the hell can you call attempted murder an accident?"

"Okay, okay, not exactly an accident," Fallon muttered. "More along the lines of a wrong-place, wrong-time thing. What I'm trying to say is that there's no sign that she was after Grace or the housekeeper. They interrupted her."

"So now it's Grace's and the housekeeper's fault that they almost got killed?"

"Damn it, stop putting words in my mouth," Fallon growled. "Grace said the Siren was in heavy disguise. That means that, as far as the singer knows, there's no way Grace can identify her. Ergo, she has no reason to go after her. Get the picture?"

"You and I both know that Grace can identify her aura."

"Only if the two of them come face-to-face again," Fallon shot back. "And what are the odds of that?"

"How the hell should I know?"

"Look, the Siren has no way of knowing Grace's identity, let alone her whereabouts or that she's an aura reader. Take it from me, Grace is not in danger. As for the Siren, Sweetwater can do a better job of finding her than I can. She operates in his world. He's got the connections it's going to take to track her down."

"How high is she on Sweetwater's to-do list?"

"Right at the top," Fallon said, flat and brusque. "Seems Harry's a tad irritated to find out that he's got some upscale sensitive competition that he didn't even know existed."

"What if Grace is right about the Siren being an obsessive type? What if she becomes obsessed with Grace because of what happened on Maui?"

"Then we would have a problem," Fallon agreed in the tone of voice one used to placate a kid who won't stop asking questions. "But like I said, we're talking about a pro. Trust me on this, she's in the wind, long gone."

Luther snapped the phone closed and tossed it onto the table. He turned his head and saw that Grace was watching him with her haunting green eyes.

"The Siren got Eubanks," he said. "Fallon says Sweetwater will find her."

"And until that happens?"

He closed his hand around her hip, savoring the firm, feminine shape of her as she lay curled beneath the sheet. "Until then you're on vacation in Hawaii."

Twenty-eight

The chef carried a large knife that looked like it had been designed to slice and dice something other than vegetables. The heavily tattooed waiter kept a gun strapped to his leg beneath his trousers. The auras of both showed above-average levels of psychic talent and unmistakable signs of permanent damage done by extreme violence. There was also evidence of an odd Zen-like acceptance of what they had done and what they knew themselves to be.

The Dark Rainbow appeared to cater to a weird crowd of misfit sensitives, most of whom looked like they had fallen off the edge of somewhere far, far away and washed up on the beaches of Hawaii. The majority of the customers had profiles typical of people whose auras had been scrambled, warped or badly dented. Most of them probably didn't even know that they were psychic, let alone that their problem stemmed from that side of their nature.

So why do I feel right at home here? Grace wondered.

She sat with Petra Groves in a booth at the back of the room, adjacent to the swinging door that opened onto the hot, steamy kitchen. It was late afternoon. Behind the bar Wayne polished glasses with scary precision, as if each was a cartridge he planned to load into a rifle and upon which his life might depend.

Petra had explained that they were in the lull between the lunch rush and the dinner service. There was only one customer in the place. He had parked his rusty shopping cart containing a stained bedroll and a number of empty soda cans and bottles outside in the courtyard. Referring to him as a customer was pushing it, Grace thought, since he was getting a free meal.

"That's Jeff," Petra explained in low tones. "Head trauma while he was doing his third tour."

"I can see the damage," Grace said softly. "He's low level. Looks totally paranoid."

"Yeah. Doesn't trust the VA. Probably just as well. Doubt the doctors would know what to do with a sensitive. When he gets one of his spells, he shows up here. Luther tweaks his aura a little. Calms him right down. On his good days, like today, he stops in and orders the fish and chips."

"Which you serve him without charge?"

Petra shrugged. "He always offers to pay but we don't need any more empty cans and bottles."

"Judging by the lunch crowd, a lot of your clientele look like they should have an appointment with one of the Society's shrinks."

Petra snorted. "Most of 'em don't even know the Society exists. What's more, if they did find out that there was such a thing, they'd probably run like hell in the opposite direction."

Grace nodded solemnly. "They become so paranoid they would probably fear anyone who tried to coax them into a clinical setting."

"A few of them have good reason to be paranoid," Petra said grimly. "A lot of our regulars got into trouble somewhere along the line when their psychic natures brought them to the attention of folks in white coats."

"You mean when other people decided they were crazy?"

Wayne paused in his polishing, eyes as cold as those of the snake that crowned his shaved head. "Couple of 'em ended up in some damned lab experiments."

Petra lowered her coffee mug. "We don't try to play doctor here at the Dark Rainbow. Me and Wayne, we put off having kids and then found out we couldn't have any. After we moved here, I guess we just started adopting folks like Jeff and Ray and the others. The customers come here the first time for a meal or a drink. They come back because they feel better when they're here."

Grace smiled. "And they feel better because the proprietors understand them and because the bartender has a special knack for calming them down."

Petra blew that off with a slicing motion of her hand. "Luckily we don't have to deal in empty pop cans a lot. Most of our crowd pays with actual cash. Enough about us. Let's talk about you. Luther says we're on the lookout for a female who can whack someone by singing opera."

"I think so. Her songs sounded like operatic arias."

"I'm into classic rock, myself. Wayne, here, is the one who likes opera."

Grace looked at him, trying to conceal her surprise. "You're a fan?"

Over at the bar Wayne picked up another glass. "I'm okay with it. Puts me in another place, y'know? Only been to a couple of live performances but I got a lot of CDs. This Siren. She any good?"

"Well, her singing certainly has a very dramatic effect on her audience," Grace said. "But her psychic talent aside, I think she is more than good. Fallon Jones believes that she's a professional hit woman, not a professional singer, but I'm not so sure. It may be the other way around."

Wayne pondered that closely while he applied the towel to another glass. "Either way, Luther is right. You shouldn't be running around on your own until J&J punches her ticket."

Grace tried not to be stunned by the casual way he referred to killing the Siren. She cleared her throat.

"Does J&J actually do things like that?" she asked.

"Fallon Jones would never admit it," Petra said. "But yeah, once in a while stuff like that gets done."

The wall phone rang. Wayne ignored it. Petra shoved herself out of the booth and took the call.

"Yeah, Julie," she said. "Don't worry about it. Hope he feels better soon. Tell the little guy I said hi. No problem."

She tossed the phone back into its cradle and heaved a sigh. "Julie can't make it in tonight. Probably not tomorrow night, either. Her kid's sick."

"No dishwasher and no waitress," Wayne said. "Comin' up on the weekend. Busiest nights of the week. Figures."

Petra shook her head. "These are the kind of personnel problems that come with success. We never used to have to worry about someone not showing up for work B.L."

"B.L.?" Grace said.

"Before Luther," Petra explained. "Who knew success was gonna be such a pain in the ass? We can squeak by without Julie but there's no way I can cook and keep up with the dishes at the same time when we've got a full house."

"I can wash dishes," Grace said.

Wayne and Petra looked at her as if she had started speaking in tongues.

"I used to wash dishes for a living," she explained. "Then I became a butler. You could say I'm a professional."

Twenty-nine

Luther used a little subtle aura manipulation to coax out the last few stragglers shortly after midnight. He walked into the kitchen and found Grace elbow deep in soapy water. She wore an oversized apron that hung almost to her feet. Her hair was shoved up under a net. Her face glistened from a combination of steam and perspiration. She looked adorable. He wanted to take her into the back room and make love to her on a couple of sacks of potatoes.

"We're closed," he said. "Time to eat."

"Almost finished," she said. "I'm on the last pan."

Petra yanked the badly yellowed chef's toque off her head, tossed it aside and dried the sweat from her forehead with the back of her arm.

"Busy night," she declared. "How'd we do?"

"Wayne is closing out as we speak," Luther said. He looked at Grace. "You must be exhausted."

"I'm okay." She finished rinsing a large pot and used both hands to transfer it from the sink to the drain counter. "Just a little out of condition, that's all. What's this about eating?"

"We're all hungry and usually a little wired after a busy night," he explained. "We generally go over to Milly Okada's place for some udon soup."

"Sounds good to me," Grace said. She dried her hands on a towel.

Luther looked at Petra. "We were swamped out there. How'd you two do in here?"

"Got ourselves a rhythm going," Petra said, looking satisfied. "Worked swell. Grace is definitely an industrial-grade dishwasher. Looks like we've got our new Bud."

"We all have our talents," Grace said modestly.

They locked up, crossed the courtyard and walked the half block to Kuhio. Without any discussion, Luther, Petra and Wayne formed a protective phalanx around Grace. The four flowed as a cohesive unit along the crowded street.

The Udon Palace was almost empty. It would fill up rapidly later as other restaurants closed for the night and the staffs made their way there for a late-night meal. Milly Okada emerged from the kitchen. She smiled when she saw Luther.

"You're back and you are no longer depressed," she announced. She turned to Grace. "And this young lady, I think, is the reason why, hmm?"

Grace looked disconcerted. Luther hurried into introductions.

"Milly, this is Grace Renquist," he said. "She's visiting from the mainland."

"Welcome to the islands, Grace," Milly said, giving her an appraising look.

"Thank you," Grace said politely.

"She needs a drink," Petra said to Milly. "The latest Bud quit on us a few days ago. Grace, here, has been washing dishes all night."

"So you're the new Bud, Grace?" Milly chuckled. "You don't look like a dishwasher."

"I've had a lot of experience," Grace said.

"Well, well, well," Milly said softly. "Isn't that interesting?" Before anyone could respond she waved them all to a nearby table. "Sit down, sit down. I'll get the beers." She looked at Grace, one brow raised. "Wine for you?"

"Yes, please," Grace said. "Thanks."

Luther pulled out a chair for her. Then he and Petra and Wayne arranged themselves around the table.

"Any luck tracking Sirens in the genealogy records this afternoon?" Luther asked.

"I made some progress during the after-lunch lull," she said.

Petra leaned back in her chair and folded her arms. "What makes you think she's a member of the Society?"

"She's a very powerful and extremely rare talent. That means there's a high probability that she comes from a long line of sensitives. There's a strong genetic component involved in powerful talents like hers."

"In other words," Luther said, "even if she isn't registered, one or more of her ancestors with the killer talent may have been a member?"

Grace nodded. "Right. If I can get a fix on one of them, I might be able to jump from the Society's genealogical records to other databases maintained by organizations outside the Society."

Petra frowned. "The other genealogical databases wouldn't tell you whether or not a person has a strong psychic talent."

"No," Grace said, "but it might help me identify a Siren's descendants. From there I can determine if any had an unusual talent for singing."

Wayne's eyes narrowed faintly. "Sounds like a long shot."

"It is," Grace agreed. "But it's something to do while we wait for word from Fallon Jones."

Milly emerged with three beers and a glass of white wine. She came back a moment later with bowls of steaming udon soup and handed them around.

"Anything else?" Luther asked after Milly returned to the kitchen.

"Not much," Grace admitted. "There are a number of references to members who possessed what was often described as a mesmerizing voice. But even today critics throw that term around routinely so I'm not sure it means much. I did find some entries concerning singers whose music can put people in a trance that resembles sleep."

"I hear that happens a lot at the opera," Petra said. "Maybe the talent isn't so rare."

Grace smiled. "The point is, I didn't find any references to singers who can literally kill with their music. I sent an e-mail request to Fallon Jones asking him to grant me access to the classified section of the genealogy files."

Luther picked up his beer. "There's a classified section?"

"Oh, yes," she said. "A lot of the records pertaining to particularly dangerous or bizarre talents are highly classified. I've been allowed to work with them on occasion when Mr. Jones was trying to identify a suspect. I'm sure he'll let me back into them for this search." She inhaled the steam off her soup. "This smells very, very good."

"Best udon on the island," Wayne assured her.

Luther watched her use her chopsticks to pluck noodles out of the soup. He didn't have to look at her aura to know that she was exhausted.

"You need a good night's sleep," he said.

She did not argue.

Wayne studied Luther. "So, what's the plan here? Do we just whack anyone who shows up at the restaurant singing something we don't like?"

"That could leave us with a lot of bodies to explain," Petra observed. "Lot of bad singing out there."

"I think the larger issue here is making sure that Grace is never alone until this is over," Luther said.

"No problem." Wayne went back to his udon.

Grace set her chopsticks very precisely across the soup bowl and looked at the three of them with a faintly baffled expression.

"It's very nice of you to do this for me," she said. "I don't know how to thank you."

"No big deal," Petra assured her. "Makes for a change of pace."

"Change is good once in a while," Wayne said. "Keeps life interesting. Forget about thanking us. You're with Luther."

She flicked a quick, searching glance at Luther and then turned back to Wayne. "That matters?"

"Sure," Petra said. "Makes you family."

Grace sat back, hands tightening on the edge of the table, shock in her eyes. "But I'm not family."

"You got your definition," Wayne said. "We've got ours. If we say you're family, then you're family."

Grace's eyes glinted with tears. "I don't . . . You don't even know me."

"Forget the mushy stuff," Petra said. "Tell us more about Sirens."

Grace grabbed her napkin, dabbed at her eyes and then cleared her throat a couple of times. She took a sip of wine and set down the glass, composed once more.

"I spent some time researching the subject of mythological Sirens in order to get some background. It occurred to me that some of the ancient legends might have a basis in fact."

"Huh." Luther looked up from his soup, intrigued. "You think there might be something to those old tales about sailors who were lured to their deaths on the rocks by the music of the Sirens?"

"Maybe," Grace said. "According to the myths, there were some folks who survived the encounters. One story states that when Orpheus heard the Sirens' music he took out his lyre and countered the effect by creating music that was more beautiful than the song of the Sirens."

"In other words, he neutralized the energy of their music by setting up a counter-resonating pattern," Luther said.

"Or maybe he just drowned out their song," Grace suggested.

"Like using one of those white-noise generators to cancel out the sound of street traffic at night?" Wayne asked.

Petra brightened. "We can crank up the rock we play at the Dark Rainbow."

"Can't hurt," Grace said. "But remember that we're not dealing with just music here. The Siren is able to infuse her singing with psychic energy. I don't think we should assume that even the Grateful Dead can cancel out those wavelengths."

"Loud noise of any kind might make it harder for the Siren to concentrate, though," Luther said. "And if she can't hold a focus, all the psychic power in the world is useless."

"True," Grace said. "Also, no singer can stay on key if she doesn't get the right auditory feedback, so she probably needs a suitable venue for one of her performances."

"Any other ideas on how to handle her?" Wayne asked.

"Maybe. When Odysseus and his men sailed past the Sirens' location, he had his sailors stuff beeswax in their ears so they couldn't hear the music."

"Simple, but effective," Wayne said. "I don't fancy the idea of walking around twenty-four/seven with earplugs, though. I like to use my ears."

Grace made a triangle with her fingers and framed the stem of her glass. "There's something else I think we can assume. According to what I found in my research, a very powerful Siren might be able to throw a whole theater full of people into a light trance but she can only project the full force of her killing talent on one, at most two people at a time. I saw proof of that at the hotel. I could feel it when she switched her attention from the maid to me. But when the elevator started to open, she panicked and fled. She knew she couldn't control any more than just the two of us."

"Stupid thing to do, trying to kill the housekeeper," Petra mused. "Wonder what the hell she planned to do with the body?"

Grace contemplated that for a few seconds. "If it had been me, I would have put it into the housekeeping cart and taken it out that way."

A round of silence greeted that statement. Wayne and Petra looked impressed.

Grace frowned. "Did I say something?"

"No," Luther said before any of the others could ask Grace why she had known exactly what to do with an inconvenient body. "Moving right along, the other fact we know about our Siren is that she seems to prefer opera because it allows her the high, killer notes."

"Okay, that's interesting," Petra said. "But what does it tell us?"

"Well, for one thing," Grace said, "it tells us that she probably has had formal musical training. It's not much but it's something. By the way, there is one thing in our favor."

Petra raised her brows. "What?"

"The laws of paraphysics. Psychic energy can't be transmitted mechanically. Like the rest of us, the Siren has to project her talent in person. She can't simply mail her victims a CD and expect them to keel over dead when they listen to her music."

Petra wiggled her brows at Luther. "Congratulations, I see you've found yourself a real glass-half-full kind of woman."

Luther grinned at Grace. "Yeah, I've turned over a new leaf. Who says I'm depressed?"

Thirty

Damaris came awake with the familiar panicky feeling. Something was wrong. But that wasn't true. Everything was all right again. The Maui operation had gone off perfectly in the end. Eubanks was dead and La Sirène was back in San Francisco. Her racing heart and the breathless sensation were due to the drug. She dreaded the next injection. It was scheduled for nine A.M.

The phone rang. She rolled onto her side and grabbed it off the bedside table. One glance at the incoming number iced her blood.

"What is it?" she said into the phone. "What's wrong?"

"Nothing's wrong," La Sirène said impatiently. "Except that I'm running around like a madwoman here getting ready to fly to Acacia Bay. Dear Newlin is sending his private jet for me." Her voice became slightly muffled as she spoke to someone else. "No, no, not those shoes, you idiot, the blue pair. Blue is my color. I'll need them for the opening-night party."

Like a madwoman. Damaris shuddered, wondering if her sister had any idea just how accurate the description was. Probably not. Crazy people didn't see themselves as crazy.

"That's great," she said, taking a couple of deep breaths to calm her racing heart. "You're going to knock 'em dead as the Queen of the Night." She winced at her own unfortunate choice of words. "I'm looking forward to the performance. I'm sure all the most important critics will be there."

"Dear Newlin has promised they will be. Has Daddy found that bitch yet?"

Damaris closed her eyes. "Vivien, please listen to me. The housekeeper isn't important."

"I told you, forget the hotel maid," La Sirène snapped. "I'm not interested in her. She's nothing to me. I want the other woman, the one who protected the housekeeper and tried to resist my singing."

Damaris got to her feet, fingers clenched around the phone. "The other woman doesn't matter, either. Let it go, Vivien. Concentrate on the Acacia Bay performance. Your career is about to take off again. You can't afford to be distracted."

"Not the emeralds, you silly creature, I'll need the sapphire-and-diamond set that dear Newlin gave me. They go with the shoes and the gown." La Sirène's voice grew louder as she spoke directly into the phone. "Damaris, this is the least you can do for me. Let me rephrase that. It's the least *Daddy* can do for me. He owes me this much."

"The important thing is that the woman has no way of knowing who you are. She can't identify you."

"This has nothing to do with whether she can identify me. She resisted me. I know she must be a sensitive. Don't tell me that Daddy can't find her."

"He's still looking for her," Damaris lied. "I'll let you know as soon as he finds her."

"Promise?"

Damaris sighed. "Promise."

The phone went dead. Damaris stared at it, wondering why it was vibrating. After a couple of seconds she realized that it was shaking because her hand was trembling.

She made herself take several deep, steadying breaths and went to the window. She stood looking out at the lights of Los Angeles for a long time, thinking.

Two things had become very clear. Her fears about using her sister to take out Eubanks had been justified. La Sirène was now obsessed with the mysterious woman she had encountered on Maui. She viewed her as a rival. Given Vivien's character, that fixation would not end until the woman was dead.

The entire plan was in jeopardy.

She went back to the nightstand and picked up the phone. Daddy answered on the first ring.

"You're awake," she said quietly.

"I don't sleep much these days. What's wrong?"

"I think we may have a problem. Vivien has become fixated on the woman who discovered her in Eubanks's hotel room on Maui. Not the housekeeper, the other one."

There was a short silence and then a soft chuckle. "Your sister may not be as crazy as you think."

"What do you mean?"

"I've been obsessing on her, myself."

"I don't understand," Damaris whispered. "Why?"

"Because it was simply too much of a coincidence that a sensitive powerful enough to interfere with your sister's singing just happened to be in that hotel on Eubanks's floor at that moment."

Shock reverberated through her. "Yes, of course. I should have realized."

"Yes, you should have thought about the possibilities."

"I'm sorry." She rubbed her damp forehead. "It's the drug, Daddy. I can't seem to think straight these days."

"I know. I told you, the first few months are a little rough. Relax, I'm not annoyed because of this small lapse. I've got the situation under control."

"You found the woman?"

"Her name is Grace Renquist. Turns out she's just a librarian in the Bureau of Genealogy. A fairly strong aura talent, though. Fallon Jones sent her to Maui along with a bodyguard to get a look at Eubanks. That means she must be able to ID auras."

"How much does J&J know?"

"At the moment, nothing. As I thought, Jones was watching Eubanks as part of a routine investigation into the death of one of the women he killed, the last victim. The woman's family hired the agency to look into it. Fallon Jones figured Eubanks for just another high-level sensitive gone bad. Now Eubanks is dead due to a stroke. As far as the agency is concerned, the case is closed."

"But what about Grace Renquist? You said she's a high-ranking aura talent. She must have seen Vivien's aura. A lot of strong auras can recognize individual energy fields. At the very least she must have realized that Vivien is a powerful sensitive of some kind. J&J would follow up on that information."

"Now you're thinking like the future director of Nightshade." Approval laced each word. "You're right. Miss Renquist has, indeed, become a problem. As things stand, she is the one person who might be able to identify La Sirène. And if La Sirène were to be discovered and identified, well, things could get a bit awkward."

Comprehension shuddered through Damaris. She had to fight to breathe. "If J&J finds Vivien—" She broke off, unable to finish the sentence.

"Yes, exactly," Daddy said gently. "It's highly unlikely, of course, but if J&J manages to track down Vivien, and if Grace Renquist were to identify her as the woman in Eubanks's hotel room, it is possible that they would make the connection to you and then to me."

Damaris's mouth went dry. "You're not . . . you're not thinking of doing something to Vivien, are you?"

"Of course not. She's my daughter. The person who needs to disappear is Grace Renquist. With her out of the picture there will be no one around who can identify La Sirène. We'll all be safe again."

She crushed the phone against her ear, trying to think like him, like the future director of Nightshade. "It will have to look like an accident, or at the very least, a Nightshade operation."

"Very good," he said. "But don't worry. I was doing this kind of thing for a living before you were even born. I'll take care of everything."

The phone went silent.

She rose and went back to the window. *I'll take care of everything.* That was what a father was supposed to do. So why was she so terrified? It was the damned drug.

She glanced at the clock. Two more hours until the next dose.

WILLIAM CRAIGMORE put down the phone, set aside his book and pushed himself up from the reading chair. He smiled at the realization that he was actually looking forward to the venture. It had been a long time since he had felt the kind of adrenaline rush that only came with fieldwork. Running Nightshade was a fascinating challenge, but he sometimes missed the old days when it was just him and the other guy playing for keeps in the shadows.

He glanced at his image in the mirror as he went down the hall. He was seventy and still in good health and excellent physical condition. It was too soon to tell if the drug would give him a few extra decades of life, but Sylvester Jones, the alchemist who first concocted it back in the late 1600s, had been convinced that longevity would prove to be a side effect of the drug. Something to look forward to, he thought, especially now that he had found his daughters. He had a genetic stake in the future. He wanted very much to live long enough to see his grandchildren grow up. His offspring, enhanced by the perfected formula, would be the most powerful people on the planet.

He keyed in the code that unlocked the vault door and entered the gallery. The lights came up automatically, revealing the objects on display in glass cases. Each was a memento of an assignment successfully carried out. The bureaucrats at the clandestine government agency he had once worked for would have fainted dead away if they had known that he kept souvenirs. They were so sure they had concealed all traces of the very existence of their operation; so certain that even the agents had all died. Fools. One agent had been smart enough to see the writing on the wall.

The item he wanted was not on display in any of the cases. He went to the back of the room and entered another code into the wall safe. The door swung open. He reached in and took out one of the objects inside.

Just holding it in his hand sent a thrill of anticipation surging through him.

Like old times.

Thirty-one

Grace shoved several strands of sweat-dampened hair back under her net and seized the heavy soup pot with both hands.

"When was the last time you cleaned the deep-fat fryer and changed the oil?" she asked.

"Can't remember." Petra emerged from the walk-in freezer with a package of frozen fish fillets. "Figure the more stuff you cook in the oil, the more flavor you get. Besides, every time it boils, you kill off all the germs."

"That's an interesting theory." She wrestled the big pot into the soapy water and reached for the scrub brush. "I'm surprised the health department doesn't take a slightly different view, however."

"We don't have a lot of problems with health inspectors here at the Dark Rainbow." Petra ripped open the package and dumped the rock-hard fillets on the counter. "They don't show up often, and when they do they don't hang around long. Generally speaking, they take a quick look in here and off they go."

"Please don't tell me that's because Luther uses his talent to urge them along."

"Okay, I won't tell you that." Petra dumped a mountain of uncooked French fries into the fryer's basket. "But that thing he can do does have its practical uses."

She dropped the basket into the hot oil and jumped back with a practiced movement to avoid the hiss and splatter.

The kitchen door swung open. A wave of rock music rolled in from the main room. Wayne appeared, an empty tray tucked under his arm.

"Order up," he announced. "Three of them." He tore three pages off his pad and added them to the long row of orders already hanging over a counter. "Gettin' busy out there. Full house tonight. Bunch of damned tourists wandered in."

He turned and stalked back out through the swinging doors, allowing another flood of hard rock to inundate the kitchen.

"Well, doesn't that just suck," Petra muttered. "What do they think I am? A machine? I can't crank out food like I'm some kind of assembly-line robot."

"Looks like an assembly line is exactly what we need," Grace said. She dried her hands on her apron. "I'm caught up with the dishes. Why don't I take over the fish-and-chips orders while you deal with the dead red?"

"Sounds like a plan," Petra grumbled. "Watch out you don't burn yourself on that damn fryer."

Grace eyed the sizzling oil warily. "I'll be careful."

Petra glanced at the remaining order slips, scowling. "Three fish and chips and five more burgers."

"Got it." Grace selected a few pieces of thawed fillets and dipped them in the batter.

"Keep the portions below four ounces," Petra said. She tossed five raw hamburger patties onto the grill. "Aim for three. We're not running a homeless shelter here."

"Isn't three ounces of fish a rather small serving?"

"Not when you're feeding tourists. They'll never know the difference. Besides, the batter blows up a lot in the fryer. Makes the portions look bigger. Then you fill up the rest of the plate with a lot of French fries. Potatoes are cheaper than fish. And since it's all fried, it's all the same color. No one notices where the fish stops and the potatoes begin."

"I can see you've got this down to a fine art."

"Damn straight."

The swinging door opened again, releasing another flood of rock just as Grace was lowering the basket of batter-dipped fish into the fryer. Luther came into the room. He frowned at her.

"Watch that fryer," he said. "It's dangerous."

"Trust me, I'm being very careful."

"Thought you were supposed to be washing dishes," he said.

Petra looked up from the burgers. "Gave her a field promotion due to the fact that we're swamped. How's it going out there?"

"Busy night. Probably peak in the next hour or so. Bunch of tourists found us. You two doing okay?"

"Do we look like we're okay?" Petra snapped. "It's hotter than hell in here and we've got orders coming out the ass."

"Now there's an appetizing visual," Luther said. "Do they talk like that on the cooking channel?"

"Damned if I know," Petra said. "I didn't learn to cook by watching the cooking channel."

"Well, hey, I'm just the bartender," Luther said. "I sure don't want to slow down the process in here. I'll leave you two to get on with the preparation of your culinary art."

He winked at Grace and went back through the swinging doors.

Petra glared at the doors. "What the hell is culinary art?"

"Cooking," Grace said.

"Oh, yeah, right. I knew that."

"Where did you learn to cook?" Grace asked, curious.

"Wayne and I hired us a real cook when we bought the place. Watched him for a while. By the time he quit—and sooner or later they all quit— I figured I could handle the kitchen. No big trick to it. So long as you put the food in the fryer or throw it on a grill, folks will eat it. Fact of life."

"I can see there's a real emphasis on healthy, organic cooking here at the Dark Rainbow. How did Luther come to join the staff?"

"After he moved to Waikiki, he found his way here like the rest of the regulars. Started coming in occasionally for a beer and sometimes a meal. On quiet nights we got to talking. You know how it is. Strong sensitives usually recognize each other."

"Yes," Grace said, thinking back to that day on the concourse when she first saw Luther. "I know."

"We had some things in common. He'd been a cop and he was doing some contract work for J&J. Wayne and me, we'd done something along the same lines. None of us had any family to speak of. Guess you could say the three of us sort of understood each other."

"You formed your own family."

"Something like that, yeah."

"But how did Luther get involved in the business?" she asked.

"After a while it came out that me and Wayne were having some problems here. There was a lot of drug dealing in the alley out back and some of the low-rent hookers had started hanging out in the bar. We had a few fights break out. Police started showing up a lot. Disturbed the regulars. They stopped coming around. All in all, we were going under. Luther fixed a few things."

"How?"

"Let's just say he got rid of some pesky problems. The regulars returned and we've been okay ever since."

Grace smiled. "Another practical application of Luther's talent?"

"Told you, that talent of his does come in handy once in a while."

Thirty-two

Crazy Ray seemed a little more agitated than usual. Luther sent a soothing pulse of energy his way before he urged him out the door along with the handful of remaining customers.

Ray went outside, trailing the others, but he stopped just beyond the entrance and looked back at Luther.

"You be careful tonight," he said.

Ray rarely emerged from his paranoid world long enough to produce a coherent sentence. Luther nodded, letting him know that he had gotten the message and would take it seriously.

"Okay," he said. "I'll be careful."

Ray vanished into the shadows.

Wayne appeared behind Luther's shoulder. "What was that about?"

"Just Ray being Ray. He warned me to be careful."

"Probably picked up on the vibes the rest of us are giving off. We're all a little jacked tonight because we're watching over Grace."

Luther thought about the occasional icy tingles he'd been experiencing all evening.

"Yeah," he said. "Let's go get some of Milly's soup. It's been a long night."

"Damn tourists."

"This is Waikiki, Wayne. You've got to expect that occasionally a few tourists will find us."

"Maybe we should put up a sign."

"'No Tourists Allowed'? Somehow I don't think the Visitors and Convention Bureau would approve."

By the time they had finished the bowls of udon, Grace was yawning.

"When this is over, I'm going to write a self-help book titled *How to Build Stamina and Lose Weight Washing Dishes and Frying Stuff Eight Hours a Day*," she announced.

"You've been living the soft life in the Bureau of Genealogy for a year," Petra said. "You're out of shape."

"I know." Grace stretched. "But it's like riding a bicycle. It's all coming back to me." She sniffed the sleeve of her shirt and wrinkled her nose. "Including the smell. Funny how the scent of fried fish permeates your clothes."

"You get used to it," Wayne said.

"Time to go home," Luther said. "I'll get the Jeep and meet you out front."

The routine had been established after consultation with Wayne and Petra. Under the circumstances, no one thought it was a good idea for Grace to be walking back to the Sunset Surf Apartments late at night even if she was accompanied by a bodyguard. The plan was simple. Luther parked the Jeep in a nearby garage. After the Rainbow closed for the evening, Wayne and Petra stayed with Grace at Milly's place while he went to get the vehicle.

He walked toward the garage, cane tapping on the sidewalk, and thought about the rest of the new nightly routine. Within twenty minutes he would be back at the condo with Grace and they would both tumble into bed together. Maybe they would make love if she wasn't too exhausted. Afterward she would press close to him and fall asleep in his arms. In the morning they would sleep late. When they woke up, they would make coffee and slice some fresh papaya.

He could definitely get used to this routine. Hell, he was already so deeply into it that he did not want it to end.

There were still a fair number of people on Kuhio. At the end of the block he turned up his senses; rounded the corner and went down the narrow street toward the old hotel garage. The hotel had been closed for a couple of years. It's upper windows were boarded up and the pool was covered. A nightclub had recently opened on what had been the first floor. It was operating at full volume tonight. The hard rock pounded into the night, accompanied by the roar of a crowd fueled by alcohol and a day at the beach.

The garage was full, thanks to the club patrons. He walked toward the far end where he had parked the Jeep, automatically watching for the flash of an aura in the dark canyons between vehicles. The deep thunder of the music spilled through every opening in the concrete walls and cascaded down the stairwell.

His leg was aching again tonight. He would have to take some more anti-inflammatory tablets when he got back to the condo. The thought made him want to snap the cane in half and hurl the pieces into the nearest trash bin. The memory of the shooter coming out of the bedroom, surprising him, flashed in his head. *Get over it. Could have been a hell of a lot worse.*

He went toward the Jeep, keys out, still on alert for movement in the shadows or anything else that didn't seem right. The garage was empty, except for the hulking shapes of the vehicles. There was nothing out of the ordinary to disturb his cop intuition or his psychic senses. So why the whisper of unease? *Thanks for giving me the willies, Ray. After all I've done for you.*

When he got close to the SUV he used the remote to unlock it. Automatically, he gave the garage another quick survey. The concrete stairwell that led upstairs to the old hotel lobby and the entrance to the nightclub was to his right. The light was off inside. It had been on earlier when he parked.

Adrenaline scalded his veins.

The narrow beam of a penlight appeared first, prowling around the stairwell landing, illuminating the concrete steps.

The person gripping the small light rounded the corner a second later and started down the steps. In the darkened stairwell he was only a tall, lean silhouette but his aura pulsed hot with the colors of violence and raw power.

Luther concentrated, getting the pattern in focus, just in case. The man halted at the foot of the stairs. Although his aura was running red-hot, he made no move that could be interpreted as violent. There was no gun or knife in his free hand. He just stood there, aiming the flashlight at Luther's chest.

Rogue waves spiked across the stranger's aura. Luther sent a crushing tide of energy at him.

Nothing happened.

In the next instant he realized that his parasenses were fading fast, going blind. It was suddenly hard to make out the stranger's pattern. That wasn't right. He should have been able to see it clearly.

"I'm afraid you have become a problem, Mr. Malone," the man said. "But I'm an old hand at fixing problems like you."

The words sounded as if they came from the bottom of an abyss. They were laced with the promise of death. Luther could barely hear them. The garage was filling with a rising tide of shadows. The gathering darkness rapidly blotted up what little light came from the overhead fixtures. Now his vision was fading. A great weakness settled on him, saturating his bones.

He knew with absolute certainty that he was dying. There was pain where the pencil-slim flashlight beam struck his chest. He realized that it had to be the light that was swiftly neutralizing his aura. When your energy field went out, you went out with it.

He tried to summon the strength to move but his muscles would not obey. His will to live was a weak and flimsy weapon against the numbing power of the penlight.

"Who are you?" he croaked.

"William Craigmore. Perhaps you've heard of me?"

"Council." He could barely get the word out. Fallon and Zack Jones were right. They had a spy in the highest of high places within the Society. "Nightshade."

"Very good," Craigmore said approvingly. "I am most certainly Nightshade, and I've been a member of the Governing Council for fifteen years. Sadly, I'll be disappearing soon. I'd have preferred to stay on for a couple more years but that's not possible now that Zack Jones is in charge. He's simply too good, much better than his predecessor. It's a damn shame, you know. I was almost able to prevent him from taking over the Master's Chair but, unfortunately, things went wrong."

Luther said nothing. He could no longer speak. He started to shake uncontrollably. His breathing was getting tight. The pain grew worse, searing his senses.

"You're stronger than I expected," Craigmore said. "Most men would be unconscious by now. Fallon Jones did a good job of covering up your true talent level in the files. But after all these years on the Council, I know most of the Society's secrets, including how to bypass the J&J encryption codes. I am aware that Miss Renquist is something more than what she appears, as well. When I've finished with you, I will remove her. That should take care of all the dangling threads."

Grace. He had to survive to protect her. *Grace.* Somehow just thinking her name clarified his fevered mind for a few seconds.

It occurred to him that the only thing keeping him on his feet was willpower and the cane. He had a death grip on the handle, knowing that if he went down, he would not get up.

If he went down.

He allowed himself to stop fighting the effects of the beam. The last of the strength went out of his fingers. The cane clattered on the concrete. Predictably, he, too, fell hard and fast onto the unforgiving floor. Pain jolted through his bad leg but for a precious few seconds, the penlight lost its focus on his chest.

His senses slammed back with jolting force. The lights came up in the garage. The thunder of the rock music and the noise of the crowd grew loud. He could *breathe* again.

He rolled under the Jeep, instinctively seeking the darkness like some night creature scurrying from the sun. Craigmore swung the penlight back and forth in an arc, trying to track and pin him again with the beam.

He sensed the slender ray slicing like a surgeon's scalpel, striking his legs and, briefly, his shoulders and back as he scrambled under the Jeep. When the killing light hit his lower body, it did not have nearly as much impact as when it glanced across his core. It hurt like hell but he could keep moving.

In the two seconds it took to get under the Jeep, all his senses sparked on and off like faulty electrical wiring, a dizzying, nerve-rattling whirl of sound and silence, sight and blindness.

Once in the narrow space under the vehicle, he kept going, wriggling beneath the undercarriage and out on the far side.

"Give it up," Craigmore ordered.

There was a new note in his voice now. Anger, maybe. Or maybe sheer outraged amazement. That was the thing about being an aura talent. No one took you seriously.

Craigmore walked closer to the Jeep but paused several feet away, keeping a wary distance. Maybe it had occurred to him that an ex-cop might carry a hold-out gun.

If only, Luther thought.

"I watched you come down the street a short while ago," Craigmore said. "We both know you can't run. Not with that bad leg. Even if you were in good shape, you're not fast enough to evade my little flashlight. You might as well come on out from behind the Jeep. It will all be over very quickly, I promise."

Adrenaline was an excellent temporary painkiller. Ignoring the stabbing pain in his thigh, Luther yanked open the passenger-side door and hauled himself up into the front seat. He made it into the driver's side and hit the button to lock all four doors, sealing himself inside.

He was about to put the laws of paraphysics to a severe test. If he was wrong, he was a dead man.

He was banking on the fact that the beam of the penlight had to be paranormal in nature. There was no other explanation for its effect on his aura. Most solid materials such as steel or concrete effectively stopped paranormal energy waves. Liquids, on the other hand, did not. Crystals and certain reflective surfaces, although solid, fell into a third category. They could be used to focus energy if you knew what you were doing.

Glass, however, was a fourth category of matter as far as paraphysics was concerned. It was neither a crystalline substance nor a liquid but it had properties of both states of matter. As a rule, a barrier made of glass dramatically slowed or even distorted waves of energy passing through it.

Unfortunately, when it came to glass, there were a lot of exceptions to the rules. The substance was still little understood by the Arcane Society researchers. The bottom line was that the material was damned unpredictable.

He cranked the engine. Craigmore aimed the flashlight at him through the driver's-side window. He started to shiver. The laser was having some effect, even through the glass, but he wasn't completely frozen. He ducked low to evade the ray, snapped the gearshift into reverse and hit the accelerator, driving blind.

The Jeep lurched backward, tires screeching. The rear seat windows exploded. Shit. The bastard had a real gun, too. What's more, the bullets seemed to be obeying the laws of regular physics. No sound, though. Silencer.

He whipped the wheel hard left and shot forward, heading straight toward Craigmore.

Evidently having concluded that the beam was no longer effective, Craigmore took aim with his pistol again. Luther ducked as the front windshield disintegrated. Glass shards littered the front seat. His shield against the light beam was gone.

But the Jeep was still in motion and Craigmore was too busy leaping out of the way to aim the flashlight.

Luther hit the brake and got a fix on Craigmore's aura. He sent a squelching current of energy at it even as Craigmore tried to line up twin shots using both the beam and the silenced gun.

Head shots were notoriously difficult. They were made even harder when you suddenly wanted nothing more than to go to sleep.

Craigmore sagged, stumbled and went down. The laser device fell from his hand and rolled away across the concrete. It winked out instantly.

Luther threw the Jeep into park, got the front door open and stumbled out. He limped toward Craigmore, using the fender of a nearby car for support.

Craigmore was on his belly on the oil-stained concrete, facing Luther. Amazingly, he still gripped the gun and was using both hands to try to aim it. His lips were pulled back in a savage grin. He managed to get off another shot. The bullet went wide but Luther jerked aside reflexively. The sudden movement caused his leg to collapse again.

He landed hard on one knee and his elbow. His concentration wavered for a few seconds. Freed, Craigmore tried to line up another shot, but the sudden relief of the compelling pressure on his aura left him disoriented.

Luther heightened his aura to full power, lurched partway to his feet and fell on top of Craigmore. He caught hold of one arm and twisted hard. At the same time he threw everything he had at Craigmore's wildly pulsing energy field.

There was a stunning flash of energy on the paranormal plane. Luther felt his parasenses go blind for an instant.

He saw Craigmore's mouth open on what was probably intended to be a shout. But what emerged was an eerie groan, the kind you expected to hear in graveyards at midnight. His eyes widened in shock. He jerked, flopped around and then went unnaturally still. His aura winked out just as the psychic laser had a few minutes earlier. The gun thunked on the garage floor.

An eternity passed.

Luther's senses came crashing back. It occurred to him that he was still gripping the dead man's arm. He released it and rolled clear of the body. For a moment he lay on the cold concrete, trying to catch his breath and steady his senses.

He heard only the merest whisper of sound on the concrete steps before he saw the flash of an aura. He did not move.

"Wayne, it's me," he said urgently.

Wayne emerged from the stairwell. He had his gun in his hand. Everything about him was preternaturally focused. He was in the kill zone.

"You okay?" he asked in a very flat voice.

"Yeah." Luther relaxed a little. "He was waiting for me. An ambush. What are you doing here? Wait, don't tell me. Petra had a feeling, right?"

Wayne came out of the zone. He shrugged and tucked the gun into the holster beneath his trouser leg.

"Both of 'em had a feeling," he said.

"Both?"

"Grace and Petra. They both got a bad vibe. Grace wanted to come with me. Petra had to damn near tie her down."

"Guess I should have paid more attention to Ray's warning tonight."

"Now, why in hell would you want to do that? Ray's crazy."

Thirty-three

"Do I need to talk to our guy in the Honolulu PD?" Fallon Jones asked.

"No," Luther said. "Craigmore had a silencer. No one came to investigate. Petra and Wayne cleaned up the scene."

He and Grace were in the apartment. He was on the phone, pacing, trying to ignore the aftereffects of the heavy burn. She was gazing into the glowing computer screen as if it were a crystal ball, contemplating her precious genealogy files.

It was taking everything he had to stay focused on the conversation with Fallon. What he really wanted, *needed,* was a stiff shot of whiskey and then sleep.

"What did you do with the body?" Fallon asked, pragmatic, as always.

"This is Hawaii. Gets a little warm here. We wrapped it in a few yards of plastic kitchen wrap and stashed it in the walk-in refrigerator at the restaurant."

Luckily Petra bought extra-heavy-duty plastic wrap and she purchased it in commercial-size containers.

"You don't do things in a discreet way, do you?" Fallon's voice rumbled through the phone. "Craigmore was a distinguished member of the Council. He served for fifteen years and was considered to be one of the most powerful men in the Society. Now it turns out he was a traitor."

"What kind of talent?" Luther asked.

"Craigmore was a crystal generator," Fallon said.

"What's that?"

"A specialized kind of crystal worker. He could channel energy through a few extremely rare gemstones. That laser gadget you described appears to have worked by disrupting and neutralizing an individual's aura."

"Where the hell did he get that thing?"

"Good question. We're still looking into it. It didn't come out of our labs, that's for sure. Best guess now is that it was designed especially for his talent in that no-name government agency he used to work for."

"He worked for the government?"

"Back in the day. There are over twenty government agencies dedicated to national security and intelligence issues. Some people in the know claim the number is closer to thirty. And they've all got black-hole departments that are used for clandestine purposes. Every so often one of them decides to experiment with paranormal research. Not that any of them would ever admit it, of course. That would mean trying to justify the funding to Congress. The media would have a field day blasting the feds for spending tax dollars on *junk science*."

Luther understood the sudden flash of anger in Fallon's tone. Many members of the Arcane community found society's attitudes toward the paranormal frustrating and, on occasion, infuriating.

"Probably hard enough to justify the Farm Bill and corporate welfare," Luther said. "Try telling people that you're spending millions on the woo-woo stuff."

"How the hell are we going to prove that people like you and me and Grace and everyone else in the Society aren't wack jobs if everyone insists on officially denying the existence of the paranormal? Talk about catch twenty-two. Talk about the emperor's new clothes. Talk about shortsighted, stupid and—"

"Uh, Fallon, maybe we could get back to the subject of what to do about Craigmore's body? I'm pretty good when it comes to tweaking auras but even I have limits. If someone from the health department happens to drop into the restaurant tomorrow, I may have a little problem convincing him to ignore a dead guy in the refrigerator."

"Sorry. I don't usually get off track like that."

"I know."

It said a lot about the situation that Fallon had allowed himself to lose his focus.

"I hate to admit it but I think this thing that you and Grace have uncovered is starting to get to me," Fallon continued, grim and glum. "The Nightshade operation is so much bigger and more extensive than we imagined. And we're on our own."

No getting around that, Luther thought. The danger posed by Nightshade was very real. The Council was committed to dealing with the threat but it was not easy fighting a battle that was invisible to the wider society.

As far as most people were concerned, the paranormal equated with entertainment. It belonged on television and in books and films. People had *real* things to worry about in the real world—terrorism and global warming. They were not going to take seriously warnings about a shadowy organization of evil psychics, especially when that warning was issued by another, equally secret society dedicated to the study of the paranormal.

There were sensitives—members of the Arcane community—working at various levels in government agencies, police departments and other venues who could be called upon by J&J, but they were usually able to supply only limited assistance. In addition, whatever help they did provide had to be strictly off the record. Being outed as someone who claimed to be psychic was, generally speaking, not a smart career move unless you happened to be running a cult.

"About the body," Luther said. "We've got two options. We can either have Petra and Wayne take it out to sea on their boat and dump it or you can arrange to ship it back to Craigmore's family."

"Craigmore doesn't have any family. He married three times but there were no children. Rumor has it that he wasn't able to have kids. His last wife died nearly a decade ago. But yes, we need to get the body back here. He can't just disappear. There would be a lot of questions. Let me think for a minute."

Luther listened as Fallon clicked computer keys.

"Okay, looks like he flew commercial," Fallon said finally. "His private jet is still sitting on the ground in L.A. That means he didn't want a record of the trip, and that, in turn, means he probably used a phony ID to get the seat on the scheduled flight. We're clear."

Luther went blank trying to follow the logic. It was a frequent occurrence when talking to Fallon.

"Clear for what?" he asked.

"No one knows Craigmore went to Hawaii so no one will think it's strange when he turns up dead in his own home in L.A.," Fallon explained. "I'll send a company plane with refrigeration equipment to pick up his body."

"Will there be an autopsy?"

"Probably not," Fallon said. "It's going to look like he died of a heart attack and wasn't found for a few hours. He was seventy. No one will question cause of death."

"But if there is an autopsy?"

"Natural causes," Fallon said absently. His attention was already on the next move in the three-dimensional chess game he was playing.

"What makes you so sure of that, Fallon?"

"You're not the first person to zap an aura."

"I'm not?" Luther glanced at Grace. She was still studying the screen but he knew she was listening to the conversation. "There have been others?"

"A few. It's an extremely rare variant of the aura talent. Requires off-the-charts power, which, as we both know, you just happen to have. Also, in every reported case, the aura talent had to be in physical contact with the victim in order to douse the whole energy field."

"There was a struggle," Luther said tonelessly. He looked at one of his hands. "I was right on top of him."

Fallon tapped merrily away on his computer. "Takes a while to recover from that kind of burn. My guess is that you're going to need to crash for a few hours."

"No shit." It was a damn shame that Fallon was so far away, Luther thought. It would have been very satisfying to throttle him.

"Couple of other things you might want to know about this kind of thing," Fallon said.

"Go on."

"I came across an old Society research paper on the subject a while back. Evidently the experience of killing someone the way you just did is described as intimate, akin to using a knife or your bare hands."

Luther tightened his grip on the cane. "Thanks for that."

"Hence the possible parapsych fallout," Fallon added.

"What the hell?"

"Posttraumatic stress and all that. The paper said that the aftereffects are highly unpredictable."

"Did it ever occur to you to warn me about any of this?"

"No," Fallon said.

"Why not?"

"Well, for one thing, there's no way to know if an aura talent can actually extinguish another person's energy field until he actually does it. That pretty much rules out experimental trials, at least as far as the

Society is concerned. For another, the records of the handful of talents who could generate that kind of energy have always been classified to the highest levels. The Society doesn't need that kind of stuff hitting the Internet or the tabloids."

"I can't tell you how much I appreciate your keeping that information from me, Fallon."

"Like I said, no way to know if you could do it until you did it." Fallon broke off again. There were more clicking noises. "Here's something interesting."

"I'm not sure I can take any more interesting news."

"According to the experts, you didn't actually kill Craigmore."

"This is starting to sound like a trip down the rabbit hole."

"Here's the deal," Fallon continued, unfazed by the lack of enthusiasm. "Evidently what you did with your aura was *reflect* the violent energy that Craigmore was generating. In effect, you created a mirror. When you came in contact with him, he got a severe bounce-back jolt. It set up a dissonant wave pattern that shattered his aura. In essence, Craigmore was the victim of a ricochet shot."

"Huh."

"Trust me," Fallon said, "there's no trace of physical evidence in situations like this. It will look like Craigmore's heart just stopped. Which is pretty much what happens at the end, anyway, regardless of what kills you."

"Craigmore was a wealthy man," Luther said. "Whoever inherits his financial empire may have a few questions about the manner of his death."

"A few years back Craigmore informed the previous Master that he intended to leave his entire estate to the Society to continue funding its research. Under the circumstances, I doubt that the Council will ask too many questions."

"Craigmore and I didn't exactly have a lengthy conversation in the garage," Luther said, "but in view of his admission that he was Nightshade, he may have changed his mind about who gets his money."

"Yeah, can't wait to see who comes out of the woodwork to collect," Fallon said. "I've got people on the way to Craigmore's home and his office to see what they can dig up. The good news is that I don't think Craigmore ever found out that you and Grace stumbled into those four other Nightshade talents on Maui. As far as he knew, you were interested in Eubanks only because J&J was investigating him for murder."

"Craigmore was on the Council. Why didn't he learn that we stumbled into the Nightshade connection?"

"Because I didn't enter anything into the computer files about the link to Nightshade and because Zack chose not to inform the Council about what you and Grace discovered," Fallon said.

Luther whistled softly. "You two really are worried about a spy, aren't you?"

"I told you, Zack sensed that there was a Nightshade plant somewhere very high up within the Society. He had even begun to think that the spy might be on the Council. Guess the big sixty-four-dollar question now is, How many other members of the organization are members of the Society?"

"Any idea why Craigmore wanted Eubanks taken out?"

"Not yet," Fallon admitted. "Just starting to work on that. Probably some kind of competitive thing. Maybe he and Eubanks were both going after the same promotion within Nightshade."

"Why the hell did he come after me?"

"Because you're guarding Grace," Fallon said with his customary devastating logic.

Luther suppressed the icy chill that slithered through his veins.

"The only reason he would have been worried about Grace is because she can identify the singer," he said quietly.

"Right. Craigmore must have been convinced that if we found the singer, we would uncover a connection that would lead straight back to him."

Luther thought about that. "Wonder why he didn't just take out the singer and cut the connection that way?"

"I keep telling you, she's a pro like Sweetwater. She wouldn't be all that easy to find, let alone remove."

Fallon clicked off the way he usually did, without bothering to say good-bye. The way you knew a chat with him was over was when the phone went dead in your ear.

Thirty-four

Grace watched Luther close the phone and sink down onto the sofa. Absently he rubbed his right leg, weariness in every line of his body. The aftermath of the confrontation with Craigmore was having its way with him, hitting him on every front. She remembered the sensation all too well.

"Fallon says Sweetwater is still looking hard for the Siren," Luther said. "He's sure it won't take long to find her."

"That's good to know."

She got up, went into the kitchen and took the whiskey down from the cupboard. She poured a healthy shot into a glass, carried it back into the living room and gave it to him.

He looked at the glass for a moment as if he didn't recognize the contents. Then he drank some of the whiskey.

"Thanks," he said. "I needed that. Or something."

Grace sat beside him. Together they looked out at the night through the open lanai windows. She put her hand on his thigh and began a gentle massage. He hesitated, as though he didn't know how to react.

Then, without a word, he let her continue. After a while he drank some more whiskey.

"Fallon sounded strange tonight," he said.

"In what way?"

"I don't know. Different. Tired. Worried. Depressed, maybe. Or maybe just a little overwhelmed. Hard to explain. Never heard him quite like he was tonight. He's always been . . ."

"Fallon?"

"Yeah, that's it. Long as I've known him, he's always been Fallon. A force of nature, like a thunderstorm or a tsunami or a shark. But not tonight."

"J&J is all we've got to stop Nightshade, and Fallon Jones is in charge of J&J," she said. "That means the outcome of this battle is on his shoulders. He needs someone."

"Who?"

She thought about it. "Someone he can talk to. Someone he can trust. Most of all, someone who can take over a portion of the responsibility. An assistant, maybe."

Luther shook his head. "He'd never go for an assistant. He works alone. Like me."

"You didn't work the Maui case alone. I was there, too, remember? And I'm still around."

"Because I won't let you go off on your own as long as it looks like you need a bodyguard," he said. He drank some more whiskey.

"No," she said quietly. "I'm still here because I want to be here."

He contemplated the darkness. "Living in the moment?"

"That's all any of us really has, isn't it?"

"No," Luther said. "We've also got our pasts."

She sighed. "Yes, I suppose that's true."

Luther swallowed some more whiskey.

After a couple of minutes she tried again.

"I know what it's like," she said.

"Living in the moment?"

"No, killing someone with your aura. I've done it, too, remember?"

He looked at her over the rim of the glass. "For what it's worth, Fallon says that, technically speaking, we didn't actually kill anyone. We used our own energy to reflect the violent energy of our attackers. The process set up a dissonant wave pattern that shattered their auras. He said it was like they were killed by a ricochet from their own weapon."

She contemplated that for a long moment. "Interesting but I'm not sure it changes anything. The bottom line is that we are responsible for the deaths of those people, and no matter how bad they were or how much they deserved to die, you and I still have to live with it."

"Yes," he said. "We do."

"He was trying to kill you, Luther. You were fighting for your life."

"His aura winked out like that damn laser. Like someone had turned off a switch."

"I know what it's like to watch that happen, too. It's terrifying to realize that you have it within you to take a life without even using a weapon."

He gazed into what was left of the whiskey. "Makes you feel like there's something inside you that's not really human."

"Oh, we're human, all right," she said. "Humans have always been very good at killing. But we pay a heavy price when we use that talent. I don't think anyone is the same after they've gone down that path."

"I know you and I and Petra and Wayne have paid a price. What about guys like Sweetwater?"

"I expect that, in their own way, the members of the Sweetwater family pay, too," she said. "Maybe that's why they're such a tight-knit clan. They need each other to survive what they do for a living. One thing's for sure, I'll bet none of them has any real friends outside the family, not even when they were children. They can't afford to trust outsiders."

"Yeah, I guess you would have to keep the truth about what Daddy does for a living from your kids. Kids talk."

"And then, later, you'd have to teach them to lie to everyone. Finding a wife or a husband must be tough if you're a Sweetwater."

"Running that kind of family business would tend to limit your lifestyle," he said. "Hard to talk business with your golfing buddies, that's for sure."

"Nevertheless, I think it's different for people like you and me. Knowing that we can kill and in such a very personal way, with our auras, makes us feel . . ." She broke off, unable to find the right word.

"Uncivilized," Luther said.

"Yes, uncivilized," she agreed. "We don't like to think of ourselves that way. It violates our sense of who we are. But one of the things that defines us is that we are survivors. When push comes to shove, that's what we do. We survive or we go down fighting. I think we need to accept that part of ourselves, too."

He did not look away from the night but he put his hand over hers on his thigh. She threaded her fingers through his, stood and led him down the hall to the bedroom.

They made love first; hard, fast, a little violent, affirming what Grace had said earlier. They were both survivors.

HIS PHONE RANG, bringing him awake with an unpleasant jolt of adrenaline. His eyes opened to the sunlight outside the window. Going on ten o'clock, he decided. He grabbed the phone.

"Package got picked up a few minutes ago," Petra said. "We watched the plane take off for the mainland. Tell Grace the walk-in's clean. No need to worry about the health inspector."

"Thanks," Luther said.

"No problem. Like old times. How are you doing?"

"Okay."

"You did what you had to do. Get over it and have breakfast with Grace."

Luther closed the phone and looked at Grace.

"Petra says I should get over it and have breakfast with you."

She smiled. "Sounds like a plan."

Thirty-five

Grace scooped the tiny black seeds out of the papaya half and set the fruit on a plate.

Luther watched her while he made coffee, his expression bleak. He was still recovering from the trauma of what had happened in the garage, she thought. He needed time.

"This isn't the kind of place you're used to, is it?" he said.

Startled, she paused in the act of carrying the plates to the small kitchen table. "What?"

"This apartment." He angled his head to indicate the cramped kitchen-living area and the small bedroom beyond. "It's not exactly your style. I could tell that first day when we checked into the hotel suite on Maui. You didn't even blink."

She set the plates down very carefully, unsure of where the conversation was going.

"Should I have blinked?" she asked, wary.

"No, because you're accustomed to that kind of first-class travel."

"Ah," she said. She smiled.

"What the hell is that supposed to mean?"

"It means I now know where you're going with this conversation. Yes, I did spend more than a decade traveling first-class. Martin Crocker knew how to make money and he paid me well. But before I met Martin I was living in an apartment that was about this size and buying my clothes in thrift shops. My cottage in Eclipse Bay is not much bigger than this place."

He gave her a head-to-toe glance, silently underlining the fact that her shirt and trousers had not come from a thrift shop.

"J&J pays me a very good salary," she said drily. "I'm sure the agency pays you well, too."

He turned back to the coffeemaker. "I've had a lot of expenses in the past few years."

"I'm told that divorce is never cheap. Guess that's what you get for being such a romantic. Is that coffee ready?"

He glared at the coffeemaker. "Yes."

She finally lost her patience. "Let's get something straight. I've lived high and I've lived on the streets. Living high is definitely more comfortable but neither place felt like home. My cottage in Eclipse Bay hasn't ever felt like home, either. This apartment and the Dark Rainbow, they feel like home. Now why don't you follow Petra's advice? Get over it and pour us both a cup of coffee?"

He didn't move for a few seconds. He just stood there, looking at her. Then he smiled slightly. His eyes warmed. He picked up the pot.

"I can do that," he said.

She watched him fill two mugs. "And while you're doing it, why don't you tell me about your accident?"

He handed her one of the mugs. "I got shot on my last J&J case."

"Shot?" Horrified, she stared at him. "I thought you said it was an accident."

"It was." He picked up his own mug, grabbed his cane, hiked around the counter and sat down at the table. "Someone pulled the trigger of a gun. I happened to be standing in front of said gun. Wrong place, wrong time. Pretty much the working definition of an accident."

"Good grief."

"I got what you might call a split-second warning," he said around a mouthful of papaya. "Time enough to dodge, at any rate. The shooter was aiming for my back. Hit my thigh instead."

"What happened?" she demanded.

"It was a routine referral from J&J. One of the low-rent private jobs. The client told me she wanted me to protect her from her ex-husband. Claimed he was stalking her."

"Claimed?"

"She thought she could sucker me into killing him for her."

"What made her think she could convince you to do that?"

"She was a level-seven strat talent. You know strats. They think they can manipulate and outmaneuver anyone. They always figure they're the smartest person in the room."

"Well, they do tend to make good chess players," Grace said. "Didn't she know that aura talents are darn hard to manipulate because we can usually see it coming?"

"Like a lot of sensitives, she didn't think much of our kind of talent. Thought the only thing we could do was perceive a little radiation. She assumed that when we look at folks, all we see are human lightbulbs."

Grace made a face. "Typical."

"When she contacted J&J, she specified that she did not want to pay for a high-grade talent. In fact, she specifically asked for an aura."

"She didn't want to take any chances, is that it?"

"Right. She would have preferred to use a nonsensitive, a P.I. with no psychic ability at all, but she didn't have much choice. She had told everyone, including her family, that she was deathly afraid of her ex. They were all registered members of the Society and they all insisted she get a bodyguard from J&J. She had to make it look good."

"Bet she wasn't expecting a powerful aura talent."

"She didn't know how strong I was," Luther said. "But she wouldn't have cared. So long as I was an aura, she felt safe. Fallon was a tad suspicious."

"Fallon is always suspicious."

"True. I shared his suspicions but neither of us could figure out what to be suspicious about, and I needed the money."

"So you took the job."

"The client assumed that I was just so much dumb muscle on the hoof."

"Bless her heart."

"I regret to report that she was not too far off in her assumption," Luther said. "She damn near got me killed."

"How?"

"The ex wasn't stalking her. He didn't want anything to do with her. When it finally dawned on me that she wanted me to get rid of him, I informed her I wasn't in that line of work. Like I said, she was a strat. She realized immediately that I wasn't just walking away from the job. She knew I'd probably warn her ex."

"What happened?"

"She lost it." Luther took a bite of his scrambled eggs and swallowed. "Flew into a rage and started screaming that I had ruined everything. Told me the whole story. That's when I found out why she wanted her ex dead."

"Can I assume you tweaked her aura a tad to prod her into losing her temper and spilling her guts?"

He shrugged. "Figured by that time I had a right to know what she was up to. Turned out the reason that she wanted her ex dead was because she stood to inherit his share of the business they had founded together."

"That's when she shot you?"

"No. While she was screaming at me and I was concentrating on manipulating her aura, her lover walked out of the hallway behind me and shot me."

"There was a *lover* involved?"

"It was a complicated situation."

"How did you get your one-second warning?"

"I was facing away from the hall. But the client was looking straight at it while she yelled at me. When she saw her lover with the gun, I saw her aura spike. I knew something had changed in the situation. Cop instinct took over from there. Caught the bullet in my thigh. Before the lover could line up another shot, I put him to sleep."

Grace shuddered. "Close call. What happened to your client and her lover?"

"They're both sitting in prison at the moment. Probably be out on an early-release program. The family has a lot of money and more than one talented lawyer on the tree."

She nodded and ate the papaya very slowly, trying to make the moment last as long as possible. It was all so perfect, she thought. The sun-warmed room, the light, floral breeze off the lanai; Luther sitting there with her. Life didn't get any better than this. But such moments could not last forever. She knew that better than most. After a while she put down her spoon.

"We need to talk," she said.

"Oh, shit."

She frowned. "What now?"

"I hate conversations that start with 'We need to talk.'"

"Sorry." She sat a little straighter in the chair. "But this is important."

"Uh-huh." He picked up a slice of toast. "Okay, let's have it."

"Fallon Jones keeps saying that this situation, at least as far as you and I are concerned, is under control. But last night you were almost killed. Because of me."

He put the uneaten portion of toast on his plate. His eyes narrowed slightly. "Last night is over. If the situation wasn't under control before, it is now."

"I don't think so. Last night was a wake-up call for me. I don't care what Mr. Jones says, I saw the Siren's aura. My intuition tells me that she is obsessing over what happened on Maui. She's powerful and she's lethal and I don't want you or Petra and Wayne to get killed trying to protect me."

"Protecting people is what I do, remember? I'm a bodyguard."

"You proved that last night. I don't want you to take any more chances on my behalf."

"Let me worry about the chances I take."

"What about Petra and Wayne? They have nothing to do with this but she might target them to get to me. I don't want to be responsible for putting any of you in more danger."

"Planning to disappear again?"

She stiffened. "It worked well the last time."

"You've built a new life for yourself. You can't be serious about leaving it behind to fire up another one."

"I've always been able to handle my own problems. I'll deal with this."

"Not alone. Not this time. J&J got you into this mess. J&J has a responsibility to protect you. And since I'm the nearest J&J bodyguard on the scene, you've got me, whether you like it or not."

"Petra and Wayne don't work for J&J," she said, desperate now.

"Remember what you said about the Society being the closest thing you've got to a family?"

"What about it?"

"Petra and Wayne are my family. As long as you and I are together, they see you as family, too. You couldn't make them walk away from this if you tried." He grinned. "Besides, they'd be crushed if you refused their help."

"I'd rather have them crushed than dead because of me."

"Trust me, Petra and Wayne don't see it that way. They may be getting on in years, but they're warriors, Grace—warriors to the bone."

She tried and failed to blink back the tears. "I was afraid of this."

"What, exactly, were you afraid of?"

She wiped one cheek with the back of her hand. "I was afraid that I wouldn't have the courage to turn down your offer."

"It's not an offer," he said softly. "It's just the way things are. I couldn't let you walk away now, even if you tried."

"Luther—"

"Hush."

She felt herself grow unnaturally calm and serene.

"Stop that." She glowered. "I'll let you know if I want my aura manipulated."

The artificial serenity vanished.

He grinned. "I love it when you do that. Gets me hot."

She glowered harder. "How can you talk about sex at a time like this?"

"You're right. When it comes to sex, talking isn't nearly as much fun as doing."

He got to his feet, made his way around the table and hauled her up out of the chair. His mouth closed over hers before she could think of a good reason to stop him.

She tried to resist for all of two seconds. Then, with a sigh, she put her hands on his shoulders and kissed him back.

She sensed the passion unfurling between them. He kissed her until she shimmered with need, until she trembled with it; until she could no longer even think about getting on a plane, let alone starting a new life.

He captured her face between his hands.

"I won't let you disappear on me," he said. "If you try to leave, I will come after you. Never forget that. And I will find you."

She went very still, her fingers clenched around his shoulders. She could not identify the tangle of emotions cascading through her. Fear? Hope? Love?

"What makes you so certain that you could find me?" she asked.

It wasn't a challenge. It was a question, an urgent one. She needed an answer badly.

"Because you and I are linked," he said. "Don't try to tell me that you don't sense the bond between us."

He covered her mouth with his own again, not waiting for an answer. Her hands tightened on him. With a small, urgent little cry, she kissed him back, holding him captive, just as he held her.

Somehow they ended up on the ancient sofa. He eased her onto her back. In the short time they had been together, he had learned a lot about what made her hot in bed and he applied the knowledge ruthlessly. The energy of passion—light and dark—flared high.

But the bond worked both ways. She knew him now as well as he knew her and she was just as ruthless.

He drove himself deep inside her. Her senses flared, fusing with his in the moment of release. And then they both fell off the edge of the world.

Thirty-six

The monster did not come from under the bed, he came down the unlit hall. She heard him unlock the door that she had locked so carefully. Frozen with panic, she watched his terrifying aura as he moved stealthily into her room.

She had just turned fourteen. She had been in the foster care system for only a few months but her survival instincts were already razor sharp. She had gone to bed fully clothed every night because she sensed that sooner or later the husband would come to her room.

In the dense shadows she could not see him but his energy field blazed with the darkness of perverted lust. He came to stand beside the bed.

"Are you awake, sweetie?" he crooned. "I came to kiss you good night."

She did not answer. She did not move. She did not think she could move. Perhaps if she pretended to be asleep, the monster would go away.

He sat down on the edge of the bed and put one hand on her leg. She trembled, instinctively shrinking from him.

"So you are awake," he whispered. "I thought so. You're a sexy young lady. All grown up. I'll bet you've had a couple of boyfriends already, haven't you?" He drew his hand up her thigh. "But you probably haven't had a real man yet."

"Please, don't." Her throat was so tight she could hardly get the words out.

"I'm going to teach you how to please a man. By the time you've had some lessons from me, you'll be able to get any guy you want."

"No."

"Don't worry, with an ass like yours, you'll be a natural."

His hand moved up the blanket, over her hip, heading toward her breast. She saw the sick pulsations in his aura. She struggled to a sitting position.

"No," she said.

It should have come out as a scream but fear partially gagged her.

"Stop it," he ordered angrily. "Stop it right now. This is how it's going to be. You're going to learn that tonight. I'm going to make a woman out of you. Believe me, in the end you'll be grateful to me."

She wanted to run but he had her trapped against the headboard. She was shivering violently to the beat of her own pulse. She struggled but he was far too strong. He forced her back down onto the pillows and yanked aside the sheet and blanket.

"Wore your jeans to bed, I see." He chuckled. "You are a nervous little filly, aren't you? But we'll get you past that, don't you worry."

He started to unfasten her jeans.

She flattened her hands against his upper chest. Her palms touched his rough, hairy skin. She realized he was wearing the grimy tank-style shirt that he'd had on earlier.

"Go ahead and struggle," he said. "It'll make things more fun."

He tugged at her jeans.

"No," she repeated. Her voice was still half strangled.

She knew a terrible sense of helplessness. She had no chance against him physically. He was too big and too strong and too aroused. Frantic, she pushed back at him with her hands and with her fully jacked aura.

As though it had been triggered by the threat, her new, rapidly developing talent flared higher than it ever had before. She felt the leap and pulse and flash of the invisible energy. She could not see the fierce veil that surrounded her—she had learned early on that individuals could not view their own auras, not even aura readers—but power could always be sensed. The effects were immediate and devastating to her attacker.

He jerked wildly, as though he had touched a live electrical wire. The scream of rage and fear was trapped in his throat. Seconds later he collapsed on top of her, a dead weight.

Her hands burned.

"Grace."

Luther's voice, laced with solid, reassuring command, brought her out of the dream. She awoke with a start, shivering. He pulled her against him, comforting her with his body and a gentling hand.

"Sorry," she said.

"It's okay." He stroked the length of her spine. "I was tempted to calm your aura but the last time I tried that you didn't appreciate it."

"No." She hesitated. "I'd rather deal with the nightmares than feel that someone else is controlling me."

"Understood."

She huddled close. After a while she stopped trembling. Her breathing returned to normal. She exhaled slowly, sat up on the side of the bed and wrapped her arms around herself.

"In case you haven't figured it out by now, I'm pretty screwed up, Luther. Are you sure you want to get involved with me?"

"In case you haven't figured it out, we're already involved." He grabbed his cane and made his way around the foot of the bed to sit beside her. Close but not quite touching. "And you aren't the only one in this relationship who is a little screwed up. So what? How bad was the dream?"

"You don't want to know."

"Yes," he said, "I do."

He had a right to know, she thought.

"I told you that I was responsible for Martin Crocker's death," she said quietly. "But he wasn't the first."

Luther said nothing. He just waited.

"There was another man. When I was fourteen."

"While you were in the foster care system?"

"Yes." She unfolded her arms and looked at her hands. "He came to my room one night. Said he was going to make a woman out of me. His aura terrified me. I fought back instinctively with talent but I had only recently come into it. I didn't know what I could do, what I was capable of. I didn't have any control."

"You fought back and he died."

"He was leaning over me, touching me. I put my hands on his chest and *shoved.*"

"With your hands and the full energy of your aura."

"It was all instinct and panic on my part. I think he tried to scream but no sound came out. He just collapsed and died." She closed her hands into small fists. "It was as if I'd touched a red-hot stove. But there were no marks on my palms. The pain faded rapidly. The worst was over within forty-eight hours. But four days later I was in a fast-food restaurant getting a slice of pizza. The clerk accidentally dropped the plastic plate. We both reached for it. Our hands collided. The burning sensation came back. Not nearly as strong but it *hurt.* I was terrified. I thought I'd been somehow marked for life."

He took one of her hands in his. "That was the first time you got sensitized?"

She looked at his hand wrapped around hers, marveling anew at how good it felt to be able to touch and be touched.

"Yes," she said.

"What did you do?" he asked. "Afterward?"

She knew he wasn't talking about the pizza incident. "After the monster collapsed on my bed, I packed the few things I owned, took the money out of his wallet and I ran."

"Smart."

"I was afraid I'd be blamed for his death." She hesitated. "And, given that I actually was guilty, I didn't think it would be a good idea to hang around to try to explain things. In the end they called it a heart attack but the fact that I was missing along with the money didn't look good. I knew I had to stay gone. I could not have gone back into that house under any condition."

"That's when you hit the streets?"

"Yes. I told you, my talent kept me alive there. It let me know who to trust and who to avoid. You could say that I was endowed with the ultimate in street smarts. I slept in shelters for a while. Washed a lot of dishes. Made some connections. Eventually I built up a successful small business selling . . . things."

"But not yourself," he said, very sure.

"No. Even if I had been desperate enough to sell myself, it wasn't an option. It's hard enough for me to touch people I like. I can't even imagine trying to have sex with someone just for the money. I wouldn't be able to stand it." She made a face. "I probably would have freaked and wound up killing off my clients, which would not have been good for business."

"What did you sell?"

"Mostly I brokered fake IDs on the Internet. My mother was a high-level crypto talent, a computer wizard. I learned a lot about navigating the online universe from her before she died. I was very good at putting buyers and sellers together."

"You took a commission on the deals you set up?"

"Yes. It was actually a fairly lucrative line of work but it was also a tad risky. One day I decided to get a real job, something beyond dishwashing and selling fake IDs."

"Why?"

She raised a shoulder and let it fall. "Mostly because I wanted to see what it was like to feel normal. I should have known better. I don't think people like us ever get to feel normal."

"What kind of job did you get?"

"Believe it or not, I went to work in a flower shop." She smiled a little, thinking back. "I loved it, even if it didn't make me feel normal. After a while I was promoted to manager. That's where Martin found me. He came in to buy a dozen roses for one of his women. He recognized me immediately as a strong sensitive. He was a high-level strat and he understood right away that I could be very useful to him. He was managing a small casino at the time and he was having problems. He offered me a position on his security staff."

"What kind of problems was he having?"

"A ring of cheats had targeted the casino. They were bleeding it dry. Martin's boss began to suspect that he was the one responsible for the losses."

Luther gripped her hand more tightly. "What did Crocker have you do?"

"I profiled the players. Pointed out the members of the ring. One thing led to another. Eventually Martin was promoted to president of the company that owned the casino. We branched out from there."

"He used you."

She shook her head. "It was an equal partnership. In exchange for my help, Martin saw to it that I made a lot of money and got an education. He used to refer to himself as Pygmalion. After he founded Crocker World, I not only got a very, very good salary, I got stock in the company."

Luther whistled softly. "A slice of Crocker World, must have been worth a fortune at one time."

"It was. When I first noticed the effects of the drug in his aura, I thought about selling off my portfolio and tucking the money away in an offshore account, but I was afraid Martin would find out. Once he started taking the formula, he became extremely suspicious of everyone around him. I had to be careful. Then I found out about the arms dealing."

Luther's hand tightened around hers. "And the bastard tried to kill you."

"After Martin's body was found, the value of the company shares plummeted to almost nothing. They never recovered."

"It wouldn't have mattered if they had bounced back. You still couldn't have sold off your portfolio. The authorities would have noticed the activity in the dead butler's accounts."

"Yes. Turns out the Arcane Society pays well, though, and it doesn't cost a lot to live in Eclipse Bay. I'm doing fine."

"Still, you had to walk away from the empire that you and Crocker built."

"Toward the end the profits were tainted by the arms deals that Martin had arranged for Nightshade. Blood money." She shivered. "Even if it had been safe to do so, I couldn't have touched those shares. Not for anything. It sickened me to realize that, for a time, I was a part of that business."

He put an arm around her and pulled her close against his side.

"Not everyone would have seen it that way," he said. "Money is money. A lot of folks would tell you that the blood washes off very easily."

"They're wrong."

Thirty-seven

Daddy was dead.

Damaris huddled on the edge of the bed, trying to stop the drug-induced shivers while she fought the tears. She'd had him for such a short period of time, only a year, and now he was gone. It was almost impossible to believe. He had seemed so strong, so powerful, so invincible.

William Craigmore had been a wealthy man. His death had made news on the Internet and then in the morning papers. "Reclusive Financier Found Dead in Home." But she had known hours earlier that something had gone terribly wrong in Honolulu. She had lived on hope for a while, telling herself that the sense of doom was just another side effect of the drug. But when the first reports started appearing online, she was forced to face the truth. Daddy was dead.

The only thing she did not understand was why the body had turned up in his Los Angeles residence. She refused to believe he died from a heart attack. She knew he had gone to Honolulu because he called her once from there to let her know he was on the ground and to reassure her that everything was under control. That was the last time she had spoken with him. The next day his body was discovered at his home in L.A.

Impossible. Whatever had happened to Daddy happened in Honolulu. And that meant that J&J was responsible.

The phone warbled, making her flinch. She turned and picked it up off the bedside table.

"Hello, Vivien," she said quietly.

"I just heard the news." Vivien was furious. "Why didn't you tell me?"

"I just found out myself. I was going to call in a few minutes." She massaged her temples. "I needed a little time to get over the shock."

"What happened?" Vivien demanded.

"I don't know. The papers are calling it a heart attack but I don't believe it."

"I don't, either, not for a minute. They got to him, didn't they?"

"J&J? Yes, I think so. I don't know how. They must have figured out that he was Nightshade."

"Do you think they know about you and me?" Vivien sounded genuinely concerned for the first time.

"No, we're safe. Daddy was very careful to keep both of us a secret. Even if they did find out about us, there's not much they could do. J&J has no evidence that we were involved in anything illegal."

"This is all so awful," Vivien whispered. "So completely unfair. It isn't right."

Damaris was surprised and touched to hear the anguish in her sister's voice. Vivien had evidently harbored more feelings for Daddy than she had let on.

"I know," Damaris said. "We had him such a short time."

"It is so damn typical of the bastard."

"What?"

"Dying like this, before he found that aura talent for me. Honestly, if he wasn't dead, I'd be more than a little tempted to give him one of my private performances."

"Vivien—"

"Was it too much to ask? A name. That's all I wanted, just the name of the bitch. But no, Daddy had to get himself killed before he found her. One lousy name, that was the only thing I ever asked of him. The bastard wouldn't even give me that much."

Damaris sank back down on the bed. "He did find her, Vivien. He also found her bodyguard. That's why he went to Honolulu. He was going to fix things for us."

"Why didn't you tell me?" Vivien demanded.

"I didn't tell you because Daddy wanted to take care of her. I can give you the name but it won't do you any good. Now that Daddy's gone we've lost our access to the J&J files. It's just a name."

"Give it to me."

"Grace Renquist."

"You're sure?" Vivien's voice sparked with excitement.

"Yes, but, I don't see what you—"

"Thanks. Bye for now. Rehearsal time. You wouldn't believe what I'm having to put up with from the conductor here in Acacia Bay. He's an absolute nobody but he thinks he can give orders to La Sirène."

The phone went silent. Damaris sat looking at it for a long time. Daddy was dead and, for all intents and purposes, so was she. He had been her source for the drug and now she was cut off. The good news was that soon there would be no more of the dreadful injections. The bad news was that Daddy had warned her that if she stopped taking the drug, she would go insane and die. She had a little more than a three-week supply left. It was just a matter of time now. She wondered if Vivien would miss her.

Thirty-eight

Luther watched Grace come out of the sea, removing the mask and snorkel as she walked through the light surf. Water spilled down her shoulders, breasts and hips. Her hair was sleeked behind her ears.

She had picked up the little black bathing suit at one of the boutiques on Kalakaua that morning. He had thrown the snorkeling gear into the backseat of the Jeep and driven her to the secluded little cove that he thought of as his private slice of paradise.

Wayne and Petra had sent them off with a couple of sandwiches, some bottled water and instructions not to come back until the dinner service. A real date, he thought.

Grace dropped lightly onto the towel beside him under the umbrella, looking fresh and vibrant, utterly feminine and wet. Incredibly sexy.

She gave him a curious look when she reached for a bottle of chilled water.

"Something wrong?" she asked,

He realized that he was staring at her.

"Nothing's wrong," he said.

"What are you thinking about?"

"Sex."

"I hear men do that a lot."

"What about women?"

"We think about it, too," she said, "but it is possible that we have broader fantasy horizons."

"Yeah? What else shows up on your horizon?"

"Shoes come to mind."

They both looked at his bare feet.

"Shoes are sort of absent from my horizon," he admitted.

"It's okay." She patted his bare leg. "You have very nice feet. Big and strong."

"You like big, strong feet on a man?"

"To tell you the truth, I never paid much attention to male feet until quite recently." She smiled somewhat smugly and slipped on her sunglasses. "But now I find them utterly fascinating."

"Good to know."

She lounged back on her elbows. "You never told me why you quit your job with the police department."

He contemplated the frothy surf while he considered. He had known the question was coming. She had told him her story. She had a right to know his. More than that, he wanted her to know it. The exchange was part of the bond.

"I told you that my talent had its uses while I was on the force," he said.

"Yep, the way I see it, you must have been the great neutralizer in any kind of dangerous situation. One stroke of your aura and the bad guy drops his gun and goes to sleep. Cool."

"There were other things I could do with my talent."

She tipped her head a little to the side. "Such as?"

"Get confessions."

"Hmm. Confessions. Double cool."

"Without laying a finger on the perp," he said evenly. "I never touched your client, Counselor. Check out the videotape of the confession. Your guy couldn't wait to tell us how he beat the victim to a bloody pulp."

"How did that work for you?"

"Great. For a while. You'd be amazed how easy it is. Deep down a lot of them *wanted* to tell me how smart or how macho they were. Robbing a convenience store is an adrenaline rush. Breaking and entering a house is a thrill. Murder is the ultimate power trip. Perps want to impress the cops. Show them how tough they are. So, on some level, yes, a lot of them wanted to talk. I just gave that natural inclination a psychic shove in the right direction."

"I always assumed guilt was the motivating factor in a confession."

"Sometimes it is." He fished a bottle of water out of the cooler. "I can work with a bad conscience, too. With a few tweaks, a little nagging regret or anxiety about what your parents will think can become crushing guilt."

"All it takes is a little subtle manipulation and the suspects suddenly can't resist spilling their guts, is that it?"

"Get it on videotape, add a little hard evidence and you've usually got a case. No rubber hoses or misleading statements required."

She looked at him very steadily, her eyes unreadable behind the glasses. "You must have been a very good cop."

"I was," he said. He drank some of the crisp, cold water. "Very, very good."

"So you quit because you felt you had turned into some kind of psychic vigilante."

He had known she would understand. What surprised him was the sense of relief that descended on him.

"Something like that," he said. "It was never a fair fight. Statistically speaking, most of the perps I came in contact with were seriously messed up, the products of horrific parenting or no parenting at all. A lot of them had been abused as children. Many had some kind of mental illness. Nearly half the suspects I caught couldn't even read a newspaper, let alone hold down a decent job."

"You felt sorry for them?"

He smiled faintly. "I wouldn't go that far but the truth is, the majority of the people I helped send away didn't stand a chance against me. I could and did violate their right to due process without anyone else, including the suspect, knowing it."

"You didn't violate their rights in the legal sense."

"No, but I sure as hell did in a very real sense."

"You accomplished a lot of good, Luther. Putting bad people away. Getting justice for the victims. Those are important to a civilized society."

"That's what I told myself for several years. But I found out the hard way that the vigilante thing carries a load of bad karma."

"Your two broken marriages?"

"Among other things. I also managed to freak out so many partners that eventually no one wanted to work with me. I got a reputation for being a lone wolf. That's not good when you're a cop. You're supposed to be part of a team. I tended to make the people around me very uneasy."

She frowned. "Did the other detectives you worked with ever realize what you were doing?"

"They knew that I almost always got results but they didn't know how I got them. Hell, they didn't *want* to know. A few concluded that I was somehow hypnotizing the suspects. Turns out no one wants to work too closely with a guy who may be able to hypnotize you without you knowing it."

"I can see where that might be an issue," she said.

"I went through partners the way the Dark Rainbow goes through dishwashers. Some of the other guys had enough natural sensitivity of their own to wonder if there might be a paranormal explanation for my string of confessions. They didn't like that idea any better than the hypnosis theory."

"Because it made them question their own mental health?" she asked.

"Most successful cops have a fair amount of intuition when it comes to dealing with the kind of folks who lie, cheat and kill. They're usually happy to admit that they have good instincts."

"Aren't good instincts viewed as an asset in the police world?"

"Sure. But no cop wants to get slapped with the psychic tag. The woo-woo factor can kill a career real fast."

She studied him intently. "You just walked away from the job?"

"There was what I guess you could call a final straw. An incident. People died. I walked away after that."

"What happened?"

He watched the sunlight flash on the waters of the cove.

"There was a man," he said. "His name was George Olmstead. He walked into the office one day and said he'd just killed his business partner. Turned over the gun. It had his prints on it. He claimed he and the partner had quarreled over whether to sell the business. He said he was desperate for the money but the partner refused to go through with the deal."

"You didn't believe him?"

"He seemed calm enough but there was something spiking in his aura. I talked to him for a while. Pushed a little. It came out that he wasn't the one who had shot the partner. Olmstead was covering up for his daughter."

"She was involved with the partner?"

"They'd had an affair," he said. "She was twenty-five years old. She had been seeing a shrink since she was in high school and she was on medication. The partner belatedly started to realize that she was very unstable. He tried to end things. She went crazy and shot him."

"And then went running to her father?"

"Who told her that he would handle things. He wanted to protect her. He saw that as his job. He'd been doing it all her life. She was his only child. The mother had died years earlier."

She nodded. "Did he know about the relationship between his daughter and his partner?"

"Yes. He'd encouraged it because he thought marriage would give his daughter some emotional stability. After the murder, he was convinced that the whole thing was his fault so he was eager to take the blame."

"But his story fell apart."

"Because of me. When we arrested his daughter, he felt he had failed in his duty as a father. The daughter committed suicide in jail. Olmstead went home, stuck a gun in his mouth and pulled the trigger."

"Thereby proving that he was just as unstable as his daughter," Grace said quietly. "But you felt responsible."

"I was responsible. I should have called in the department shrinks and let them handle it. Instead, I went ahead and prodded the weak points on Olmstead's aura until I got my answers. Another case closed for the lone wolf."

"It was your job to get the truth," she said calmly.

"Sure. It was just too bad a couple of people committed suicide because I was so good at doing my job."

"Yes, it was too bad. But it was not your fault. One of those two people murdered a man and the other tried to cover up the crime. You were not responsible for their actions."

"Maybe not technically."

She brandished her half-empty bottle of water. "Hold it right there, Malone. You were not responsible technically or otherwise. You used your talent, a natural ability that is as much a part of you as your eyesight or your hearing or your sense of touch, to do your job and to bring some justice into the world."

"I told you, the bad guys were broken losers for the most part. I rolled over them like a train."

"Works for me," she shot back. "They were bad guys, remember? Just their bad luck they ran into someone who could see through their lies." She paused, lowering the water bottle. "But I do understand why you felt you had to quit the force."

"Yeah?"

"You're stuck with the instinct to protect and defend. It's part of who you are. But like I keep telling you, you're also a hopeless romantic. You want to go after what you consider fair game. Working for J&J gives you that satisfaction. You get to go up against bad guys who possess talents that are the equivalent of yours. You're doing your hunting on a level playing field now."

"I think of it more as a level jungle."

She smiled. "Good visual."

Thirty-nine

The following afternoon Luther suggested they close the restaurant for a couple of days. Petra and Wayne didn't have any issues with that decision.

"Could use a break," Wayne said. "Some of the tourist customers are startin' to irritate me. I think I'm losin' that aloha spirit."

"Same here," Petra said. "Been a long time since we took a vacation."

It was four o'clock, the lull after the lunch rush. They were all standing around in the Rainbow's kitchen. Grace looked at the three of them and felt a sudden, inexplicable urge come over her.

"I think I found something important in the classified J&J files today," she said. "It's a long story. What do you say we have dinner tonight and I'll tell you all about it. I'd like to get your thoughts before I contact Fallon Jones."

Petra grinned and clapped Luther on the shoulder. "Looks like you've got yourself a date."

"No," Grace said. "All of us. At Luther's place. I'm cooking. You know, like a family dinner."

. . .

SHE BORROWED THE COOKWARE she needed from the Rainbow's kitchen and hauled it back to the apartment in the Jeep. She made lasagna—a vegetarian version with feta cheese and spinach—and served it with a big bowl of Caesar salad and a loaf of warm, crusty bread.

Bruno the Wonder Dog's ferocious barking announced the arrival of Petra and Wayne. Luther opened the front door to let them in and handed around some bottles of beer.

They drank the beer and talked about unimportant things, saving the serious stuff until after dinner. The balmy night air was warm and comforting against Grace's skin. A faint breeze stirred the magnificent green canopy of the banyan tree.

When she brought out the large pan of lasagna, Luther, Petra and Wayne gazed at it as if it were the Holy Grail. She used a spatula to serve large slices.

"Can't remember the last time I had lasagna," Petra said reverently. "My mom used to make it when I was a kid."

They all looked at her.

"What?" she said.

"Hard to imagine you as a little kid," Luther said. "With an actual mom."

Petra used her fork to cut off a large bite of the lasagna. "Everyone has a mom."

"Where is she now?" Grace asked.

"She died when I was sixteen. Cancer."

"Forgive me," Grace said. "I shouldn't have pried."

"Don't worry about it. Been a long time. After she died I went to live with my dad and his second wife, but we didn't get along so good. He kicked me out when I was seventeen. Don't blame him. I'd have done the same. I was not in a good place. He said I was a bad influence on his other kids, the ones he and his new wife had."

"I had a mom, too," Wayne said around a mouthful of bread. "She didn't cook much, though. She was more into martinis and pills. Called 'em her little mood elevators. She used to hide the bottles around the house so my dad wouldn't find them."

"That had to be hard for you," Grace said. She reached for the salad tongs and told herself she would not ask any more questions.

"Dad knew about the pills and the booze," Wayne said. "He told me a few years later that was why he took off with his secretary when I was eleven."

"You're not supposed to call 'em secretaries anymore," Petra informed him with an air of authority. "They're administrative assistants or somethin'."

"I knew that," Wayne said.

She should definitely change the subject now, Grace thought, but she couldn't seem to stop herself from asking one more question.

"What happened to your mother, Wayne?"

"Pretty much what you'd expect." He shrugged. "A few months after Dad split, she took a lot of pills and made a really big pitcher of martinis. I found her dead on the sofa the next morning."

No one said a thing. Petra and Luther concentrated on the lasagna on their plates. They all knew one another's stories, she thought. And now she knew them, too. It was one of the ways they were linked together.

On impulse she set the tongs aside.

"I'm so sorry you had to be the one to find her," she said quietly.

"Like Petra said, it was a long time ago."

She realized all three had stopped eating. They were staring at Wayne's heavily tattooed forearm, which happened to be resting on the table next to her. She looked, too, and saw that her palm was resting on his warm, bare skin in a comforting gesture that partially covered a portion of a skull and crossbones.

"Why can I touch you?" she asked. Slowly she raised her hand and held it in front of her face. "Why can I touch all of you without pain? After that incident with the housekeeper, I should have been sensitive for at least a week or longer."

Petra's expression tightened in a knowing look. "When did you get burned the first time?"

Her first impulse was to say she didn't want to talk about the past. But they had shared their stories with her. They had a right to know; she *wanted* them to know.

"In a foster home," she said, automatically putting both hands out of sight under the table. "I was . . . attacked. When the bastard touched me I sort of . . . touched him back. He died."

Petra nodded, unperturbed. Wayne looked equally unconcerned. He forked up another bite of lasagna. Luther drank some beer and waited.

"How old were you when you did the guy in the foster home?" Petra asked.

"Fourteen," she said, wincing a little at the expression "did the guy."

"You would have been just coming into your talent," Petra said. "The Society shrinks believe that a traumatic event during that time can really screw up your senses, sometimes for life. My guess is the shock of the attack together with the psychic jolt you must have got when you whacked the SOB who tried to rape you left you with a real delicate sensitivity to touch."

Luther looked at Petra. "You talked to a Society psychologist?"

"Wayne and I both went for a while after we retired from the agency," Petra said. "We were having trouble sleeping and some other problems. The doc explained a lot of stuff to us."

"That's right," Wayne said. "She told us that, what with our dysfunctional childhoods and the kind of work we did for the agency, we both had a lot of issues. Said she couldn't cure us but she kept us from eating our own guns."

Petra turned back to Grace. "Thing is, what with having been a foster kid and then having a couple of little psychic incidents, you're probably a tad messed up, too."

Grace clamped her hands very tightly together in her lap. "Little psychic incidents? I *killed* two people with my aura."

"And I used a rifle," Wayne said. He ripped off another chunk of bread and reached for the butter knife. "Doesn't matter how you do it. Sooner or later, you're gonna have to pay for it in the psychic zone. Looks like, in your case, your sense of touch was permanently affected."

She stilled. "Then why is it I can touch Luther and you and Petra without having to brace myself?"

Petra smiled. Light glinted on the gold ring in her ear. "I'm no expert, but I'm thinking that's because you feel comfortable with us. You know us for what we are and we know you."

"Survivors," Luther said.

"Yeah, that's right." Wayne nodded. "One way or another, we're all survivors. We understand each other. When we're together, there's no need to hide. No need to pretend you're not damaged."

"No need to be afraid," Luther said, watching her.

The sudden rush of tears startled her. She blinked them back.

"Family," she said.

"Yeah," Petra said. "Family. Can I have another slice of lasagna?"

Grace gave her a misty smile.

"Yes," she said. "You may have as much as you want."

"Don't tell her that," Wayne said quickly. "She'll eat the rest of it. Luther and I haven't had seconds yet."

"Nobody likes a whiner," Petra said. "You know, maybe we should put lasagna on the menu at the Rainbow. Got a hunch the regulars would go for it. It's not fried, but it's not bad."

Forty

After dinner Petra and Wayne washed and dried the dishes. Grace put the clean things away in the cupboards while Luther made coffee. They took the mugs into the living room and sat down while Grace brought them up to date on her genealogical research.

"Mr. Jones granted me access to the confidential files," she said. "I found only one record of a singer J&J knew for certain had killed with her voice."

"Who?" Luther asked.

"Irene Bontifort. But it's safe to say that she was not the Siren who killed Eubanks."

"What makes you so sure?" Luther asked.

"Bontifort was a star back in the late eighteen hundreds. She's been dead for well over a century. In her time she was hugely famous. Right up there with Melba."

Petra's mug paused halfway to her mouth. "She was as famous as Melba toast?"

Grace laughed. "You could say that. Melba toast was actually named after another opera singer, Nellie Melba. So was the dessert peach Melba."

"Well, dang," Petra said. "Learn something new every day."

"Irene Bontifort was an absolute sensation," Grace continued. "She toured all the capitals of Europe."

Luther looked at her. "Did this Irene Bontifort die of natural causes?"

"Not exactly," Grace said. "She was one of J&J's early cases. That's why she caught my eye. According to the file, she was believed to have murdered at least one cover, another singer she thought had tried to upstage her."

"What's a cover?" Petra asked.

"An understudy," Wayne said.

"Show-off," Petra muttered.

"Covers are always ambitious, of course," Grace said. "Naturally they want to be stars, too. Evidently Bontifort thought one particular up-and-comer was a serious threat. The other singer died under mysterious circumstances but the death was ruled to be from natural causes. There were a couple of other suspicious deaths among Bontifort's circle of associates, too—a rival who was starting to gain fame, a critic and a lover."

"Bontifort had a lover?" Petra asked.

"Several of them," Grace said. "Divas are known for their big appetites, and we're not just talking about food here."

"Damn. I thought rock stars were the wild ones," Petra said.

Wayne rolled his eyes.

Grace glanced at her notes again. "It was the death of one of Bontifort's lovers that caught the attention of J&J. The victim was Lord Galsworthy, and he was a member of the Society. His death, like the others, was ruled to be of natural causes but his widow, Lady Galsworthy, asked J&J to look into the matter."

"Did J&J find any proof that Bontifort killed Galsworthy?" Luther asked.

"According to the file, the agency was satisfied beyond a shadow of a doubt that she was guilty," Grace said. "But they never came up with any hard proof that could be turned over to the police."

Petra was intrigued. "How did J&J stop her?"

"They didn't," Grace said. "Someone shot her before they could deal with her."

"Who whacked her?" Wayne asked, looking interested.

"Lady Galsworthy." Grace checked her notes again. "After J&J informed her that they had psychic evidence against Bontifort but no proof that would be admissible in court, she decided to take matters into her own hands. One night she waited in the bushes outside Bontifort's town house. When Bontifort got out of her carriage and started up her front steps, Lady Galsworthy emerged from the shrubbery and shot her twice at point-blank range. By all accounts of the incident, Bontifort was taken completely by surprise. She never had a chance to sing a single note."

"What happened to Lady Galsworthy?" Luther asked. "Was she arrested?"

"No. She went to the town house dressed from head to toe in mourning, including a hat with a heavy black veil. No one at the scene knew who she was. There was so much commotion after the shooting that she was able to escape. No arrest was ever made, although there was a long list of suspects. In the end the newspapers claimed that she was murdered by one of her rivals. The police went with that."

"What did J&J do?" Luther asked.

"The notes in the file are a little cryptic but it appears that J&J knew what had happened and took steps to ensure that Lady G.'s name did not appear on the suspect list."

"How the hell did J&J figure Bontifort killed the lover?" Petra asked.

Grace smiled. "Get this. The agent who tracked her down was completely deaf from birth but he was exquisitely sensitive to the psychic residue left by violence. He could literally read a crime scene. He was one of J&J's most effective agents."

Luther stretched out his legs. "Did he ever confront Bontifort?"

"Yes, as a matter of fact. Toward the end of the investigation, she became suspicious of him and tried to kill him with her voice. He wrote in his notes that he could see that she was singing at him and he could sense some dangerous energy pressing against his senses but that was all."

"So if you can't hear the sound, the music can't kill you," Luther said. "That's interesting. Maybe there was something to Odysseus's approach to dealing with the mythological Sirens. Wasn't he the one who had his sailors put beeswax in their ears?"

"Right." Grace looked up from the notebook. "And that's exactly what J&J concluded. The full force of a Siren's talent only works if the victim can actually hear the music."

"What was J&J planning to do with Bontifort if Lady G. hadn't come through with her pistol?"

"It seems that the Bontifort case was not the first time J&J was obliged to deal with a killer who was a high-grade talent and who, for one reason or another, could not be handed over to the police. The firm had a very special agent they called in to deal discreetly with such problems."

Luther raised his brows. "The Harry Sweetwater of his era?"

"How did you guess?" Grace said.

"Guess what?"

"The agent's name was Orville Sweetwater, Harry's many times great-grandfather."

Petra grinned. "Small world, the Arcane Society. Go on, why are you interested in this Bontifort woman?"

"A couple of reasons," Grace said. "First, she had a daughter by Lord Galsworthy. Which was probably why Lady Galsworthy got so pissed off, by the way, but that is not important now. Bontifort managed to keep her pregnancy and the birth a deep, dark secret, fearing that it would not be good for her public image. Even J&J didn't know about the baby at the time."

"What happened to the kid?" Petra asked, frowning.

"The infant wound up in an orphanage. When she became an adult she somehow discovered the truth about her parents. She blamed the Society for their deaths. She confronted the Master." Grace checked her notes again. "That would have been Gabriel Jones. In essence, she told him that the Society owed her, big-time."

"Probably didn't get far with that tactic," Petra said. "Can't see a Jones paying blackmail."

"As a matter of fact, Gabriel Jones thought she had a legitimate case. He told her that the organization had an obligation to take care of its own. He offered to register her with the Society. When she refused, he gave her a rather large sum of money. She took the cash and sailed for America."

"Any indication that the daughter inherited her mother's talent?" Luther asked.

Grace tapped her notebook. "She did not become an opera singer, but she did make her living singing in nightclubs and cabarets. She was very popular. The critics loved her, too."

Petra raised her brows. "Did they describe her voice as 'mesmerizing'?"

"As a matter of fact," Grace said, "they did."

"Any sign she used her talent for something other than singing?" Petra asked.

"It's not clear. She had a number of lovers and eventually married an extremely wealthy industrialist in San Francisco. But six months into the marriage, the industrialist dropped dead, apparently of natural causes. The singer inherited his entire fortune, much to the irritation of his family."

"I think we can assume he might have been given a strong shove into the grave," Luther said. "Any kids?"

"The widow never remarried but she had a daughter by one of her lovers. The girl grew up in the lap of luxury. She never went on the stage, presumably because she never had to work for a living. But she took music and singing lessons and frequently performed at private gatherings. Like her mother and grandmother, she never lacked for lovers."

"Anybody drop dead in her vicinity?" Luther asked.

"There were a couple of interesting incidents." Grace flipped a page in the notebook. "At one point she fell in love with a handsome film actor whose star was on the rise. She bankrolled a couple of his movies. But when he became famous, he dumped her in favor of a well-known actress. The actor turned up dead in his Hollywood mansion soon thereafter. The death was attributed to a drug overdose. The lady also had a daughter."

"And so it goes?" Petra said.

"And so it goes." Grace closed the notebook. "Right down to the present day. The trail gets a little murky in places but I think I've found our killer soprano. If I'm right, she's the descendant of Irene Bontifort. Her name is Vivien Ryan."

Wayne frowned. "La Sirène?"

They all looked at him.

"You never fail to amaze us," Luther said. "Who the hell is La Sirène?"

"She was a major star up until a couple of years ago," Wayne said. "I've got some of her CDs. Incredible voice. But she has sort of faded from the scene lately. Haven't heard much about her in a while."

"According to what I found online, she's trying to make a comeback," Grace said. "She's going to sing Queen of the Night at the opening of a new opera house in Acacia Bay, California. The premiere performance of *The Magic Flute* is two days from now. Oh, and there's one more thing."

"What?" Petra asked.

Grace clutched her notebook to her chest. "La Sirène just happens to be the title that was bestowed on Irene Bontifort."

"Anybody die of natural causes in the vicinity of this Vivien Ryan?" Luther asked.

"Oh my, yes," Grace said.

LUTHER GOT ON the phone to Fallon as soon as Grace had finished reporting the results of her research.

"I don't like it," Fallon complained. "It just doesn't fit into the pattern. Whoever killed Eubanks has to be a pro. Craigmore was smart. He wouldn't have risked so much by using a notoriously temperamental diva."

"Maybe he didn't have a choice after Sweetwater bailed on him," Luther said. "He had to move fast. There was no time to shop at Hit Men 'R' Us."

"Then how did he find the diva?" Fallon asked. He sounded not just impatient but supremely weary. "It's not like killer sopranos advertise in the yellow pages."

"We're still working on that angle," Luther admitted. "Look, there's one way to find out if La Sirène is the singer Grace saw in the hotel. All she needs is a good look at Vivien Ryan's aura. We need to attend the opening-night performance of that opera in Acacia Bay."

Fallon was silent for a time. Eventually he spoke. "I'm ninety-six percent sure it's a waste of time but I'll authorize the flight to California. Attend the performance. Let Grace get her look."

"There's just one small problem," Luther said.

"Now what?"

"The opera is sold out for every performance. We need tickets. Good seats. Grace has to be close enough to read Ryan's aura. We have to be sure of this."

"What? Now I'm a concierge?"

"Hell, you're better than any concierge. You're the head of J&J."

"Just remember, it's customary to tip the guy who can deliver seats to a sold-out performance."

Forty-one

The small, exclusive city of Acacia Bay was located on a picturesque stretch of the southern California coast, just north of Los Angeles. Determined to make a name for the city in the arts, its citizens had spared no expense on its new opera house. The arched and colonnaded entrance to Guthrie Hall gave the structure an air of architectural gravitas suitable for a theater devoted to *serious* music. The lobby glowed like the inside of a box full of velvet and jewels.

Grace stood with Luther on one side of the elegant room watching the opera patrons as they awaited the start of the performance.

"You were right," Luther said, studying a distinguished silver-haired man in formal attire. "An aloha shirt might have looked a little out of place here. Not sure the jacket and tie is enough. Should have brought my tux."

"You own a tux?" Grace asked.

"No."

"Didn't think so." She smiled. "Don't worry, these days you see everything from jeans to tuxedos at the opera, especially here on the West Coast."

"Mostly I'm seeing tuxes that don't look like they were rented. I'm also seeing a lot of fancy gowns and about a million bucks' worth of glittery stuff on the ladies."

"People dress up more for opening nights. We're fine. You said the important thing is that we don't stand out in the crowd. Trust me, no one will look twice at us."

That wasn't quite true. She had looked more than twice at Luther tonight. It was the first time she had seen him in anything other than casual island wear. She had been more than a little surprised when he produced a well-tailored jacket, crisp white shirt, tie and trousers from his duffel bag.

Back in Hawaii, dressed in a short-sleeved sport shirt, khakis and running shoes, he had looked like a homicide detective on vacation, albeit an injured homicide detective. Tonight, in the jacket and tie, he looked like an injured homicide detective going to the office. Clothes might make some men but they had no effect at all on the aura of power that radiated from him.

She had done some hasty shopping at the Ala Moana shopping center before catching the flight to the mainland. Luther had accompanied her, exhibiting remarkable patience while she conducted a series of surgical strikes on the various designer boutiques and high-end department stores. She had targeted the sales racks, unwilling to pay too much for an outfit she might never wear again. She was dressing for the mission, she reminded herself. But some part of her that she could not suppress insisted on finding a dress that would cause Luther to sit up and take notice, even if it meant exposing more of her sensitive skin than she would have liked.

Eventually she had emerged from the dressing room at Neiman Marcus wearing a sleek black number with a wide, ballet neckline and a slim skirt that ended just above her knees. In a bow to her ever unpredictable sense of touch, the dress had long sleeves.

The faint narrowing of Luther's eyes and the very satisfying spike in his aura told her she had discovered the right dress.

"Let's go find our seats," he said.

"I need to make a trip to the ladies' room first. I'll be right back."

Luther dutifully walked her to the swinging doors marked "Ladies." She zipped inside and came to a sudden halt. Awed, she gazed at the seemingly endless ranks of gleaming stall doors.

"Wow," she said to a well-dressed middle-aged woman at the nearest sink. "There must be fifty commodes in here."

"And more in the other restroom on the other side of the theater," the woman said with satisfaction. "I gather you're from out of town."

"Yes, but I've been to enough opera houses to know that there are never enough stalls in the ladies' rooms to take care of the demand during intermission."

"The mayor of Acacia Bay is a woman. She refused to throw her support behind Guthrie Hall unless the planners guaranteed that there would be enough restrooms for the female patrons."

"My kind of politician," Grace said fervently. "She has her priorities straight. Let's hope she runs for president."

She emerged from the restroom a short time later and joined Luther.

"You look awfully cheerful, considering the fact that we're here to ID a murderer," he said.

"I didn't have to cut off all liquids after three o'clock this afternoon, after all."

"What do you mean?"

"There were at least fifty stalls in the ladies' room. I counted. And there's another restroom on the other side of the theater."

"So?"

"So, it means that I won't have to get totally stressed out at intermission assuming we're here that long."

Luther frowned. "Are you okay?"

"Never mind, it's a woman thing."

"I'll take your word for it."

An usher directed them to their seats on the aisle twelve rows back from the stage. Luther was satisfied.

"Close enough to get a good look at her," he said.

Grace's stomach suddenly did an odd little flip. Her senses fluttered uneasily. Ever since Fallon Jones had authorized the trip to Acacia Bay, she and Luther had been consumed with preparations, the long commercial flight to L.A. and the drive up the coast. Now the reality of what she was about to do suddenly hit her like a splash of glacial melt. What if she was wrong? What if she was *right*?

"Don't worry about it," Luther said. "If she's not our hit lady, there's no harm done. Just another night at the opera."

"And if she is the woman I saw in Maui?"

"Then we report the info to Fallon. He'll take care of things from there. You and I will fly back to Honolulu tomorrow and have dinner with Petra and Wayne."

And then what? she wondered. She didn't live in Waikiki. She lived in Eclipse Bay, Oregon. Alone. *Don't think about it. Live in the moment.*

"This doesn't make any sense," Luther said.

Startled, she turned toward him. "What? I thought we just agreed—" She broke off when she realized he was reading the plot summary in the program. "Oh, the story line. No one ever said *The Magic Flute* made sense. But it's Mozart so operagoers don't quibble about little details like plot logic."

"I'll keep that in mind."

"The experts in the Society are certain Mozart was a sensitive, you know," she added.

"Yeah?"

"How else can you explain his preternatural musical talent?"

"Did he ever join the Society?"

She smiled. "I think he chose the Freemasons instead."

"Well, the good news is that La Sirène appears in the first act." Luther closed the program. "It won't be long before we'll have our answer."

The lights went down and the crowded room hushed. The overture began, showering the audience in glorious, sparkling energy. *Music had power.* Like some weird combination of a freezer and a microwave appliance, it could capture and preserve the brilliant energy of a long-dead composer, warm it up and serve it again and again to generation after generation.

The curtain rose on ancient Egypt. The story unfolded on an elaborate stage that incorporated all the latest and greatest technology. Grace knew that opera audiences expected over-the-top extravagance, not just from the singers but from the sets and costumes, as well. The Acacia Bay opera company had delivered.

It was the perfect setting for a killer coloratura soprano, and when the Queen of the Night took the stage it was all Grace could do to resist the urge to duck behind the seat in front of her.

The Queen's costume was an elaborate confection of tiered silks and velvets in luminous shades of sapphire blue. The gown was trimmed with gold and studded with glittering beads. The ornate black wig redefined the term "big hair." The glittering crown was cleverly woven into the tower of fake curls, producing an effect not unlike lights on a Christmas tree.

Everything about the Queen of the Night flashed and sparkled and glittered in an ominous, stage-dominating way. And all of that energy, including the incredible power of her dazzling voice, blazed just as violently in her terrifying aura.

The audience sat, transfixed, when the florid notes of "O zitt're nicht" flooded the house to the highest balcony. La Sirène did not just squeak out the impossibly high F, she sang it full voice.

Grace did not move so much as a finger. She almost stopped breathing, half expecting to hear the sound of shattered crystal. There was psychic power in the musical fireworks, not enough to kill, but more than enough to mesmerize the audience. Her skin prickled and burned. All her senses were shrieking that she was in the presence of a predator, a *crazy* predator.

She knew that she and Luther were safely hidden in the shadows; knew that the intense stage lighting made the audience largely invisible to the singers; knew that La Sirène had no reason to suspect that she was being hunted tonight. But the logic did little to satisfy her survival instincts. Death and madness walked the stage.

She did not attempt to whisper to Luther. For one thing she was fairly certain that the people around her would be extremely annoyed if anyone in the audience so much as coughed, let alone spoke to a companion.

Luther's right hand closed around her left. She realized then that she was shivering. He tightened his grip, letting her know that he had received the message loud and clear. She knew that he could no doubt detect the power of the Queen's aura, if not all the detailed lights and darks. He could probably see the crazy stuff, too.

He shifted a little and tugged lightly on her hand, indicating that he intended for them to leave. She tugged back, letting him know that they could not walk out while the Queen was onstage. There was too much risk that their departure would be noticed.

When the scene changed, they slipped out of their seats and made their way back up the aisle. Grace pretended not to notice the glares of disapproval. She breathed a sigh of relief when they reached the lobby.

"Tough crowd," Luther observed.

"Opera has a lot of audience protocols. Walking out in the middle of a performance is frowned upon."

"If those people knew what the Queen of the Night could do with her voice, they'd all be stampeding for the exits."

"I'm not so sure," she said, struggling to calm her breathing. "This is opera. People expect larger-than-life performers. Now what?"

"Now, as ever, we call Fallon."

They went outside, crossed the street and entered the discreetly landscaped parking garage. In spite of the fact that the Queen was still onstage and would be for some time, Grace found herself scanning every shadow with her senses. When they reached the rental car, Luther got behind the wheel and took out his phone.

Fallon answered on the first ring.

"Well?" he asked.

"Grace says it's her," Luther said. "No question."

"Damn." Shock reverberated in Fallon's voice. "Is she sure?"

"I know it's hard for you when things don't work out the way you anticipated," Luther said. "Get over it. We're the ones sitting here half a block from a woman who can kill us with a lullaby. What now?"

"Harry Sweetwater says he hasn't been able to turn up anything on anyone in his line who fits the description of the Siren."

"Probably because Grace was right all along. She isn't a professional hit woman. She's a professional opera singer."

"It just doesn't make any sense. Why the hell would she go all the way to Hawaii to kill Eubanks if she's not a pro?"

"Maybe Craigmore knew what she could do with her talent and was somehow able to convince her to take out Eubanks for him. Maybe he was her lover. Grace says she's had a long string of them. The bottom line is that she's a killer."

"There are just too damn many questions here," Fallon insisted. "A big piece of this puzzle is missing. We need to find the connection that brought Craigmore and an opera singer together. Your diva has a town house in San Francisco. I'll get someone inside as soon as possible."

Luther checked his watch. "La Sirène is going to be tied up onstage for quite a while. After that, Grace says she'll probably spend another hour backstage with her fans. Then she's scheduled to attend a private reception. Plenty of time for me to see if I can get into her suite at the hotel where she's staying."

Grace turned very suddenly, gripping the back of the seat with one hand, her eyes huge in the shadows.

"No," she whispered.

"Do it," Fallon said. He ended the connection.

Luther gave Grace a reassuring smile.

"Relax," he said. "What could possibly go wrong?"

Forty-two

Grace stalked back across the hotel room, arms twisted around her middle. She could not seem to stop shivering. Luther had dropped her off nearly twenty minutes earlier. Surely he was inside Vivien Ryan's suite by now. He was an ex-cop, she reminded herself. He knew what he was doing. Besides, the second act of *The Magic Flute* hadn't even concluded yet. Right now the Queen was probably onstage singing her shattering aria about making her own daughter kill her father.

There was plenty of time, Grace thought. Ryan would not leave the theater until she had received her awed fans in her dressing room. She was a diva in the truest sense of the word; she needed adulation the same way she needed oxygen. It was all there in her aura.

Grace reached the far wall, turned and started back across the room. Why couldn't she get rid of this terrible, creeping unease? All her senses were raw. Only deep breathing and the near-constant pacing were keeping the incipient panic attack at bay. It dawned on her that what she was experiencing was something quite new. She was used to looking out for herself. But now, for the first time since her mother had died, she was terrified because someone else was in danger.

As close as she had been to Martin Crocker, she had never known this kind of anxiety, not even when she realized he was sliding deeper under the spell of the drug. She and Martin had been friends and business associates. There had been affection between them but never love. In the end all she had felt for Martin was a sense of sadness and regret and betrayal. And then her razor-sharp survival reflexes had taken over, as they always did.

But with Luther, everything was different. His safety mattered more to her than her own.

I'm in love.

The realization brought her to an abrupt halt in front of the desk. She gazed down into the glowing screen.

I'm in love.

A strange sensation of release flashed through her. So this was what it was like to fall in love. It wasn't the passion she had experienced in Luther's arms. It wasn't the fact that they understood and accepted each other's talents and each other's pasts. What she felt for Luther encompassed all those things but there was something else, a bond that was truly, unmistakably psychic in nature; a connection that hovered just beyond the reach of mere words. Love was as close as she could come to a description but even it wasn't enough. She knew then that whatever fate might bring, she would carry Luther in her heart for the rest of her life.

No wonder they wrote operas based on over-the-top emotions like this, she thought, dazed. At the same time, there was an unnerving downside. She was now vulnerable in ways she had never known before.

It's not just about me anymore, she thought, and smiled a little.

"Okay, so I'm in love," she said to the illuminated screen. "That still doesn't explain why I'm standing here talking to a computer and having a panic attack."

Her phone rang, jarring her so badly she gasped aloud and jumped at least half a foot. Feeling like an absolute idiot, she hurried to her purse and fished out the device. Fallon Jones's code was displayed on the small screen.

"Mr. Jones," she said. "This is Grace."

"You okay? You sound breathless."

"It's nothing. I'm waiting for Luther to get back from searching Vivien Ryan's hotel suite. I'm a little anxious."

"Calm down. Luther knows what he's doing. I'm calling because the agent I sent to check out William Craigmore's house found a wall safe. One of our cryptos was able to open it. They found some interesting records inside. Craigmore was La Sirène's father."

Shocked, Grace sank down onto the bed. "Are you serious, sir?"

"Grace, you should know by now that I am always serious. There's more. Vivien Ryan has a half sister. Her name is Damaris Kemble."

"Is she a singer, too?"

"No. Evidently Damaris got a version of Craigmore's talent. She's a Crystal generator."

"Do you think she's involved in any of this?"

"We're looking into that angle now."

Grace shoved her fingers through her hair, trying to think. "There was no record of Vivien Ryan having a half sister in the genealogy files. I thought you told Luther that Craigmore couldn't father children."

"Turns out that when he was in his early twenties, before he went to work for that no-name government agency, he deposited his sperm at a clinic that was run exclusively for members of the Society."

Grace froze the way she had when La Sirène sang the high F.

"The Burnside Clinic?" she whispered.

"Right. Place burned to the ground years ago. All the records were destroyed. But I've got a hunch that Craigmore may have been responsible for that bit of arson because he had the files on his own offspring tucked away in his safe. Looks like he went in, grabbed the records he wanted and then burned down the clinic."

"Why would he do that?"

"I told you, the man spent decades working for a clandestine government agency. The business teaches you to be paranoid. He probably wanted to make sure there was no way one of his offspring could blow his cover."

"How . . . how many daughters did he have?" Grace whispered. She realized she was holding her breath.

"Two, Vivien and Damaris."

Grace squeezed her eyes shut, not knowing whether to be relieved or dismayed. "You're sure there were only two?"

"He was very clear about it in his notes. He was determined to track down all of his progeny and was disappointed to find only the two girls."

"I see."

"You're not his daughter, Grace." Fallon's voice was disconcertingly gentle. "Think about it. I'm sure you checked out your father's profile. Your mother put it into the genealogical records when she registered you. It's very different from Craigmore's. For starters, his eyes were brown. And he was a crystal generator, not a strat."

She felt like the *Titanic* shortly after it encountered the iceberg.

"You know that I came from the Burnside Clinic?" she managed.

"I'm trying to run an investigation agency here. I make it a point to know as much as possible about my agents. The future of the Society and maybe the whole damn world depends on me getting at least some of that kind of stuff right."

"But how did you discover that I was a Burnside Clinic baby?"

"Easy. Once I knew who you were before you became Grace Renquist, there was no problem finding out about the clinic. It was in the file under your first identity."

"Oh." She couldn't seem to process that. Slowly it dawned on her that if he knew about Burnside, he knew everything.

"Yeah, I know about you and Martin Crocker," Fallon said, as if he had read her mind, which was supposed to be impossible. "The SOB was running guns or drugs, wasn't he? Which was it?"

"Guns," she said weakly. "But—"

"You found out about the guns so he tried to kill you and you beat him to the punch. Thought that was how it went down. Good job, by the way."

She was vaguely horrified by his casual acceptance of what had happened that day in the Caribbean.

"I wasn't on a mission," she said. "I was just trying to save my own life."

"Works for me. But I really don't have time to reminisce. We've got a situation here." Fallon paused. "I can't believe I said that. I need to get more sleep. The point is we've got the connection between Craigmore and La Sirène."

"Craigmore's other daughter," Grace said quickly. "Damaris Kemble. What happened to her?"

"Trust me, we're looking for her real hard right now."

"Good." Another shiver flashed through Grace. She pushed aside all thoughts about Craigmore and the Burnside Clinic. Luther was in danger. She was sure of it. "I've got to go, Mr. Jones. I need to call Luther right now."

"Wait, you don't want to do that. He's on a job."

"I need to warn him to get out of Ryan's hotel suite immediately."

"Why?"

"I have no idea."

She ended the connection and punched in Luther's code.

There was no answer.

Forty-three

"This is a little inconvenient," the woman said. She held the laser steady on Luther's chest. "I had a slightly different plan in mind but since you've gone out of your way to come here tonight, I'm sure we can work something out. I hope you enjoyed my sister's performance. She's brilliant, isn't she? Crazy but brilliant."

"You're Ryan's sister?" Luther was weak and shaky but thus far he had been able to resist the worst of the laser's effects on his aura. The woman was evidently not as powerful as Craigmore had been.

"Damaris Kemble," she said. "Vivien and I are half sisters, sperm donor kids. William Craigmore was our father."

Damaris looked relatively composed on the outside but her aura was an unstable inferno. A variety of fierce emotions—rage, despair and fear—pulsed along the entire spectrum interspersed with the dark energy of the drug.

The laser device she held appeared to be identical to the one Craigmore had used on him in the garage. Thus far Damaris didn't seem to realize that he was employing his own talent to ward off the worst effects of the beam.

She had insisted that he drop the cane so he was propped against the corner of the desk. His hands were in the air, which also affected his already lousy balance. But aside from those precautions, Damaris did not seem unduly concerned. No one took aura talents seriously. Given how easily she had surprised him, maybe there was some justification for that lack of respect.

Damaris had not appeared overly astonished to find him in her sister's hotel suite. His reaction, on the other hand, aside from the obligatory *Oh, shit,* was a flash of adrenaline and anticipation. The missing pieces of the puzzle were falling into place at last. Now all he had to do was stay alive long enough to get the whole picture.

"You're some sort of Crystal talent, not a singer," he said.

"A generator, like my father," she said proudly. "When he found me he was thrilled to know that he had passed on his talent."

"When did he go looking for you?"

"A few years ago. He told me that he had taken the precaution of depositing sperm at the clinic because he knew there was a strong possibility that he might not survive his work as a spy. He said that, just in case, he wanted to leave a genetic inheritance. Turned out he survived the spook business but the enhancing drugs his handlers gave him had some major side effects. One of them was sterility. For years, he refused to believe it. He married three times before he finally gave up and came looking for me and my sister."

Luther looked at her in disbelief. "The government agency he worked for had a version of the founder's formula?"

"It operated a lab that was run by a scientist named Hulsey, a descendant of Basil Hulsey. Does that ring any bells?"

"Sure. Basil Hulsey is a legend within J&J and not in a good way. He created a lot of trouble back in the late eighteen hundreds. Classic mad scientist."

"His descendant managed to re-create the old formula for the agency." Her mouth twisted. "But the good doctor never quite got the bugs out."

"No one ever does," Luther said. "But that never seems to stop folks from trying."

"When the agency suddenly shut down the black hole operation, Daddy's supply of the drug was cut off. He had stockpiled some of the drug but he knew that he was going to die within the month if he didn't act. His handlers expected him to go insane and take his own life."

"Thus neatly cleaning up all traces of the government's little psychic experiment."

"Exactly," Damaris said bitterly.

"What happened? How did your father survive?"

"His handlers gave him one last assignment. They wanted him to get rid of Dr. Hulsey. But by then Daddy had his suspicions about the drug. He and Hulsey had a conversation. Hulsey explained exactly what was going to happen once the last of the drug was used. Daddy agreed to let him live as long as Hulsey continued to brew the drug for him."

"Sounds like a win-win for both of them."

"The only thing Dr. Hulsey cared about was being able to continue with his experiments. All he wanted and needed was a lab. He and Daddy made a deal."

Comprehension struck with the force of an explosion.

"I'll be damned. You father wasn't just a member of Nightshade, he founded it, didn't he?"

"Yes." Pride and rage flashed across Damaris's face and aura. "For years he hoped that the Council would come to see the true value and potential of the drug. He was convinced that eventually the Society would authorize research on it."

"What the hell for?"

"He had a vision of what the Arcane community could have been. An organization of elite, powerful sensitives capable of controlling governments, corporations and scientific endeavors of all kinds."

"But that never happened and it's not going to happen."

"No," she said wearily. "The only reason my father established the organization you call Nightshade was because he was finally forced to acknowledge that the Council would never permit its scientists to work on the formula, at least not in his lifetime. He was determined to build what the community refused to create. He wanted to leave a lasting legacy. Now he's dead because of you. Tell me what happened in Hawaii."

"No wonder Nightshade got such a head start on J&J. As a trusted member of the Council, Craigmore had access to all of the Society's secrets from the start."

Anguished fury leaped in Damaris's eyes. *"Tell me about Hawaii."*

He was sweating now. Cold chills alternated with spikes of fever. Nevertheless, he used some of the energy that was holding the effects of the beam at bay to calm Damaris's aura. She blinked a couple of times and then grew more composed.

"First tell me why your father wanted Eubanks taken out," Luther said.

"Eubanks had become very ambitious and very dangerous. He had developed a new, capsule version of the drug in his lab. He was using that, along with his own enhanced strat talent, to demand a place on the board of directors."

"Craigmore didn't want him on the board?"

"No. My father didn't trust him. Eubanks didn't know who Daddy was, of course. Only the members of the board are aware of the identity of the CEO of the organization. The others at the top thought Eubanks had proven himself worthy. They were getting set to vote him into the highest circle of power."

"Your father didn't want that to happen."

"He wanted Eubanks taken out but he wanted it done in a way that could not be traced back to him."

She fell silent. He could have sworn that she was shivering.

"You tried using Sweetwater to remove Eubanks," he said, coaxing her to start talking again.

"It was Daddy's idea to use Sweetwater," she said, sounding dispirited now. "Worst-case scenario was that the board would suspect J&J. Either way no one would think that the head of Nightshade had anything to do with it. But something went wrong. Sweetwater called off the operation."

"So you turned to your sister."

"We didn't have any time to set up something more elaborate. Eubanks had to die on Maui. The board of directors intended to vote on whether or not to give him a seat the following week."

"So you decided to keep it in the family. Well, your sister was certainly successful."

Damaris tensed. "She's had a good deal of experience. Daddy said she's a natural. He thought all she needed was direction."

"A target."

"I don't think Daddy ever really understood Vivien. My sister is nothing if not self-absorbed. Until Eubanks, the only people she had killed were those she thought were standing in her way professionally. But yes, she does seem to have an instinct for the business. Probably a side effect of her talent. After all, what's the point of having the ability to kill with the power of your voice if you don't have the inclination to do it once in a while?"

"No offense, but your logic is a little weak. Anyone can commit murder with a gun. But not everyone has the *inclination* to do it. Your sister's talent is freakish but evolutionarily speaking, it was probably designed to be a psychic self-defense mechanism."

Damaris's smile held no humor. "You don't know my sister very well, do you? In her mind she does use her Siren talent for self-defense. It's not her fault that the people she finds threatening happen to be rivals, critics and irritating managers."

"So why did she agree to do Eubanks? As a favor to Craigmore?"

"No. She and Daddy never bonded. They were never close. Vivien did it for me. I'm the one person in the world La Sirène cares about, aside from herself, of course."

"Hell of a favor, killing someone for you."

Damaris shifted uneasily. Her focus weakened. Luther grabbed a deep breath and jacked his senses a little higher.

"It wasn't like Eubanks was an innocent victim," Damaris said, oddly defensive. "Daddy told me that he murdered two wives for their inheritances and another young woman with whom he was having an affair. Evidently she found out about Eubanks's Nightshade connection."

"Did Craigmore know that J&J was watching Eubanks?"

"No, not until after my sister was seen in that hotel room on Maui. He concluded that Vivien encountering a woman who could even partially resist her singing was too much of a coincidence. He checked the J&J files and discovered that the agency was investigating Eubanks."

"That must have worried him."

"Why? It was clear that J&J was only interested in Eubanks because of the murder of the young woman. The agency didn't know that Eubanks was Nightshade. He was concerned, however, that if J&J pursued the investigation too deeply, they might uncover the link to Nightshade. It was just another reason Eubanks had to go, as far as he was concerned."

The ice-and-fire sensation was still sending chills through him but Luther relaxed a little. Fallon and Zack Jones had pulled it off. Craigmore had gone into that parking garage thinking that his only problem was Eubanks's ambitious nature. He never realized that Eubanks and four members of Nightshade's upper management had been identified. Score one for J&J.

"Craigmore came after me because he knew he had to get through me to get to Grace," he said. "He was afraid Grace would be able to identify La Sirène."

"Yes." Damaris's hand tightened on the laser. "He said we had to get rid of the aura talent who saw Vivien. He decided to take care of that problem himself. But you murdered him, didn't you? *How did you do it?* He was powerful."

"Everybody screws up occasionally. Take me, for example."

"Daddy wasn't a screwup," she shot back, very fierce now. "He survived for years in a dangerous job and again in the very heart of the Arcane Society. He was on the *Council.* No one even suspected him."

"Well, actually, that's not entirely true. Shortly after he became the new Master, Zack Jones sensed that he had a problem high up within the Society. He started taking precautions immediately."

She looked shaken. "He didn't suspect Daddy. He couldn't have. My father was too smart."

"Craigmore was good and he'd had plenty of time to cover his tracks before Zack took over. But Zack and Fallon were keeping an eye on everyone on the Council. It wouldn't have taken them much longer to figure out that your father was the traitor."

"He wasn't a traitor, damn you. He did what he had to do in order to survive. He would have died without a steady supply of the drug. He knew he would never be able to persuade the Council to brew it for him."

"But he didn't just make enough of the formula to keep himself alive, did he?" Luther said softly. "He founded Nightshade. He saw a path to power and he took it."

"Shut up. You killed my father and you're going to pay for that. But first I want to know how you did it. I have to know."

He spiked up his talent again and took another look at her aura.

Damaris was still running hot, energy bleeding back and forth across the spectrum. The erratic panic was getting stronger. So were the dark pulses.

"How long have you been taking the drug?" he asked quietly.

That caught her off guard. She went very still. Then the laser in her hand started to tremble. Luther felt some of the pressure go out of the beam.

"You can tell?" she whispered.

"Aura reading isn't considered a high-end talent, but occasionally it has its uses."

"Daddy didn't want me to start taking the formula. He said there were side effects. But I insisted. I was only a level seven. I wanted to be his true heir in every way."

"Craigmore was right about the side effects. The chief one being that withdrawal's a bitch. You stop taking the drug and then you die. How much do you have left?"

She seemed to pull in on herself. For the first time the panic and despair in her aura manifested itself on her face.

"Enough for the next three weeks," she said flatly. "The liquid version of the formula won't keep any longer than a month, even under ideal conditions. That's why Eubanks's capsule version was so important."

"Why aren't you at the theater watching your sister's performance?"

"I wanted to go," she whispered. "But I'm not feeling very good. I think I'm allergic to the formula." Her mouth twisted. "Maybe it will kill me before I run out of it."

"Maybe we can do a deal," Luther said.

"No deals. In three weeks at the very most, I'll be dead. You have nothing to offer me. I came here to say farewell to my sister."

"How about a chance at a normal life span? That interest you?"

"Are you talking about the antidote? Daddy said the Society labs were working on one but it hasn't been perfected yet. Even if it does work, there's no way the Council would give it to me."

"It's not the Council's decision. Zack Jones could authorize it and he would if Fallon Jones recommended it. I've got to tell you that at this point it's highly experimental, however. There are a lot of unknowns. But it's not like you have a lot to lose, is it?"

Damaris stared at him, hardly daring to hope. "Why would Zack Jones allow me to try the antidote?"

The beam was very weak now. Damaris was focused almost entirely on the possibility that she might survive, after all. Luther stopped shaking and started to breathe evenly again.

He revved up his senses to the max and sent a suppressing tide of energy at Damaris's aura. The laser fell to the floor at her feet. She did not notice because she was fighting to keep her eyes open.

He grabbed his cane and went toward her. "The Master will give you the antidote because you have something the Society wants very badly."

"What?"

"Inside information about the highest levels of Nightshade. Now that your father is dead, you don't owe the organization a damn thing. What do you say? Do we have a deal?"

"It would be stupid to say no," Damaris whispered, hugging herself.

He asked her a few more questions. When he was finished he eased more suppressing energy across her aura. She closed her eyes and went to sleep.

It would be stupid not to tie her up while she was out, Luther decided. Once a cop, always a cop.

He secured her wrists and ankles using his belt and the tie he had worn to the opera. Then he took out his phone and called Fallon Jones.

"Craigmore was the *founder* of Nightshade?" Fallon sounded truly stunned, a rare state for him. "Damaris is his daughter. Hell, yes, she can have the antidote if she's willing to talk."

"Figured as much. First things first. You need to send someone to Acacia Bay to pick up Miss Kemble. She's unconscious at the moment. She told me her sister has no way of knowing that Grace is in town so we're okay on that front for now."

"I'll get someone out from the L.A. office as soon as possible to bring Kemble in to the lab. Probably take an hour or more to get anyone on the scene, though, depending on traffic. Keep an eye on her until then."

"She said her sister probably won't come back to the room until morning but there's no way to be certain of that."

"Listen up, Malone. I do not want you having a confrontation with Vivien Ryan unless there's no alternative. We pay Sweetwater to handle problems like that. Get the Kemble woman out of there."

"Fine. But I can't exactly walk out through the hotel lobby with an unconscious woman over my shoulder."

"Got any other ideas?"

"How about getting me another room here in the hotel? I'll check in and then come back here, collect Kemble and move her."

"Move her how? You're on a cane, remember?"

"Trust me, it's not something you forget. I'll use a laundry cart."

"Good idea," Fallon said. "How'd you think of it?"

"Just came to me."

"I don't want Kemble left alone for a minute. She's too valuable."

"Don't worry, she's not going anywhere. Call downstairs to the front desk and get me a room on a different floor."

"I wish to hell you'd stop treating me as if I was your personal concierge."

"One more thing," Luther said. "If the Siren does happen to come back here tonight, she'll realize that something has happened to Damaris."

"Let her worry about it."

"What if she disappears?"

"Give me a break. She's a diva. Probably incapable of going into hiding for longer than ten minutes. We'll find her."

"Right. From now on, she's your problem."

Moving fast, Luther managed to cut the connection before Fallon could do it.

Forty-four

Damn the Renquist woman. Once again she threatened to ruin everything. How dare she show up in Acacia Bay tonight of all nights?

La Sirène glared at Newlin Guthrie in the dressing room mirror. "Are you sure she's here?"

"Yes, my love, and the bodyguard, too." Newlin spread his hands wide, half appeasing, half in supplication. "I had no trouble getting into the J&J files. Two tickets were purchased by the agency in the name of Mr. and Mrs. Kerney last night. Honolulu to L.A. Kerney is the name Miss Renquist and Malone are using for a cover. I'm sorry, my love, but I think we have to assume the worst."

"It is all so unfair. I don't deserve this. I was brilliant tonight."

The trip to Maui had turned out to be very good for the Voice. Using her power to its full extent on Eubanks had reinvigorated her talent in the most amazing way. She should have realized long ago that the Voice needed to be properly exercised to its maximum strength quite frequently in order to keep it in top form.

"You were flawless, my love," Newlin said. "You are, after all, La Sirène. They adored you almost as much as I do."

She'd received a standing ovation; she'd taken bow after bow, all the while feeling as though she really were the Queen of the Night. Afterward, Newlin and the stage door guard had been forced to shoo the last of a seemingly endless string of admirers from her dressing room. As she had hoped, the important critics from L.A. and one from San Francisco had attended. Her new manager had called during intermission, ecstatic. He had assured her that the publicist had booked back-to-back interviews with the press for the following day.

Everything had been perfect and now this. She had intended to deal with the Renquist creature after she finished her engagement in Acacia Bay. She was an artist. She was not supposed to have to tolerate distractions of this sort.

She took another swipe at the heavy makeup with a tissue, wave after wave of rage crashing through her. She wanted to scream. But that was not good for the Voice.

She crushed the tissue and tossed it aside. Her fingers closed around the hairbrush. Before she could even think about it, she had hurled the brush straight into the mirror. The wooden handle struck the glass and bounced off without leaving so much as a chip. She grabbed a bottle of makeup and threw it at the same target. This time there was a sharp splintering sound. A very satisfying crack appeared.

Newlin winced and took a step back, looking more uneasy than ever. What a wimp. It was all too much. Callas had Onassis for a lover, a worldly shipping magnate, one of the legendary tycoons of the last century. What did La Sirène have to work with? Not a rich Greek but a rich *geek.* It was not right. This was not her true destiny.

She had to admit, however, that, in addition to his adoration and his billions, Newlin had one immensely useful attribute. He knew his way around cyberspace. After Craigmore had turned up dead, Damaris had been unable to monitor J&J and thus lost track of Grace Renquist. But dear Newlin had hacked into the agency's confidential, highly encrypted database with ease. It was not terribly surprising since his company had designed the software.

She pulled herself together with sheer willpower and forced herself to think.

"We've been through this. You know why she's here." She turned around on the stool and looked straight at Newlin. "She is stalking me."

"Dearest, are you absolutely certain of that?"

She leaped to her feet, tightened the tie of her dressing gown and began to pace the lush room. "I told you, Grace Renquist has been haunting me for weeks."

The stalking scenario had started out as a minor fib intended to explain the situation to Newlin. But somewhere along the line it had become a reality. There was no doubt in her mind that Renquist, driven by jealousy, was stalking her.

"Perhaps it's time to call in the police," Newlin suggested.

"The police are useless in situations like this. Believe me, I know. This is not the first time I've had to deal with this kind of thing."

"Then at least allow me to hire around-the-clock security to protect you."

She was pushing too hard. The last thing she wanted was a security detail.

"I told you, that would only cause rumors and scandal," she said quickly. "I can't afford that, not at this delicate point in my career."

That certainly ranked as one of the most outrageous lies of the twenty-first century. Generally speaking, there was nothing like a juicy scandal to perk up a career in the world of opera.

Newlin was almost wringing his hands now. "But your safety is paramount. I can afford the best in security. They'll be very discreet, I swear."

She waved that away. "No, no, now that I think about it, you may be right. I do have to consider the possibility that Renquist is simply a devoted fan who admires my art so much that she flew in from Hawaii to catch my performance tonight," she said soothingly.

Fat chance. There was only one reason Renquist was in Acacia Bay. She was pursuing her. While it was deeply gratifying to know that the woman comprehended La Sirène's power, she simply could not be allowed to live.

She stopped at the wardrobe and spun around to face Newlin. The practiced motion sent the skirt of her blue satin dressing gown sweeping out in a dramatic fashion.

"I have an idea," she said, "but I will need your help, my love."

"Of course, my dear. Anything."

"I can see only one course of action." She eased compelling energy into her voice. The result was a delicate, melodic singsong effect. There was some natural power in her speaking voice but the full strength of her talent could only be accessed when she moved into the higher ranges. "I must meet with Grace Renquist face-to-face, woman-to-woman. If I talk to her, perhaps I can find out the basis for her obsession with me."

Newlin glowed with admiration. "That's a wonderful idea."

"I'll record the conversation." The words came out in a light, lilting, sparkling pulse of energy. "With luck I'll be able to find out whether she's a fan or a dangerous person. If she is a stalker, I'll have proof that I can take to the police."

"Brilliant, my love, absolutely brilliant."

He was already helplessly enthralled. She could see the longing in his eyes.

She began to thread more energy into each word. The Voice took on strength, resonance and raw power.

"You must bring her to me," she sang.

Newlin's dark brows crinkled together over the rims of his glasses. For an instant his own considerable intelligence rose to the surface.

"Wouldn't it be simpler if you just called her at her hotel in the morning?" he said plaintively. "I'm sure Miss Renquist would probably be thrilled at the chance to meet you in person."

She was suddenly and completely Verdi's Lady Macbeth, faced with the maddening challenge of trying to urge her lover to overcome his foolish scruples. She launched into the sleepwalking aria, energy soaring through her.

. . . You tremble?

. . . Shame

Toward the end she sailed on the wings of the high D-flat. Even Callas, La Divina herself, had found it difficult to hold on to that exposed note. But it was nothing for La Sirène, nothing at all.

Newlin was transfixed.

"I would do anything for you," he whispered. "Anything."

No doubt about it, she still had the Voice.

Forty-five

Luther swiped one of the laundry carts from the housekeeping closet down the hall and stuffed the still sleeping Damaris into it. When he had her safely locked away in another room on a different floor, he took out his phone and punched in Grace's number.

She answered halfway through the first ring.

"Luther? Are you okay? I've been worried sick. I had that terrible feeling again, the same one I had the night you ran into Craigmore in the garage. I tried to call you but your cell was off. Then the sensation just sort of evaporated."

A sense of deep satisfaction warmed him. Bonded for sure. It felt good.

"It's a long story," he said, "but yeah, I'm okay."

"I just had a call from Fallon Jones. He said they found some files in Craigmore's safe indicating that Vivien Ryan is his daughter. He was a sperm donor years ago. What's more, there's another daughter around somewhere."

"Her name is Damaris. We just met."

"*What?*"

"She's going to be the first person to enter the Society's version of a witness protection program."

There was a brief silence on the other end.

"You've been busy," Grace said.

"And the night is only going to get busier. Don't take this the wrong way, but it looks like I'll be spending the next hour or so in a hotel room with a blonde."

"Okay, that's going to take some explaining."

He gave her a quick rundown of events, deliberately finessing the confrontation over the laser. Unfortunately, Grace could read between the lines.

"She tried to kill you."

"She's on the drug, Grace," he said quietly. "Her supply was cut off when her father died."

Grace sighed. "She's dying."

"Her only hope is the antidote. She's willing to talk to J&J and Zack Jones and anyone else in order to get it. She's not a complete sociopath like her sister. Her spectrum is complete. This was all about trying to please Daddy."

"William Craigmore."

"Turns out he wasn't just a traitor to the Society. He was the founder of Nightshade."

"Well, that's going to be a little awkward to explain at the Society's next general meeting."

"I think so, yes. Fortunately, we don't have to worry about the politics of the situation. Start packing. I'll come back to the hotel as soon as someone arrives to collect Damaris."

"We're checking out tonight?"

"I'm going to take you to L.A. I don't want you in the same town as Vivien Ryan any longer than necessary. We've got some time, though. According to Damaris, Ryan doesn't know we're here. She also said La

Sirène probably won't return to her hotel room until very late tonight if at all."

"Because of the reception we read about in the newspapers?"

"Right. It's being thrown by her current lover, Newlin Guthrie."

"As in Guthrie Hall, the new opera house?"

"As in. Guthrie made his fortune in software and high-tech gadgets. He owns half the town."

Forty-six

It was going to be a long night. Now that she was no longer worried about Luther's safety, Grace became aware of the combined effects of the long flight from Hawaii and the adrenaline rush following the identification of La Sirène's aura.

She started a pot of coffee in the little machine that sat on the granite counter and went into the bathroom to take a reviving shower. She was not looking forward to the drive back to L.A.

The sense of throat-tightening urgency hit her a short time later when she turned off the water. For no discernible reason, all her senses were suddenly revved sky-high. Intuition worked that way.

She grabbed the white spa robe that had been thoughtfully provided by the hotel and opened the door to the bathroom.

There was a man dressed in a tuxedo in the bedroom. He held an odd-looking box in one hand.

"My apologies, Miss Renquist," he said. "But I really have no choice."

"Who are you?" she managed.

"Newlin Guthrie." He glanced at the strange device. "This is my latest invention. It's going to be huge in the security market. Similar to a

Taser except you won't feel a thing after the first jolt. Puts you out like a light for a couple of hours but with no lasting side effects."

She couldn't believe it. He sounded genuinely apologetic. There was nowhere to run so she launched herself at him, hands outstretched, mouth open on a scream for help.

The twin probes of the electroshock gun struck her before she was halfway across the room. Pain scorched her nerves and her senses for what seemed like an eternity.

Then she plunged into darkness.

Forty-seven

Notes of pure, crystalline energy drew her up out of the depths of an unnatural darkness. Madness and death pulsed and flashed in the music. The power of the singing dazzled and riveted Grace's disoriented senses.

She realized in a rather vague way that she was sprawled on her side on a carpet. Beneath the carpet she could feel an unyielding concrete floor. Panic splashed through her, briefly pushing back the nearly overwhelming energy of the singing.

She opened her eyes and levered herself to a sitting position, one hand braced on the carpet. She was vaguely aware that she was still wrapped in the hotel bathrobe. The first thing she saw was a luminous beam of energy slicing through the night. For a few heartbeats the hot ray of light got tangled up with the impossibly brilliant notes of the music. Her senses could not seem to separate the two.

Martin Crocker came to stand in front of her. He smiled his I-can-give-you-anything-you-want smile.

"You're dead," she whispered.

"Am I?" he asked.

"Yes."

She had intended the word to come out as a defiant shout. Instead, it emerged as a breathy gasp of sound that was drowned beneath the torrent of mad psychic energy that swirled around her.

"You were very useful to me," Martin said. "But all good things must come to an end. Unfortunately, you're no longer an asset. You've become a liability."

This was not a dream. She was officially going insane. The music was making her crazy.

She clamped her hands over her ears. As a defense mechanism it was pathetic. The singing dimmed a little but it was still too powerful. It flooded through the atmosphere around her.

"You're dead," she repeated, louder this time. Her senses pulsed in response, sending out sharp spikes of energy.

To her amazement, the image of Martin Crocker winked out. Relief shivered through her. Shaking, she took her hands away from her ears and clamped her fingers around the nearest object. It turned out to be the arm of a theater chair.

The scalding music continued to soar and flash, drawing her deeper into a hell fashioned of purest crystal.

She turned her head to follow the beam of light and found herself looking at a stage. A woman in a white gown that appeared to have been splashed with blood stood in the center of the light beam. Her blond hair was loose around her shoulders. She gripped a knife in one hand as she poured the psychic energy of her Siren's music out into the theater.

Vivien Ryan, La Sirène.

In a fleeting instant of horrible clarity the memory of one of the online film clips that she had viewed while researching coloratura sopranos slammed through Grace's fevered brain. Vivien was singing the famous Mad Scene from *Lucia di Lammermoor.* The blood on the virginal white gown looked all too real.

So did the body sprawled in the shadows of the stage. A man, Grace realized. His face was turned away from her.

She clutched the seat arm, feeling as though she were about to drown. In the opera the scene she was watching takes place *after* Lucia murders her unwanted bridegroom. What if she was too late? What if Luther was already dead?

No. She would know if he was dead. In spite of the relentless power of the music, she was certain of that much. The knowledge gave her a curious strength. Her senses pulsed more strongly. It was not Luther who lay so unnervingly still on the stage.

Vivien released another cascade of high, delicately pure, eerily shattering notes. The music was accompanied by dangerously erratic spikes in her aura. Like Lucia, Vivien was driving herself deeper and deeper into insanity with her song, and she was trying to pull her audience of one down with her. It was all there in the music and in the aura. Grace could see it, hear it, fear it; but she was not sure she could resist it.

There was a terrible kind of power in madness, and La Sirène was exulting in it.

Grace pulled herself to her knees but before she could get all the way to her feet, the monster who had tried to rape her in the foster home appeared. He started up the aisle toward her, grinning. She trembled. Please, not again. She could not deal with another ghost. She had to focus on surviving.

"Don't worry, you're going to like what I'm going to do to you," the monster promised.

"You're dead," she said. She had made Martin disappear. She would make the monster vanish, too. She managed to summon a sharp pulse of will that translated into a strong flare of psychic energy. *"You're dead, damn it."*

The monster dissolved, just as the image of Martin had.

Pay attention. There's something important here, something that could help you fight back.

She was on her feet now but still under the compelling spell of the music. She was moving down the aisle toward the stage, not fleeing to safety. She struggled to resist but only succeeded in slowing her steps. She could not stop the inevitable. She was being summoned to her doom just as surely as the sailors in the myths had been drawn to their deaths.

Onstage, Vivien raised her arms. Her song of madness soared ever higher.

Grace put her hands over her ears again and concentrated on pulling her scattered senses together so that she could jack her own power higher. She pushed energy out against the storm of the music, trying to create a bulwark against the waves. It seemed to her that the force of the singing lessened a little. Encouraged, she threw more energy at it. Her mind cleared. She was able to think more clearly.

There was no way she could stand firm against the great rolling breakers of the Siren's call, but it might be possible to skim through the psychic pulses that energized the song, like a surfer riding the pipeline.

Even if her theory was correct, she knew she could not neutralize Vivien's power from this distance. Nor could she turn and run. The compulsion of the music was still too strong. There was only one chance, and that was to get closer to the stage.

Face the music and dance, Grace, dance, as fast as you possibly can.

She watched Vivien's aura, not her face, focusing on the patterns of the flaring, flashing pulses. Cautiously she sent her own energy into the valleys between the spikes on the Siren's raging spectrum. It was like firing arrows at a machine gun, but she knew she was making progress when she felt the compulsion ease further.

Vivien stopped singing. The abrupt silence was electrifying.

"Do you really think that little trick will work against my talent?" she asked, amused.

Grace stopped in front of the dark well that was the empty orchestra pit. Opera singers cannot allow themselves to get genuinely emotional when they sing, she reminded herself. Powerful emotions tightened the throat and chest, destroying both breath and sound.

"You know, Viv," she said, "the clothes are great and the theaters are classy, but when it comes right down to it, you're just another singer in a band."

"*Shut up, you stupid woman.* I am La Sirène."

Grace looked at the motionless man lying in the shadows. "Who is he?"

"Newlin Guthrie."

"You killed your lover?"

"Oh, he's not dead. Just unconscious." Vivien smiled. "Why would I want him dead? He's very useful to me. He's the one who found you. Imagine my surprise when he told me you were in the audience tonight. I'm so glad you had a chance to hear me sing the Queen. Astonishing, wasn't I?"

"Give me a break. Your career is on the skids. Everyone knows it. That's why you're singing here in Acacia Bay instead of at the Met."

"That's a lie," Vivien shrieked, her aura sparking with fury. "I am La Sirène. No other singer alive can do what I can do with my voice."

"Come on, we're talking about opera, remember? You may have been good once upon a time but you're losing it. Remember how they booed you at La Scala? The claque could hear the weakness in your voice."

"I silenced an entire section of the audience at La Scala with my voice," Vivien shouted.

"I'll bet there are probably a couple dozen sopranos coming up behind you who can take your place. What's more, a lot of them are ten years younger."

"Stop it," Vivien shrieked. "My voice is flawless."

"Maybe a few years ago but not any longer. I've got a theory about that, by the way. I'm something of an expert on the laws of psychic genetics, you know."

"Shut up."

"My theory is that every time you used your voice to kill, you made yourself a little crazier. People who go insane lose control. That's what's been happening to you these past couple of years, Viv. You're losing control of your voice."

"I am not crazy," Vivien screamed.

"Sure you are. It's all there in your aura."

"I'll show you what I can do with my voice," Vivien shrieked.

"Be careful. I doubt if screaming is good for the throat."

Vivien clenched her hands in the skirts of her bloodied gown and erupted into song. The high notes of Lucia's descent into madness exploded from her once again.

Grace shuddered and clamped her hands more tightly over her ears in an attempt to lessen the impact of the mesmerizing song. It was the musical equivalent of watching a volcano erupt while trying to hide under a piece of cardboard. She had braced her senses for the hellish rain of crystal fire but she could not stop all of it. The music fell on her in a molten torrent of sharp crystals.

She was going to die if she did not destabilize Vivien's aura.

She shoved hard at all the weak places on the Siren's spectrum.

Vivien went higher. The notes she sang were still piercingly clear but they began to grow fainter, weaker. Her fury was interfering with her ability to project her astonishing talent. She was literally choking on her frustration and rage. One very high note and then another fractured.

Still singing, Vivien whirled and stalked to the stage steps. It didn't take a psychic to see the madness and murder in her aura now, Grace thought.

Vivien descended the steps with theatrical deliberation as though she was in the middle of a dramatic production. When she reached the bottom she advanced toward Grace, the dagger held high for a killing blow. The jagged notes of her mad song spilled forth in mere squeaks.

Grace felt the last of the compulsion evaporate. She could move freely now.

She jumped up onto the nearest seat, stepped over the back into the next row and rushed toward the aisle. Running between the closely packed rows proved complicated. Her thigh collided painfully with one of the chair arms.

Vivien was screaming now, her voice hoarse, her power almost gone. She grabbed a fistful of her bloody skirts and raced toward the far end of the front row, dagger poised to strike, clearly intent on intercepting her quarry at the aisle.

Grace scrambled to a halt, climbed up onto another seat and jumped down into the third row. She vaulted into the fourth, trying to put more distance between herself and her pursuer. She gained ground quickly, her bathrobe flying around her.

Vivien was reduced to hoarse screeching.

A blinding light spilled from the lobby entrance. The silhouette of a man appeared.

"Grace," Luther shouted.

"I'm okay," Grace shouted back. "Be careful, she's got a knife but she can't sing worth a damn anymore."

Vivien floundered to a halt in the aisle. Her harsh breathing seemed very loud in the sudden silence of the theater. The light from the lobby illuminated her stained gown and disheveled hair. Her aura was a rainbow comprising all the colors of a nightmare.

"I am La Sirène," she whispered.

She dropped the dagger, turned and fled back down the aisle toward the stage.

Luther started forward, cane in one hand, gun raised in the other. His aura was flaring, an icy-hot spectrum of violent hues.

"No," Grace said quietly. "It's not necessary. Let her go."

For a few seconds she was afraid he wasn't going to pay any attention to her. Then he lowered the gun and his aura.

Vivien raced up the short flight of stage steps and vanished behind the bloodred curtain.

Forty-eight

J&J sent out more people from the Society's L.A. offices to deal with Newlin Guthrie. The minute they arrived on the scene, Luther briefed them and then bundled Grace into the car.

"Are you sure it's necessary to drive back to L.A. tonight?" she asked, yawning.

"As long as that Siren is still on the loose, we are not hanging around Acacia Bay."

It was a command decision. She was too exhausted to argue. She rested her head against the back of the seat and looked out over the night-darkened Pacific.

"I'm so glad to know that wasn't real blood on her Lucia outfit," she said. "It was just a costume from the wardrobe department."

"Fallon Jones thinks your theory about her descent into insanity is right. She was unstable to begin with. Using her voice to kill people for little or no reason just made her crazier. And with craziness comes loss of control on both the normal and the paranormal plane."

"How did you find me?" she asked.

"I'll always be able to find you," he said.

She smiled. "You are such a romantic. I'm serious."

"So am I."

She turned her head to look at him. "Come on, tell me how you knew that Guthrie had taken me to Guthrie Hall."

"Process of elimination. She had a limited choice of venues. It's a small town, after all. There was a big reception going on at Guthrie's house so she couldn't use it. Smuggling you into her hotel room would have been dicey. Where else was she going to go? You told me yourself she loves the spotlight. And Newlin Guthrie had access to the finest stage in town."

"That was brilliant."

"Yeah, I used to be a detective once."

She rested her hand on his injured leg. "Once a detective, always a detective."

Forty-nine

La Sirène looked down at the cauldron of crashing surf far below. A swath of cold moonlight stroked the scene; the perfect spotlight for her final performance. The cliffs were not the ramparts of the Castel Sant'Angelo that Tosca used after discovering that her lover had been shot by the firing squad, but they would do.

It was over. The Renquist woman had proved too much for the Voice. Her power was almost gone now, and she knew it would never recover. La Sirène was doomed. Better by far to depart the stage tonight. Tomorrow the critics would make her famous once again as they rhapsodized about her Queen of the Night and simultaneously mourned the loss of her incredible talent. Her death would make headlines.

She spread her arms wide and sang her own death song as she flung herself over the castle wall.

Really, she had always been so much better than Callas. She was La Sirène.

Fifty

The three-way conference call with Fallon took place the following day in their hotel room near the L.A. airport.

"Ryan's body was found washed up on the rocks at a place called Hellfire Cove," Fallon said. "Evidently it's a major scenic attraction in Acacia Bay. Lots of rough, dangerous surf. Photographers love it. Strictly off limits for swimming or diving."

"Tosca flinging herself from the castle wall," Grace said. "A fitting stage for La Sirène's final performance."

"You knew she was going to jump?" Fallon asked, sharply curious.

Across the room, Luther looked at her, too.

"I didn't know how she would do it," Grace said quietly. "But yes, I was fairly certain that she would commit suicide. It was there in her aura when she ran back toward the stage."

"Well, it looks like we won't need Sweetwater's services on this case," Fallon said. "That simplifies matters."

"What about Damaris Kemble?" Luther asked.

"She's being debriefed as we speak. She'll get her first injection of the antidote later today."

"So soon?" Grace said. "I thought she still had a three-week supply of the drug."

"It was her decision," Fallon explained. "She wanted to get started on the antidote as quickly as possible. Apparently she's been experiencing some unpleasant side effects from the Nightshade drug. She gave her remaining vials to the lab techs to study. They've been trying to figure out how Nightshade genetically tailors the formula for each individual. The information may be useful for tweaking the antidote."

"How did she take the news of her sister's death?" Grace asked.

"One of the Society shrinks who is talking to her told me she was sad but not surprised."

"Poor Damaris," Grace whispered. "She lost her father and her sister within a year of finding them. Now she's alone again."

"She's alive," Fallon pointed out drily.

"Thanks to Luther," Grace said.

Luther frowned. "How the hell did Craigmore manage to slip past all the scrutiny that would have been given to a member of the Council?"

"Good question," Fallon said, sounding more than a little annoyed. "But bear in mind that he was appointed fifteen years ago."

"In other words, before you took over J&J?" Luther prompted.

"My uncle was running the West Coast office at that time. He was good but he didn't have the research capability I've got now. In addition, Craigmore came out of the depths of a government agency that specialized in creating false backgrounds. He had the perfect résumé, literally. And it was solid. Those who knew he'd worked as a spook figured him for a patriotic hero. Which is exactly what he was when you get right down to it, at least until he fired up Nightshade. And last but not least, he pulled off the oldest trick in the world."

Luther looked at Grace. "He hid in plain sight."

"Right. I've recently initiated deep background checks on all Council members. The process probably would have uncovered Craigmore or at least raised some red flags. According to Damaris, he was getting worried and planning to disappear."

Luther made his way across the room. He lounged against the edge of the desk and hooked his cane over the back of the chair. "Is Newlin Guthrie all right?"

"Yes. Pretty badly shaken up, though. Turns out La Sirène nailed him with his own electroshock gun. Our people from L.A. talked to him. He feels terrible about the kidnapping. Said he knew what he was doing but just couldn't seem to help himself."

"That is the truth," Grace said. "When I found him waiting for me in the hotel room, his aura seemed weirdly frozen, which would not be normal for anyone committing an act of violence. He was under La Sirène's spell."

"He wanted to turn himself in to the police but the J&J agents talked him out of it. They told him that you were fine and that no one was going to report the incident. With Vivien Ryan dead, it's all moot, anyway."

"How did he get into my room?" Grace asked.

"Through the connecting door between your suite and the neighboring room."

"That door was locked," she said. "Luther and I both checked it."

"Guthrie owns the damn hotel. He had no trouble getting a master key."

"He's a smart man," Luther said. "How did the agents explain what had happened to him?"

"They told him he was the victim of a unique kind of hypnotist. That depressed him even more because guys like that don't like to think they can be hypnotized. He perked right up, though, when he was informed that J&J was interested in purchasing some of his electroshock devices."

"For what it's worth, from the brief look I got at his aura, I'd say he is a high-level crypto talent," Grace offered. "Probably never realized he's a sensitive."

"Funny you should say that. One of the agents who spoke to him suggested that he get tested at the L.A. lab. Guthrie seemed enthusiastic about the idea."

"What happens next?" Luther asked.

"Case closed as far as you and Grace are concerned," Fallon said. "Send in your bill. J&J will cover your airfares home. Check the Society's travel agency site online. Your reservations have been made."

"Luther meant what happens now with Nightshade?" Grace said.

"On that front, things are moving fast." Fallon sounded weary and determined, not excited. "Since Craigmore handled the Eubanks operation privately, the board of Nightshade doesn't have any idea that we have four of their people under observation, and we're waiting to see who takes the place of the fifth. They may not even realize yet that their founder and CEO is dead."

"There's going to be some interesting political infighting at the top to see who takes his place," Luther observed.

"Especially after we start taking apart those five labs."

"What five labs?"

"Forgot to tell you. Those four Nightshade execs that you ID'd?"

"What about them?"

"Looks like each of them is responsible for a lab that is either conducting research on the formula or producing it. They're all small operations. Evidently Craigmore liked to keep things decentralized for security reasons."

"Smart."

"Zack and the Council authorized action an hour ago. J&J agents will go into all the labs, seize whatever computers and notes they can find and burn everything else to the ground. Standard procedure when dealing with a formula lab."

"And no one involved with Nightshade will run screaming to the cops because no one wants an investigation that would turn up proof that some kind of illegal drug lab had been operating," Luther concluded.

"Yeah, that's pretty much how it works," Fallon agreed.

"That's going to be a big blow to Nightshade," Grace said.

"The problem is, we don't know how many labs are currently operating. You're right, though, between losing their founder and five of their labs, they're going to be in disarray for a while. The goal now is to identify as many operatives as possible. We still don't know who sits on that damn board."

"Can't Damaris Kemble tell you?" Luther asked.

"She said Craigmore didn't consider her ready to receive that information. The debriefing people believe her. I've got people tearing apart Craigmore's mansion, his office, his computer and his entire past. We're getting information but we've got a long way to go. He was very good at keeping secrets."

"Lot of work ahead for J&J," Luther said.

"Tell me about it," Fallon muttered. "I'm going twenty-four/seven here."

"That's not good, Mr. Jones," Grace said. "Sooner or later you're going to burn out. That would be a disaster. The Society needs you at your best in the months ahead."

Fallon snorted. "Not like there are a lot of options here."

"Yes, there are," Grace said. "You just need to focus on the problem for a couple of minutes the way you focus on other issues. Start by getting yourself an assistant."

"Forget it. I work alone."

Grace smiled. "That's what Luther used to say, too. At least until you assigned me to work with him. You've got to admit that we made a pretty good team."

"There's a reason I work alone," Fallon said bleakly. "No one can stand working with me for longer than about five minutes."

"That's not true. I've been your research assistant in Genealogy for several months. I didn't have a problem working with you."

Across the room Luther grinned but kept quiet.

"You're different," Fallon grumbled.

"So? Find someone else who is also different. You need an assistant, Mr. Jones. Make hiring one a priority. Think of it as a puzzle that needs to be solved as soon as possible."

"It would have to be someone I could trust with the Society's secrets," Fallon said, unconvinced.

"Of course. But it won't be the first time. Keep in mind that the founder of J&J, Caleb Jones, eventually acquired a partner who became his wife. She was the second Jones in Jones & Jones, remember?"

"You don't need to tell me my own family history. I'm sure as hell not looking for a wife."

"We're talking about you getting an assistant, not a wife," she said soothingly.

There was a long pause on the other end of the line. "I'll think about it. Oh, by the way, I need you to set up a new identity for Damaris Kemble. She says Craigmore never told the Nightshade board that she existed but I don't want to take any chances. Bury her deep in the Society's genealogy files for me, will you?"

"Uh." Grace stopped. "I thought J&J had people on staff whose job was to invent new IDs."

"Well, sure, for routine things like giving an agent a temporary cover for a case. But I'm talking about a whole new personal history here. I want it solid all the way back for several generations. Far as I know you're the best there is at that kind of thing, at least when it comes to creating a phony past within the Society."

Grace's mouth went dry. "Excuse me?"

"Hell, the one you did for yourself after you got rid of that son of a bitch Martin Crocker was damn near perfect. If I hadn't been keeping an eye on Crocker at the time because I had a hunch he was into some illegal business activity, I never would have looked twice at the circumstances of his death, let alone started to wonder about his butler. Have a good trip home."

The phone went dead in Grace's ear. She closed it slowly and looked at Luther.

"That's Fallon for you," he said. "Mr. Personality."

"He knows everything," she whispered. "He has all along. He even knew about the Burnside Clinic."

"Yeah, that's also pure Fallon. Now, I don't know about you, but I'm more than ready to get out of here." He looked down at the computer sitting on the desk. "What do you say we pull up those reservations and see what time our plane leaves?"

Reality sluiced through Grace, leaving her chilled.

"Okay," she said quietly.

She got up and crossed the room to the desk. Quickly she entered the address for the travel agency. When it came up, she keyed in the code for Luther's reservation.

"You're leaving at two-fifteen," she said.

"Great." He collected the cane. "Time for lunch."

"Not for me." She straightened slowly. "My flight to Portland leaves at one o'clock."

Luther looked at her, expressionless.

"Portland," he said. "Forgot about that part."

She nodded, afraid to say another word, terrified not to speak.

There was a short, heavy silence.

"I've been thinking," she started carefully.

"What a coincidence," Luther said. "So have I. What do you say we both go to Portland—"

"I could pack a few things—"

"You could pack everything you own. Then you could fly home to Hawaii with me."

She smiled, her eyes misting.

"Yes," she said. "Yes, I could do that."

His hands settled on her waist. He drew her to him. "You do know where this is going, don't you?"

She put her arms around his neck, happiness soaring like a glorious operatic aria through her. "I think so, yes."

"I love you," he said. "But you probably already know that also, what with you being such a hotshot aura talent and all."

"I love you, too." She brushed her mouth lightly against his and drew back slightly "And for your information, no one can see actual love in an aura, not even a high-grade aura profiler like me. That's why you have to say the words."

"I can do that," he promised. "And I will. Often and always."

"Often and always," she vowed.

Fifty-one

The knock on the door came just as Grace was wedging a pair of boots that she would probably never wear in Hawaii into a suitcase.

"I'll get it," she said to Luther.

He straightened from the box of books he was taping and glanced out the window. "Looks like an old lady in camouflage, dark glasses and a black raincoat. I think she's carrying."

"My landlady," Grace said. "And it's not a gun, it's a special camera."

"Interesting landlady."

Grace opened the front door. "Hello, Arizona. Come on in. It's wet out there."

"You got that right." Arizona stomped into the small foyer, shaking water off her black raincoat. "I've been out doing recon all morning. Days like this I've got to stay extra alert. Folks up at the institute like to schedule a lot of clandestine deliveries on rainy days. Probably figure there's less chance that someone is doing surveillance."

"I'd like you to meet Luther Malone," Grace said. "Luther, this is my landlady, Arizona Snow."

Luther nodded politely and held out his hand. "A pleasure, ma'am."

Arizona took off her mirrored glasses and gave Luther a squinty-eyed look. "So you're the one, huh?"

"The one what?" Luther asked.

Arizona snorted, stripped off her thick leather gloves and shook his hand with great vigor. "No need to play games with me, young man. I recognize another pro when I see one. Minute I spotted you coming up the walk with Grace, I knew you were the one she's been waiting for all this time while she was lying low here in Eclipse Bay."

Luther smiled at Grace. "Actually, I think I was the one doing the waiting."

Arizona winked. "Got it. Going undercover is a real pain, isn't it? But since you're here now, I reckon it was mission accomplished, eh?"

"Yes, ma'am," Luther said.

Grace went into the kitchen. "How about a cup of coffee to warm you up, Arizona? I just made a fresh pot."

"Thanks. I could use it." Arizona surveyed the boxes and suitcases. "Well, looks like you two are shipping out together this time."

"We're going to get married," Grace said. "We're moving to Hawaii."

"Still working for the agency, though, right?"

Luther raised his brow in silent inquiry. Grace smiled.

"Definitely," she said smoothly. She handed the filled mug to Arizona. "But we'll also be running a little restaurant on the side in Waikiki."

Arizona looked down at where their fingers had brushed. Grace followed her glance and suddenly realized she had felt nothing unusual when she accidentally touched the older woman.

"My little phobia seems to have finally disappeared," she said.

Arizona nodded, pleased. "Good thing, what with you two getting married and all."

Luther laughed and took the coffee Grace had poured for him. "A very good thing."

"Waikiki, eh?" Arizona sipped her coffee and assumed a meditative expression, as though she was looking back into the past. "Knew a couple of folks who retired and moved to Waikiki."

"That right?" Luther said.

"I seem to recall them talkin' about maybe buying themselves a restaurant or a bar. Petra and Wayne Groves. I'll never forget 'em. Best sniper team there ever was. I retired from the agency right after they did. They were a few years younger than me. Probably in their sixties by now. Guess we were all a little burned out."

Grace stilled. Luther's mug stopped in midair. He looked at Arizona as if she were a ghost.

"You knew Petra and Wayne?" he asked without inflection.

"Hell, yes. They were like you two in a way." Arizona tapped the side of her head. "Had a sixth sense. This country owes them more than it knows. Folks like that don't get ribbons or stars but they sure as hell deserve 'em."

Fifty-two

The wedding took place in the little cove Luther had discovered and made his own. The bride was barefoot and blissfully pregnant.

They closed down the restaurant for the day and invited the regulars and Milly Okada and Julie Hagstrom and her son. Altogether some eighteen people showed up for the sunset ceremony. Everyone got a lei. The bridal couple got eighteen leis each. The fragrant blossoms were stacked so high around Grace's throat she had to spit out a few petals when she took her vows.

The guests stood around in the warm sand while the sun went down and everyone paid close attention while the minister conducted the service. Afterward Crazy Ray took out his guitar and launched into "Hawaiian Wedding Song," sounding just like Elvis.

Later they repaired to Milly Okada's for udon soup. At the close of the meal Milly surprised everyone with a massive cake emblazoned with the words *Grace and Luther, Happy Ever After.* There was a bottle of champagne and a lot of beer to go with the cake. Milly and Julie shared the champagne. Grace stuck with sparkling water because of the baby. Everyone else went for the beer.

There were a number of toasts, but Wayne delivered the one that made the day perfect.

"Here's to Grace and Luther," he said, hoisting his beer. "And to the baby who's due to arrive in seven months and eight days, not that anyone's counting. The kid's going to have himself one hell of a family. We're gonna take good care of him. Teach him all the stuff he needs to know."

"Got a feelin' about that," Petra said.

They all looked at her

She chuckled. "A good feelin'."

Watch out for the following
books by
Jayne Ann Krentz,
also available
from Piatkus Books

SIZZLE AND BURN

Raine Tallentyre, recently dumped, knows her gifted Aunt Vella was right –
she should always keep her paranormal abilities a secret. And now that Vella,
her last relative, has died, Raine's resigned herself to a lonely life. Then, while
clearing out Vella's house, Raine's sensitivity leads her to a horrifying
discovery: a young woman, bound and terrified, in the basement. The victim
has survived, but the culprit is on the loose.

Suddenly, a new man enters Raine's life: psychic investigator Zack Jones. But
there's one complication – Zack's working for a secret organisation that
shattered Raine's family. She's wary of his motives, but as a killer makes her
his target, and a group of psychic criminals operating in the shadows surrounds
them, Raine and Zack must rely not only on their powerful abilities, but on
each other…

978-0-7499-0900-0

WHITE LIES

Petite, thirty-something Clare Lancaster is a gifted psychic and a 'human lie detector'.

Until recently, Clare had never had much to do with her estranged father, Archer Lancaster, so when he summons her from California, she is reluctant to say the least. But after meeting Jake Salter, Archer's financial consultant, Clare is convinced that things aren't what they seem. Something sparks and sizzles between them – something more than just casual flirtation between a man and a woman.

Caught in a dizzying storm of secrets, lies and half-truths, Jake and Clare must work together in an investigation that demands every bit of their special gifts. Together they must overcome their mutual distrust in order to unravel a web of conspiracy and murder.

978-0-7499-3845-1

ALL NIGHT LONG

After the violent deaths of her parents seventeen years ago, Irene Stenson left the tiny lakefront town of Dunsley, Oregon. Now she's back and she's determined to discover the truth about what happened that night. Armed with a shocking new lead and her experience as an investigative reporter, Irene dives straight into the mystery and finds herself in trouble up to the collar of her black trench coat.

Luckily, ex-Marine Luke Danner is on hand to pull her out, and his calm, quick-thinking response in the face of danger makes him the perfect ally. And as the intrigue deepens and the secrets turn deadly, Irene will need all the allies she can find if she is to lay the past to rest.

978-0-7499-3739-3

FALLING AWAKE

Isabel Wright spends her days at the Belvedere Centre for Sleep Research analysing the dreams of others. It's satisfying, lucrative work, but it can be emotionally draining at times – especially when one of her anonymous subjects, known only as Client Number Two, captures her imagination through his compelling dream narratives.

Client Number Two's real name is Ellis Cutler. A loner who learned long ago not to let anyone get too close, he works for a highly classified government agency with an interest in the potential value of lucid dreaming. And he has just been ordered by his boss to make contact with Isabel, who's been fired after the sudden death of her boss, Dr Belvedere.

When they meet in the flesh, the dream becomes real enough to touch. And a waking nightmare begins. For a suspicious hit-and-run leads them into a perilous web of passion, betrayal and murder, and forces them to walk the razor-thin line between dreams and reality.

978-0-7499-3622-8

TRUTH OR DARE

Zoe Luce, an interior designer with a unique sense of style, has an even more uncanny sense of what's going on under the surface, the secrets a house can hold.

At the moment, though, Zoe is more concerned about what's going on in her own house in Whispering Springs, Arizona, where she lives with her new husband, private investigator Ethan Truax.

But newlywed life is suddenly interrupted when a shadowy figure from Zoe's past shows up in Whispering Springs and her closest friend is put at terrible risk. For Zoe and Arcadia Ames share a shocking secret. And as they seek to protect the truth, they must join together, and with Ethan's help, accept a very dangerous dare…

978-0-7499-3496-5

LIGHT IN SHADOW

Zoe Luce is a successful interior designer, and when she senses that one of her clients may be hiding a dark secret, she enlists private investigator Ethan Truax to find the truth.

But Ethan's investigative skills start to backfire on Zoe. She never wanted to let him find out about her former life. Or to reveal to him her powerful, inexplicable gift for sensing the history hidden within a house's walls. And she certainly never wanted him to know that 'Zoe Luce' doesn't really exist.

But now, Ethan may be her only hope, as just when Zoe started to dream of a normal life and think about the future, her own past starts to shadow her every step – because the people she's been running from are getting close to finding her…

978-0-7499-3392-0